C000078562

HOUSE
OF
STICKS

HOUSE
OF
STICKS

MARC SCOTT

Copyright © 2022 Marc Scott

The moral right of the author has been asserted.

Apart from any fair dealing for the purposes of research or private study, or criticism or review, as permitted under the Copyright, Designs and Patents Act 1988, this publication may only be reproduced, stored or transmitted, in any form or by any means, with the prior permission in writing of the publishers, or in the case of reprographic reproduction in accordance with the terms of licences issued by the Copyright Licensing Agency. Enquiries concerning reproduction outside those terms should be sent to the publishers.

This is a work of fiction. Names, characters, businesses, places, events and incidents are either the products of the author's imagination or used in a fictitious manner. Any resemblance to actual persons, living or dead, or actual events is purely coincidental.

Matador
Unit E2 Airfield Business Park,
Harrison Road, Market Harborough,
Leicestershire. LE16 7UL
Tel: 0116 2792299
Email: books@troubador.co.uk
Web: www.troubador.co.uk/matador
Twitter: @matadorbooks

ISBN 978 1803131 016

British Library Cataloguing in Publication Data.
A catalogue record for this book is available from the British Library.

Printed and bound in Great Britain by 4edge Limited
Typeset in 11pt Adobe Garamond Pro by Troubador Publishing Ltd, Leicester, UK

Matador is an imprint of Troubador Publishing Ltd

For

Amie and Marissa
My two beautiful shining stars that guide me every day.

And with special thanks for the inspiration and support of Gina
Blackmore, Michael Ricketts, Morhib Miah, Toby Frost, Robyn
Leigh and Tammy Dickerson.

CHAPTER ONE

Some say she was pushed, but most thought she had jumped. Whichever was the sad reality, the wiry-framed girl with the soft voice and the ever-teary eyes was gone. She was, in the words of Karen Walpole from B Wing, 'As dead as a doornail.' Only two people would ever know the truth behind her demise.

Just one cell door was unlocked, slightly ajar, that bright August morning. An enforced, but welcomed, lay-in for the rest of the inmates. Poppy peered through the small gap in the doorframe, across the landing to where her former cell mate had fallen without grace to her bleak fate the previous week. Glancing down at the empty bed beneath her bunk, she pondered on that curious phrase, 'As dead as a doornail.' Nobody, not even Smart Sheila, the corrupt accountant, seemed to know what that expression meant. But it would be the only epitaph used to describe the short life of a hopeless soul whose only true sin was to fall in love with a man who prayed to a different God. His crimes, though extreme, were not her crimes, but guilt by association would determine her destiny. In truth the frail and timid twenty-one-year-old should never have been locked up in an institution that had been purpose built for the hardest and most dangerous female criminals in England. But government cuts and overcrowding at lower category prisons sealed her fate.

Her untimely death, however, would become just another in a string of negative statistics hanging over the heads of the staff of Wallsgrave Prison. There would be an enquiry of course, standard practice, but nothing would ever come of it. The name of the poor girl would soon be forgotten, almost as quickly as the other two women that had died during Poppy's tenure in this bleak establishment.

Strange thoughts can fill your head when you live in dark places. Poppy had found herself continually wondering what that expression really meant, 'As dead as a doornail'. There were certainly no nails in those large clunking sheets of metal that had kept locked her away from society for the past two years. She checked again, just to make sure. No, there were definitely no nails. But that's the problem with prison, too much time to think, too much space inside your head to ponder on the craziest of notions. Just one out of place word or innocuous comment can send your mind spinning into an eternal overdrive.

Maybe today was a good time for this troubled girl to reflect on her stay in this place. She remembered the day that she was transferred here from Downview Prison, the words of the Chief Prison Officer Ray Callard had rolled around inside her head ever since. 'You are a nobody here, Jarvis,' he told her. 'Forget your reputation as a hard nut in those soft places, here you are nothing, a nobody. You came in as a nobody and you will leave as a nobody. Stay off my radar and you will get through your time here just fine. Fuck with me and I will come down on you like a ton of bricks.'

Callard was old school, an army veteran with medals to prove his worth. He was proud of his reputation as a 'hard and uncompromising bastard'. In fact, those very words were used on his application form for the role he held at this establishment. But Poppy never was very good at following orders, especially those dished out by a uniformed thug. It only took three weeks for her to cross his lines and start a conflict she was never likely to win. Maybe the heavy-handed prison officer would be pleased to see the back of her today. Her presence here had certainly undermined his authority and he had other problems on his plate. Apart from the media attention attracted by the unexplained death of another inmate, he had to deal with a lack of capacity caused by an outbreak of mumps.

So, he for one, would be happy to wave one of his problem captives a cheery goodbye, when she was let loose on society today. But he knew that her double cell would not remain empty for long. Two prisoners were already on route from a remand centre in Nottingham, more fodder for the rehabilitation machine. Callard would never admit to defeat when it came to keeping his inmates in check, but he had certainly had his work cut out where Poppy was concerned. Her blatant refusal to fall into line with his orders had not gone unnoticed amongst the other inmates. The last thing he needed now was a mutiny on his hands. So, it would be goodbye and good riddance to the departing criminal today.

The birth certificate for Poppy Jarvis would show that she was twenty-eight years old now, but to look at her rugged washed-out features and dark shadows beneath her eyes you would add several years to that number. The stern expression on her face wasn't helped by her poorly groomed shoulder length brown hair, which had never grown long enough to hide the two deep scars she bore on her neck. Some might say that she would feel better about her appearance if she covered them up. But Poppy wore those battle scars proudly, like medals of honour. They warned off would-be attackers, reminding them that she was a survivor, that she feared nobody.

At five feet nine and weighing no more than ten stone, one might be mistaken in believing that her fierce reputation was nothing more than a myth. But it wasn't just strong arms and a solid determination that won Poppy her fights. She had stealth and cunning. Her torrid experiences growing up on the violent streets of South London had taught her well. Why take five seconds to threaten someone that you are going to do something when it takes less than two seconds to do it. And those who did oppose her would soon realise that Poppy had no filter to her violent outbursts. She was like an unkempt alley-cat when it came to a scrap. A fearsome temper that protected her wherever she went. Every encounter she faced in her troubled mind was a fight to the death.

Five fights, three resounding victories, an honourable draw and one defeat was her record within these walls. No Queensbury rules in here of course, makeshift weapons, fists, feet and heads were all you had to make it count. It is amazing the amount of damage you can cause to somebody's face with the sharpened edge of an empty toothpaste tube. Her only loss inside the prison came at the hands of a trio of stocky Rumanian women who ambushed her at the back of the laundry room. Poppy spent three days in the local hospital ward after she suffered a hefty beating. She did, however, take some comfort from the knowledge that two of her attackers did not come off unscathed. One of the Eastern European women needed several stitches in an eye while another would be keeping the visiting dentist busy for the following few weeks.

But violent encounters like these were commonplace in here, where madness and mayhem often reigned supreme. HMP Wallsgrave was the brainchild of some crazy government officials who believed that, if you bring together the most violent and mentally challenged category A prisoners within the same confines, they would be easier to manage. At the last count there were the one hundred and seventy-six inmates housed here, at least eighty per cent of them had been convicted for violent crimes. Murderers, child abusers, drug runners and habitual criminals that had probably gathered more column inches of coverage in the tabloid newspapers than the whole of the British Government and the England Football team put together.

But the young girl who left the prison for the last time in the back of an ambulance the previous week was no hardened criminal. Her only crime had been to harbour a man whose extreme beliefs led him to ignite an explosion causing dozens of life-changing injuries to a group of innocent onlookers at a ballroom dancing competition. The man in question had been her childhood sweetheart since the tender age of thirteen and the couple had lived together in a dingy basement flat in North London. Her boyfriend, barely out of his teens himself, had been brainwashed by an on-line religious group. Converting to Islam, he had come to believe that western civilisation was the devil incarnate. He had been encouraged to use extreme methods to gain recognition. The explosion at the side of a packed dance floor certainly did that for him and he was seen in the eyes of his peers as a martyr. But the fact that all the paraphernalia for bomb making had been found on his girlfriend's laptop meant she was treated as his accomplice. Many believed that the harmless girl needed support and re-educating rather that the six-year custodial sentence that was handed down to her. More than that, this den of iniquity was no place for the girl to be housed. Her empty bed was just another symbol of the failure of a system that was cracked at the core. Poppy glanced down at the lone pillow and recalled how the terrified girl had wept every single one of the twenty-seven nights she spent in this cell. The broken and helpless young woman had entered the prison to a chorus of catcalls and death threats. But she left in stony silence less than a month later in an unmarked body bag.

A modern purpose-built structure HMP Wallsgrave was testament to a Tory government that had tried to reverse its previous string of spending cuts. Set in twenty acres of prime Kent countryside, the newly built prison was described as a 'detention complex', a term which made it sound more like a home for naughty school children than seasoned criminals. But in truth this place was no more than a last resort, a final throw of the dice.

It was the badly judged brainwave of a judicial system that was on its knees and had seen its sentencing powers undermined for years. The numbers of repeat offenders were growing steadily year on year, and something had to be done. Wallsgrave was to be a return to no nonsense prison rhetoric of yesteryear. The simple logic was hard-line rehabilitation. There were no comfy beds or multi-channel television sets in the cells. You earned merit point for hard work and good behaviour and inmates were allowed one three minute monitored phone call each week. If you were caught with contraband or a mobile phone in your cell you would have six months added to your sentence, which was doubled each time you broke the rules.

And then, just when you thought your bleak existence inside this place could not sink any lower, there was 'The Blue Room'. The clever bods who devised this new prison establishment proposed that all inmates should undergo, 'friendly counselling'. It was an attempt, no doubt, to rid every offender of the evil demons that had made them turn bad. Once a week you would be greeted with the plastic smile of a thirty something would-be university professor, who would coerce you to 'open up' and talk about your past. You would be encouraged to speak openly about your childhood, your hopes, your fears and, of course, all your regrets. All this while an eighty thousand pounds per year busybody sat in a designer suit scribbling furious notes that meant nothing to anybody. These would-be psychoanalytical experts would make recommendations that a six-year-old child observer could have made. Many inmates left their two-hour sessions in floods of tears, while the counsellors would feel they deserved a firm pat on the back for helping another lost soul on the way back to recovery. Some inmates said that it was called 'The Blue Room' simply because it was decorated and furnished with a blend of soothing shades of that colour. But the reality was that it was just an ordinary ten by twelve cubicle where your darkest thoughts were laid bare. Inmates would often remark that, 'If you didn't feel 'blue' when you went in for your regular session, you certainly did when you came out'.

Poppy hated these weekly rituals, psychoanalysts had been having a field day with the troubled woman in every institution she had been housed. But these counsellors were savage, intrusive, unrelenting. These so-called experts loved interviewing her in the Blue Room. After all she ticked all their boxes. Neglected and abandoned as a child by alcoholic parents, pushed from pillar to post through the care system, where she was frequently abused both physically and sexually. Petty crime led to drug abuse, harder crime led to harder drug abuse. Youth Offenders Institution, soft prison, hard prison and now, this place, whatever this place was. Yes, this was all in her social services casebook and crime folder, but none of it ever came out in the Blue Room. Poppy was no pushover, she would drip feed them enough each week to make sure she earned her merit points. But there was no way she would ever discuss the reasoning behind her criminal past and what was going on inside her head. In truth, if she had ever revealed the darkest of her thoughts, those do-gooders would never have believed her. Because, if they did, they would surely be compelled to lock her up and throw away the key.

During her incarceration Poppy had tolerated constant abuse from both fellow inmates and the hard-line staff that Callard had assembled to control his captives. But there was one girl that stood out in her mind, Sherrine Marchant, or as she would refer to herself, 'Queen Shayla'. A foul-mouthed girl in her early twenties, Shayla was covered almost head to toe in anarchistic tattoos. The sides of her head were shaved bare, and she had large holes in her nose where several ring piercings had been. She had arrived at the prison having thrown battery acid in a rival musician's face, following an altercation over an unfaithful boyfriend. Her alter ego Queen Shayla, she informed anybody who would listen, was the undisputed queen of grime in her native northeast. She often referred to herself as, 'the truth of the streets.' She had a scratchy voice that belted out self-penned anti-establishment lyrics' morning, noon and night. Apparently, and it was never proven, she had become a huge success on the internet by 'sending for' other rappers. She would spit out cutting put-downs for her music rivals, 'dissing' their lifestyles and lack of musical abilities. She would think nothing of insinuating through her lyrics that her on-line opponents were ugly smackheads with body odour and lived with paedophile families. She boasted that one of her songs had clocked up more than a million views on YouTube and that at the time of her incarceration she had more than nine thousand subscribers to her music stream.

Most of the inmates found the girls spontaneous lyrical outbursts mildly amusing for the first few weeks. But she made a massive error of judgement, 'sending' for Poppy, in verse form. She suggested, in prose, that her fellow inmate had been the child of alcoholic drugged-up mother who deserted her to live a life as a prostitute. They say that truth hurts and maybe those comments had been a little too close to home for Poppy. Her parent had indeed abandoned her when she was just eight years old. Her last memory of the woman that gave birth to her, was of a half-dressed lady stumbling down the roads to the local shops, with a promise that she would be back in ten minutes. That memory would never leave her, no matter how hard she tried to erase it. Those ten minutes became ten hours, ten days, ten months, ten years. She knew by now that her mother had to be dead, although it had never been confirmed.

And so, if the 'Queen of Grime' had bothered to do her homework she would have avoided Poppy like the plague. Maybe too busy in her own little world, the self-acclaimed, 'truth of the streets' felt immune to the harsh brutality that lurked around every corner of the prison. But the wayward singer with the cropped hair and unruly swagger never got the chance to write a second verse of her ode to her latest subject. She came out of a shower one morning to find an enraged Poppy lying in wait for her. The altercation lasted less than the chorus of her one of her songs did. The only thing Queen Shayla was spitting out that day was two back teeth and a mass of fleshy blood.

A prison officer helped the poor girl to the medical room, but she refused to make a statement of accusation. She insisted that she had slipped on the wet floor and had hit the side of her head on the sink tap. And then, crazily, had done the same thing again, only this time to the other side of her face. As with most altercations in HMP Wallsgrave that was the end of the matter. Case closed. The golden rule in this establishment was to accept your beating and see what the next day brings. Strangely, the feisty girl with all those adoring subscribers to her YouTube channel decided to take a break from her budding music career. She never uttered another word in anger for the rest of her duration at the prison.

It was nearly time to leave now, Poppy sensed it, and with only a few moments left to savour the dank smell and lifeless beige walls in her cell, she found a moment to recall the last time she had left the confines of the prison system. She remembered that it rained the morning that she was allowed to attend her father's funeral at a small church in Battersea. She was on remand, awaiting sentencing for her vicious assault on her ex-boyfriend, Cameron Turner. A red-haired prison guard escorted her that day, they were handcuffed together for the whole of the excursion. She remembered that he had a good voice, he needed one, he was, after all, the only one of the five people in the chapel that was singing at the service before the cremation. She didn't know the other people in the church at the time but found out later that they included her father's landlord and a representative of HM Customs and Excises. Both men were no doubt angry that they were there to watch their overdue debts go up in flames. She recalled that the prison van driver had a kindly face and a sympathetic smile and that he bought her a packet of chocolate digestive biscuits to take back to her cell after the ordeal was over. He described them as comfort food and told her they always got him through bad times. Poppy could not remember which lasted longer the memory of watching the man who had neglected and physically abused her a child pass by in a cheap wooden casket on his way to the furnace or the lingering taste of those biscuits. She traded half of them with the inmate in the adjacent cell when she returned to the prison. The tobacco she received in the swap deal being the only comfort food that made any real impact on her.

As news of her impending release had spread around the prison that week, the rumour mill amongst the inmates had been rife. All the gossip seemed to be centred around Neddy, a notorious South London drug dealer who had sworn to exact his revenge against Poppy the moment she stepped foot outside the protective surroundings of the prison. One of the inmates had heard that the departing prisoner was going to be, 'chopped into tiny pieces and fed to the pigs,' as retribution for Poppy's violent assault on the villains lifelong best friend Cameron, who now needed a walking stick to get around. Others said the planned attack was more about the youth she had stabbed to death six years previously. Billy Keyes was barely seventeen years old when he was laid to rest and although his notorious brothers were now safely under lock and key, they had left one man in charge of their death wish. All roads now led to that one daunting name, Neddy.

A jangling of keys at the far end of the corridor and the measured approach of heavy footsteps told Poppy that the time had finally arrived for her to go. Like most of the monotonous sounds inside those four walls, the footprints of prison officer Meade were instantly recognisable. An overweight woman with an oversized ego, Meade's large clumpy feet barely left the ground as she shuffled her away towards Poppy's cell. Twenty plus years in the prison service had wiped any shine from her features. She wore a downcast expression, a permanent frown which never broke and added years to her visible age. The large and rounded prison officer stared long and hard at the departing inmate as she ushered her out of her cell. There was no love lost between these women, so there was no smile of congratulations for her imminent release. Poppy followed Meade, the sour-faced prison guard who was clearly counting the moments from the time she started work that day until the time she would finish. She was another member of staff who would not miss Poppy Jarvis when she locked the gates behind her. She had got under her skin on A Wing from the moment she set foot in the prison. And so, the walk to the outside world began, Meade setting the slow pace, those clumpy feet leading the path to freedom.

Poppy was not surprised to see Callard behind the custody desk, she knew he would not let her leave this place without testing her resolve one last time. She was right.

'This is 774552 Jarvis, due for release today, Mr Callard, sir.'

'I can take it from here, Meade,' he replied, opening a thick grey folder on the desk in front of him. 'You can let the other animals out of their cages now.'

Ray Callard looked as he always did, neatly pressed white shirt with perfectly folded cuffs, a stranglehold dark tie giving him just enough leeway to breath and a shock of Bryl Creem in his neatly combed black and grey steaky hair. He always stood tall and proud, as if he was on an army parade, the chiselled expression on his face, no doubt used to intimidate those under his control.

Meade shuffled off, hardly lifting her solid heels from the floor. Poppy stood expressionless, she knew his methods by now, she was not going to bite back, not today. But this was her nemesis within these walls of degradation, she knew he would not let this moment pass without giving her a final roasting with his sharpened tongue. It took less than ten seconds for the prison chief with the steely look to sound off. 'You're a misfit, Jarvis,' he said. 'A menace to society. Trash like you should never be allowed back out on the streets.' Turning his head away from the hovering CCTV camera, the stone-faced prison officer was careful to ensure that no lipreader was going to be privy to the utter contempt he held for the delinquent standing before him. 'You see I have read your notes, from cover to cover, you are just a pain in the arse. Stabbing that poor kid to death and crippling your ex-boyfriend, made you feel good did it, Jarvis? Made you feel like you were top dog? Well, I told you before, you and all these other scumbags in here. You are nobodies. You mean no more to me than that the dog shit I wiped off my shoe last night.'

Poppy stood rigid, showing no emotion. She was never going to be intimidated by an arrogant bully like him. She looked in his direction, but her stare took her beyond his face, determined that she would not been drawn into conflict.

But Callard was far from done with the departing prisoner. 'You see, I have dealt with pondlife like you all my life, Jarvis. Trust me, you're nothing special. You may have fooled the idiots on that parole panel, but you don't fool me. I know you're a fucking wrong 'un, bad to the core.'

A stalemate ensued. It was becoming clear that his goading was having no effect. But Callard had witnessed first-hand the wrath of the woman stood before him, he knew her volcanic temper was likely to erupt at any moment. He knew, however, that he would need to rethink his strategy. Yes, he would have liked to have seen her react and give him the chance to keep her under lock and key, but the truth was he needed her cell. He was conscious that those two new inmates would be halfway down the M1 Motorway by now. Space was already tight on both wings of the prison, he needed to choose his parting words carefully.

Some formalities still needed to be carried out. 'You have that bag, so you been given your clothing back and some donations from a local charity organisation. This small bag here contains three pounds and forty-four pence, the money that was taken from you when was arrested and taken into custody. You need to sign here for that.' Poppy leaned forward and scribbled her name on the release sheet. 'You also need to sign for this envelope. Inside is one hundred pounds cash for your first two weeks living expenses and a travel card for fourteen days to get you two and from Plumstead Police station. Under the terms of your release you will need to attend there every Wednesday morning between ten and eleven o' clock.' Poppy slipped the envelope in her pocket and signed again. She glanced across at the large grey door to her right, a beam of sunshine began to sneak beneath the cracks in the bottom. This that would be her exit route. Nearly there, she thought, nearly there.

But Callard was back on the attack again, the hardened expression on his face showing no compassion. His poisonous putdown continued. 'Spend the money on pills or booze if you like. I don't give a shit. In fact, it would do us all a favour if you had a drugs binge and did yourself in.' His next comment was the lowest blow he could strike, he knew it would hit home hard. 'That is what your friend did, isn't it? That girl from that shitty estate where you lived. That's what you told the judge, that crackhead who killed herself, she was your mate.'

Poppy rolled her tongue around the inside of her cheek and bit hard on her lip, so hard she drew blood, but she still refused to react.

'You are to reside at number three, Albermarle Court, Oxley Village and your sponsor will be Miss Brianna Nylund. She will call your case worker every week to confirm that you are still living there. I have already told you that you will need to sign on at Plumstead Custody Suite every Wednesday morning. Nobody knows why a charming young lady like that Miss Nylund would want a piece of shit like you living in her house. God, she needs her bloody brains tested if you ask me!'

Then suddenly, something snapped inside her head, her tormentor had finally hit a nerve. The missing red mist appeared in full view and a small voice inside Poppy's head told her she had to say something. It was time to retaliate, to bring this thug down a notch or two. 'They still ache ya know.' she said in her course and raspy South London accent. 'My ribs, they still ache. That

13

shooting pain goes right though me, every time I cough or sneeze, or laugh, which I don't do very often.'

Callard wasn't interested in her rant, he kept himself busy with the forms beneath him, it was a welcome distraction

'So, yer did a good job that night, Mister Callard, sir, the night of the power cut, did a right good job. Taught me a lesson, really put me in my place.'

The prison chief tried his best to ignore her, every word she uttered seemed to be tinged with venom, they travelled through his body causing an uneasy feeling which grew by the second.

Poppy wasn't done. 'You see I knew it was you. I'd recognise that pissy smelling pound shop aftershave you wear anywhere. I knew it was you. I have always known it was you.'

The six-foot brute seemed to have shrunk a half a dozen inches in height during this exchange. His demeanour began to change, he looked slightly nervous. He scribbled furiously on the release papers in front of him, clearly not keen to pursue a counterattack at this point. Suddenly, Officer Meade appeared from the corner of the room and stood alongside Poppy. It was obvious to her that there was an atmosphere, but she said nothing.

Callard did gather some momentum, maybe still determined to have the last word. After all, he had never suffered insolence of this kind from his subordinates during his military service and he was not prepared to start now. His voice, however, lacked authority as he gave the parting prisoner his final thoughts on her leaving. 'I would love to think I never see you again, Jarvis, but crackheads like you can't help yourself. You will be back, either here or another place like this. I just hope I never lay eyes on your ugly face ever again.'

Poppy stood tall, she smirked broadly as her opponent finally caved in and raised his head, the pair made full eye contact with each other. He ran a finger around the inside of his tightened shirt collar as he found himself on the end of a dark and lifeless stare that sent freezing cold chills running down his spine. The inmate who had caused this man so much grief during her incarceration here was far from done with this battle. Poppy never minced her words and there would be filter for her foul mouth now she was rattled. 'Nah, nah, don't say that, Mister Callard, sir, don't say that. I hope we do meet again, soon. Somewhere quiet, an alleyway maybe. Somewhere dark, like that night of the blackout. Somewhere you can't hide behind that uniform and you aint got those two big fuckin' gorillas to hold me down while you belt seven bells of shit out me.'

The departing prisoner cracked a sinister smile that turned those small watery particles running down Callard's spine into blocks of solid ice. 'I look forward to that,' Poppy concluded. 'I really look forward to that, Mister Callard, sir!'

Meade took that as her cue to defuse the situation and she grabbed the angry inmate's arm in a bid to remove her from the building.

'Get your hands off me!' Poppy snapped. 'Get your fuckin' hands off me now!'

The bulky prison guard followed her advice, not wanting to inflame the situation further. She walked towards the exit door, her prisoner followed, never once losing eye contact with a stunned and bewildered Callard. He laughed to himself as she left the prison for the last time, but it was certainly not the laugh of a confident man.

Walking at a snail's pace behind the woman with the mardy look on her face, Poppy felt some early morning sunbeams catch her cheeks. It felt refreshing, its rays felt warmer than the sunshine in the exercise yard, the fresh air felt cleaner.

As those large gates closed behind her, Poppy lit up her celebration roll-up, the one she had prepared the previous night, and inhaled her first real intake of clean living in more than two years. Her immediate instincts told her to survey the domain and she noticed a large grey van and a long shiny black vehicle perched precariously to her right. Nothing to her left. She took several long drags on her cigarette before tossing it into the kerb. Strange thoughts began passing through her head and she found herself biding her time before moving on.

Nothing resting between those four walls behind ever unsettled the departing prisoner. Not Callard and his heavy-handed goons. Not the next queue of psycho bitches wanting to test the waters with her inside the prison. Not even the overzealous do-gooders who wanted to rehabilitate her in the Blue Room. Trawling through the murky waters of her harrowing childhood in a bid to find her some sanctuary. No, none of those things ever worried the hard-faced girl who carried the deepest of scars, both physical and emotional.

There was only one thing that really bothered Poppy Jarvis, the unwritten future.

Freedom.

It scared her more than anything in the world.

CHAPTER TWO

I t started, the revving of the engine on the grey transit van, the noise started the second Poppy took her first steps away from the prison gates. A similar sound followed, this one more refined, as the large dark vehicle, slightly obscured, also came to life. No banners and welcoming party to celebrate her release, Poppy thought, probably just a couple of thugs with baseball bats. Undeterred, she made her way to the bus stop at the end of the road and boarded the first bus bound for the London area. The driver refused to accept her travel pass, so she scrambled through her coins and found enough money to cover the fare. As she looked down the aisle of the almost empty bus, she noticed a scruffy youth wearing a black hoodie sitting next to a young girl. She seemed agitated and was clearly intimidated by the boy. He was touching her knee and trying to wrestle with her hands. A few of the lecherous young lad's friends, probably no older than sixteen or seventeen, sat a few seats behind the cocky youth, goading him on. The driver could clearly see what was happening, but, maybe fearful of the consequences, chose to ignore the situation.

As Poppy moved down the middle of the aisle, she took one long look at the rear window and noticed that both vehicles were now in convoy, moving at ridiculously slow speeds rather than overtake the bus. She had a clearer view of the windscreen of the van now, three, possibly four heads bobbing around in the front seats. Not good, not good at all. The number plate on the dark vehicle at the rear was also more noticeable as they turned a corner, three number fours stuck in her mind.

Even though there were twenty or so empty seats she could have chosen to sit in she found herself hovering above the youth who was on the mission to rile the young girl next to him. Poppy watched as he tried to slip his hand beneath her skirt, the frightened teenager was almost in tears.

'You're sitting in my seat,' Poppy said, leaning down to make sure the lecherous lad heard her clearly.

'Fuck off!' came his swift reply. This lad was braver than most.

Poppy bit the inside of her lip and repeated herself, a little louder this time. 'Know your place, little boy, you're in my seat, now move yer fuckin' arse.'

'There are loads of fucking seats. Go sit somewhere else.'

'Listen, shithead, I have told you twice now, I won't tell you again, move!'

A roar went up from the boy's friends, all daring him to challenge her. He responded to their calls 'Or what?' he asked, 'Or fucking what?'

Poppy smiled, that sinister smile that had frightened bigger and braver men already that morning. Her head moved downwards, closer to his, inches away, her breathing was heavy, their faces so close the boy could almost taste the fresh tobacco on her breath. 'Do you really want me to show you what?' she asked. 'Do you really want your friends to have to scrape you up off the fuckin' floor?'

Suddenly his demeanour changed. Maybe it was that look, the stare he faced, that grisly dark expression, dead behind the eyes, evil to the core. His show of bravado disappeared faster than a sinking vessel full of holes. He slipped beneath her and retreated to the back of the bus, much to the amusement of his friends. Poppy sat down, shaking her head as she heard him try to cover his cowardly shame by suggesting that the two girls were probably lesbians and he had lost interest. The distressed girl straightened her clothing and mimed the words, 'Thank you' to her new travel companion. Poppy found no need to respond, she thought she might have left all that bullying and intimidation behind her when she walked out of HMP Wallsgrave. But in just a few short moments she remembered that life can be just as hard outside those walls as it was in inside the prison. Poppy had no further interest in the noisy group of teenagers behind her now, she concentrated on the mirror at the side of the bus, it gave her a clear view of the pursuing vehicles. She was no longer in any doubt, the ensuing entourage were on the warpath. Her self-preservation mode kicked into overdrive, she told herself she needed a weapon.

A few stops later the girl she had rescued left the bus to some nasty cat calls from the bunch of brats in the back seats. But those insults halted the very second Poppy swung her head to confront the heckling crew. If there had been an Olympic award for synchronised cowardice, then the four youths at the rear of the bus would surely have won a gold medal, when their heads bowed as one and their eyes stared firmly on the floor for at least twenty seconds.

When Poppy began to realise that the journey was nearing her destination, she opened the small bag of clothing that Callard had handed her. She discarded the charitable cast-offs on the seat left vacant by her thankful travel companion and pulled out the only item that she needed. It had been dry cleaned, the scruffy looking green jacket with the air force badges on the shoulders, cleaned thoroughly by the looks of things. But the dried-in blood stains on the right sleeve could still be seen, they stood out, forming a scrambled pattern that told a story. The story of a man that had raised his fists to her once too often. A big man she had once shared a bed with, once shared a life with, once shared a dream with. But he was a man who could not say no to the devil's poison. A man who had scalded her head with burning hot water and used her as a punch bag one time more than he should have done. But now he was a man that needed a walking stick to help him when he had to get to the bathroom. A man who surely regretted the day he ever met Poppy Jarvis. She had never given him a second thought until that she saw those bloodstains, not even in those moments of extreme boredom in her cell. One thing was for sure, she had never regretted beating him to within an inch of his life with a sold metal tyre iron. She couldn't care less that Cameron Turner would limp for the rest of his life or that his speech was slurry and almost incomprehensible. All she could think about for the remainder of this trip was the day her friend had stolen this jacket from an upmarket clothing store in Clapham and given it to her as a peace offering after they had argued. This piece of clothing was all she had left of that girl, it made her feel safe when she slipped it on. It was her comfort blanket. Nikita was watching over her now, she knew things would be OK.

Once the bus had passed into South London Poppy felt slightly more at ease, she didn't know why, she just did. She decided that the time was right to test the waters and left the bus. The van stopped some hundred yards or so behind her. The other vehicle however seemed to have left the welcoming party. Poppy was not disappointed. She walked a few hundred yards and noticed a few small shops behind a large green. Most of the outlets had not opened yet but one small convenience store seemed to be bustling with customers. As she neared the shops she noticed a bald man struggling to tie his large dog to a lamppost. The poor animal had no dog collar, just a thick metal chain wrapped around its neck. The hound was pulling hard on the chain, choking himself in the process. He clearly did not care to be restrained in this manner, barking his discontent as loud as he could. The dog abuser was not happy with the animal's behaviour, swinging out a hefty kick into the ribs of the struggling animal and ordering the suffering hound to 'Shut the fuck up.' The angry man disappeared into the newsagent store, cursing his four-legged friend continuously on route.

Poppy was not really a fan of animals, least of all dogs. An Alsatian had once bitten her leg during a short stay with a foster family in Chatham. She revenged the attack by adding chilli powder to the dog's food for several days, before her new carers caught her in the act and sent her packing. But for some reason she was drawn to the helpless hound today, she felt compelled to assist the growling beast. So, before she had time to think about that incident in her past, she found herself stroking his head. There was genuine sorrow in his eyes, it was a strange kind of sadness, it reminded her of her last cellmate, and that had not ended well. Within a matter of seconds Poppy had slipped the chain loose from the dogs bulging neck and tucked it away in her jacket pocket. But to her surprise, the animal did not bolt into the distance as she expected it to. His tail wagged, he seemed to have found a new and caring friend. 'Fuck off stupid mutt,' she shouted. 'Scram!'

Realising his initial poor judgement, the animal seized his chance and a runaway stocky bulldog scampered across the green in the direction of a nearby housing estate. Poppy bid him farewell with a simple but prophetic comment. 'Time for both of us to be off the leash today, mate,' she said.

As Poppy entered the shop, she passed the bald-headed man. 'I think your dog's done a runner, mate,' she said, matter-of-factually.

'What!' asked the man, his face turning beetroot red, he looked as if he was about to explode.

'Yeah, he fucked off down that way,' Poppy explained, pointing into the opposite direction to where the dog was last seen.

The red-faced bald man started running, well in truth it was more of a slow jog, cursing his apparent best friend again and threatening all sorts of punishments when he caught up with the creature.

When Poppy opened the fridges inside the shop, she winced at the cost of the cans of soft drink. She slipped one inside her jacket rather than pay the extortionate prices on offer. She did, however, need to find the money to pay for some tobacco and some rizla papers. She spent some time scouring the shelves, looking for a large knife or an iron bar, oblivious to the fact that she was unlikely to find those in what was little more than a newsagent shop. She had no doubt when she left the relative safety of the convenience store that an encounter of some kind was inevitable. What she needed to do now, in some way, was to level the playing field. Her mouth was dry, but she chose not to open her can of juice just yet. She needed to be fully focused.

And so, the game had started. Only three heads in the van now, one sturdy individual in a grey sweatshirt on foot. He was following her and the van was following him. The black car had probably been a rare error of judgment on her part, it was no longer in the hunt. Slowly but surely Poppy's feet gathered momentum, her walk turned into a jog which quickly became a sprint. The man on foot followed her lead and within a few seconds the race was on. She picked up more speed as she raced past some bewildered bystanders and turned left at a small pathway between some terraced houses. Her chaser was not shaken off and pursued her down the narrow alleyway. In front on her she could see a green wire fence blocking her escape, several tennis courts behind the fence, but no gate. As she neared the perimeter she spotted a gap in the wire mesh at the bottom of the fence, but she had no intention of getting down on her hands and knees.

It is said that in times of danger that your brain instinctively sends you two messages, fight or flight. Poppy Jarvis was done running.

In a split second she used the tennis court fence as a springboard for her feet and bounced around at pace to face her opponent. His momentum carried him forward and he was just inches away when Poppy swung the can in her hand with an almighty force.

The weighty tin of fruit juice cracked hard against the side of her pursuers nose, breaking it instantly and sending spurts of gushing blood all over the place. The chasing thug fell to his hands and knees in agony. Almost instantly he felt the power of Poppy's solid boot crash against the side of his skull, sending him reeling sideways. Another swift kick to his head followed, causing her would-be attacker to curl up in a ball to protect himself. Poppy looked beyond the moaning mess beneath her and took a deep breath as three full sized figures grew larger as the other pursuers approached the battleground. Just as they arrived Poppy raised her leg and bought her heel stomping down on the shoulder of the injured attacker. A sickening noise and a howl of excruciating agony confirmed that she had snapped his collar bone in two. She had set out her stall, there would be no mercy shown in this conflict today. Her brutal assault had an immediate effect. The sight of their semi-conscious friend screaming in pain in the gutter slowed down the oncoming trio. It was obvious to them now that their opponent was going to be no pushover.

Cautiously they descended on the battle scene, anger in their eyes, snarling, like a hungry pack of wolves baying for blood. The facing parties danced around for a few seconds, eyeing one another up. Poppy, as always, looking for any signs of weakness in her enemy. Without thinking twice, she pulled the dog chain out of her pocket and wrapped it around her wrist, the chunks of metal were loosened and slowly gathered momentum as she began to swing her new weapon by her side. There were no words, no threats, both sides knew exactly why they were there.

Showing no fear at all, Poppy, studied her opposition more closely as the standoff ensued. Heavy guy, balding head, large fists, tattoos on his fingers, scars across the cheeks of his angry face. He is the threat, she thought, he is the hard man. Black guy, tall, skinny, smart tracksuit, gold rings, holding a metal bar, he is doing this for the money. Third man, nervous, scruffy hair, pale spotty skin, no eye contact, a druggie, a visibly shaking wreck. He is the weak link, probably just the driver. He is not up for this fight, she thought, take that fucker out first, then it will just be two of them.

Poppy changed the angle of the swinging chain and raised it above her head, she was alert now, her senses fully heightened. She homed in on the scruffy youth and lashed out viciously with her weapon. Her first strike missed the target, but she saw the fear in his eyes as the second swing of the dog chain caught the corner of his head. Almost instantly the dance routine changed shape as the blow took its toll and the reluctant fighter took two steps backwards. A voice suddenly rose from the concrete floor beneath the dancing quartets feet. 'She's broke my fucking nose, bruv, shank that bitch, kill that fucking slag.'

Black Guy found his voice too. 'Neddy said no blades.'

Hard Man now joined in, opening his mouth and displaying a line of crooked teeth hemmed together by two oversized jagged incisors. 'Fuck Neddy!' he shouted. 'Done is done, bruv! This is the mad bitch that carved up Billy. She's gonna pay, she is gonna fucking pay big time.'

The mutiny in the ranks had not go unnoticed by Poppy, she quickly realised that this conflict was more personal than she first thought. There were a few seconds of switching eye-contact amongst the quartet before Poppy broke her own silence. 'You had better finish me today then, shitheads,' she said. 'Cause thanks to mouth almighty down there, I know where to find you now.' With those words she swung her arm and bought the chain back into the fray, narrowly missing the tall black lad's neck as she lashed out with a vicious strike.

The trio of aggressors regrouped once again, changing positions, perhaps in readiness for a masterpiece ending for their violent dance finale. Gurgling noises were now emulating from below as the wounded youth began to cough up some blood that had trickled into his mouth. The distraction gave Poppy her chance and she aimed the chain once again towards her attackers, determined this time to score a hit. But as the chain travelled beyond her line of vision, she caught sight of something which put her off her stride. The shiny black car had reappeared, three number fours on the plate. It had found them, it was perched precariously at the end of the alleyway, engine purring, as if it was waiting for somebody to lower a starting flag. An eerie thought flashed through her mind, and she remembered how vicious and brutal Neddy could be. Suddenly her head-to-head with this rag-tag bunch in front of her seemed irrelevant. The main man was here himself, here to exact his revenge.

In that split second that Poppy lost concentration the whole tide of the battle wave changed. Hard Man had snatched her weapon from her hand and was now standing behind her with the thick links of the chain pressing hard against her neck. She found herself gasping for air, instinctively she slipped her fingers beneath the metal in a bid to stop herself being throttled. But danger loomed all round her, Black Guy was lashing out with the solid metal pole. One of the strikes caught Poppy on her arm as she tried to defend herself. Scruffy had also come to life, finding the courage to launch some token kicks at her, no doubt trying to justify his pay packet for the day. Even the battered whinger on the floor was screaming out loudly for them to finish her off. And, to top it all, to her left she could see that black carriage, no doubt carrying the executioner that would finish the task.

But that's when it happened, that's when Poppy noticed them, that's when the tattoos on the fingers of the Hard Man who was squeezing the life out of her, came into full view. Large, inked letters that spelled out a word, a tattooed word that told its own story. A tale of an innocent young girl that was brutally passed around a gang of laughing hyenas. They were using her, systematically abusing her. Her former flat-mate, Nikita, the closest of friends she had in her life, was the helpless victim. She was being traded around for the sexual gratification of others. She had only ever seen those tattoos once before, on the tiny screen of a mobile phone, but she had played that sickening event over and over in her head. She remembered those ink marks, she would never forget them, the letters L I O N S.

They had appeared a thousand times in her darkest moments. And with those tattooed knuckles came the sound, the voice was there too, right behind her head. It was that voice that had accompanied those big fat fingers and those tattoos in that haunting small screen nightmare. The hand that had pushed Nikita's poor head backwards and forwards on his sweaty unwashed penis, while he uttered those terrible words that would never leave her memory. 'Gag on that ugly freak,' he had said, as he thrusted his manhood down her throat. 'Gag on that ugly freak.' Poppy could see that tiny screen again in her head, replaying the incident, it was as clear as anything. Him, the ringleader, the sickening laughter of the onlooking crowd, patiently waiting their turn to abuse her defenceless friend. The sound of Nikita sobbing as she begged them to release her from her torment. It was him, the Hard Man with those marked fingers pressing firmly against her neck. It was him and Billy Keyes, it was them to blame, they were the reason Nikita had been shamed and humiliated into taking her own life.

Poppy was still in the thick of the onslaught, she should be finished off by now, she had almost turned blue. The blows were still reigning in on her body from every angle. In the car, Neddy was surely just biding his time, menacingly waiting to take her carcass away. But the sight of those tattoos changed everything. Suddenly Poppy found a renewed strength, a mighty surge of unbridled rage ripped through her body and exploded with extreme venom. She was single-minded now, forget Black Guy, forget Scruffy and the loser on the floor. She wanted blood, she wanted Hard Man's blood, she wanted rivers of blood. She wanted so badly to drain his body of all life, to cut him into pieces as she had done to his fellow abuser Billy. That inner strength raced through her body and doubled the size of every muscle, she suddenly found she had the strength of the warrior queen, Boudica, and the whole of her Iceni army. She let out an ear-piercing scream as her hands slipped further under the chain, her neck swung forwards and then backwards with a mighty force, catching the Hard Man fully in his face with the back of her head.

The chain on her neck was loosened, enough for her to wriggle free, allowing her to lash out with her right foot, catching Black Guy off balance and sending him reeling to the floor. She was released from his grip now, free to finish this battle, her arms begun swinging wildly, like runaway windmill sails, her fists catching everything in her path. She turned her attention fully on the Hard Man with the inked fingers who was desperately trying to find his feet. Blow after blow reigned in, each punch, each kick for Nikita. The big lump was struggling to defend himself. But with this single-minded attack mode driving her on, she lost sight of Black Guy who crept in behind her back and launched his weapon with a powerful swing. Poppy felt the force of the metal bar crack against her skull, she slumped forward on to her knees. Another strike followed swiftly, and she doubled over in pain.

In a complete daze, Poppy stumbled forward, expecting another round of blows to thrust down on her. But at that very second, when her head was spinning and her body was screaming out in agony, she heard a loud shout. Her ears were ringing inside, but she swore she heard someone shout the words, 'feds' and 'run'. Pushing down on the concrete path she was struggling to find her feet, her legs buckled, and she fell back down on her knees. Confused and stunned she tried desperately to focus. Through her cloudy vision she could just about make out the shapes of four blurry figures burrowing their way through the small hole in the tennis court fence and scurrying across the courts. Poppy was completely disorientated, semi-conscious, she tried to pull herself up but fell forwards again, that blow to her head had grounded her and now she was helpless.

And then, just when she thought the conflict was over, alarm bells sounded out loudly inside her head, as she heard the purring engine on the car die. A deafening silence ensued, she waited, her heart pounding loudly inside her chest as she tried to regain her composure. Somewhere inside her bruised and battered mind a voice told her that her final destiny had arrived. She knew Neddy would never relent, she had witnessed his anger at close quarters, she knew he was a man who would not think twice about ending her existence. Her fate was sealed.

Through a melee of screeching and buzzing noises rattling inside her head she made out the sound of a car door opening and closing, she knew her time was near. Footsteps followed, her heart raced faster and faster, she tried desperately to find some inner strength to protect herself, she had no intention of dying without a fight. But then, during those next few seconds, mixed signals raced through her brain, she became confused. They were not heavy footsteps as she had anticipated, they were light, measured, moving slowly, moving closer and closer. And then a pungent odour found its way into her returning senses. A familiar smell, a perfume, strong, laced with almonds, sweet, yet to her it could prove more deadly than the traces of napalm that kissed the killing fields of Vietnam. Slowly but surely her vision became less blurry, and she could make out a welcoming grip. Long outstretched fingers, perfectly painted nails adorned the helping hand. And finally, the voice, soft, refined, educated, a small hint of drama. 'Oh, my beautiful sister, what have those monsters done to you?'

Maybe Poppy should have been grateful that this was not the demon that she had expected to encounter at that moment. Thankful that she had been spared the merciless brutality of Neddy. She should have been whispered a prayer of redemption for the angelic creature that had just rescued her from an horrific fate. She should have been grateful, but she wasn't. Every ounce of self-preservation in her battered body screamed out to her now.

'Throw me back to the wolves,' she thought to herself as she clambered up off the stony ground. 'Throw me back to those bloody wolves, I'll be safer there.'

CHAPTER THREE

A renowned philosopher once shared his belief that, 'Life can only start on the other side of despair.' But how far? How could you ever measure how many days, weeks, months or years it would take? Or how many miles you would need to run to distance yourself from a moment that broke your heart into a million tiny fragments and left you wanting to end the misery of your pitiful existence.

Brianna Nylund was no wiser. It had been exactly nine hundred and eighty-six days and nights since the tragic accident at the Maple Crossing near her home in Oxley Village. But every morning still felt as if it was the day after. She had been consumed by grief from the moment it happened. Confined to her bed for almost five months as she struggled to cope with the pain of watching her twin brother, Jamie, die amid an act of heroism. Someone she loved more than life itself, simply vanish from her life in a few short seconds.

Her mother, Krista, thought she knew the answer, counselling, counselling and more counselling. But the kind words and understanding smiles of strangers could not bring him back. Her life had been an empty vessel floating on a sea of sadness since that dark November day in 2018. She knew that her brother was forever lost to her. She felt as if nothing or nobody could ever fill that void in her life.

And to pour the sharpest of salts into her open wounds, shortly after her brother was buried, she would discover that the only other man in her life that she had ever loved, ever truly respected, was not her real father. But maybe it had been a moment of serendipitous fortune when Brianna found a twenty plus year old photograph of her mother and a strange man, both looking 'loved-up' at an awards ceremony in a posh London hotel. She put two plus two together and came up with her own theory. 'My mother was a cheating whore and the man that had cared for me since I took my first breath was not my real father.' That man that had raised her and her brother was Per Nylund. So smitten was he with Krista that he dropped out of college and followed her to England in the early nineteen nineties. He even changed his name by deed-poll to match hers because she continually refused his offers of marriage. But Per was no longer in Krista's life. Finally, after thirty years of chasing a dream life with his childhood sweetheart, he had accepted that he had never been anything more than her comfort puppet. He had allowed Krista to pursue her career while he parked his to bring up two children, he knew were not his own. He always seemed happiest when he was back in his native Finland and perhaps there was a twist of irony that he had now found belated love and consolation in the arms of one of Krista's friends from her hometown, Tampere. Bree still loved Per, as much as anybody can love an absent guardian or stepfather. She was genuinely happy that he had escaped the manipulation and humiliation that her mother had cast on him. Per still sent her the odd text message, which she appreciated, but never answered.

It was no secret that Brianna and Krista did not have a harmonious mother and daughter relationship. She rebelled at an early age against her parent's obsession with perfection. Her mother was forever scolding her daughter if she lost in a sports event or wasn't the best dressed at a special occasion. Tensions heightened when she reached her teens and she refused to answer to the name 'Brianna' anymore, saying that she found that tag highly embarrassing. Luckily, most of her close friends and her twin called her Bree. Her mother, however, refused to march to her tune. Some might say she revelled in the drama of the mother and daughter rivalry. Maybe there was truth in that assumption, until things started to turn nasty.

It was not long after her brother's tragic death that Bree discovered the truth about her mother's sordid affair and cut off all ties with her. Krista did what she was best at, she won back her daughter's affection with cold hard cash, buying her a luxury flat from the proceeds of the sale of the family home. Even though she could have purchased a similar property for a knockdown price in a new development in Guildford, Bree stood her ground and insisted that she had to live in Oxley. It was, she reminded her mother, where all her happiest memories had been with Jamie. The luxury two-bedroom abode in Albermarle Court was just one of six in the block. It had beautifully bright and well-maintained communal gardens and a breath-taking view of the surrey countryside. It set Krista back a little over four hundred thousand pounds, but she saw this as a small price to pay for a new start with her estranged daughter. This new start, however, lasted less time than it took for the first bottle of milk to be replaced in the fridge. Like mother like daughter, Bree had got what she wanted and now her parent's affection was surplus to requirements.

To find out that her mother had cheated on Per and that she and her beautiful twin brother came from the sperm of a total stranger had fuelled the fires of burning hatred inside the hurting girl. She had felt an empty hollowness since Jamie died, sleepwalking her way through her mundane life until that discovery of that incriminating photograph. Brianna had found a twisted kind of comfort in the knowledge that the random man

31

that her mother had cheated with had a child of his own. She had inherited a sibling, a half-sister, from nowhere. A dirty secret locked away from her for the past twenty plus years. Poppy's father was, however, no run-of-the-mill fling for Krista. Her mother had managed to fall for a low-life member of society. A man who could not hold down a job, a man who put alcohol before everything in his life, including his wife and daughter. A selfish man, who, when things got tough and his spouse left him, dumped his eight-year-old daughter into care without a second thought. But in Brianna's eyes Karma played an ace when her unknown father died of cancer of the liver. Not only did it rid her sibling of a parent who deserved nothing, but it would be the catalyst that would finally bring the sisters together.

In the past, Brianna had always had Jamie to rely on, they were more than brother and sister, more than just twins, they were true soul mates. But as a child she always felt as if there was something or somebody missing in her life. Jamie would often say she was weird because she seemed to be talking to imaginary friends in her room. He often teased her that nobody at their school liked her and those ghosts in her bedroom were the only real friends she had.

If only Brianna had known at the time that her estranged sister was never far from her. She was there, in plain hiding, living just a short drive away from her front doorstep in a run-down council estate in South London. That was of course when Poppy Jarvis was not being detained in one of Her Majesty's secure bed and breakfast institutions. And since their first encounter and Poppy's latest incarceration, Brianna had been a regular visitor to the establishments that housed her troubled sibling. This she did, even though Poppy would often feign illness to avoid her sisters prison visits. But, like a faithful puppy who had been ignored by its owner, Brianna would return the following week bearing small gifts of expensive chocolate and news from the outside world.

Brianna Nylund was twenty-five years old, but despite the traumas of the past few years retained the youthful looks of a teenager. Her admirers would say that her long wavy locks of golden blonde hair and heightened cheekbones gave her the look of a Scandinavian Princess. Perfect soft skin to match her perfect body, she looked and walked like a sophisticated cat-walk model. Never seen in anything other than the best co-ordinated designer clothing, she certainly took after her mother in one respect. She had an untameable wildness about her, a hint of danger in her mesmerising deep brown eyes, that seemed to melt like large chocolate buttons when she glanced your way. She could steal your heart with one twist of her smile. To add to her awesome beauty she was spritely, full of energy, full of life. One of her counsellors once described her as, 'the epitome of beautiful craziness. A girl that had been to the depths of despair and back to conquer her deep depression. She had been like a single blood-red rose, lost and alone in a dark and barren wilderness.'

While Poppy was sleeping soundly in her new bed, Bree had made a trip to Heathrow Airport to collect her boss from the publishing company where she worked. Kendra de Jerez was returning from a shopping trip to New York. Brianna often did this, not for the duty-free gifts she was showered with but because she had the use of Kendra's top of the range Mercedes car during her absence. Brianna would never tell her boss, but she often raced the high-powered vehicle along narrow country lanes, reaching speeds of 140 miles an hour. She found it exhilarating, it tested her resolve, danger was just a word to her. She thought that the vehicle would also be an impressive gesture for collecting her sister at the prison gates. Although for one reason or another that had not gone according to plan. When she returned home that night, she had no more than three hours sleep before her body dragged her out of bed and out into the early morning sunshine for a steady five-mile jog.

If there was one thing Brianna had, it was an eye for perfection. You only needed to look at the array of high-brow designer clothing and shoes in her wardrobe to see that she had impeccable taste. So, when it came to decorating the spare room for her new housemate it had to be 'Une oeuvre d'art,' it had to be perfect. She hoped her sibling might appreciate that she remembered the things that she had told her during her prison visits. Definitely no bright pinks and purples, she knew that her sister would not approve. Pastel colours were fine, so Poppy's new bedroom was decorated in lilacs, pale mauves and two different shades of cream.

Since returning from her jog and shower Brianna had sat quietly on the corner of her sister's bed, drying her hair with a hand towel while watching over her sibling like a mother would over a child at bedtime. The fresh smelling Egyptian cotton bedclothes covering her sister had fallen slightly to one side, revealing a mass of battered flesh on her body and legs. She tried to look away but was drawn to the yellowing bruises and mouldy grey skin abrasions. She ran her fingers gently across her sister's wounds knowing that it would take more than a jar of Geranium Oil to heal those marks. She had been sitting by her side for more than twenty minutes now, watching her sibling's pallid cheeks twitching, listening to her heavy breathing as she wrestled with the soft pillow supporting her head.

'Morning, sleepyhead,' Bree whispered as she noticed her sister's eyelids begin to flicker.

'What the fuck!' her new guest replied in a throaty voice, pulling up the duvet to cover her exposed body.

'Sleep well?' Bree asked, moving over to the window and drawing the colourful Laura Ashley curtains.

'No!' Poppy barked. 'I had an 'orrible dream and my 'ead feels like I have been hit by a car.'

Bree laughed politely. 'I am not sure if your head was down to those bullies that were bashing you around yesterday or the two bottles of Merlot you guzzled down last night.'

'Awww, fuck!' she said, clearly suffering as she retreated beneath the covers. 'I need some fuckin' aspirin.'

'I did say we should take you to A and E, but you wouldn't go.'

'I don't do hospitals.'

'But you were in a real mess when we got you back.'

'Look, have ya got any headache tablets or not?'

'Eggs benedict OK for brunch?' Bree asked, busying herself by bringing some fresh towels to her patient's bed. 'I showed you where the bathroom is, why not have a nice shower before we go out.'

Strange sounds, coupled with several X-rated expletives emulated from Poppy's mouth beneath the cosy duvets. She desperately wanted her sister to leave her in peace. But Bree was persistent, much to her sibling's distaste. 'Your clothes were covered in blood, so I threw them in the wash. You can have a rummage through my wardrobe for something to wear today. Oh, I had better find you some painkillers.'

Poppy made no attempt to leave her comfy den, she simply pulled a few faces and mimicked her sister's well-spoken accent.

When she thought it was safe to emerge from her bed, Poppy looked around and studied her surroundings. Clean, everything so clean. Fresh, everything smelled of flowers and pleasant scents. She noticed that every item in the room seemed to be colour co-ordinated, right down to the lamp on the bedside cabinet. Her attention was suddenly drawn to two large pictures on opposite sides of the bedroom wall. They were pastel-coloured illustrations, simple but eye-catching. Both were pictures of a young woman, immaculate features, hair in different poses. The clothes she was wearing were not modern, they wore strange lacey type outfits. At first, she thought they might be portraits of her narcissistic sister, but on closer inspection dismissed that theory. She found the pictures very strange but also enticing. The eyes in the paintings had a sorrowful look about them, they fascinated her. She felt a compulsion to study them closer, as if she was being drawn in.

Poppy double-checked the locks on the bathroom door before enjoying a fifteen-minute shower. Unlike her sister she spent no time at all studying the new bruises on her battered frame. She wrapped herself in the clean smelling towelling robe left by her sister and joined her for brunch. Hoping above all else that her sister would be busier eating than she would talking. She had been in her new home less than a day and the sound of her sibling's voice was already grating on her.

During their meal Bree handed her sister a brand new I-Phone. She told her that she had left the charger in a box in her new bedroom. She was happy to show her how the device worked and not to worry about the amount of calls she made as everything was billed to her main account. Bree also showed her that she had included herself as the first contact's name on the handset and pointed out the small picture of her that would appear every time the phone rang. She told her that the contact log stored up to three hundred names, a comment which received a blank expression from her new housemate. Poppy may well have been struggling to think of anybody else she would or could add to the single contact she already had in there.

When the girls had eaten, and Poppy had swallowed some much-needed Ibuprofen, they found themselves in Bree's bedroom. More perfectly designed themes, more carefully blended colour schemes and two more of those pictures that had fascinated her so much. Poppy wasn't really interested in an explanation but found herself asking the question. 'Fuck! You've got those all over the house, even in the bathroom. Did you get them as a job lot or somefink?'

Bree laughed. 'No, no, those are my Luna Sards.'

'Who?' her sister asked.

'Luna Sard, a highly reputable artist, I have the full collection. They were not expensive but it took me ages to track them all down.'

'They all look a bit weird to me. It is the same girl right, in all the pictures, the same girl?'

'How perceptive of you, Poppy, that's exactly what they are, self-portraits, they all display a different mood'

'Nah, I meant, you know the bird in them. It's all the same bird innit? Loves herself or what!'

36

'But that's the enchanting thing about them, Poppy. You see it was a man, not a woman, a man painted those pictures. He wanted to express his true feelings. He wanted to show the world how he would look if he was a female. So, he made pictures of himself as a woman in all those different outfits. The different clothes expressed the different moods he was having at the time. There are twelve of them altogether, I have the whole collection.'

'What, was he some sort of nut job?'

'No, no, no, he is renowned for this collection. People believe that he was confused about his sexuality. That he was trapped in a body he didn't want to be in. So, this was his way of expressing himself as a woman, like an alter-ego'

'He sounds like a right nutter to me.'

Both girls found themselves staring at the same picture for a few seconds, Bree was deep in thought. 'I find them comforting, spiritually comforting. It's as if they are trying to tell me something.'

Poppy shook her head. 'Yeah, that the geezer who painted them is a sandwich short of a picnic.'

'Clothes,' Bree said, changing the direction of the conversation. 'What's mine is yours, you know, sisters are meant to share everything.' She opened a large, mirrored wardrobe housing a wall-to-wall array of stunning outfits. Dresses, trousers, jackets, all neatly pressed and colour co-ordinated. Perfectly pressed, as if they had all been dry cleaned that morning.

'Half-sisters.' Poppy said under her breath, just loudly enough for her sibling to be reminded that the girls did not share the same mother.

Bree had already chosen her outfit for the day, a smart paisley print Michael Kors dress and knee length Moncler boots. 'It is lovely outside today, Poppy, what about a nice summery dress? This is Dior, it will go really well with your hair colour.'

'I don't do dresses,' Poppy replied. 'Some jeans or leggings will do me, we are about the same size, aint we?'

'Yes, but, Oh, wow! This Cardin dress, I have only ever worn it once, it will bring out the …'

Bree's persistence enraged her sister. 'What! Are you deaf?' she yelled. 'I don't do fuckin' dresses.'

The ringtone of Bree's mobile saved the moment from becoming anything more than a difference of opinion. Bree would usually ignore this caller, but it gave her an excuse to leave her sister to browse through her outfits.

'Yes, mother, what do you want? I am going out shortly, so I haven't got long.'

Poppy began rummaging through her sister's wardrobe and sizing up a couple of garments that drew a disapproving glare from her sibling. Bree was answering her mother's questions very much in a 'yes' and 'no' fashion, hoping that she would see she had not time for small talk. 'Yes, I am pleased you liked the feature. Yes, Kendra was very impressed. No, I didn't have to have any jabs mother, they are homeless people not lepers.'

Clearly riled be her parent's comments, Bree pulled several faces as the conversation rolled on. 'I can't speak for long, I am going over to Kayleigh's house, she is helping me with some things I need to get sorted. Oh, but you knew that, didn't you? There's you again mother, calling my friends for a chat whenever you feel like it. Can't you get some friends of your own?'

Bree covered the phone with her hand while she guided her sister through her search 'They are yoga pants, Poppy, not really for going out.'

It became obvious that a comment from Bree's mother had angered her daughter and Bree raised her voice a couple of notches. 'Yes, I did watch that documentary you told me watch, but I don't get what it has to do with me.'

A thumbs up from Bree as her sister slipped on a powder blue Versace top, but a frown when her sister had decided that the leggings should stay.

'I know those pills are dangerous, I told you before that I

stopped taking them ages ago. God, I don't think you can even get them anymore, mother. Will you stop treating me like a five-year-old, I am OK now. In fact, today I am in a happy place. What! God, no, no, you can't stay with me when you come over, you will have to stay with Aunt Milly. It's not convenient. Why? Well, I have someone staying with at me the moment.'

Bree was looking for an excuse to end the call and help Poppy find something other than the mis-matched garments she had prised from her collection. But now her mother had begun digging for clues to who her house guest might be, so she decided to be blunt. 'No, not Preston, why on earth would it be Preston? It's not a man, mother, just someone, you don't know them. 'Yes, yes, I know, yes, yes, right, I have to go now, bye.'

When she finished the call, she rolled her eyes and shook her head, hoping that her sibling might see the contempt she held for the woman that had bought her into the world. 'God, that woman drives me to despair. Sometimes, I wish she would just take the hint that I don't want her in my life.'

Bree wasn't totally convinced by the sweat top and leggings that her sister had chosen to wear, but she was conscious of the time and wanted to get to her first destination as soon as possible. She had promised Poppy that she would take her to pick up some items that a friend was looking after for her later in the day and her gut feeling was that it was not going to be a simple task. Before the girls set-off Poppy grabbed an apple from the fruit bowl and stood in the hallway looking long and hard at another of those strange self-portraits.

She found herself snarling and pulling faces at the woman in the illustrations. She certainly did not share her sister's enthusiasm for the collection of pictures, she found them to be most unsettling.

CHAPTER FOUR

'An ordinary house in a very ordinary street.' That's how Bree described the location where her sat nav had delivered her car to. Twenty-One Marlow Close was indeed an ordinary house in a quiet cul-de-sac in Anerley, a small suburb of Southeast London. The brickwork could do with a makeover, the front door was a fading shade of orangey brown and the grass covering the small front garden had been neglected for some time. The black metal gate was buckled in places and was hanging loose from its hinges, a definite danger to passing children. This run-down Victorian abode was ordinary indeed, but maybe not to its residents. The couple that lived here were solid honest people. They had scrimped and scraped to find the deposit for this two-bedroom house, both working two jobs for a year or so to buy purchase their first home together. But things became tougher for the pair when their plan took a diversion with the unexpected, but welcomed, news that their family would be having a third member

Bree pushed hard on the front doorbell for the third time 'I know they are in,' she said. 'I heard the baby crying when we first arrived.' Poppy said nothing, she was not as keen as her sibling at the prospect of a reunion with the girl who had suffered a broken cheekbone when the pair had first met. To make matters worse she had promised her pushy sister that she would apologise for leaving her friend Kayleigh's face with an unsightly bump and a permanent scar.

'Come on,' Bree insisted. 'There is a spare key around the back, follow me.' The women walked along a narrow side path which led to the rear of the house. On route they passed a couple of teenage boys sat on the neighbouring wall. The youths were nodding their heads to some repetitive techno sounds on their mobile phones and sharing a badly cut joint. Their adolescence became evident as the sisters passed them by. 'Oi blondie,' the elder youth with the ginger hair shouted. 'Come and have a blaze with us.'

The girls ignored their comment and let themselves in to the property via the back gate. Bree couldn't help but share her thoughts on the home they were visiting. 'I told you, it's disgusting, this area, I hate coming here.'

Retrieving a spare key from under a loose brick on a small rockery in the garden, Bree began to let herself in through the back door. But before she could turn the key the door was pulled open, and Poppy was shocked to the core when she was greeted by a familiar voice from her past. It caught her completely off-guard. 'Hello, trouble, welcome back to the real world.'

At a little over six feet tall, Matt Jameson would probably not stand out amongst other men, but his broad yet gentile Geordie accent did. In those few seconds Poppy was confused, she hadn't seen him since the incident at the Chez Blanc restaurant two years previously. For a short time before her incarceration, Matt had been her work colleague, her friend and her sexual sparring partner. He was her comfortable port in a storm when her boyfriend at that time was high on drugs. He was also present the night she lost control and smashed up the bistro where the unlikely duo had worked. But it wasn't just the sight of the strapping lad with the beaming Cheshire cat grin that had taken her by surprise. No, it was the bundle nestling tightly in his arms. 'This is Willow,' he declared proudly. 'This is our beautiful pride and joy.'

The sisters were ushered in, the fact that neither Matt nor Poppy could take their eyes off one another did not go unnoticed. Maybe the fires of a burning inferno that fuelled their sexual past had been re-ignited. Their awkward re-union was interrupted by the appearance of the co-owner of the property, Kayleigh. It was clear from the expression on her face that she was far from impressed with the entrance of the girls and she aimed her angst at her best friend. 'You can't keep doing that, Bree, babe, you can't just come up through my back door whenever you feel like it.'

Almost simultaneously Matt and Poppy laughed out loud at the seemingly harmless remark she had made. Bree smiled to herself when she realised that the giggling pair had enjoyed the sexual innuendo and were clearly somewhere on the same wavelength.

'Chill out,' Bree said, angry that her host was making an unnecessary scene. 'I told you I was going to bring my sister around today.'

'I know, babe,' Kayleigh replied, trying not to overreact. 'But you really should have called me first. Matt is off to the gym in a minute, and I still have all of the rooms upstairs to clean.'

'Poppy has something she wants to say to you, don't you Poppy?'

Three adults and a babe in arms seemed to turn their heads in unison, all waiting for some heartfelt speech or humble apology. Poppy bit the inside of her lip and muttered a few words, reluctantly. 'She', no doubt meaning her sibling. 'She said I had to say sorry.'

If the quartet of onlookers were waiting for more than that then they would be waiting for a very long time.

Bree shrugged off the awkwardness of the moment much to everybody's relief. 'I think that's the best you are going to get, Kayleigh. Any chance of a cup of coffee? Not that instant crap, make some fresh stuff.'

Her friend nodded before reaching out for Matt to pass her the baby. 'Help yourself,' she said. 'You know where everything is. I am going to put Willow down now, it's way passed her napping hour.'

Matt explained as his partner whisked the baby upstairs to a waiting cot. 'We read about the benefits of napping hours for Willow. She has a disorder, you see, where she falls into very deep night sleeps if you don't make her take naps a few times through the day. Sometimes, it is almost impossible to wake her. Bree knows, don't you Bree? When we first bought her home from the hospital, we rushed her to A and E a few times, she just wouldn't wake up.'

Poppy caught the attention of her sister, rolling her eyes and mimicking a fake yawn. Having agreed to be the baby's Godmother, Bree had suffered chapter and verse of every moment of the baby's journey into the world right up to her three-month celebration party the previous week. She felt like telling Matt that she didn't have the slightest interest how much the baby weighed or what colour her stools were that week. But she needed some help from him and her bestie, so her thoughts were best kept to herself, for now, anyway.

Kayleigh took her time when settling the restless infant upstairs in the main bedroom, she was in no hurry to return to the homecoming party downstairs. She for one was not impressed with the fact that Poppy had gained an early release from prison. She wished that the authorities had never released the girl with the mounting history of violent assaults and thrown away the key. To make matters worse her boyfriend had seemed to be a little too enthusiastic to be re-acquainted with his sordid past.

When Kayleigh reached low points, she would often visit the long mirror on the back of her wardrobe door. For her, it was, in the strangest of ways, the 'mirror of truth'. She studied her reflection more closely than usual. It screamed out to her, 'Frumpy cow'. She never argued with its findings, it knew her better than anybody, why would it lie? But the mirror of truth had been much kinder in previous years, it told her nicer things. That was until she put on more than twenty five pounds of weight during her pregnancy, when it had all but told her to 'give up'.

Kayleigh was in her mid-twenties now, a plain Jane who never bothered too much with make-up, even though those sleepless nights comforting her new-born were taking their toll on her features. Without realising it, she was beginning to dress like a middle-aged woman. She had even found a hairdresser that managed to age her twenty years with a variation of no-frills cuts for her mousy brown hair. It seems that the mirror of truth was telling her repeatedly that she was getting old before her time, but it never told her what to do about it.

She sometimes wondered where her youthfulness and energy had gone. It seemed that in just a short space of time, she had lost her tag as a carefree teenager with no morals and an extremely high sex drive, and simply grown old. She seemed to have woken up one morning and found herself in a dead-end relationship, living with a man she no longer trusted. The one, sometimes the only thing, that her and Matt had to fall back on when the conversation dried up, was their animal instincts. But her once sex-mad partner had not satisfied her needs in months.

The pair had become an item after Matt had, in true gentlemanly fashion, escorted her to the hospital after she had been beaten black and blue by Poppy in that terrifying ordeal at the restaurant. Despite Matt considering himself to be a sex crazed stud who had the stamina to perform long and hard all night, it was Kayleigh that instigated almost every sexual tryst they had in those early days. To say she had a high sex drive at the time was an understatement and, on many occasions, they would lock themselves away in Matts flat for days on end, only breaking from their erotic marathons for takeaways and toilet breaks.

Kayleigh often wondered if she had chosen the wrong girl to be her bestie. Bree was, after all, breathtakingly stunning from the moment puberty arrived. Long blonde silky locks, a perfectly formed body for figure hugging designer clothes. She didn't need to be witty and intelligent, but of course she was. In their mid-teens her schoolfriend had drawn the attention of everyone around, a countless number of teenage boys who would declare her as their first real crush. But for Kayleigh she would always have to play second fiddle, fighting for the scraps. She would often find solace in the arms of the lads that Bree had rejected. After all, any attention was better than none. But she soon realised that boys wanted more than kisses and cuddles from the geeky second bester and she reluctantly gave away her virginity when she had only just turned fourteen. By the time she took her final college exams Kayleigh had lost count of the number of one night stands she had enjoyed. Yes, she craved attention, but after a while she realised that she genuinely enjoyed the sex.

Whether it was all in her mind or just the inset of post-natal depression she wasn't sure. But since the arrival of baby Willow, much had changed. Matt had become increasingly distant, the small bunches of flowers and heart-warming messages had all but disappeared. He had become less adventurous and downright selfish between the sheets. He would often climax while she was giving him head with no chance of an encore. Matt would simply say that he was too tired, working more than sixty plus hours each week to support his little family. The mirror of truth, of course, would put her straight and tell her that his excuses were, 'pure bullshit'.

But Kayleigh never regretted the arrival of her beautiful new-born for one moment. Although, maybe selfishly, she would give anything to spend an uninterrupted night of pure unadulterated lust with her partner. To feel the surge of his oversized manhood thrusting away inside her wet cavity and to wrap her legs so tightly around her Geordie lover's torso, that she risked breaking every bone in his ribcage. But no matter how much she wanted to recapture that feeling, she simply didn't know how to tell him, and when she did try the words would come out all wrong. She would sound just like any other woman moaning at her partner for no reason.

And now, when her insecurities were at their lowest point, there was Wednesdays to worry about. Every Wednesday afternoon, Matt would disappear off the radar for hours on end. He offered excuses that didn't make logical sense. Visits to the gym where nobody had seen him, catering courses that didn't exist. One lie after another. The icing on the cake was the fact that he seemed to be working much longer hours and providing less money for them to live on. Despite his denials, Kayleigh didn't need the mirror in front of her to tell her what she already knew. Matt was seeing somebody else.

She knew of course that it could not be her arch-rival sitting on her sofa downstairs. Poppy had, thankfully, been locked away for the past two years. Her incarceration, however, had not stopped Matt talk about those sex excursions when he and his former waitress had worked together. 'Mad in the head, means bad in the bed,' was the expression he used. Maybe not realising that his current partner did not want to have to compete with the bedroom shenanigans of a deranged woman, that was clearly one step away from being locked-up in a Mental Health Institution.

Revisiting the reliable mirror, Kayleigh brushed her hair and applied a small amount of blusher to her pale cheeks. She didn't know why, but at that moment in time she wanted to scream out very loudly. But something in her head doubted that anyone would really hear her cry for help or if they would really care. Painting on a plastic smile she skulked downstairs to join the adults in the living room.

The main topic of conversation had turned to the youths on the side wall and the loudness of the beats being played on their mobile devices. Matt complained that there were inconsiderate, often playing their music until the early hours of the morning. It was always the same two lads, one of them lived just three doors up the road. Sometimes their number would grow to six or seven and the whole neighbourhood would be kept awake by the offending din. The big man who in his prime could bench press three hundred pounds of weight did not want to admit it but he felt intimidated by the youths. A local resident had been stabbed in their road the previous month and the police enquiries had been met with a wall of silence.

Kayleigh bypassed her lover and her enemy and made her way into her kitchen, closely followed by her best friend who closed the door tightly behind them. 'You have to give her a chance,' Bree insisted. 'Honestly, Kayleigh, she has been through so much over the years, she just needs a fresh start.'

Her bestie was not convinced. 'She is trouble, babe, you know it, she is going to be big trouble. I have shown you all those news reports of the things she has done in the past. Mark my words this won't end well.'

'Wow! Whatever happened to that Christian girl who used to go to Sunday school? The one who was always banging on about forgiveness and stuff.'

Kayleigh did not want to be drawn into an argument but there was something she needed to ask. 'Have you told her yet?'

'Told her?'

'You know what, babe, don't play with me. You really need to tell her. She has the right to know.'

'She is not ready yet, just give her time to find her feet.'

'But that is not fair, she should know.'

'I will tell her soon, just give her time to settle in at my place. Oh, and tell that dimwit boyfriend of yours not to say anything, not until she is ready.'

Kayleigh poured herself half a mug of coffee and topped it off with a splash of oat milk. It was clear that her friend was calling the shots, she always had done, she always would do. The girls exchanged some small talk and Bree shared with her friend some details for a new photography assignment that would take her off to Tuscany at the end of the month. There seemed to be a friendly vibe, but as Kayleigh reached into the cutlery drawer for a clean spoon, she found the drawer snap sharply and press against her hand, trapping her fingers in a vice like grip. Bree pushed hard on the outside of the drawer and issued her bestie with a warning. 'You never listen to me, Kayleigh, do you?'

Kayleigh was clearly in pain. 'You are hurting me, babe. You are really hurting me!'

Bree squeezed the drawer tighter on her friend's hand and watched as her knuckles began to turn red. She looked sternly at the suffering on her friend's face. 'You are such a disloyal friend, I told you, I warned you not to speak to my mother anymore.'

'She called me, I didn't call her, she called me. She wanted to see if I had seen that documentary, you know about those pills and all the dangers.'

'How many times do I have to tell you?' Bree asked with a soft silky voice which did not mirror the venom in her eyes.

'She was worried babe, she thought you was still taking them. That programme said that over a thousand people had committed suicide in America, all down to those pills, it was all in that documentary.'

'Jesus, that bloody woman, she is such a drama queen!'

Kayleigh's face was starting to turn the same shade of red as her hand. 'I told her you threw them away, ages ago, you got rid of all of them. I told her, I know you don't take them anymore, I told her that.'

'Well, in future, Kayleigh Hardy. you don't take her calls, you don't speak to that bitch, ever! I won't tell you again, is that clear?'

'Yes, yes, yes, I get it! Please let go babe it is really hurting now.'

Bree's warm and friendly smile returned as she released her grip on the drawer and allowed her friend to escape any further punishment. Kayleigh ran to the sink and soothed her throbbing fingers under the cold tap. She felt a compulsion to tell her best friend what she really thought of her, how her constant intimidation and bullying had plagued her ever since they became friends at school. How she deserved better, having always been a loyal and trusted friend. How it broke her heart to see the girl she had loved like a sister since primary school become so nasty and vindictive. She wanted to tell her. But she never did and probably never would.

'Now, shall we get your magic fingers busy on your laptop?' Bree asked, brushing aside the awkward moment. 'Let's see if we can find a suitable job for my sister?'

In the living room Matt and Poppy sat awkwardly at opposite ends of the sofa, they had exchanged nothing more than a few wayward glances. It seemed that any sort of conversation that might follow would have to be one that hid the fact that there was clearly still a connection between them. Matt finally cleared his throat and picked a topic that he felt safe with. 'Isn't she beautiful, Willow, she is such a beautiful baby?'

Poppy couldn't have looked more disinterested if she had tried. She shrugged her shoulders. 'Dunno, all kids look the same at that age.'

'She was three months old on Sunday.'

Matt received a lukewarm response from the visitor who clearly wasn't bothered. 'Really!'

'Kayls doesn't like me telling people, but our baby nearly died at birth. She stopped breathing four times, she was in intensive care for weeks. She has to have two different types of medication every day now. But she is a fighter, Willow is a real fighter.'

'She'll have to be a fighter with a name like that. Jesus, she is gonna get the piss ripped out of her at school, mate, you know that dontcha?'

Matt smiled, remembering perhaps that his former lover never minced her words. 'Narcolepsy', that's what they call it, her deep sleeps. It's not really an illness, it's a condition. She has been through so much in such a short space of time, she is so tough inside though, she is a miracle baby.'

Poppy showed no interest at all, yawning loudly and stretching her arms outwards. She was beginning to wish she had stayed in bed and not agreed to this tedious excursion. When she looked around the living room, she couldn't help thinking that it could do with makeover from her houseproud sister. The carpets were grubby and torn and the woodwork was riddled with holes. A toolbox sat beneath a leaning curtain rail that looked as if might fall down at any moment.

A sudden blast of drum and bass from the side of the building gave Matt a chance to change the subject. 'They get on Kayleigh's nerves, those kids, out there every day with that bloody music.'

'So do something about it,' Poppy said. 'Don't let them take the piss.'

'They are just kids, Poppy, they don't mean any harm.'

She shrugged her shoulders. 'Well stop fuckin' moaning about it, if you aint got the bollocks to sort them out.'

Their awkward banter was interrupted by Bree and Kayleigh who shuffled past them and headed for the laptop on the table in the corner of the room. Bree reminded her friend why they had turned up unannounced that day. 'It makes things easier with her release conditions if Poppy has a job. But she doesn't need to work full time, just part time and not too far, she needs to be close to my place.'

Kayleigh's 'magic' but slightly sore, fingers thrashed out several options on the job search pages and the two girls became absorbed in a wide selection of varied vacancies. The girl with Poppy's future employment prospects in her hands tried to seem enthusiastic. 'We will need to do her a CV, everyone asks for a CV these days.'

'I know all my sister's information,' Bree boasted. 'Just ask me what you need.'

'And we need to make a list of the things she is good at. Make a list of all her positive points. Lists are important, aren't they Matt?'

Her boyfriend nodded. 'Yes, Kayls, I haven't forgotten. I have both lists, the one for shopping and the one for the DIY stuff. I will get Preston to stop off at the supermarket on the way back from the gym.'

'Oh, God!' Bree said, shaking her head. 'Don't tell me that moron is coming round here.'

'It will make his day, seeing you, babe.' Kayleigh replied, smiling to herself. She knew more about the twisted love-hate relationship that existed between her two close friends than any living soul. Suddenly, her aching fingers began to feel slightly better.

Poppy was still in Matt's line of fire, he moved from the sofa and toyed with his mobile phone, trying hard to find a distraction. However, he found himself continually staring at his ex-lover and was finding it difficult to concentrate. Poppy was bored by now, she looked it too. She was happy to leave her career prospects in the hands of others. She decided it was time to break up this monotonous chit-chat about babies and noisy neighbours, it was time to have some fun. Without saying a word, she raised her hand and inserted her index finger into her mouth, sucking hard on it to make it wet. Her hand then slipped down her front until she reached the waistband of the yoga pants. Staring at Matt with the wickedest of smiles on her face, she slid her hand inside her underwear until she found her target. Her eyes rolled as she slid her finger in and out of her dampening crack, never once breaking eye contact with the quivering wreck of a man perched awkwardly on the adjacent armchair. The mindless chatter of the unsuspecting girls sitting behind her added real spice to the moment. Matt's embarrassment suddenly became obvious, and he reached for a cushion to hide the growing bulge in his trousers. Poppy smiled, she was in control now, she knew it. She could hear the girls behind her chattering on about working hours and minimum wage, but all she was focussed on was the damp patch inside her knickers. She slowly pulled out her hand, revealing a moist sticky substance on her fingers. 'Is it hard, Matt?' she asked cheekily, a question that made his face turn several shades of bright red.

Poppy smiled warmly and toyed with his libido a little further 'Getting a job nowadays, ya know, after that pandemic thing and all that shit. Is it hard, like to find a job now?'

'Really hard,' Matt replied, glancing over Poppy's shoulder in the hope that his girlfriend was still concentrating on the job search in hand.

Kayleigh was oblivious to the banter in the room, but Bree wasn't. She had noticed the sexual tension and sideways glances between her sister and her besties boyfriend since the moment they had arrived. She mischievously decided to stir the pot. 'Can't Matt get her a job at his place? He told us before that she was a really good waitress.'

'No!' Kayleigh snapped, not realising how her loud her objection had been voiced. 'They are always fully staffed there, aren't they Matt? Besides it is a vegan restaurant, they only employ people that don't eat…'

'And how do you know my sister isn't vegan?' Bree asked. 'God, Kayleigh, you can be so judgemental sometimes.'

It was a good moment for all present when the front doorbell rang. Kayleigh sprinted out of her chair to greet the guest. 'It will be Preston,' she explained. 'He is running Matt to the gym.'

Preston Edgell entered the arena, a strapping man in his mid-twenties, with a perfectly toned body and face to match. He smiled churlishly as he nodded at Bree and made his way across the room. She sneered and seemed to look straight through him, clearly not a fan of the tanned Adonis type.

But the visitor's tort physique and rugged good looks had caught the attention of one of those present, Poppy saw him as a welcome distraction from the fun family day out crowd.

'That's Poppy,' Kayleigh confirmed. 'Matt told you about her didn't he?'

'Oh yeah, Bree's sister.'

'Half-sister,' Poppy said, the first clean words she had spoken for several minutes. 'We aint real sisters.'

Preston felt slightly awkward when he caught Brees puzzled expression, but he was curious to know if the stories about the new visitor were true. 'You just got out of, err, err, Matt said you was in, err...'

'Nick,' Poppy responded, saving the man the embarrassment of using the word. 'I got outta prison yesterday.'

'How bad was that, must have been tough being locked away from all your friends and family?'

'Not really, I aint got no friends or family.'

'Except me.' Bree declared with a small frown on her face.

'Oh yeah, except her.'

Matt was not happy that Preston was stealing the limelight and found an opening to join in the conversation. 'There must have been things you missed, Poppy, when you were inside.'

'A good hard shagging,' was the immediate response, a comment that had mixed reactions amongst the audience.

Preston decided to push her for more information, keen to spice up the heated exchange. 'I bet there were some women in there who turned, you know, got themselves a bit of girl-on-girl action.'

Bree gave Preston a harsh stare that told him he had crossed a line. 'My sister is not like that,' she said. 'Don't try to satisfy your own sexual fantasies by thinking she is.'

But Poppy was in full swing now, enjoying all the male attention. 'Yeah, but this geezer is right though. When you get a bit bored it's nice to have a bit of tonguing. Let's face it, if its dark, you don't really notice if it's a bloke or a bird.'

Matt was trying to hide his smutty smile, he was mentally searching for a cushion, hoping that embarrassing bulge in his trousers did not make a sudden re-appearance. After all, his own sex life had been somewhat mundane since the arrival of his daughter and the slightest hint of any kinky sexual activity would send his testosterone levels soaring through the roof. He made himself scarce for a few seconds, fetching his gym bag from the hallway and holding it in front of his waist.

The tall handsome visitor suddenly realised that he had forgotten something important, he reached in the pocket of his gym shorts where he prized three crisp twenty-pound notes and handed them to Kayleigh. 'I had a good win on the horses yesterday,' he said, proudly. 'Put this in my beautiful little God-daughters trust fund.' The money was accepted with a small hug and a smile of gratitude.

Kayleigh then opened a cupboard door and pulled out a large jar with Willow's name plastered on the side. Poppy noticed those notes would not be alone in that canister, a large stack of paper money caught her eye. 'Matt has been struggling for tips lately,' Kayleigh exclaimed. 'He never seems to have any spare cash to put into her savings these days. So, we really appreciate that.'

All eyes were smiling as the lid of the jar was closed and returned to the shelf inside the cupboard. All but one of those onlookers were thinking about the baby's future.

Kayleigh had not joined in the free-for-all investigation of Poppy's prison life, she was listening to the conversation and studying the eye contact exchanges between her house guests. Preston, as always, remained his usual composed self. There was a time when the new mother thought that he had a soft spot for her. But that vanished almost immediately when Matt appeared on the scene. She was intrigued to see how everything had suddenly become centred around Poppy, a girl who she had zero respect or compassion for. She couldn't help but wonder what it was about her, why everybody was drawn to her, like moths to a flame. Kayleigh had always been inwardly jealous of Bree's stunning beauty and persona but now there was another threat to any attention she was likely to receive, in the form of an ex-drug addicted murderess. She wasn't even pretty, in Kayleigh's eyes, in fact, to her, she looked downright rough. Her poorly groomed mass of manky hair and her pale complexion did nothing for her blotchy skin and deep scars in her neck. She had a nasty tongue and an arrogant manner that seemed indelible. Yet there was something about Poppy, she couldn't work out what it was, but it fascinated her. It was almost as if someone had told you not to put your hand in a glowing flame. But you can't help it, you have to do it, just to see if it will really burn your fingers.

Preston reminded Matt that they were collecting his work colleague, Devon, on route to the gym, so they needed to be setting off. Matt was still finding it hard to take his eyes off his former lover. Bree said nothing on the subject when the men headed for the door, maybe she thought there would be a better time and place.

Kayleigh was quite relieved when her daughter started crying for attention in the upstairs bedroom. It gave her an excuse to snarl at the mirror of truth and punch the fluffy pillows on her bed, seeing Poppy's face staring up at her from every one of them.

When the sisters left the house, they went through the back gate and strolled the length of the walkway towards the car. The volume of the music playing on the ginger boys mobile phone seemed to have been turned up a few more levels. The duo of hooded youths had been joined by a third track-suited delinquent. A few unwitty sexual innuendos were aimed at Bree as she glided gracefully back to her vehicle. But the red-haired lout wanted to show that he had more ammunition in his armoury, more caustic one-liners. This time Poppy received some unwelcome jaunts from the drug-fuelled teens. 'That munter looks like she haunts houses for a living.' followed by 'Oi, Frankenstein, show us your bolts.' The new addition to the alley crew, not wanting to be left out, added one cutting comment of his own, 'Hashtag.Uglybus.'

'Ignore them,' Bree said, inwardly pleased that no snide comments had been aimed in her direction. 'As Matt says, they are just kids.'

Poppy took her sisters advice but not without delivering one long hard stare at the unruly trio. She lit up a cigarette and thought long and hard about the people living in the ordinary house. Meeting up with Matt had sent some strange thoughts running through her mind. She began to wonder what might have been had things turned out differently. Maybe it would be her now, scrubbing those upstairs rooms and coaxing the baby to have a sleep. Maybe she would be the one sharing the cheery northerner's bed each night. But then she remembered how sickly the smell of the soiled nappy had been and she counted her blessings that she had escaped that fate.

Bree was back in the driver's seat of her Saab SUV, applying some cherry lip balm and busying herself with the dials on the sat nav. There was something bothering Poppy when she joined her sister in the car. 'Why didn't you say nothing, yer know, about them two? Why didn't ya tell me that Matt had shacked up with yer mate?'

'Oh, sorry, I forgot, Poppy, you knew him from before, didn't you?'

'Yeah, bit sneaky that, not telling me.'

'I don't know what she sees in him really, he is so thick, you know. Like, the elevator works but it doesn't go all the way to the top floor. Trust me, Poppy, I could tell you things about your friend Matt that would make you change your opinion of him. He is not as squeaky clean as he makes out.'

'What do yer mean?'

'Oh, it's not for now, Poppy, I am going to save that little gem for a rainy day. One day when little miss prim and proper really pisses me off, I shall tell her the truth about Mister Matthew Jameson.'

'Fuck, you can be a real nasty cow when you want to.'

'Now, where is this place you need to go to?' Bree asked, with her fingers at the ready.

'Woolwich, South Woolwich, just get there and I will show you the way to the Marfield Estate.'

CHAPTER FIVE

It was that unique smell that Poppy recognised. The unmistakable blend of rotting meat from the kebab shop mixed with unwashed urine stains on the pavement and the sweet yet sickly odour of stale cannabis. It filled the air, wafting in and out of the passenger door window, causing the over-dramatic Bree to gag repeatedly. But for Poppy, those pungent smells made her feel welcome here. This was a comfort zone, she was home.

Nothing seemed to have changed, it was as if she had never left this hallowed turf. The parade of shops at the entrance to this infamous housing estate in South Woolwich seemed to have frozen in time. Children of every age, colour and creed strutted the filthy walkways. Obese tattooed women carrying carved out expressions of a hopeless existence etched on tired faces. Stray dogs plundered overfilled rubbish bins down the sidewalks and alleyways that were littered with takeaway wrappers. Thumping notes blared out from an open window in the side street, treating allcomers to a drum and bass extravaganza. This was the notorious Marfield Estate.

Poppy lit up her third roll-up since the girls had arrived in the parking bay usually reserved for taxis, ignoring her sisters constant whinging about the time they had spent there and the cost of illegal parking. She stared intently at the narrow walkway between the run-down chicken shop and the grubby looking discount store. She was closely following the antics of a young lad in a dark hoody who was perched on a shiny pushbike at the entrance to the pathway. The youth was clearly a popular fixture, constantly chatting to passers-by and furiously texting messages on his mobile.

'You smoke too much,' Bree observed.

'And you talk too much,' came the blunt response, which put the younger of the siblings firmly in her place.

She did not want to admit it to her sister, but Bree felt intimidated by these surroundings, she hoped that their visit here would be a short one. Darkness had begun to fall, and she did not cherish the thought of being amongst the 'riff-raff' as she called them, on these filthy streets.

Still focusing on the busy walkthrough between the shops, Poppy shared an observation that had been playing on her mind 'This aint the motor we were in yesterday.'

'No,' her sister replied. 'I had to take the Mercedes back to Kendra. She is my boss by the way. That's where I was while you were sleeping off your hangover this morning, I picked her up from Heathrow airport at four o clock. She had been to a fashion show and then on to New York to…'

'Alright, alright!' Poppy said abruptly. 'I don't need a long story about it. I just said, it was a nicer car than the one you had yesterday.'

'Are we going soon?' Bree asked, trying to think of any excuse to get her away from the estate. 'I need to get some prep work done for a client for tomorrow.'

Poppy ignored her comment, she was busy calculating her move. Her sister tried again. 'We haven't eaten since brunch, Poppy. I am hungry now.'

Poppy nodded at the grubby looking chicken shop next to where they were parked but received a sharp response from her sibling. 'God, not from around here, no!'

'Right,' Poppy said, zipping up her jacket and opening the car door. 'You wait here, I will be back in ten minutes.'

'No, I am not waiting, I am coming with you.'

'Suit yourself, just don't start whinging at me if you get hurt. And don't say nothing, nothing at all, just keep your mouth shut, OK?'

Bree locked her car and then repeated the exercise for good measure, looking over her shoulder as she followed her sister in the direction of the boy on the bike. The lad looked out from his hoodie as the two women neared. He was fresh faced, a bad case of acne on his chin, probably no more than fourteen or fifteen years old, his voice had barely broken. 'What yer looking for?' he asked.

'Some Ket and an eighth,' Poppy replied, watching her sisters face drop like a large boulder into a small lake.

'Kets done on this turf, love,' the lad responded. 'Can do you some Es, good gear, top notch.'

Poppy nodded. 'I'll try a few.'

'Forty' the young lad said reaching his hand down the handlebars and making a small shape for Poppy to place the two twenty-pound notes she had prized from her pay-out from the prison.

'Down to the rockery, Cheyenne will sort you out.'

'Cheyenne?'

'Asian bird, cocoa coloured girl, white tracksuit, you can't miss her.'

Poppy nodded and marched along the walkway followed by her angry sibling. 'Drugs?' Bree asked, clearly angered by the transaction. 'You never said we were buying drugs, what the hell are you getting me into Poppy?'

'I told you to keep yer mouth shut. Now listen, if that fuckin' twat on the bike comes down when it kicks off, you need to slow him down. Don't let him get through the end of the alley, it's a shortcut, slow him down, right!'

'Kicks off?' Bree asked in a panic-stricken voice 'What the hell, Poppy, what the hell!'

But there was no time for further explanations as the girls reached the flower beds in the middle of a small square halfway through the walkway. Sure enough, a girl with jet black hair and a tacky fake designer tracksuit turned to greet them. She was busy checking text messages on her mobile and unaware of the approaching threat.

'Cheyenne,' Poppy yelled, as she swung the back of her fist directly into the startled girl's cheek, causing her to wobble slightly. Poppy followed up with a clenched fist to the other side of her face which took the young dealer off balance and sent her crumbling to the floor. The Asian girl's phone flew several feet across the pathway. Poppy swung her lag and caught the startled girl in the small of her back with a hefty kick. The dozen or so onlookers, enjoying their takeaways, followed the action, but nobody moved a muscle to protect the wounded girl.

Poppy crouched over her victim and made her intentions very clear. 'Listen, Cheyenne, it aint personal, I just want the gear, all of it.'

'Go fuck yourself!' the plucky Asian girl screamed.

'Wrong answer,' Poppy yelled, springing to her feet and launching another well aimed kick to the side of the girl's torso.

Cheyenne was no pushover, she shouted up loudly at her aggressor. 'Neddy will kill you, bitch! I swear down, he will cut you into little pieces.'

Poppy was angry now, she knew that time was limited, there would be no more messing around. She reached down and dragged the plucky girl by her hair to the flower bed. In a matter of a few seconds, she had smashed her head twice into the side of the rockery, a large bloody gash appeared on the side of her face. Cheyenne had been braver than most, standing up to her attacker, but she knew she was a spent force. 'Alright, alright,' she cried out, reaching inside her tracksuit pocket and throwing half a dozen small bags of cannabis on to the floor in front of Poppy.

'Don't take the piss, girl,' Poppy yelled, aiming another kick at the girl on the ground. 'Get your bottoms off, now! I want all the gear.'

The last kick had the desired effect, the searing pain in Cheyenne's back finally knocking any resistance she had to offer. She took off her tracksuit bottoms and gingerly put her hand inside her underwear to retrieve the rest of the booty. Casting out one small bag of white pills followed by another. But Poppy's patience was wearing thin, she bent down and ripped the side of the beaten girl's knickers, completely tearing the frilly garment off her in one yank. A dozen or more cachets of drugs flew into the air and Poppy was quick to scoop them up.

While all eyes were on the centre stage Bree picked up the discarded mobile phone at her feet, frantic with worry that this was all going to end badly. She had been switching her attention form the half-naked girl on the concrete paving to the far end of the alleyway. Her heart raced faster as she saw a speeding bike appear from the entrance to the walkway, swerving in and out of bystanders, clearly making for the short cut exit. Bree froze for a split second but then noticed a large metal rubbish bin behind her. Without thinking, she grabbed the lid and launched it sideways, like a huge metal discuss. It had the desired effect, causing the spotty lad to slam on his brakes and fall headfirst over the top of his cycle. She looked on as the angry youth cursed at her as he turned to run, leaving his damaged bike behind him as he made off into the distance.

Poppy smiled at Bree's quick-thinking, she would never tell her so, but her sister had done well. The two women marched back to the parked car at a military two-step that Prison Chief Callard would have been proud of. Bree wasted no time in driving away from the scene of the crime. She wasn't sure what she had just witnessed, but somehow it didn't feel wrong. Filled with a strange rush of nervous excitement she followed her sister's instructions and drove to the south side of the estate. As she turned a corner which seemed to be leading them away from the dangers behind them, she noticed three run-down tower blocks surrounded by cranes and scaffolding.

'Stop!' Poppy yelled. 'Stop here, I need to get out.'

CHAPTER SIX

This was once her playground.

A forgotten wasteland of urban decay and multi-cultural degradation. It was a council housing project that had been doomed to failure since the first cheaply made bricks and mortar were laid in its foundations in the late nineteen fifties. Badly spelled graffiti covered the rotting walls encasing a generation of tenants on the bottom rung of the social ladder. Broken windows mirrored the broken dreams of snotty-nosed kids on the wrong side of the poverty line. Dysfunctional families of a multitude of colours and religions trod the same filthy walkways. Used condoms and syringes littered the stairwells of multi-story flats which should have been condemned a decade ago. But the underfunded council felt that dignity could be restored to these tired looking buildings with a new coat of bright paint every few years. This tacky refurbishment had no more than the effect of putting a sticky plaster on a six-inch-deep gash.

The Marfield Estate was a place where the screaming of police sirens was heard far more frequently than the tones of the ice cream van. Ferocious looking animals, both two legged and four, patrolled these streets, protecting their own. Even seasoned bailiffs thought twice about doorstep visits here. Battered wives and single mothers, struggling to manage the fortnightly benefit pay-outs, hoping their money would arrive in time for a weekend of essentials. Booze and baccy were top of the list, of course. Plenty of frozen fish fingers and tins of beans to keep their offspring alive and well. Money for the electric and gas meters was a must and if there was any left, give your local dealer a call. After all, you could do with a break from the harsh reality of your existence here. But the golden rule was never to buy your gear on tick. The last thing you needed was the Bagman banging down your door at midnight.

To most this was an estate to avoid, a cut-throat collection of low-life rejects encased in a tomb of false hopes and despair. A place where you could buy anything from a small bag of weed to an AK47 assault rifle, if you had the money and knew the right person. But, to Poppy, this had been her sanctuary. This dingy two-bedroom flat on the thirteenth floor of Rutland Towers was a place she could call home. There was something about this dark shrine that had bought life to her weary features when she was just a lost and troubled teenager. The people here had welcomed her with open arms, made her one of their own.

This was once her playground.

One friend was all she needed, one was all she found, a soulmate for life, however short that tragic life would be. Nikita Pearson, a pint-sized girl who weighed next to nothing, yet could stand out in a Wembley Stadium crowd. A precocious bundle of energy, with weird and wacky hairstyles, piercing emerald-green eyes and her own mad theories on the working of the human mind. The troubled teens had met at a Youth Offenders Institution and found something in one another that others never saw. They became 'besties' without ever using the word and showed their love for each other one crack-rocked evening by having a local tattoo artist ink the others name inside a purple heart on their thighs.

They shared countless drug-fuelled nights of crazy mischief and mayhem. Halcyon days filled with boozy parties and shoplifting sprees. The girls had all but perfected a scam at an expensive baby clothes shop in London which had poor security. At that time toddlers on the estate were wearing designer clothing more suited to the offspring of celebrities and politicians than a squalid council neighbourhood. The pair spent their ill-gotten gains on a cocktail of drugs and alcohol. Two girls, out of control, living the dream in their own little world. Their shoplifting scam ended abruptly, however, when an off-duty police officer spotted them stealing and chased them the full length of Kensington High Street. Nikita gave herself up and allowed her friend to escape, knowing that Poppy would have been hauled back into prison if she had been caught.

But then, without warning it all ended. Nikita, desperate to score a high after the social services had removed her son for neglect, simply took her own life. To score, she had traded a half-dozen blowjobs for a bag of bad brown. The precocious tiny girl with the crazy runaway bunches in her hair was found dead amongst the discarded litter in a dark alleyway. But she left behind a broken girl who would never find the glue to mend her shredded heart. Poppy would never tell anybody but there was never a day that went by when she didn't hear her tiny friend's voice scolding her. She could almost hear her now, reciting some prophetic masterpiece she had read on a toilet wall. There was never a day that went past when Nikita was not in her thoughts. Her happy memories of her lost friend could never be tainted.

Poppy stood motionless on the balcony of the squalid abode she once shared with that lost soul. Pushing aside the tired looking security netting she took a long drag on her roll up and looked down on to the estate below. It had been the first time she had been here since that night her life changed. The first visit since her friend had found a better place to confess her sins and she had taken a hunting knife to look for the youth that she blamed for her death. Billy Keyes may have only just turned seventeen years old when his friends witnessed her frenzied attack on him. But the youngest of four criminal brothers would not live to see his next birthday. An out-of-control Poppy stabbed the youth two dozen times and left him in a pool of blood. Maybe the kindly judge had seen her as a victim herself. He handed her down a minimal sentence for her vicious crime. But maybe he should have asked her for her thoughts on her actions before showing such leniency. Poppy Jarvis would, in her own words, have given him no doubt that she was not repentant for her sins. That she would never feel the slightest morsel of remorse during the years that she spent in prison.

Bree had complained at the bottom of every flight of stairs that had bought them to this dirty flat. Not just because the service lifts were not working, it was also the fact that the building was clearly being demolished, as the warning signs on the entrance doors had boldly stated. She swore she saw at least three large rats amongst the rubble on the stairwells and she was also aware that they were likely being hunted by a gang of enraged drug dealers. From all that she had heard the last thing she wanted was to come face to face with this nasty 'Neddy' character.

With her sister clearly in a headspace which carried a 'do not disturb' sign on the door, Bree busied herself with trying to uncover some graffiti that was on the back wall in the living room. She had identified the names of *Popsy* and *Nixie* in what looked to be childish crayon marking and had now unveiled further text which seemed to be a list of objects. 'Your name is on this wall, Poppy,' she exclaimed. 'And I have found a list of some sort.' Curious to get the full picture of the caveman type findings she scraped away more of the peeling wallpaper. The filthy walls in the room were covered in grease and grime and all sorts of unknown fluids. Bree made a mental note to soak her hands in antibacterial handwash the minute she arrived home.

But her sister was in another place now, another world, some would say a happier time in her life, although those words 'Happy' and 'Life' were rarely found in the same sentence in Poppy's vocabulary. From the balcony, beneath the darkening skies, she could make out the large grass quadrant at the back of the estate. A memorable moment on a notorious day suddenly breezed through her head. It bought a small smile to her face.

She was barely fifteen, she had served her first term in a Youth Offenders Institute. She was an angry child that had been bashed from pillar to post, physically and mentally, for most of her life. But the Marfield represented a new beginning, Callard, would be sorely disappointed to know that she was never a 'nobody' at this place.

She had hooked up with Cameron and Neddy, two best friends, bad boys on their way to becoming bad men. The thrill of an older lover, an endless supply of free drugs and a roof over her head was the young girls dream ticket. She was at the time, like the proverbial 'pig in shit! The trio were inseparable, she would run errands, usually delivering small cachets of weed and whizz to residents on the estate. The strapping six foot plus lads would use the only assets that God had gifted them with, their size and strength. Recruited by the local drug kings they would become enforcers. Hard-hitting no-nonsense bullies who terrorised the hopeless addicts who never paid their bills on time.

That large field that had once provided a play area for the children of the estate was wasteland now, no doubt waiting for a property developers bulldozer to move in and erase it from the minds of residents. But it had once been the scene of a famous battle, not one that would have made official history books, but it had become folklore in the hearts of the social misfits that lived in this run-down fortress of degradation.

The war had been declared the night that four large men in long dark coats from the travelling community walked into the Eagle Public House, one of two bars that bordered the estate. The owner, Big Bazza, refused to serve them, he had good reasons. His young son had seen his brand-new bike stolen by some of the traveller's wayward offspring and traded off for a third of its original value. It was not the first case of theft since the free-spirited roamers had rocked up on Cranford Fields and it surely would not be the last. Action was needed and refusing to serve the undesirable illegal tenants from his pub would show he would the first to make a stand. The quartet of heavy-set bruisers took objection to his ban and set about the landlord and his bar staff with a ferocity that sent shockwaves throughout the estate.

Enough was enough. Big Bazza started recruiting a task force to oust the travelling community from their rent-free site. He was a popular figure and respected businessman in the area and the list of volunteers grew rapidly. Cameron and Neddy, strapping eighteen-year-olds at the time, signed up for combat as did a dozen or so of his regular punters. All the recruits were fed-up up with the itinerant antics of their new neighbours on the camp site.

It was rumoured the council had spent more than four hundred thousand pounds, over a two-year period, to obtain an eviction order for the thirty or so caravans and mobile homes, which had parked on the green field behind the local sports facilities. But neither council officials nor a burly team of bailiffs had any success trying to remove these undesirables. It seems that they were there to stay, brazenly sticking up a middle finger at the authorities as well as the local community.

Nobody knew who would be brave or sober enough to show on that chilly Tuesday morning, but by half past four the numbers of able bodies had passed fifty and was growing steadily. Albeit some of the vigilante army was suffering from a lack of sleep. Others, still off their faces on drugs or booze, may have simply thought it was a long queue for a free burger bar. A few heavies, mercenaries, unknown to residents of the estate, were enrolled by Nathan and Mitchell Keyes. They were the two brothers that ran the drug trade on the estate and were worried that the permanent fixture of these travellers would be bad for business.

Whether it was the promise of free booze in the Eagle bar or a handful of uppers nobody knew, but as the clock struck five and the sun began to rise the Marfield army of misfits were on the march. Knives, baseball bats, some laced with barbed wire, iron bars, a machete or two and an assortment of metal rods was the armoury on display. Druggies rubbed shoulders with shoplifters and violent youths. Even the two waiters from the local Chinese restaurant were there, both carrying nasty looking meat cleavers by their sides. Somewhere between the giant figures of Cameron and Neddy stood a five feet nine girl with a carefree attitude and a ferocious look on her face. Poppy, holding a sold metal crowbar, was ready to face the enemy.

It was a heavily intoxicated, Jimmy the Liar, who broke ranks as they arrived at the campsite. He led the charge with a scream of, 'Kill the pikey bastards,' a comment which would surely have earned him a reprimand and fine in any magistrates court. But on this day, it was one of the less offensive exchanges that were made between the warring tribes.

The dawn attack had caught the travelling community off guard and the Marfield volunteers gained an early advantage in the battle. They had turned over a couple of light weight caravans and had freed a couple of the guard dogs, letting them loose to flee from the onslaught. But within a few minutes the real men of the campsite had joined the fray, some half-dressed others in just their underwear, looking like boxers from another century. Fists and heads clashed, swinging blades glistened in the early morning sunshine. Wounds opened, blood from both sides flowed, bodies fell and bounced back up again. Carnage ensued as the battle raged on.

It would later be revealed that a call had gone into the local police station from a busybody onlooker who reported that, 'All hell had broken loose on Cranford Fields.' The message was passed along the line and within ten minutes half a dozen police cars should have been arriving at the so-called Armageddon in progress. But, although they would never admit it, the shrewder of the officers who had knowledge of the participants involved, took a leisurely drive through the scenic route and did not arrive until the fracas was almost at an end. By the time the senior police officer gave his boys in blue the signal to join the fray it was all but over. Each side taking care of their own wounded. Miraculously, despite a lengthy casualty list, there were no fatalities

No statements were ever taken from the travelling community as none were ever offered. They had taken a severe beating that morning and took their humbling defeat with pride and pain

Cameron and Neddy carried young Poppy on their shoulders as the entered the Eagle pub, she had certainly earned her spurs that day. A nasty looking black eye and cuts and bruises all over her body, her battle scars were shown off proudly to the rest of the returning heroes. Big Bazza informed his bar staff to give unlimited free drinks to all who had participated that day, while his wife patched up poor Jimmy the Liar on the pool room at the rear of the pub. Despite needing stitches and a tetanus jab, the brave, but foolish, old sod made do with a bottle of Bells Whisky and an oversized plaster.

The celebrations continued through the day, even the Keyes Brothers welcomed this distraction from their usual business practices. Although their frequent trips to the pub's toilets would suggest their celebratory presence was more to do with cash than glory.

At a little after midday the Eagle Public House fell silent when the side doors were thrust open, and the senior man of the travelling community entered with two bruised and battered companions. Walking to the bar he looked around him at the rag-tag rabble that had done so much damage to his community. 'I'll have a large whisky for the journey,' he said. His distinct Irish voice booming out over the murmurs inside the pub.

Big Bazza excused the shaking barmaid and poured the drink himself. The journeyman guzzled the alcohol down in one gulp and slammed the glass on the bar. 'We were thinking of moving on, anyways,' he said, offering his hand to the landlord.

The bar owner nodded and shook his hand firmly. 'Safe journey mate,' he replied, with a glint of pleasure in his eyes.

And with that the trio of travellers exited the pub to a waiting cavalcade of vehicles parked in the street outside. A huge roar erupted inside the bar and pandemonium ensued. Families and friends rejoiced in the victory, sworn enemies hugged one another and the landlord rang the bell continuously as he revealed he intended to hold a full-blown lock-in that night. It was the first and only time that the residents of the estate would ever came together as one to defeat a common enemy.

That memory of better times was interrupted by the shriek of Poppy's over-dramatic sibling. 'A rat!' she screamed. 'That was definitely a rat that time, look, there, in the corner.'

Poppy wasn't listening, she looked across the estate with a tinge of sadness. They were good people form her past, gone, all gone now. Nikita had left her. Cameron had not deserved her and now Neddy was her sworn enemy. But her and the big man had been so close in those hazy days, like a brother and sister. He had looked after her when her boyfriend served time in prison, and she had understood him when he shared his insecurities about his monstrous features. But now they were at war, both knowing the other well enough to know that neither would ever wave a white flag. It would only be a matter of time before their paths crossed, Poppy knew she would need every ounce of her courage and strength to survive.

Her sister had used a long nail file from her bag to scrape the mould on the walls. She had managed to strip one section bare and was taking pictures of the graffiti. A dozen scribbled names were listed in what looked like a child's crayon. One name at the top of the list had been re-written in bold with an angry marker pen. 'Wow! This *Houghton* fella, you really didn't like this one, he is top of the list. What did he do wrong?' Bree asked.

A short sharp shock of reality suddenly hit Poppy when she

heard that name. 'Houghton,' she said, trying hard not to show her true feelings. 'He was nothing, it was just a game that me and Nixie played.' She turned her head away from the scribbled list that her and her friend had devised over a three-day drunken binge. She didn't want reminding, she had tried desperately to forget him over the years, but now that ghost was back to haunt her.

'It says '*sick fuck peedo*, next to his name,' Bree declared. '*Paedo* is spelt wrong, but I can see what you meant.'

'It's the past.'

'Please, tell me everything, Poppy, I want to know. I want to know who he is. I want to know who they all are. Why you wanted to kill them all.'

'You need to keep your beak out of my business.'

'But if he did things to you, Poppy, you know they can still arrest him, it doesn't matter…'

But Poppy was adamant. 'Just leave it girl! It's in the past. Come on we need to get going.'

Bree took a few more photographs and rushed to catch her sister on the stairway, squealing loudly when she saw some newspaper move amongst the litter in the hallway.

CHAPTER SEVEN

The two women exited the tower block with Bree continuing her condemnation of the hazardous building and trying her best to convince her sister that she had seen a rat the size of a Jack Russell dog. Poppy was never one for sentiment, but she felt as if of her part of her life was about to be erased. She knew that the demolition of Rutland Towers would bury many memories of better times. It gave her a hollow feeling inside.

The girls had taken a different route back to the car and were coming to the end of a dank and smelly subway when a voice called out to them in the cooling night air. It gave each of the sisters a different kind of emotion.

'I thought you was still in the nuthouse.'

The throaty Scottish tones bought a small smile to Poppy's face as a wiry figure appeared from the shadows. Bree was alarmed at first, but quickly realised the women knew each other.

'Lulu fucking Lush,' Poppy responded, grinning from ear to ear 'Jesus, aint you fuckin' dead yet?'

The approaching woman responded with a beaming smile of her own and shared a double fist bump and a touch of elbows with her old acquaintance. 'Still alive and kicking girl. You know me.' She looked to the rear of her old friend and noticed the worried expression on Bree's face. 'Who's the posh frock?' she asked.

Bree feeling slightly awkward and left out lifted her arm and offered a handshake to her sisters' friend. 'I am...'.

'She is nobody,' Poppy barked, interrupting her sister's introduction and angering her in in the process. 'You aint still working these streets are you girl?'

'Got no option lass, no work no food.'

It was obvious to Bree from looking at the scrawny woman with the drawn and gaunt expression on her pasty face, that the food she was referring to was hard drugs. Studying her as closely as she could from a safe distance, she could see the dark saggy bags beneath her lifeless grey eyes. There were needle marks on her arms and she had had badly pockmarked skin. She had seen enough addicts at the homeless shelter to know that this girl was hooked on heroin. She wanted to join in the conversation but felt she would have little to offer.

Poppy seemed genuinely concerned for the old friend. 'I heard the Lithis had taken over this patch.'

'Yeah, but their bitches don't like the dark. Their blokes get them set up in cosy little bedsits. Don't get much competition out here now. Hey, who else is gonna offer a blowie for a score?'

Poppy shook her head, 'Fuck me, Lulu, you aint serious?'

'Needs must girl,' she said, scratching at her arm.

'Just came back over here to see the old block before they knock it down.'

'You don't wanna hang about here too long, words out on you already.'

'Neddy?'

'Yeah, he is furious as fuck, aint many people come into his back yard and nick his gear.'

Poppy shrugged her shoulders, 'Fuck him, lanky streak of piss.'

'He aint messin, he has put a call out on you, you got a price on yer head girl.'

Bree was alarmed, she pulled her sister's arm. 'Come on, you heard her, we need to get going.'

Poppy gave her sibling a harsh stare and responded in a loud tone. 'Wait! Can't you see the grown-ups are talking.'

Her comment gave Lulu a reason to laugh which set her off into a spluttering coughing fit. Poppy reached into her pocket and pulled out the bags she had taken from Cheyenne in the square and offered them to her Scottish friend. 'There's no brown but you can trade this off. Give that fuckin' ugly mouth of yours a rest from those smelly dicks tonight.'

Lulu didn't hesitate, the catchment of substances was taken and hidden safely inside her brazier within seconds. 'I owe ya,' she said. 'You always were a goodun, Poppy, girl.'

Bree was becoming more anxious, she was seeing figures in the shadows that were not there, her paranoia was working overtime. The rats in the tower block would seem to be the least of her worries now.

'Posh frocks getting edgy,' Lulu said. 'She aint cut out for this shit.'

Poppy pulled a face and again told her sister to be patient, there was something on her mind. 'There's a bloke on Neddy's payroll,' she said. 'Big bloke, not much hair, funny teeth, got tattoos on his fingers.'

'Shark,' her friend replied, before Poppy could finish her description. 'Don't fuck with him, girl, he is a proper mental case.'

'Yeah, I thought he might be a bit heavy duty.'

'Bit some blokes ear clean off in a fight, headcase Poppy, best you swerve that bastard.'

'I need to find him, just business, ya know.'

'Fuck off Poppy! This is me yer talking to. If you've got beef with that bloke, bury it, he aint worth it.'

'I just wanna know where he hangs out.'

Lulu thought long and hard before she shared her information. It seemed, however, that the gift of those free drugs had been enough to jog her memory. 'The Coconut Teaser, the pub that used to be The Greyhound, on Vincent Street. He is a regular, you will always find him there after Millwall games.'

'Millwall?'

'That's the tattoos, Lions, he has them on both hands.'

'Lions?'

'It's the nickname for Millwall Football Club. He goes to every home game, mixes with some right fucking nutcases there. But he always goes back to that pub afterwards.'

'The Greyhound, yeah I remember it, been in there a few times. So, it's called the Coconut now?'

'Yeah, they've done it up, the Coconut Teaser. It's a bit more upmarket now, they play music and all that shit. One of my regular punters sees him in there, Shark, always making a fucking nuisance of himself. Nasty cunt he is, fucking sex pest.'

'Sex pest?'

'Yeah, he got off a rape case last year, the feds had him bang to rights, but the girl topped herself before it went to court. Neddy sent round some heavies to put the frighteners on the parents. They reckon that's what sent her over the edge. She hung herself with a couple of her dad's belts, so there was no case. She was only fourteen, poor bitch, just a fucking school kid. He likes 'em young, Shark, it's the third time he's done it, young girls, all just kids really, got off all three times, thanks to Neddy.'

'Why is Neddy bothered?'

Lulu gave her friend a solemn look. 'Shark is Nathan Keyes cousin, he used to knock about with Billy when he first came to the estate. If he knew who you were, girl, he wouldn't stop til…'

'He knows who I am, trust me, he knows.'

'Seriously, girl, don't fuck about with him, lots of bad stories, just let this one go.'

'Aint my style, Lulu, I owe him, he needs sorting.'

The former friends shared another fist bump and exchanged a few more friendly insults before, much to Bree's relief, they parted company and headed in separate directions. Half-way back to the car Poppy led her sister on a small diversion at a piece of wasteland next to a second subway entrance. They walked through a poorly lit alleyway where Poppy stopped and looked down at a small patch of grass that was badly in need of cultivating. She had no intention of sharing the fact that this was the spot where Nikita's sad life had ended. Bree had said nothing while her sister had her moment of remembrance, she was busy looking over her shoulder, maybe expecting a gang of knife-wielding thugs to appear in the distance.

Poppy soon noticed her sibling's nervousness. 'Come on Posh Frock,' she joked. 'Let's get some grub and go home.' Her sister did not need a second invitation and her feet shuffled along in double time. But as she followed her sister strutting merrily through the debris of her old stomping ground, strange thoughts began to cross her mind. She was worried that her sister was going to be returning to this awful place, hell-bent on retribution. She was also concerned that Poppy would be back to visit her prostitute friend and maybe get embroiled in the drug-fuelled life-style that she left behind.

But what worried her more than anything was that, although she had felt scared, she also felt a tinge of excitement coursing through her veins. She couldn't work out why, but she was high on adrenalin, loving this new danger. Living on the edge of a world where seriously nasty people were called Neddy and Shark. Where street hookers gave her affectionate nicknames and drugs were rife. As she reached into her pocket for her car keys, she suddenly realised she still had the mobile phone she had picked up in the square. She thought about handing it over to her sister, but her instincts told her that there had been enough drama for one day. When she sat in her car, she suddenly felt emotions that she had been missing. For the first time in a very long time Bree

76

had a feeling of being alive, really alive. She wanted to share that emotion with someone.

*

There was no coincidence that Bree chose to take the long route back to Oxley Village that night. After all, if Poppy was prepared to share the highs and lows of her past, so was she. Besides, there were some things that she still struggled to talk about with her mother and best friend. But sisters, now they can share anything, can't they?

The familiar long and darkly lit short cut home led them to the Maple Railway Crossing. The clock on her dashboard showed that it was a little after eleven o clock. It was, in her mind, the only appropriate time to ever come to this hallowed place.

Poppy was puzzled when Bree slowed down as they entered the road that led through the tracks on the railway line. She was even more perturbed when her sister bought the vehicle to a sudden halt. 'Dah, the lights are green, missy, you can go,' she said, pointing at the traffic light hovering over the gates.

Her sister smiled and took a long hard stare down to her left, along the dimming shadows of the railway sidings. She looked down at the time on her mobile phone and then back into the dark distance. Her sister was becoming impatient. 'I am dying for a wazz,' Poppy moaned. 'You don't want me to piss in your car, do you?'

Again, her comment was met with complete silence. Poppy was getting angry. 'For fucks sake! I have been holding this in for ages, come on girl the fuckin' light is green.'

And just then, a sequence of small, insignificant noises followed, they were as familiar to Bree as the sound of the postman delivering the morning post. The lights on the control system suddenly started to flash and the barrier began to lower, slowly, stickily, as if it was fighting a hidden force of nature.

'It's never late,' Bree declared with an all-knowing smile. 'This train, it's never late.'

'Brilliant!' her sister replied with the face of an angry emoji. 'And now the lights are fucking red!'

'It's always on time, it's never late,' Bree said again. Her eyes shut tightly, her mind in a distant headspace, as the headlights of a speeding locomotive were seen in the distance.

The level crossing traffic lights were showing a solid red now and the noises around them grew louder and louder until the headlamps of the train grew in stature and the front of the train became clearly visible. Poppy suddenly realised where they were and why they were there. She thought back to those hours and hours of arduous prison visits where her sister's tedious conversation would be littered with an ever-growing list of small details she had remembered from the night of Jamie's tragic death. She had heard those tales so many times, she felt she had been there and witnessed the entire event herself. But Poppy said nothing, she watched on as her sister's eyes remained closed as the passing train threw up a strong gust of wind, blowing small particles of debris and some empty crisp packets into the air as it rattled through the tracks in front of them.

Poppy looked across at her sister, she was visibly shaking, as if she was frightened to look outside the vehicle. And then her lips began to move, murmurs, barely audible, it was if she was talking to herself, arguing with herself. The vibration of the final carriages of the train caused the car to vibrate slightly. 'It's my destiny, I know it's my destiny.' Bree whispered. Poppy shook her head and dismissed the moment of high drama, believing that, not for the first time that day, it was her sister being overdramatic.

A few seconds of stony silence followed before Bree was back in the land of the living. But there was something strange about the way she looked, a hint of blind panic, almost as if she had seen something she should not have seen. There was a frosty silence for the remaining few moments of the journey back to Albermarle Court.

When the girls had settled into the cosy home comforts of the flat, Bree rustled up a late-night snack, which Poppy woofed down in less than sixty seconds. She could clearly see that her sister was restless and still seething with anger, adamant that she needed to return to the estate to, 'sort out those muppets.' Bree tried several distraction techniques in a bid to calm her sibling down. The introduction of the remote control for the fifty-inch screen television proving the most effective. And the battle for a return to some sensibility was won when she produced a large bowl of expensive choc chip mint ice-cream, which her siter devoured before retiring to her bed for the night.

It had been an eventful first day together. Maybe these two lost souls had found a real connection, albeit a weird and distorted one. Somehow, this strange new partnership had provided some mental stability for each of the duo. Things felt right, life suddenly felt good for them both.

CHAPTER EIGHT

The still of the night can be a lonely place for a restless soul. Despite the warmth of the luxury duvet wrapped around her, Poppy was struggling to achieve a peaceful slumber. Maybe it was the eerie jangling of a brisk midnight breeze rushing through the noisy wind chimes in the neighbour's garden that had made Poppy open her eyes. She felt a sudden chill, ice-cold, rushing through her veins. She slipped deeper into the snug bed clothes for some comfort. She tried to close her eyes, but the chimes were getting louder, it was as if they were calling out to her, tormenting her. The sound of a distant church bell joined in the chorus. It was a familiar sound, one that reminded her of bad places, bad people.

Moths, two, maybe three, fighting for prime position at the flickering shade-less light above her bed was the first thing she saw when her vision was restored. She was confused, this was not the place she had rested her head, yet everything around her seemed familiar. Small voices, starting as a whisper, gradually grew louder inside her head. Some she recognised, others, strangers, seemed to know her name. Their torturous taunting began to alarm her. Echoes of their angry words reverberating through her subconscious, telling her she was not alone.

The smell of paint and the sound of children chattering suddenly found their way into her senses. Amongst the laughter party inside her head, she recognised the voice of Mrs Palmer, her primary school teacher. She had an angry voice, she was telling Poppy that had been bad, that she had been very bad. Poppy was struggling to find peace in her mind. Then suddenly the childish laughter of a couple of familiar primary school pupils jumped into the crazy orchestra of sounds rattling through her brain. She felt unbalanced, as if she was sliding down a slippery waterfall.

Her thoughts had turned to a place, long ago, before she had been taken into care, it was not a happy time in her life. The classmates in the art room had been teasing her that morning, mocking her, making up nasty jokes about her clothing. They had laughed at the sight of a small hole in one of her dirty scuffed shoes and had asked her why there was always a greasy black mark around the collar of her school dress. They liked to poke fun about her father, who always stunk of booze when he picked her up at the school gates. To make matters worse he had become the laughingstock of the school when he had fallen out of his seat during the Christmas play. They asked if her mother knew that she only had carpet slippers on when she was seen staggering around the local supermarket the previous week. Poppy never responded to their cruelty, what was the point when she knew they were only telling the truth.

She could see herself placed at a small round table, sitting on a tiny wooden chair, her hands were marked with watery paints. Mrs Palmer was standing over her, looking on as she added the final touches to her colourful painting. Lauren Kebble was sitting opposite her, the two girls were not friends, far from it. She couldn't see her face, but she knew it was Lauren because of the bright fluorescent pink coat that hung across the back of her chair. She remembered that her other classmates used to comment on the clothes Lauren wore. Everything was a dazzling shade of bright pink. The girl had long silky blonde hair with small pink clips tied to two bunches. She once heard a couple of teachers joke that her mother believed that her daughter was a real-life, Barbie. The girls may have laughed about Laurens colourful attire, but never to her face. Lauren was a popular girl, nobody makes fun of the popular girl, do they? Every Friday Lauren would invite some of her classmates to join her for a meal at McDonalds and then her mother would take them on to the cinema or let them stay at her big house for a sleepover. Poppy was never invited of course. She swore it never bothered her, but it did, deep down it really hurt her.

Mrs Palmer had been studying her picture for some time, making humming and harring sounds behind Poppy's back. Maybe she liked her drawing, maybe she was thinking of a suitable compliment for the girl's hard work. 'Goodness me, that's an interesting picture, Poppy. Which cartoon character is that based on?'

Poppy was puzzled, surely it was obvious. 'It's Peter Pan, miss, everybody knows Peter Pan.'

'Oh, I see, and what is the long green thing here with the big teeth? It looks very frightening.'

'That's the crocodile miss.'

'Yes, of course, it's the crocodile. Oooh, he has very scary eyes. And here Poppy, here at the end of the crocodile, what's this?'

'I told you, miss, that's Peter Pan, he is in the crocodile's mouth.'

'In his mouth, Poppy?'

'Yeah, look miss, all that red stuff, that's all his blood, see the crocodile has bitten Peter Pan in half.'

Lauren decided to butt in at this point and stir the pot. 'You know, Miss Palmer, she has some very funny ideas, our Poppy. She is a bit, well, you know, a bit funny in her head.' Her comment caused some laughter amongst her fellow classmates, but Poppy was not laughing. She gave the girl opposite a steely look that assured her that she was far from amused. She made a mental note to borrow the sharp art scissors on her desk and cut a hole in Lauren's prized pink coat. See if she finds that funny, she thought.

The teacher was still studying the painting, she was curious 'But why would the crocodile eat Peter Pan, Poppy? Everybody loves Peter Pan, the crocodile wouldn't eat him.'

Poppy looked slightly upset and studied her masterpiece before declaring. 'But he is a wrong 'un miss, Peter Pan, like you know he wears tights and things. My dad say he is a fuckin' nonce, you know, 'cause he likes to mess about with little kids and stuff.'

Laughter erupted in the classroom, but Mrs Palmer was certainly not amused. 'Poppy Jarvis, I have told you before, I will not tolerate your filthy language, leave this classroom immediately and wait for me in the corridor.'

'But miss, what about my painting?'

'Get out, get out of this classroom now!'

Lauren was the cheerleader of the hecklers at Poppy's expense, which continued long after the unruly girl's departure from the art class.

It was the first time that Poppy had been sent home from her primary school, but it would not be the last. It was the first time that her father had been called away from his work and told that he had to collect the wayward child for her inappropriate actions. But it would not be the last. It was the first time she saw her dad lose his temper and scream and shout so loudly that he made her cry. But it would not be the last. It was the first time that her angry father hit her across her bottom with the buckle on his belt. But it would not be the last.

Poppy never did forget the cruel jeers of her classmates that day, nor did she forget the cutting comments of Lauren Kebble. Something inside of her told her that the prim and proper schoolgirl with long blonde hair and the large Barbie lunchbox would not have the last laugh. And sure enough, one afternoon, on a crowded school stairway, just as the home time bell rang, young onlookers would witness a bright flash of pink, plunge at great speed from the top of the stairs to the bottom, as if it had been fired from a cannon. Lauren landed in a heap and let out a painful scream that children around her did not forget in a hurry. The badly injured six-year-old child had to wear a plaster cast on her broken arm and a neck brace for the rest of the that term. Her new fashion accessories certainly looked out of place with her bright fluorescent coat.

Poppy never did receive that Friday invitation for a McDonalds meal or a trip to the cinema.

*

The room had become bitterly cold, small particles of freezing water seemed to be coursing through Poppy's veins, pausing in her chest, it was as if an icy hand had grasped her heart. She looked around and suddenly realised she had woken up in her childhood bed. The walls looked a different colour, and the smell was much cleaner and fresher, but this was the place where all her dreams had been sunk into a dark oblivion. The wind-chimes continued to rattle outside the walls, Poppy could see a swinging light outside her bedroom window and could hear the brushing of the overgrown bushes as they were gripped by the howling wind that thrashed against the window frame. A mellow voice began calling out to her, she found herself sitting on the edge of her bed, looking down at small feet at the end of tiny legs, she was confused. Those strange feet suddenly lifted her away from the warm bedclothes and carried her, unwillingly, towards the window. It was as if a strange force wanted to share something beyond the glass. A large swinging light was visible in the garden below, it moved gently, backwards and forwards, like a swing. She raised her arm to clear the mist on the window, her fingers were tiny, her hands were small, childlike. Her hand barely covered one pane of glass. She looked more closely and saw that the bruises on her knuckles had gone, there were no longer any cuts on her soft skin. She felt her neck and could no longer feel her scars. She looked down and saw five tiny toes on each foot, she was a child again, her innocence had been restored. But strangely she was not alarmed, confused but not scared. The swaying light outside seemed to be calling to her, making promises of sweet and beautiful things for her to visit. And then that same force that had taken her to the window moved her half-dressed body again, first to the bedroom door and then downstairs, all the way to the open back door. She hesitated slightly, her feet were bare, the stony path was ice-cold. She wanted to resist, but a voices told her that she would not be harmed. That calming voice inside her head told her, 'not to worry.' It reassured her that 'this was an adventure, and she would be safe.' But the voices had been deceitful, the paving stones were like blocks of frozen ice, they sent chills running through her small toes all the way up her legs until they met her spine.

She looked towards the end of the garden and noticed a large rabbit cage, the door to the hutch was open, it looked empty inside. She noticed a long trail of blood leading away from the cage and stopping at the side of a stained house brick. It did not cause her concern. When she looked down at her hands, she could see the same shade of red on the tips of her fingers. She suddenly remembered why the rabbit cage was empty.

The wind began to rattle around the garden, sending empty wine bottles crashing from a small stone wall. The glass shattered ahead of her, on to the path she was about to take. But she still believed that she would not be harmed. She trod carefully across the tiny shards of glass but found some tiny fragments ripping into her flesh. She felt a stabbing pain in the souls of her bare feet, but a small voice whispered in her ear and told her not to complain. This was her punishment. It told her that this was no more than she deserved for being a bad child.

Hushed voices seemed to be all around her now, but she could see no faces. She suddenly noticed a large figure on a small swing in the middle of the garden. She knew it was a woman because she could see a flowery dress through the mist. The swing began to move backwards and forwards, not gathering speed nor height, just drifting at a steady pace. An outstretched hand suddenly pointed in her direction and beckoned her to come closer. She continued across the path of broken glass, still feeling stinging pains from the tiny fragments of glass trapped in her feet. When she was near enough to see more clearly, she could see that it was a very old woman perched on the swing. She seemed very frail and skinny. She had an untidy mop of straw like silvery hair flapping around her head. As Poppy drew even closer, she could see the skin on the old woman's face was badly burned, charred, as if she had been trapped inside a raging fire. Her hands were burned too, scarred and blemished. The woman continued to beckon Poppy to join her. Her tiny cut feet moved forward, but not as fast as before, the pain in the soles of her feet was becoming unbearable and her toes were covered in thick red blood.

The old lady peered forwards through tiny slits in her wrinkled face. She noticed the sudden hesitation in her visitor's approach. 'Do I frighten you little girl?' she asked, in a creaky voice that could barely be heard above the din of the windchimes.

'No!' Poppy replied firmly.

'You don't remember me, do you?' the old woman asked again, the swaying light momentarily falling on the side of her face, revealing a mass of dark peeling skin.

'I know you. I have seen you before.' Poppy said, still finding it strange that the age of her voice matched that of the body she was trapped in.

Cackled laughter met her answer, the woman on the swing seemed to be amused. 'Oh, my child, you can only see me when I want you to.'

Poppy suddenly heard some rustling in the bushes at the back wall, she turned her head to see a large white shape scamper across the garden path. As the figure came into view, she could see it was a furry animal, but it seemed to have no head. And then she heard the squealing and scrawling of at least a dozen large black rats as they chased the headless animal around the garden. The rodents continued their chase until the helpless white creature landed at Poppy's feet. When she looked down, she could see the fur on the poor animal was covered in thick mounds of dried red blood. The rabbit had stopped moving, his carcass laid bare, sprawled out, at the mercy of his pursuers. The pack of rats descended on the dead animal beneath her bloodstained feet and began feeding on the corpse. As they gnawed away at the rabbit's flesh, Poppy looked across at the old lady, she was still balancing on a swing, but it had lost its momentum. They exchanged a long stare that told them that they both knew why they were there that night.

The noises grew louder around the garden as the shadows began to close in on those present. The large clanging of church bells were almost deafening now, they had drowned out the gnashing of the teeth of the blood hungry rodents devouring the headless corpse. The wind chimes came back in to play as a constant breeze rushed through the dark night and swirled around the brickwork of the neighbour's house. Laughing voices started up from beyond the shadows joining in the torturous orchestra of sounds. Small whispers, voices that had been heard before, did not want to be left out. Their sharp tongues and spiteful words reminding Poppy they were never going to leave her thoughts. The cacophony of screaming sounds ran around inside her distorted brain, increasing in volume, goading her, tormenting her soul.

The old woman called out once more, louder than before in order to be heard. She asked her visitor the question again. 'Do I scare you little girl, do I frighten you?'

But all Poppy could do was to sneer as she looked back at the strange figure with the burnt features. 'No' she replied defiantly, with a sinister smile on her young face, that did not look out of place in this circus of damnation. 'Why, do I scare you?'

CHAPTER NINE

Drumbeats, loud thumping drumbeats, banging and twanging around inside her head, as if someone had turned up the bass to maximum on a distorted sound system. Poppy's eyes peeled open slowly but shut tightly when the stinging rays of the morning sun beams found the small gap between the curtains and blinded her vision. Her body ached, her arms felt heavy, her throat felt as dry as an empty well. She tried to return to her slumber, desperate for some respite.

And then a long buzzing noise, screeching at full volume, searing a hole through her brain. It repeated, over and over again. She wanted to dismiss it but that haunting one key melody would not be silenced. Suddenly as reality began to register, she recognised it as the sound of the intercom. She hid her head beneath the pillow, anxious to escape the monotonous racket. She desperately wanted the visitor at the front door to, 'Fuck off and die.' Those very words escaped from her mouth and were shouted aloud.

A pause, a short respite, but then that buzzing sound started up again. Poppy, face like thunder, had suffered enough. She threw off the bedclothes, dragged her feet across the floor and headed for the instrument of her torture. She was more than angry and relayed her fury when she answered the intercom 'What! Who is it? What do you want?'

Another pause before a softly spoken voice breezed its way through the small speaker, it caught her off guard. 'Brianna, that's not Brianna, who are you?'

Poppy was struggling to register any clear thoughts, her head was still thumping inside. Not knowing nor caring who the unwelcome visitor was, she pressed the button to open the downstairs security door and left the front door ajar. She had a craving for aspirins and an immediate intake of tobacco. The last thing she needed was an uninvited guest. Despite the fact her brain was playing host to a noisy rock concert, her sense of smell was clearly unaffected, she could almost taste the aroma of strong perfume as it wafted through the front door and into the living room. Her visitors face appeared and within seconds she knew exactly who she was. Her features instantly revealing that, unless her absent half-sister had climbed into a time machine and aged twenty or thirty years, this had to be Bree's mother, the likeness was uncanny.

The two women sparred for a few seconds, looking each other up and down, an awkward silence ensued. It was a surreal moment for Poppy. She had heard her sister berate her mother more times than she cared to remember. But this stranger didn't look like the devil incarnate that her sibling had painted her out to be at all. She was not tall in stature but held a commanding presence. She was elegant, refined, sporting a grey designer jacket that would have carried a hefty four-figure price tag. Her hair was immaculate, as though she had just jumped out of a stylist's chair. But it was those eyes that gave away the game completely. Beaming brightly, like huge balls of soft brown luxury chocolate. There could be no mistaking that this was her sibling's mother. Since the day she discovered that the man who had deserted her as a child had fathered twins during his illicit affair, she had often wondered how she would react if she ever met the 'other woman'. Her curiosity need wait no longer.

It had taken less than thirty seconds for Poppy to work out who the unwelcome visitor was, but Krista was treading more carefully. She remembered that her daughter had talked about taking photographs at a hostel for the homeless in Southwark. Maybe Bree had taken in a stray, a random act of kindness. It would be rare for her self-obsessed daughter to be so charitable. But maybe she was wrong, maybe Bree had turned over a new leaf.

'Is she looking after you, OK?' the visitor asked Poppy who was frantically looking for her lighter.

'Yeah, it's alright here,' was all that Poppy was going to give her, hoping the conversation would end there. But it didn't.

'That's one of Brianna's tee-shorts isn't it, the one you're wearing?'

'Er, it was 'er brothers I think.'

'It's a lovely area, around here, such beautiful surroundings, don't you think? Oxley, it's very peaceful.'

The reply this time was a simple nod of the head. Poppy found what she was looking for and retreated to her bedroom and opened the window to let the smoke out. Her sister had been whinging at her for days about the smell of stale tobacco in the rooms. Her throbbing head told her she needed peace and quiet today, not an inquisition.

Krista placed her Mulberry bag down on the dining room table, but after second thoughts grasped it tightly and kept it close to her side. She looked around the flat, appalled at the untidiness of the living room and the unwashed dishes on the kitchen side. She wanted to say something but thought it better to save her thoughts for her daughter. She did however have a rummage through the kitchen drawers to see if Bree had acquired any new forms of medication, none were found. She also nosed her way through a collage of photographs that been printed on press sheets and were lying on the coffee table. She studied them closely to see if the strange girl in the flat was amongst them, she wasn't of course. Her last task was to try to peek in her daughter's bedroom, but she found the door was locked. Krista, being Krista, could always see the worst in those she did not know. She automatically assumed that the door was locked because her daughter would be protecting her expensive jewellery and camera equipment from her houseguest.

Poppy slipped some jogging bottoms on and made herself some tea and toast, she was after all playing the reluctant host now. However, she chose not to offer any form of refreshments to her visitor. Her head was still hurting inside but several minutes later the Ibuprofen she had taken was starting to kick-in. It seems that the bass player and the drummer inside her brain had started to pack up for the day.

An awkwardness of proportions ensued, the women were both lost for conversation after just a half a dozen exchanges, but the sound of a key in the front door bought a smile to one of their faces and broke the frosty silence. 'Thank goodness, Brianna is home.'

Krista stood to greet the arrival with outstretched arms but did not find her daughter in reciprocal mood. Her reception was frosty to say the least. 'I told you not to come here, mother.' she said with a look of disdain on her face.

'I know, Brianna, darling,' she replied in a defensive manner. 'But I have been staying at Aunt Millie's house for the past few days and I couldn't come to London and not visit you, could I?' She rummaged through her bag and produced a small box. 'I bought you a small present from that lovely store in Helsinki, it is beautiful, such delicate features. I thought you could put it on that glass unit in your bedroom to remind you of home.'

'This is my home, mother, not Finland, not Tampere, this is my home.'

'Look, it's a tiny piano, with a small girl sitting on the seat. She has long hair, just like you used to have. I couldn't resist it when I saw it. It's pure crystal, it wasn't cheap.'

Bree was not as impressed as her mother hoped she would be and she would be even less impressed by the speech her unwelcome guest was about to make to Poppy. 'She was a star when she was young, a real star, my daughter.'

Bree shook her head. 'Not now mother, for Christ's sake!'

'The teachers said that when she was just nine years old, she could have been a piano master. Everything she played was so beautiful. Do you remember, Brianna, darling when you played that beautiful piece, what was it? Oh yes, that was it, Beethoven's Moonlight Sonata. It was just so perfect, more than two hundred people watched that recital, do you remember darling? How they all stood up and gave you a standing ovation. She was just a child, just nine, a star, a superstar in the making.'

'Why do you do that?' Bree asked, screwing up her face.

'But Brianna, I just like to let people know how...'

'Lie. I mean why do you lie all the time about things mother?'

'Oh, but darling, you were a special child. You were so clever, so amazing. The piano, ballet, gymkhana, do you remember, all those lovely rosettes? You were so talented at everything you did.'

Bree was clearly angered by her overbearing mothers' stories 'The piano, my ballet, horse riding, just all lies, mother. I was never any good at any of them and you know it.'

'But...'

'For God's sake give it a rest! Just accept me for what I am.'

Krista was silenced, she had hoped that her daughter would appreciate the small souvenir. But she was becoming accustomed to her daughter's dogmatic approach to their relationship now, she knew she needed to keep her cool. 'I just thought you would like it. I can never do right for doing wrong with you, darling, can I?'

Bree looked in Poppy's direction and rolled her eyes. 'You see what I have to put up with?'

'So,' Krista asked, slightly perturbed that her daughter was sharing her thoughts with a total stranger. 'This is your new, eh, houseguest, friend, she seems to have made herself at home, is she staying long?'

'As long as she wants mother, and she is not my friend.'

'Oh, I thought it might be something to do with the shelter and work and.'

Bree suddenly felt bullish, she knew her next comment would not gone down well. But she was going to savour this moment, she wanted to remember every twisted expression of hurt and pain on her mother's face. She couldn't wait to reveal the identity of the girl stretched out on her sofa. 'No, mother, she is not my friend, she is my sister, this is Poppy, my sister, mother, my sister.'

'Half-sister.' Poppy mumbled, feeling a bit left out at that moment. 'We are half-sisters.'

Krista did not know where to look, she scowled as she moved her eyes between the two girls, feeling more than foolish for not realising the truth of the situation. The revelation had put her on the back foot now and her daughter was determined to make her suffer. 'This is the girl you kept hidden from me for all those years, the dirty secret, the one you never thought I would find out about. This is Poppy, this is my sister, and she lives with me now.'

'But Kayleigh told me she was back in pris…'

'And there you go again, mother, talking to my friend behind my back. I sometimes think that you see Kayleigh as part of the family. She is not your daughter, she is my friend, disloyal sometimes, very disloyal sometimes, yes, but she is my friend, not yours.'

Krista's demeanour began to change, she stared long and hard at the bewildered girl sporting her dead son's tee-shirt. She was far from happy with her daughter at that moment, 'Mitä hän talla tekee?' she asked.

'English mother, we don't speak Finish here do we Poppy?'

'Oletko hullu? Hän on murhaaja.'

'No, anything you want to say you can say to her face. Maybe you can start with an apology. Explain why you kept her a secret from me. You can also say sorry to her for shagging her father and breaking up her happy home. Do you know, mother, do you ever stop to wonder what you did? All the lives you ruined back then with your sordid little affair.'

Krista was still transfixed on the new tenant, she resorted once again to her native tongue to express her anger at the situation, but her daughter was not having any of it. 'She is telling me you are dangerous, Poppy. She thinks you might steal all my jewellery, or you will kill me in my sleep.'

Poppy showed little emotion, she had made herself comfortable with her feet up on the sofa and was halfway through her breakfast. She didn't want to say anything, she was loving every moment of the unfolding drama.

Krista knew that this was not the time and place for this confrontation, she was furious at Bree for putting her in this situation. However, Kayleigh had previously filled her in on the background of the violent outcast who was now sharing a flat with her daughter. The worried parent feared she was too caught up in the moment to see the danger on her own doorstep. Part of her was angry with her daughter's best friend for not warning her of the situation. Her motherly instinct was to protect her daughter from this monster. She wanted to make a scene, shout, yell. She wanted to pack a bag full of clothes and drag her daughter, kicking and screaming, away to a safe place. To take her on a plane, if necessary, all the way back to her beloved house overlooking the lakes in Tampere

However, at that moment Krista thought it better to withdraw herself from the situation. She knew she would only make things worse if she stayed. She tightened up her smart jacket and headed for the door. She was hurt and confused. She had hoped that her daughter's interest in her newfound sibling had waned since she moved into her new flat. She felt a sick feeling in her gut as she began to relive the nightmare of the day that she had revealed everything to her. She had no intention of heading for Heathrow the next day to return to Finland, she needed to stay close, she needed to know her daughter was safe. At that moment she felt that there was only one person who could make her feel better. She was thankful she still had her best friend Milly to rely on. She needed someone who knew the whole story, someone who always understood her, someone to help her get through another dark moment in her life. When she reached the front door, she turned back to speak, but the angry expression on her daughter's face told her that it was best to say nothing and leave.

Poppy had said few words since the return of her sister but there was one burning question in her head that she had reserved for the departing woman. The words just found their way out of her mouth. 'Did ya love him, my dad, did ya love him?'

Krista wanted to ignore the comment from the scruffy looking urchin on the sofa. She despised her, she owed her nothing, least of all to lay bare her innermost feelings. But as she placed her hand firmly on the catch of the front door, that question paralysed her from her head to her toes. She became lost in those few seconds. Part of her wanted to denounce the torrid three-year affair she had with Poppy's father, to claim that it was the biggest mistake of her life and that she had regretted it every day since. But she found her heart calling out to her at that moment and a sudden reality that the nagging pain that ripped her soul from her body all those years ago had never left her. And for once she decided to speak a truth that she never shared with anyone other than Milly. Her eyes glazed over, and the tone of her voice mellowed as she answered the question.

'I loved your father more than I have ever loved anyone in my whole life.' she said in a shaky voice, which stunned her audience and drew a gasp of despair from her daughter.

But she was not off of the hook just yet, Poppy needed more from her. 'More than yer daughter? More than yer son?' she asked.

Bree stood open-mouthed, hands-on hips, studying her mother's expressionless features, fully expecting the startled woman to laugh off the crazy notion. But nothing happened, the three women seemed to be trapped in that moment of surreal drama.

Krista chose to remain tight-lipped. Totally oblivious to the fact that her stubborn silence would erupt the volcano of hatred that had been building up inside her daughter's head. But the lost expression on her weary face told a story of a million words. A tale of unrequited love, of a doomed affair that was never meant to be. A beautiful time in her life when she felt alive. A time when she would have walked barefoot on broken glass to share an embrace with the man who could make her head go giddy with just the sound of his voice. But that man's betrayal had wrecked her very soul and left her emotionally scarred for life. As Krista exited the flat, the sparkle in her eyes had been replaced with a look of bitterness and sorrow, as if she had been dragged screaming through the burning ashes of a memory that she has always held sacred.

Slamming the front door to leave, Krista heard the smashing of glass against the frame behind her as her daughter launched the tiny crystal piano figurine with an almighty scream. A lengthy tirade of abuse followed as Bree stormed around the living room, tugging clumps out of her own hair and kicking the furniture. 'I hate you, I really fucking hate you, don't come back you bitch, don't ever come back! I hope your plane crashes, I hope you die, I swear that's the end now, I wish you was dead!'

Bree retired to her bedroom, slamming the door enroute as if to tell her sibling she needed time alone. She wouldn't tell her sister, but she was disappointed that she the appearance of her mother had not enraged her. In truth she would have rather seen Poppy lash out at the woman who had cheated with her father and caused the break-up of the family home. And, of all the questions to ask, she had picked one that would further fuel the burning fires of hatred she had for her parent. She didn't want to hear that her mother had loved the man who was at the root of all the heartache that followed. She didn't want to believe that it could have been true love between them and not just a few fumbled sexual encounters in the back of a car. She locked herself in her room and looked for any of her mother's precious memories to destroy. She settled for two family photographs which she tore in to confetti-sized pieces.

Poppy wasn't bothered, she wasn't bothered at all. She had no intention of consoling her heartbroken sister. She couldn't help but laugh when she thought how the entertainment that morning had been so much better than the daytime television programmes that she had watched that week. She curled up on the sofa with a smirk on her face and wrapped two pillows around her aching head.

CHAPTER TEN

She was beginning to feel stifled, she needed to breathe fresh air, Poppy needed to get out of the flat. Strange thoughts were continually running through her aching body. She was feeling so weak, she barely had the strength to get out of bed. For once her throbbing headache could not be put down to an excess of alcohol. She could barely remember a thing from the previous night, although the meeting with her sister's mother was still fresh in her memory. Krista's strange comments, however, had not helped. She had been convincing herself for the past two years that her father's mistress was an ogre, a horrible vindictive selfish homewrecker. Bree, during her numerous prison visits, had painted a picture of a monster, when in truth she was just a woman, a very pretty woman, vulnerable and insecure. The fact that she had fallen for her father's patter reminded her just how charming he could be during her early childhood. That was, before he chose the comfort of alcohol over the love of his wife and daughter.

Maybe it was good thing that she had to report to the police station today. After spending the first week with her sister, part of her wanted to offer her wrists and ask them to lock her up again.

She was, after all, beginning to feel like a prisoner in this abode. Her money had run dry along with her patience. The conversations with her sibling were becoming stranger by the day and her sanity was being tested to the full.

She wasn't quite sure why she had crept along a small ledge to break into Bree's locked bedroom through the small window overlooking the flat roof. There was at least a thirty-foot drop to the patio below where a neighbour was filling one of the communal wheelie bins. Once inside the perfectly colour co-ordinated boudoir, she found herself surrounded by Bree's belongings. A generous spray of a sickly tasting scent had welcomed her into the room. More illustrations by that weird artist. The stares of the unknown girl in these ones much more intense, almost fierce, they seemed to be trapping her in their line of vision, draining her energy. She couldn't escape them now, they were everywhere in the flat.

The drawers to her sister's smart white chest of drawers were locked, but she didn't need to search long to find the key. Hardly hidden, it was sitting under the mouse mat on the computer desk. She was not sure what she was looking for, but the way she was feeling that morning she was hoping for a pile of cash. She had spent most of her prison leavers money buying those drugs she had given to Lulu, the rest divided between tobacco and cheap alcohol. She knew she would find it hard coping with her sisters' one-way conversations for much longer. If the stash of cash was large enough, she would be sorely tempted to 'do a runner'. She could jump on a bus, a train, steal a car, go anywhere, just to get away from this mind-numbing madness.

But there were no wads of cash in the drawers. She did find a couple of pairs of expensive looking earrings and two nice bracelets. Worth knowing, she thought, in case things get desperate. She made a mental note to look out for a pawn shop close by. While her search continued, she uncovered some weird photographs of homeless people with scribbled notes attached to each of them. Poppy knew nothing at all about photography, but she could see that her sister was indeed talented in this respect. Changing backgrounds and making faces stand out amongst dismal surroundings. She understood now why Bree had a well-paid job and drove such a nice car. It was strange, but it was the first time she had ever felt jealous of her newfound sibling. Her search of the back of the drawer produced a couple of bank statements. Studying the balances, she saw that the four thousand pounds in a current account was dwarfed by the twenty plus thousand in her sister's savings account. But no ready cash. Her search for treasure continued.

In the middle drawer she found some small trinkets and a heavy gold neckless carrying her sibling's name. She guessed that this must have been a present from her mother because it carried her full name, *Brianna*. She knew how much her sister hated the name she was christened with. It was another one of her repetitive rants during her prison visits. There were several medical prescriptions, several unopened boxes of tablets. She recognised one set of pills she had been prescribed herself during her time in Bronzefield Prison. She was drip fed the tablets daily, a precautionary measure to protect inmates. Poppy never swallowed the tablets in the medical room of the prison, she accumulated them over a two-week period and swapped them with a fellow inmate for some tobacco. She had, during her drug-fuelled teen years, taken enough substances to take her to an imaginary moon and back. But she was done with that now, since the night Nikita overdosed, she had not touched a hard drug of any description. Certainly not ones like these anti-depressants, that could clearly temper the rage that held inside during her incarceration. It was her anger with the world that kept her alive. Her rage was her survival safety blanket.

At the back of the bottom drawer, she found a long plastic tube labelled with an official looking printed name, 'Peclosaperidone'. She was curious why this was kept separate from all of the other tablets. It carried a small health warning. Poppy replaced her sister's arsenal of assorted pills and formed her own conclusion. 'Nutty pills for the nutty girl,' she said to herself with a small grin. 'I knew she had to be on something.' As she was about to close the drawer, disappointed with the lack of hidden cash on show, she noticed some handwritten envelopes bearing her sisters name and address. The postmarks were not clear on them, but the handwriting made Poppy curious. Her sibling had never mentioned any boyfriends to her before and her intuition had told her that there was more to her friendship with the good-looking man who had turned up at Matt and Kayleigh's house than she was telling. The words in the birthday and valentines' cards did not hold back either. They were heartfelt expressions of undying love. 'Forever in my heart, my beautiful soulmate.' 'My love for you grows more each moment of each day.' Poppy winced as she read them out aloud, some of the words were too long for her to fully comprehend, but she saw enough to realise that her sister did indeed have an admirer. But the odd thing was that the sender didn't sign them, just kisses and the word, 'Always' at the end of each of the cards. 'He's fuckin' married.' Poppy said aloud. 'Oooh, the goody-two shoes bitch is shagging a married bloke.' When she placed the cards back neatly in the drawer, something made her look twice at the envelopes, she knew she needed to remember the address of the place she was staying in case she ever got lost. But there was something about that postscript on the cards that bothered her. The word 'Always'. There was a familiarity about the lettering. For a moment one crazy thought went through her head. Could these cards have been sent by her former lover? Was Matt cheating on Kayleigh and treating himself to some posh totty. Her head told her she had seen that handwriting before. She remembered Bree's comment about saving the gossip on Matt for a rainy day. She began to think about things in a very different way when she climbed out of the window and risked life and limb for a second time that day.

A twenty-minute soapy shower and a plate of beans on toast was all she needed to set her up for the ordeal ahead of her. This was to be the first of twenty-six visits to Plumstead Police Station, a ritual she would never enjoy, but one she had to endure. The solicitor that her sister had hired had not been cheap by all accounts, but he certainly earned his fee when he persuaded the parole panel to give Poppy more freedom and not fit her ankle with an electronic tag. He had argued that the repentant girl was desperate to find a job and pay her own way in society. He suggested that curfew times would restrict her employment opportunities in a workplace that had been ravaged by the effects of the Covid Pandemic. Nobody was more surprised than Poppy when the self-righteous do-gooders on the panel agreed and set her up with a weekly check-in at the police station for her first six months of freedom.

Without a car, the day would be a long and arduous one. Her sister, with the assistance of busy-body Kayleigh, had planned her out the bus route she needed to take and even listed the times of the buses for her. Kayleigh, it seems, felt an urge to prepare a list for almost anything. Poppy never said anything when her sister handed her the timetable, but she felt as though she was being treated like a ten-year-old schoolgirl. When she had departed the first bus to link up with the second one at Eltham Green, she lit herself a cigarette and studied the timetable, before the complicated layout got the better of her and she was forced to ask a bystander for help. But just as the bus she needed was pulling in, something caught her attention on the other side of the road. It was a dark blue BMW, it was Matt's car, she was sure of it. The vehicle was parking in a layby next to a small park. The bus came and went but Poppy was not on it. There was something strange going on here and her growing curiosity got the better of her. She was right, no sooner had Matt left his car, she saw a girl approaching from the park gates. She was slim in build and had shiny blonde hair, but it was not her sister. But then why in God's name would it be her sister? she thought to herself, self-doubting her earlier instincts. This girl was skinny, very skinny and petite, nothing like her sibling. She was dressed in a figure-hugging black PVC jacket which looked as though it had been bought from a market stall. She wore ripped jeans, hardly an up-to-date fashion statement. But the small girl was not alone, she had her hand wrapped firmly around the tiny wrist of a small boy who was dressed in a replica football shirt and oversized shorts. Matt made no contact whatsoever with the girl but lifted the toddler high above his head and swung him around twice before returning him to earth. There was a fair distance between the bus stop and where the trio were standing but Poppy could see Matt's unmistakable grin, it seemed to be beaming brighter than ever. A small conversation ensued before Matt placed his hand in his pocket and took out a small number of notes, handing them to the waiting girl. He walked off with the young lad into the park area while she strolled away and made several calls and texts on her mobile phone.

Something in her head told her she had to get on the next bus and report to the police station. After all, Callard would be expecting her to 'fuck up' the very first week, and she didn't want to give him that satisfaction. But before she boarded the bus, she remembered where she had seen that slim figured blonde girl before. 'Chantelle,' she said under her breath. 'It's that fuckin' skanky waitress from the restaurant.'

The journey to her destination was a little over twenty minutes and by the time she departed the bus she had worked it all out. Two years and three months since the incident at the Chez Blanc Bistro. It was the same day she had caught the sneaky waitress strolling half-dressed out of Matt's bedroom at his flat. It fits, it suddenly made sense to her. The piggy-faced little slut has had his baby and now he is having to live a massive lie. No wonder he is always broke, Poppy thought. 'I bet that wasn't on one of your fuckin' lists, Kayleigh,' she said to herself. 'You dirty bastard, Matt.'

Despite her excursion she arrived at the police station, within the permitted time period. It was the first of her routine visits where she needed to report that she was, number one, still alive, two, not taking hard drugs and, three, hadn't killed anybody that week. It was a weekly ritual that she knew she would never get used to, but it was a better option than a tag, or even worse, re-visiting her old probation officer. Those weekly hour-long sessions with the bible bashing do-gooder really would have tested the patience of a saint.

She wasn't sure why, but Poppy found herself on a different return bus route to the one which had taken her to the police station in Plumstead. Before she had formulated any sort of plan, she found herself entering a small cul-de-sac in an ordinary road in Anerley. Her initial thoughts were to confront Matt when he returned from playing happy families with the young waitress and the little boy. But this was not out of any misguided loyalty to Kayleigh. No, this was for pure gain. She may not have struck gold when she rifled through her sister's personal belongings earlier that day, but she had found a solution to her cash flow problem. Fifty pounds would buy her silence for that week. It would be enough for a few days' supplies of alcohol and tobacco. She might even treat herself to a large Kebab as a reward for coming up with the idea. Besides, if this was the 'rainy day' secret that her sister was keeping under wraps, she wanted to make sure she would be the first to benefit.

As she waited, slightly hidden by a large hedge, opposite the small terraced house, she noticed Kayleigh. She had her coat on, little Willow in her arms, being bundled into a large pram. The frumpy woman began heading in the direction she had just arrived. Maybe, she thought, everybody wanted to take Matt's offspring to the park today.

She walked along the small alleyway, the smell of burned skunk and the tones of a repetitive beats getting ever louder. Sure, enough the boy with all the not-so-funny one-liners and his black friend were parked on the wall again. They were blazing away on a large joint and giggling to themselves like junior school kids. She was greeted once more with a torrent of unwelcome abuse which she ignored as she passed them by. Their childish rants were hardly likely to unsettle her. She had other things on her mind, stopping for a chat with a couple of chavs was not one of them.

The spare key was where it had been the previous week and Poppy let herself in through the back door. Time was not on her side so her mission would need to be executed swiftly and without leaving a trace of her visit. The first thing she did was help herself to three twenty-pound notes from Willows' savings. Insurance, she thought, just in case Matt did not buy in to her blackmail plan. However, when she had a rummage around the living room, she was suddenly drawn to Kayleigh's laptop, which was still open on the computer desk in the corner. There was a picture of an elderly looking woman sporting huge rimmed red spectacles that looked far too big for her narrow face. She thought she recognised the woman in the screenshot but could not remember where from. The picture was supported by an array of technical jargon which knew she had neither the time nor the inclination to study. She moved to the hallway, but that photograph stuck in her mind.

Even though she knew that both Matt and Kayleigh were not at home she still crept up the stairs in the stealthy manner of a good burglar. The first door she entered was a small room full of gym equipment. Her guess was that this would soon be the baby's nursery as one wall had a large mural embracing several painted Disney characters. She stepped over some of the equipment and noticed a foot long solid metal bar, she picked it up, it was a very heavy weight. It would make a good weapon, she thought, and slipped it in to an empty carrier bag. Her next port of call was the couple's bedroom. It was not as fresh smelling as the rest of the house and the curtains had seen better days. When she looked in some drawers and searched underneath some of Kayleigh's underwear, she noticed several sex toys and a large spikey purple vibrator, it was at least ten inches long, it made her smile. She smelled the sex toy to make sure it had been cleaned since its last use and threw it in with the steel rod. In the same drawer, amongst a selection of KY jelly and lubrications, she spotted some handcuffs. She had seen enough of those in her time to know they were the real thing, sturdy metal, solid at the joints. She took out the key for safekeeping and placed the cuffs into her new goody bag.

Poppy left through the same back way she had entered the property. She carefully placed the door key back under the loose stone. She closed the back gate firmly behind her and headed home. Her intention had been to make a swift exit, but halfway down the alleyway two voices called out to inside her head, one screamed out loud but the other was mellow and controlled. That voice of reason was winning the battle, it told her she had taken what she needed, to make her escape, buy some booze and chill out for the evening. But that voice was silenced when the youth with the scraggy red locks dished out a parting message. 'Oi,' he shouted as she passed him by, 'have you escaped from Battersea dogs' home? Shouldn't you be wearing a muzzle?'.

In an instant Poppy swung around and headed back to confront her abusers. The puzzled black lad hardly had a chance to speak before he felt the full force of Poppy's clenched fist strike the side of his face. He crumbled backwards over the wall, landing in a heap on the concrete paving stones. The loudmouthed youth reacted quickly to the sight of his buddy tumbling, rising to his feet to confront the aggressor. But Poppy was on him in a split second, yanking his arm and twisting it up firmly behind his back with one hand, while grabbing his ungainly mop of greasy red hair with the other. His face was thrust against the solid brick wall, once, twice and a third time for luck. She dragged the stunned lad sideways scraping his cheek against the side of the brickwork until his skin was raw and his face began to bleed.

'You should know your place, you little toe-rag,' Poppy yelled. 'You aint got no respect.'

The youth was suddenly tongue-tied, no witty banter to counter with. Dumbstruck and helpless, he was in fear of his life now. Poppy leaned down and looked at the fear in his eyes, he looked as if he would burst into tears at any second. She pushed his face up hard against the bloodstained brickwork and handed him a 'not-so-friendly' warning. 'These people that live next door, they are alright,' she said. 'They aint got much, but they work hard, ya know, like they do their best. Their kid needs its sleep, to give em a break sometimes, do ya get that? Their baby needs its rest. So, if I find out that they have so much as heard the ringtone on your mobile, I will come back here and shove that phone so far up your fuckin' arse, they will need to cut you in 'alf to get it out. Do you get me, shithead? I said do you fuckin' get me?'

The terrified youngster nodded and mumbled that he understood. Poppy looked sternly at the other dishevelled youth as he climbed back over the wall, fully prepared to dish out further punishment. But the clearly shaken lad raised his hands firmly into the air as if to show he was ready to surrender. 'I'm cool!' he said loudly, clearly not wanting to suffer the same fate as his accomplice.

And so, not for the first time in Poppy's life, the voice of reason inside her head was dealt a knockout blow. No matter how hard she tried to avoid confrontation it seemed to be waiting for her around every corner.

When she boarded the first of two buses that would get her back within walking distance of Oxley Village, Poppy looked through her new bag of guilty pleasures. She allowed herself a small grin when she worked out what she wanted to do with items she had taken from the house. All she needed to do now was to track down her target. A quick search on the internet football pages on her new I-phone gave her all the information she needed.

CHAPTER ELEVEN

The world we live in is full of saints and sinners. Some bad people, judged by others on the path they have chosen to take, may have good intentions. While others, seemingly clean-living folks, seen as pillars of our society, may have evil thoughts that are masked by their chartable deeds. But in truth there is a darker side to every living soul that ever walked the earth. Whether shallow or deep-rooted it is always there, inside each of us, making us all vulnerable, capable of committing the most horrendous sins imaginable.

Neddy was no saint, that's for sure. Just the image of this six-foot seven beast with mangy unkempt dreadlocked hair and fists like shovels was enough to frighten those who crossed his path. Despite being in his early thirties he looked much older than his years, his long-term drug abuse paying a heavy toll on his features. He had smoked his first joint at the tender age of eleven and during his crazy teen years binged on just about every illegal substance that had found its way on to the streets of South London.

He was indeed a frightening sight to behold. One of his eyes was always half closed. This was not an injury received in battle, merely a rare eye disorder that had maligned him as a child. He had often been teased about his features in the school playground when he was young, tagged with the cruellest of nicknames by so-called school friends. But the bullying soon stopped when young Neddy grew in size and stature at a rapid rate. Even back then his retaliation on those that mocked him was brutal and merciless.

He started year seven at school as Neville Edwards and finished that term as Neddy, a name he had not chosen but one he carried with pride. He was expelled from that particular establishment when he was fourteen years old, following an altercation with the woodwork teacher during a lesson. The foolish tutor having made the cardinal sin of laying hands on the angsty teen. Within a few short months of that incident, he was behind bars, locked away in a Youth Offenders Institute for a brutal assault on a neighbour of the foster family who cared for him. The fact that the attack had been racially motivated fuelled the judge to hand out the harshest sentence possible for the crime. This set the wayward youngster on the crooked path he still followed today.

Conspicuous by his gangly height, Neddy wore a full-length black trench coat and knee length Dr Marten lace up boots, come rain or shine, he was never seen out of them. Some say this gave him the appearance of a soldier about to lead a march into battle. But it is unlikely that any platoon would have followed a man with unwashed hair tails hanging halfway down his back. His crazy hairstyle certainly attracted its fair share of attention. After all, a white man with long dreads strutting down the streets is not something you see every day of the week.

Neddy had a ruthless reputation, feared by all who had dealings with him. It was rumoured that he once kicked a dog to death in front of its owner, simply because the animal had interrupted his sleep. Members of his gang would often say he was single-handedly responsible for the death of at least two rival gang members. Any bad-mouthing of the giant enforcer would need to be done in very dark corners.

The Keyes brothers were both serving time and had left Neddy to 'babysit' their domain. On this bright but breezy evening he had summoned his team of drug pushers to a regular meeting place behind the derelict factory on the north side of the Marfield Estate. A fire burned in a large trash can in the centre of a concreted area once used as a loading bay. The grey van which had stalked Poppy was parked in the corner of the yard. Loud shouting and banging could be heard from inside the vehicle. Someone was clearly not happy to be caged in there.

Those members of the gang who had failed so miserably to stand up to Poppy were all in attendance. They were sat around like naughty primary school children waiting for a telling-off from their headmaster. Cheyenne, sporting a bruised cheek, was wearing the same tacky tracksuit that had been hauled across the pathway. A disfigured Keelan was present, his broken nose and matching collar bone giving him excess pain and discomfort. Scruffy sat on his own, the others had refused to be placed anywhere near the prideless man who badly needed a scrub in the bath. The tall black guy, Fitz, along with his buddy, Shark, stood at the rear of the van awaiting instructions from their self-appointed leader. The assembled crew did not add up to much, but it was around half of a once finely tuned drugs operation that was slowly falling apart at the seams. Two of Neddy's top earners had joined the Keyes brothers behind prison walls and a third member had fled the set-up after a blade-to-blade run-in with the gangs' Lithuanian rivals.

They had all been on the sharp end of Neddy's vicious tongue that night, Fitz being the only gang member who escaped a full blown rollocking. So, it was now the turn of the captive making all the noise in the back of the Sprinter van. Everyone presents knew what crime the loud man had committed and looked on as their leader rose to his feet like a man mountain and prepared himself.

Neddy sucked on his teeth and spat out a large ball of phlegm on to the ground. 'Let him out,' he said, 'and bring me the cutters.'

There was a commotion when the vehicle doors were sprung open as the prisoner in the van tried desperately to escape. But a couple of heavy punches to the side of his head delivered by Shark put paid to his brave intentions. The two guards dragged the helpless captive across the yard until he was, maybe appropriately, parked on his knees within reach of the angry giant.

The gang leaders face was stern, he rubbed the knuckles on his fingers and clenched his hands together. A long and crooked smile cracked across Shark's face, he for one was going to enjoy the following torture show.

In his head the frightened prisoner began to pray and then decided it might be a better idea to beg. 'I swear down, bruv, man was mugged, it was three of those Lithi bastards. I put up a fight, but there was three of them, man had no chance.'

The gang leader said nothing, he stared long and hard at his unfaithful gang member. The audience in the cheap seats knew what was coming next. 'The cutters, Shark,' the big man roared. 'Hand me those bolt cutters.'

Sudden panic ripped through the captured man's body and his voice broke into a stuttering shrill. 'I will pay it back, Neddy, every penny, I swear down, bruv, give me a couple of days, I've got a mate, he owes me.'

Neddy opened the steely looking weapon in his hand checking that the teeth had been sharpened. 'The truth,' he said, with a steely stare aimed at his cowering corporal. 'I want the fucking truth.'

Everyone's eyes were fixed on the renegade pusher begging for forgiveness. Fear had set in, he began to slur his words, his speech was almost incoherent. 'It was me kids' birthday, my missus, she told me if I didn't find the money for a present and a party, she would leave me. She said she would take him away to her mums in Clacton. I would have never seen him again. I swear down, bruv, that's the truth.'

His explanation seemed to amuse the first in command. 'So you took my money for a fucking kids birthday party?' The onlookers laughed, as if their master had delivered a funny punchline at the end of a joke.

The grovelling gang member tried harder. 'I swear down, I got bare money, bruv, but I'm owed. On my kid's life I will pay every penny back. Just give me a couple of days.'

Neddy circled his captive, his towering figure blocking out the beams of light from the van's headlights. He pondered for a few seconds, sucking hard on his teeth before turning towards the rebellious gang member. In a split second he swung back his leg and launched one of his size eleven boots into the head of the traitor on the floor, just as if he was launching a football into the air. The impact bought a howling cry of pain from the man, who curled up into a small ball to protect himself. Neddy was far from done with him, he pressed his boot down on to the shaking prisoner's cheek and then slid his foot down until it was pressing firmly against his throat. The frightened captive's gaggled sound told the watching crowd that this was not going to end well for the thief in their ranks.

'The second time!' Neddy barked. 'This is the second time you have stolen my fucking money.'

Shark was gloating, loving every minute of the torture and degradation being dished out. He leaned down and took the arm of the cowering man, swinging it upwards behind his back and grabbing his wrist tightly, offering the thief's hand to his master. Neddy looked over to make sure his troops were witnessing the event. A squeamish Cheyenne faced him, but her eyes were fixed firmly on the makeshift firepit to the side of her. Without a second thought the big man placed the sharp teeth of the industrial pipe cutters around the prisoner's middle finger on his right hand and squeezed them tightly. The beaten man cried out loudly, the echoes of his screams heard far and beyond the boundaries of the estate. In less than five agonising seconds half of the man's pinkie fell to the floor. Shark was in his element now, grabbing the severed finger and holding it aloft like a prize trophy. Blood began gushing out all over the place, the desperate man on the floor had almost passed out with the excruciating pain he was feeling.

But the angry head of the gang had not finished. As the thief in his ranks began sobbing like a child beneath him, he grabbed his other hand and re-opened the cutters. The man became frantic and started struggling until a hefty fist on the end of Shark's arm caught him full on his cheek and he accepted his fate. Neddy leaned over his captive and asked him a question. 'Your mum,' he said 'she still lives in that big fuck-off house in Sutton, don't she? She drives that silver Merc, a top of the range motor, it's always parked on the drive.'

The terrified man was fighting to save the finger on his other hand now, he would say anything to escape further punishment. 'She will lend me the money, five hundred quid aint nothing to her, bruv. I will get it from her, Neddy. I will go there tomorrow, I swear. I need an ambulance, fuck, geezer, I'm bleeding out here.'

The big man pulled the shivering wreck to his feet and called to his second in command. 'Shark, drop this cunt off outside the A and E, he aint worth doing a stretch over.'

'What about his finger?' Shark asked, pretending the take a bite out of his prized trophy.

'Take that up to his mum's gaff. Tell her this cunt has fucked with the wrong people. Tell her you want a grand by the morning or she will get another piece of her son, a bigger piece.'

'What if she goes to the filth?'

'Mention my name, she won't go the old bill, trust me, she fucking knows what will happen.'

The prisoner was trying hard to stop the flow of claret from his hand but still wanted to argue one point. 'It was only five hundred, bruv, that's all it was.'

'Well, its doubled now,' Neddy yelled loudly. 'For all the fucking aggro you've given me.'

The prisoner saw no sense in arguing as Shark and Fitz led him to the van and tossed him back into the rear of the vehicle, slamming the doors closed to drown out his screams.

Those that were gathered at the trial were now dispersed in silent order, but the punisher dished out a final warning. 'Tell all the others what happened here tonight. Tell them I aint taking no more shit from them. Next time I'll take the whole fucking hand.'

The walls were closing in on Neddy, nothing, nothing at all was going his way. The lad with the dismembered index finger was not the first of his drug mules to be caught with his hand in the till, it was becoming a common occurrence. The takings of his ill-gotten drugs trade had halved in the past year and losses like that were making big dents into the gangs' profits. He re-counted the takings for the day and began to wonder where all the good times had gone. He didn't have to think too hard to realise that he was fighting a losing battle. During the reign of the brutal Keyes brother's regime, this was hallowed turf, nobody else dared trying to take a slice of the drugs pie. Nathan and Gary Keyes ruled this domain with an iron fist. There were no second chances for tourist pushers, retribution was swift, punishment was harsh. But back then Neddy was simply 'muscle'. He wasn't paid to think, he wasn't paid to deal or ferry class A merchandise around. No, the fearsome giant was just a thug, a big hard bastard who collected the cash and dished out brutal beatings to late payers and those who stepped out of line.

In those days every run-down house, flat and rat-infested squat on the Marfield Estate was their trading arena, but now it was a shared territory. Times had changed over the past three years. The Keyes brothers were incarcerated, both serving lengthy prison sentences for violent crimes that were so gruesome that national newspapers withheld their graphic details. It took less than a month for a black gang, the SW Buzz Crew, from neighbouring Brixton, to muscle in on the east side of the estate. Their bid for a share of the spoils was soon joined by a firm of violent Lithuanians, who settled on the south blocks, where most of the newly built flats and bedsits were situated. The Lithuanains or Lithis as they were not so affectionately known, were much more organised than their two sets of rivals. This may have been because they operated similar set-ups in their home country. The first thing they did when they arrived was to scare off all the street girls and replace them with their own 'cash cows'. Poppy's friend, Lulu, was one of only two working girls that ignored the threats of the heavy-handed gang members and continued working the streets. Neddy had a certain degree of sympathy for the fiery Scottish streetwalker, and she was often given special deals on her weekly supply of heroin. Mind you, he knew that she was a hopeless addict and that she spent almost all of her hard-earned cash on the devil's drug. Everyone who knew Lulu felt that she was probably just one fix away from the cemetery. Even though her days might be numbered Neddy never refused her credit. She was, in his eyes, a special case.

So, with takings down and the recent revelation that a couple of 'friendly local police officers,' were no longer in his pocket, Neddy had to work hard to make ends meet. The Bagman was unlikely to wait for his money and the worst sin of all sins amongst dealers is not to have drugs for their punters. After all, nobody would wait long in a pub in they were told that they were waiting for the lager to arrive from the brewery.

Even though his first lieutenant had followed his orders without question, Neddy knew that, behind his back, his authority was being undermined. Him and Shark had not seen eye to eye since the moment the loudmouthed football thug turned up on his doorstep. The big man had to tread carefully around the tattooed bruiser though, he was, after all, related to the Keyes brothers. The gang leader was no fool, he expected Shark to attempt a takeover coup at any time. Keeping his enemy close was his only option. After all, Neddy had no real friends to worry about. But he was angry inside that he had bailed out the pervert with an eye for pubescent girls one too many times and received little or no gratitude for his efforts. Maybe the giant enforcers patience began to wear thin when one of Sharks' victims killed herself rather than face the sicko in court. His guilt got the better of him that week and he sent an anonymous wreath and mailed an envelope full of cash through her parents' letterbox to help cover the funeral expenses. A kind deed from a bad man trying to lighten the burden on his heavy heart.

To add salt to his bleeding wounds the big man now had Poppy to deal with. He had history with her, a lot of history. She had been the plus one of his best friend Cameron ever since he could remember. But she had stepped over the line in big muddy boots the day she took a tyre iron to his buddy's head and left him fighting for his life in intensive care. Neddy found it hard when he visited his battered mate at his aunt's home in Portsmouth. He was now just a shadow of his former self and struggled to get out of the house. Poppy's brutal attack on him while he was sleeping off a drugs binge had left him brain damaged and barely able to walk. Neddy would never tell anyone, but he had tears in his eyes the first time he saw Cameron lift himself out of his wheelchair in the hospital. He would never forget that moment. It was another reason for him to hate Poppy and seek revenge. No matter how many good memories the three of them had shared as young tearaways in their teens, he knew that he could not rest until he had put things right.

Karma was heading Poppy's way and it was carrying a very large, sharpened blade. She was living on borrowed time.

CHAPTER TWELVE

'There is no K in tequila, but I knew what you meant,' Bree remarked in her know-all manner, as she emptied the shopping bags into the kitchen cupboards.

'What?' Poppy asked, more interested in what was happening on the television than in the kitchen.

'Your text, with the things you wanted, you spelled the word teq...'

'Yeah, yeah, did ya get that ice cream, the mint one with the chocolate sprinkles?'

'Yes, Poppy, it's in the freezer. I thought you would have at least got dressed today. God, this place is a real mess. Are you going to get off the sofa today or have you lost the use of your legs?'

Her witty remark was clearly lost on her sister whose attention was fully focussed on the television screen.

'Oh, Poppy, it was so funny on this photo shoot this morning, these two new models started arguing and...'

'Shhhh I'm watching this.'

'Oh, so sorry to interrupt your busy day. What is this rubbish anyway? It looks like people trying to sell caravans or...'

'Shhhhh…'

'Oh, I'm sorry to disturb you madame,' Bree remarked sarcastically. 'Is it OK if I have a shower now or does madame require anything from the catering section?'

Bree looked around her flat and noticed several more things that irritated her. Unwashed plates and cups left in the sink, dirty clothing sprawled out beside the washing machine and worst of all small trails of tobacco lining the floor by the coffee table. It had been a hectic day at the studio, and she had not expected to be deep cleaning her rooms at this time of night. She was livid inside but thought it best to hide her anger. Poppy had locked herself away in her bedroom the last time she mentioned her poor housekeeping. She decided to try a different approach.

'I thought I would make vegetable fettuccine again tonight, you said you liked that last time, Poppy. Oh and I can show you some old photo albums this evening. There are lots of pictures of Jamie in there, I am sure you would like to see what a handsome guy your brother was.'

'Nah, not really, that's boring.'

'OK, well let's get you away from that rubbish on the television, what about a board game or something?'

'Game? Yeah, aright, I am up for that. We can play a proper game if you want.'

'Oh, OK, what do you have in mind?'

'A drinking game.'

'What like truth or dare?'

'Didya? Wouldya? Couldya? I used to play it with Nixie.'

'Nikita?'

'Yeah, it's a real laugh.'

Bree bought in a bowl of kettle chips, another of her sisters shopping list demands. 'What do we need to play the game?'

'Nothing, oh, yeah, we need the drink of course, bring the bottle of tequila, we need that.'

Bree was slightly bemused but nevertheless delighted that her sibling had agreed to participate in something other than watching poorly scripted soaps on the television that night. She showered and slipped on one of her brothers oversized tee shirts, brushed trough her drying hair and prepared herself for their game. She was fascinated to see just what level of drinking would be required to compete, maybe a little apprehensive that her sister might be setting her up for a fall. But it wouldn't matter to her tonight, she was just pleased that her sister had chosen to share a game with her, the same one that she had played with her 'irreplaceable' soulmate Nikita. In truth Bree was slightly jealous of the relationship that Poppy had shared with the girl from the council estate. Part of her was pleased that she was no longer alive and a major part of her sister's life. Maybe she was hoping she could feel those massive shoes that her sisters departed friend had left behind. Poppy always gave the impression that her 'bestie' was a faultless angel, when in fact she had been a hopelessly addicted crackhead who overdosed on heroin.

'You should really have a proper meal each day Poppy, you can't live on takeaway burgers, kettle chips and ice cream,' she remarked, as she delivered a tray of freshly cut lemons, two shot glasses and a salt dispenser on to the coffee table with a large bottle of tequila.

'What the fucks that?' Poppy asked.

'You lick the salt then drink the…'

'Nah, nah, fuck all the fancy stuff, let's play proper like.'

'OK, just go easy on me with the drinking I have an early photoshoot tomorrow. So, what happens next? I guess this is like truth or consequences.'

'Yeah, sort of, you ask three questions, Didya? Wouldya? Couldya? And if the one asking thinks your answer is a lie you have to swig the bottle and pay a forfeit.'

'Right, so it's did you, would you, could you?'

'Yeah, you go first if you like, ask me three questions.'

Bree thought for a few seconds. 'OK, so did you ever go to the zoo when you were young? Would you prefer to go on a sightseeing holiday or the beach? Could you…'

'Fuck, nah, nah, nah, what's that shit? We aint nine years old, girl. Do you wanna play the game proper or not?'

'Yes, yes, I do, of course I do. You go first then, Poppy, to give me a better idea.'

Poppy took a swig of the alcohol before choosing her questions 'Right, so, didya ever shag the pretty boy, what's his name, Preston? Would ya spit or swallow? And could ya ever go down on another bird?'

Bree tried not to look too shocked but suddenly realised that she was going to be way out of her depth here. However, she did find some answers to appease her sister. 'No, I wouldn't touch Preston with a barge pole. Urghhh, spit, spit, definitely spit, and I would never do that to another woman, not in a million years, Urggghh.'

Before that last word had left her mouth Bree found Poppy's hand reach out, slip inside her tee-shirt and grab her left nipple, twisting it backwards and forwards and causing her sister to scream out loudly in pain. 'Arrggghhhh, that hurt, Poppy, that really hurt, what's that for?'

'Liar, liar, pants on fire! You must have shagged pretty boy. That's your punishment, for lying, now you have to take a drink.'

Her sister's face was like a dark cloud of thunder as she rubbed on her swollen nipple. She took a small sip of the tequila, followed by a whole mouthful. 'I'm not lying,' she said. 'He is not my type.'

'Bullshit!'

'Besides, there are things I know about Preston that would make you sick.'

'Like what? Spit it out, girl.'

'Oh, no, Poppy, I have to save that one for a rainy day,'

'You love keeping your little secrets, dontcha?'

'Yes, until the time is right to bring him down a peg or two. My boob really hurts, Poppy, you really hurt me there.'

'Well, don't tell no more lies then.'

'Right, my turn now.'

'Yeah, but no shit questions.'

'Alright, the same questions to you. Did you have sex with Preston? Spit or swallow? Would you, you know, do things to another women, truthfully?'

'Well, ya know I aint shagged pretty boy, obviously, but I wouldn't say no if he was up for it. I'd sort him out good and proper, I would ride his dick 'til it was red raw and…'

Bree shook her head in disgust. 'OK, OK, I think we get the message Poppy!'

'Spit when I'm sober, swallow when I am pissed, and yeah, if I was in the mood, I could handle a bit of muff diving.'

Poppy took a large swig of the alcohol but was put in her place by her opponent who pulled the bottle away from her. 'No, you only drink if you don't tell the truth, remember?'

Her sibling laughed and released her grip on the bottle 'OK, my turn again now. Dldya ever wank off someone for money? Wouldya ever rub one out thinking about a big black dick? Couldya ever do two blokes at once?'

'Wow! Let's add racist to the list of things that Kayleigh left off of your CV. Really, Poppy!'

'Nah, nah, don't get me wrong missy, nothing wrong with a big black dick, but I doubt you could handle one. So come on answer the questions or shall I give yer other tit a tweak. Remember, tell the truth and shame the devil.'

'What?'

'Tell the truth and shame the devil, it's a saying, he used to say it all the time.'

'Who?'

'Oh, nobody, let's just play, do yer want the questions again?'

'No, I want to know who used to say that.'

'My dad, well your dad as well I suppose. He had lots of stupid sayings like that.'

'What made you think of him?'

'Nothing, for fucks sake, let's just get on with the game.'

Poppy was eager to bypass her slip of the tongue, the last thing she wanted was a lengthy conversation about her late father. She knew if she started a conversation about him her sister would pounce on the chance to ask questions, hundreds of awkward questions. She would want to know chapter and verse of all her childhood memories. Not today, Poppy thought to herself, not today nor any other day.

The game continued and the contents of the bottle of alcohol began to disappear along with the drunken duo's inhibitions. Two hours later and the women found that they had covered just about every taboo subject known to mankind. Bree found herself doubled over with laughter at one point when her sister bought bestiality into the playing arena and suggested that Kayleigh would look good giving oral sex to a donkey on Blackpool beach. 'Now I would love to get that picture in a big frame to stick on those shitty white walls in their house,' Bree said, much to the amusement of her sibling.

It was indeed a strange evening, neither one of the girls would admit, it but it was beginning to feel like this union was always meant to be. But as the last drops of the tequila passed between Poppy's lips Bree noticed that her sister was struggling to keep her eyes open. She didn't want to spoil such a special evening, but she sensed that her sisters guard had been lowered. She felt this might be the time and place to ask the questions that had spun around inside her head since they had visited the flat in the tower block. The names on that 'Kill list' were still fresh in her mind and her curiosity was burning her up inside. 'Tell me about him,' she asked. 'That man, the top of that list, Houghton, what did he do that was so bad?'

Poppy shook her head, 'Its old news, girl, it's gone now.'

'Please, Poppy, I tell you everything.'

'Nah, don't wanna talk about him, ready for bed now.'

'What about the others on the list, Mrs Gill or something?'

'Gillacuddy, old Mama Gillacuddy. She was alright, she wasn't that bad.'

'But she was on the list.'

'Did some bad things, but not to me. Nixie hated her, she made her eat hot chilli peppers and put soap in her mouth when she thought she was telling lies. She did shit like that, old Mama Gillacuddy. She put pepper in some boy's eyes once 'cause he said he had seen her do something, dunno what! She liked doing stuff like that, bit nasty, yer know.'

'But didn't anyone complain?'

'Nah, weren't worth it. That's where I met Lulu, at her gaff, at Gillacuddys.'

'You do know that's not her real name, Lulu Lush, you know she made that up, don't you?'

'Course I do. Her name is, eh, eh, Louise, eh, Louisa, Mac or something. Oh, I don't know. She picked that Lush name up when she started, ya know, shagging for money.'

'How old was you, when were you at this Gillacuddy woman's house?'

'Dunno, 'bout twelve I suppose. We ran away, me and Lulu, we ran away, slept in an old laundrette for a couple of nights.'

'Why?'

'She was renting her out, Lulu, she was really pretty when she was a kid, so she rented her out.'

'I don't understand.'

'Mama Gillacuddy used to know some blokes that liked to take pictures and things, they said that some girls, the pretty ones, could be models and shit like that.'

'I don't get it!'

'Always late at night, they would come when everyone was in bed, take someone off, you know like Lulu or one of the other girls. They would go off in a car and then come back the next morning.'

'For photo shoots, in the middle of the night, that doesn't sound right to me.'

'Dunno, something like that, she would always come back with lots of makeup on. She was always like, well, dipsy, sort of drunk, but not drunk.'

'What, you mean they drugged her, Poppy?'

'Dunno, but she always got a few quid off Mama Gillacuddy. She would share the money with me and some of the others. She told us all she would look after us when she was a famous model.'

Bree sneered. 'Huh, that didn't work out too well for her then?'

'She's alright, Lulu, got mega fucked up on the gear, ya know, never been off it really, but she is alright.'

'And Houghton?'

Poppy suddenly felt something snap inside her head, it was an urge to share something she had never told any of her carers, never told a counsellor. It was something that happened to her, a day that was more painful than all her other harrowing experiences put together. And then, struggling to keep her eyelids from closing, she found herself staring at one of the strange pictures on the wall. It seemed to be calling out to her, telling her that it was alright to feel ashamed, to hurt as much as she did inside, to feel vulnerable. For a few seconds she looked beyond the picture, as if she was staring into oblivion. Maybe she was waiting for a voice to pipe up, to guide her, tell her not to share her horrific tale, but it never came. She looked neither right nor left, almost as if she was in a hypnotic trance. Her voice was softer than usual when she spoke, but Bree latched onto to every word.

'It was blue, like a light blue, like the sky, my dress, it was blue.'

Her sister sat up straight, she thought about moving closer to her sister, maybe put her arm around her, but she knew Poppy would not want that.

'It had three, no four, it had four buttons, down the front. She bought me that dress, Mrs Houghton, she was always buying me dresses, loads of em' She used to call me Poppet, ya know, like her little Poppet. I thought she was nice.'

Poppy drained the final remnants of tequila and cradled the empty bottle in her arms as she continued. 'He liked me in dresses, Mr Houghton, he liked me in short dresses, the shorter the better. I hated them, I really hated them, but it made him happy.'

She paused for a few seconds. This was clearly taking its toll on her emotions. But she felt compelled to continue. 'Sundays, it was always Sundays, the bells at the church used to go fuckin' doolali on a Sunday morning. He would rush around to get her, yer know, Mrs Houghton, off to the train station. See, she used to go and see her sick mum every Sunday, up in London, she was gone for hours. Then it was just me and him.'

Her sister could hear her sisters voice beginning to break up, she had never seen her look so pale. 'Poppy, you don't have to...'

'You wanna know about that nonce or not?'

Bree nodded gently, trying her best to keep her own emotions in order.

'It started as just tickling games, he tickled me, and I tickled him. Ya know like funny and stuff. But then it was touching, lots of touching. I knew what he was doing, it had happened before in one of the kids homes where I stayed. So, this one Sunday, after she had gone, he was in a right fuckin' mood, I could tell his face was all red, like angry. I'd done something to piss him off, dunno what it was. He dragged me in his music room, where the piano was, that's where he used to do things. See he could lock the door and stuff. He told me I was a little whore and that's why my mum and dad had left me. He said I was lucky to be living there in the big house with good people.'

Poppy shook her head, her face twisted as her vivid memory of that day became clearer. 'But they weren't no good people. So, he pulls this face and says 'cause I had done something wrong he would treat me like a little whore.'

Bree's lip began to tremble, and she felt an overwhelming impulse to grab her sister tightly and hug away her pain. But she sat still through the heart-breaking silence that followed before asking her the question that she feared the answer to. 'Did he hurt you, Poppy, did Houghton hurt you?'

Poppy looked down at the empty bottle of alcohol, wishing it was still full and that she could escape the overwhelming pain she had carried in her heart since that day. 'He raped me,' she said in little more than a whisper. 'I was ten years old, and he raped me. He held me down on that chair in his music room and fucked me in my arse, so hard, so fuckin' hard, I was still bleeding three days later.'

Bree could no longer control her emotions. 'Jesus! No Poppy! she screamed.

'You wanted to know about him,' Poppy said, hanging her head in shame. 'So now you know.'

Bree composed herself, she was determined not to show the overwhelming disgust and anguish she was feeling. She looked away slightly to disguise the fact that her eyes had glazed over, the sight of tears might stop her sister revealing more 'But, surely you reported him, you must have told someone.'

'Nah, I told yer, it wasn't worth it back then. Besides I was a troublemaker weren't I, they would have said I was lying.'

'Not the carers, Poppy, the police, you should have told the police.'

'I never told no one. They moved me away that night, it was a long drive. I remember that they put me with some other people, nice people as it 'appens. They had twins, girl and a boy, like you and whatsisface, Jamie. I didn't stay there long, but I remember they were really nice people.'

'But, now Poppy, now, you can still report him now.'

'What's the point, they would never believe me over him and his wife. Best to just leave it, it aint worth the aggro.'

'But he might have done it to other girls, other children, you need to do something.'

'Don't be a twat, I was just a kid, I can't even remember where he lived. All I remember was it was right next to a big airport cause the planes used to make a fuckin' racket when they took off.'

'The town, Poppy, was it big or small? Try to remember.'

'It was nearly twenty years ago; I can't remember that stuff. Oh, yeah, there was a big garden with a silly fuckin' windmill thing in the middle, not big, just like small, ya know the size of me when I was kid. I broke one of the wing things on it once and he made me sleep in the shed. I didn't get no dinner or nothing, just locked me in the shed. Yeah, and that church with those noisy fuckin' bells. It wasn't big, just a couple of small shops there. That's all I remember. Yer aint gonna find him so there's no point trying.'

'The road, Poppy, try to remember the name of the road.'

'Nah, I'm tired now, don't wanna talk about it no more.'

They found themselves seated at opposite ends of the sofa, both staring into the same void. No further words were exchanged between the sisters, perhaps neither one of them knew the right thing to say. Poppy felt exposed, her emotions were laying naked, stripped raw. Bree's brain was clearly struggling to come to terms with the revelation, but she knew she had to restrain her emotions. She felt that if she started crying, she would never stop.

A good half-hour passed by before Poppy lost her battle with the excess amount of alcohol she had consumed, and her head fell into her sister's lap. Bree stroked her sibling's face before running her hands gently through her hair. And then, when she was sure Poppy was asleep, she stopped fighting back the waterfall of tears she was holding on to. They trickled, one by one down her cheek and slithered slowly down on to her sleeping sister's face.

Strange emotions began to evolve inside Bree's head, her sister's revelation had left her feeling hollow inside, as though someone had ripped out her heart. She found her siblings recollection of her harrowing experience emotionally draining. Especially as she realised that the woman who could not remember what she had for breakfast the previous day could recall every small detail of that terrible morning from nearly two decades ago. It was the first time she began to understand why her sister had so much pent-up anger inside her. At that moment she despised the low-life father she had never met. She hated him for abandoning her sister into the care system and let her suffer such horrific abuse. She also hated Poppy's missing mother for choosing alcohol over her daughters' welfare. But as she remembered word for word the heart-breaking ordeal that her sister had endured, her burning hatred was focussed on Poppy's abuser, Houghton. She swore to herself that night that, no matter how long it took and how much it cost, she would find the sick and twisted paedophile and he would pay for his evil sins. Nobody was going to do that to her sister and get away with it.

CHAPTER
THIRTEEN

When you are employed by a high-brow fashion magazine, albeit one with a dwindling circulation, choosing your outfit for a lavish dinner with the owner of the publishing house was not a simple task. Bree was always conscious of the clothes she wore, that oversized wardrobe in her bedroom housed some of the finest designer clothing money could buy. She could spend more on a pair of shoes that many women would spend on a whole summer wardrobe. But she always took longer when she was meeting with her boss, one misjudged match of labels or colours might destroy the confidence that the magazine had in her. She had settled on a Dolce and Gabbana silk top and black Moschino leather trousers. She was pleased with her choice.

Bree did not like the idea of leaving her sister alone in the flat but was also conscious that she did not want to suffocate her. Poppy had remarked a couple of times during her first three weeks of freedom that she felt that that she was still a prisoner. She told her that she thought the mattress might be softer and the food more palatable, but she still needed to report each week to Plumstead for a pointless grilling. She told her she felt as if her every movement was being monitored. Bree had treated her sister to a Cantonese takeaway meal before she left the flat and made sure there was plenty of chilled wine in the fridge. Poppy had enjoyed two bowls of her newly favoured ice cream before falling asleep in front of a blaring television set. Bree was hesitant at first, but felt it was OK for her leave her unattended now. She was beginning to feel like the single parent of a teenager who might get up to mischief the moment their mothers back was turned.

You might only need to meet Kendra de Jerez once to remember her for the rest of your life. You would never forget her, however hard you might try. She left an indelible impression that might make you cringe. But one thing was for sure, she had class, she had style in abundance. Somewhere in her mid-fifties, she never revealed her true age to anybody, she could be mistaken for an ageing film star. Fellow patrons at the restaurant had commented on the beautifully aligned pink tints that highlighted her well-groomed ash blonde hair. The successful businesswoman had perfect skin, high cheek bones and was always seen in branded clothing and expensive jewellery, including a full handset of glittering rings. She reeked of cold hard cash.

Kendra was a regular at the Blue Parrot Restaurant overlooking the River Thames, she had dined here with many well-known dignitaries and television personalities in her time. She always demanded a seat with a front view of the river at this high-class London diner and was never disappointed. Waiters feared serving her, aware of her sharp tongue and impatience. She may have been a generous tipper. but they had seen her 'bite,' and all knew it was so much worse than her 'bark.'

Some of her associates may have been cruel, but certainly not within earshot, when they described Kendra as, 'mutton dressed as lamb.' But she had, through numerous sacrifices and, as she constantly boasted, a healthy sex life, managed to retain the hourglass figure she had developed as a struggling model in her twenties. She had the buttocks of an eighteen-year-old thanks to her personal trainer. Her clever use of expensive make-up and her nightly moisturising routine took at least ten years of her age. Taking no chances, a regular dose of Botox cleverly disguised the worry lines of her sordid past. She had endured everything from laser eye surgery and liposuction to lip filler and breast implants. But in truth, nobody could say she did not look good for her age. A fact she never tired of telling people herself.

She part-owned and edited a leading fashion magazine aimed exclusively at the modern working female. Her subscribers would be professional businesswomen with a more than comfortable income. Littered amongst the up-market fashion features and advertisements for exotic holidays would be editorials on issues of the day. Climate change and transgender coverage, it seems, would always appease the more liberal readers of the magazine. Coupled with the fact that Kendra seemed to be involved in just about every charitable organisation that existed, these factors helped her gain continued advertising revenue from renowned brands.

These regular monthly meetings may have seemed like a chore at times to Bree, but she was grateful to her employer for giving her the opportunity to frequent exotic locations and showcase her talents. Besides, who would turn down the chance to cleanse the soul and sample escallops washed down with the finest vintage wines in this high-class restaurant. Kendra loved Bree's raw enthusiasm for her role and had put her at the forefront of her plans to expand her monthly magazine. She also trusted her protégé enough to let her have the use of her eighty thousand pounds Mercedes car when she travelled abroad, which she did often. It was an unwelcome task for Bree sometimes, to have to pick her up from an airport in the early hours of the morning. But part of her revelled in the fact that her neighbours at Albermarle Court were green with envy when she showcased the vehicle in the courtyard.

Despite the age difference between the women, they had a surprising amount in common. Both fashion connoisseurs and free and easy with small talk. But in truth some of her employers' outrageous stories made Bree blush. She was fascinated that a classy woman with such good breeding and a privileged background could be so obsessed with sex. Not just normal sex, rough stuff, bondage, water sports, weird stuff.

The main conversation between her and Bree had centred around the on-going features that the monthly magazine was carrying on poverty aligned fashion. The concept was aimed at persuading top designer brands not to discard their end of line stocks, but to distribute them amongst the homeless and unemployed. Headlined, 'Street Life,' it was proving to be one of Kendra's better ideas and had attracted advertising revenue from a number of left-wing organisations, keen to throw their money at life-changing innovations. Bree had spent several weeks on the project and produced some stunning photography which had put her firmly in her bosses' good books.

'This place is going to the dogs,' Kendra said, throwing down her cutlery on to her plate and snapping her fingers at a passing waiter. 'It would never have happened if Raymond was still here. They made a huge mistake letting him go.' As the server arrived, the fussy woman thrust the plate into his chest. 'The salmon is not fresh, don't bring me poisonous garbage like this. Take it back to the chef and tells him his job is on the line.'

Bree discarded her cutlery and scowled at the waiter. She didn't want to let her boss know that she had been enjoying her starter but now felt obliged to follow suit. She handed her plate to the terrified looking server who scurried off to the kitchen, muttering under his breath in an unintelligible language.

Kendra turned her head to see if she still had an audience, waited a few seconds, then produced a small silver box from her Louis Vuitton bag. She rubbed some white powder on her fingers and, in clear view of all of her fellow diners, snorted it, unashamedly.

'You are outrageous, Kendra, totally outrageous,' Bree said, shaking her head at her carefree antics.

Her boss smiled. 'Just a little pick-me-up for later. You are still joining me at that new wine bar in Bond Street, aren't you?'

'I would Kendra, but, well I have to look after my sister now, you know, keep an eye on her until she has settled in.'

'Worried she might run off with all your jewellery?' her boss asked teasingly.

'No, nothing like that, I think she is a bit lost now, it's very quiet where I live, and she is used to…'

'Drugs and gun fights,' her dinner partner said, continuing a theme that seemed to excite her.

'No, no, nothing like that. Poppy has been clean for seven years now.'

'They are never clean, cutie, you have seen that first-hand with all those lazy reprobates at the homeless shelter. Once they are hooked, they are always hooked.'

Bree was keen to move the conversation away from her sister, so played along. 'I know, some of those people have lost everything, it's crazy when you hear some of their stories.'

'Good shots though,' Kendra said approvingly. 'You have an eye, Bree, a talent for catching that look of despair in the eyes of those unwashed scabby creatures. I think your montage in the last issue was your best work to date.'

The smug look on Bree's face showed she was happy with the compliment. 'We start shooting next week for the follow-up, I am looking forward to that.'

'Did you find a suitable location?'

'I think I have found the perfect place; it's run down and squalid, it will make the prefect back-drop for the shoot. I may have also found a couple of suitable models at the shelter, one of them is a young girl who…'

Kendra interrupted Bree's patter with loud cackled laughter, gaining an uninvited audience for a few seconds. 'Oh, my dearest,

Bree, we are not letting real street urchins within a hundred feet of those Prada dresses. God, lover, it would be sacrilege to have to burn all those lovely garments. No, we are flying in three models from Ukraine. They are complete unknowns, very frail looking, skinny as rakes, so nobody is to the wise. You will need to get some tatty stuff from a charity shop or something, dirty them up a bit for the before shots.'

'OK, I just thought that you wanted the vibe to be completely authentic.'

'Poverty is one thing darling, credibility is another. Don't be fooled by all these goodwill gestures in the current issues. If it wasn't increasing my advertising revenue by forty percent, I would drop it like a hot brick.'

Kendra could see that her dinner companion looked a little perturbed by her statement. 'But you are still joining me in Tuscany next month for the big show, it is going to be spectacular.'

'Yes, of course I will.'

'Drop your passport details on an email to my PA, she will book the tickets.'

'It's three days, isn't it?'

'And nights, three long nights, three wonderful nights surrounded by some of the most beautiful male species on the planet. If you don't get laid out there, cutie, there must be something seriously wrong with the world.'

As the replacement starters arrived in the hands of a humbled chef full of grovelling apologies, Bree was beginning began to wonder if she should really spend so long away from her sister. It was bad enough having to attend this dinner evening, but three nights away from Poppy might did not seem like a good idea, regardless of the fact she had always wanted to sample a fine bottle of wine in the Piazza Grande.

Brees feisty dinner partner had suddenly been distracted by a handsome young waiter who had topped-up the women's half-empty wine glasses. Kendra smiled, the smile of a cougar on the prowl. 'You are new here, aren't you?' she asked him.

The well-tanned young man nodded and replied in a broken Latino accent, 'I starta at dissa place one week ago.'

'And,' the woman with a saucy glint in her eye asked, 'do you enjoy looking after people like me?'

'Very mucho so.' was the response before the embarrassed young waiter scurried back in the direction of the kitchen.

Bree found the flirting of her boss amusing, or at least that's what she wanted her to think 'You are incorrigible, Kendra, he is just a kid.'

'Not judging by the size of the bulge in those tight trousers. God, he is packing horsemeat down there.'

Both of them laughed loudly before the ageing woman treated herself to another small pinch of Columbia's priciest export. 'He is never Italian, not in a million years,' Kendra observed, wiping small traces of powder from beneath her nostrils and running it around her gums. 'Probably grew up in a council house in the east end of London and spends all his spare time on the tanning bed in his sister's bedroom.'

Her unruly behaviour unsettled Bree, but she knew that this was always the danger of a night out with her employer. She had seen the best and worst of her over the past couple of years and knew that it was always prudent to laugh at the right times and just go with the flow of the evening. Despite her provocative behaviour Kendra had always been something of a role model for her. She had also been a source of comfort to Bree during the darkest of days after her brother died. Most sisters who had lost their twin brother would have turned to their parent for solace after such a heart-breaking experience. But Bree appreciated her boss's brutal honesty at a time when everyone around her was treading on large eggshells. The magazine owner had also been instrumental in finding a freedom loophole for her sister. She called in a favour from her publishing companies' highly paid lawyers to secure an appeal and an early release for Poppy. She never asked her star pupil for a penny towards the cost, telling her to put it down as a loyalty bonus.

*

Fulfilling her, not quite so, moral obligation to her boss, Bree found herself sharing an overpriced bottle of Champagne in the recently opened, Zastros Wine Bar, in Central London. The taxi fares were always covered by the company on such nights out, so she did not have to worry too much about the free-flowing alcohol. Her aim was to fake a dizzy spell somewhere around midnight and grab the first available cab back to her flat. She was sure that her sister did not need babysitting, but since the revelation of the previous week she found herself becoming more and more protective towards her. Maybe in some crazy sort of way she felt responsible for the damaged girl's childhood being such a harrowing experience. Some might say her sibling's life had turned out to be a car crash experience. In Bree's eyes it seemed as if it was more like a motorway pile-up.

But her plan for an early night was scuppered when a smartly dressed Preston and his friend Devon appeared completely out of the blue and joined the two women at their table. A tipsy middle-aged woman with a wicked laugh made an instant beeline for the handsome tall black lad sporting a sweet-smelling aftershave. Whether it was his smart Armani shirt or the fact that he had sparkling brown eyes seemed insignificant to Bree. She couldn't help noticing though, that Devon, like the waiter in the Restaurant, had a huge bulge in his trousers. Or at least he did once the sex-hungry cougar had pressed her body against him. Both in smart attire and of similar height and build, the two good-looking lads could have passed for brothers, apart from the fact that Preston's tan was fake and the strapping bodybuilder standing at the bar with Kendra was of African descent.

Preston stayed true to form, his eyes never leaving Bree's face once, hoping for the tiniest hint of encouragement from the ice maiden. He had been mesmerised by her captivating beauty since the day Jamie introduced them when he had started working at the local sports centre in Oxley. Like a faithful puppy the strapping lad hung on to her every word, despite the efforts of an overzealous MC doing his best to blunt the conversation.

But Bree was determined not to send out any mixed signals. She had recently been his plus one at a charity event, but only because he never seemed to tire of listening to her childhood memories with Jamie. However, on that night Preston saw a green light when in truth she was displaying a solid red. She embarrassed him in front of dozens of people and the usually self-confident man, who many young girls swooned over, was left to perform solo in the middle of a crowded dance floor. He forgave her of course. When you are as besotted as he was, humiliation was a small price to pay to be close to her.

Bree, being Bree, had already had enough of playing charades and saw an opportunity to bring her evening to an early close without insulting the woman who employed her. Preston was the designated driver for the lads that night and lived less than three miles from Oxley. She might not make her self-planned midnight curfew but if she feigned a migraine now, Bree estimated, she could be home before the clock struck one.

She would need to give a convincing performance. Kendra might be half-cut, but the excess amounts of cocaine coursing around her veins was keeping her on high alert. So, changing her plan slightly she began to show an uncommon interest in Preston, something that surprised everybody present, including the man himself. With her plan B in full swing, she was ready to leave her boss with the smiling toy-boy clinging on to her and reluctantly grabbed Preston's hand to escort her through the bar. However, the new plan went astray once more when Preston, being the perfect gentleman, offered to drop his friend and the vixen in his arms back home on route to Oxley. Once inside his car he asked for Kendra's postcode, raising an eyebrow when he realised that the address was close to Cheyne Walk in Chelsea. Even he knew the location was often referred to as 'millionaires row.'

The conversation was almost not existent from the back seat, and one might have thought that the passengers were asleep, had Bree not checked and seen her bosses head moving up and down at a steady pace. Switching the passenger mirror slightly she could see Devon's trousers halfway down his legs and a mop of ash blonde hair bobbing backwards and forwards. And, if that didn't convey the full story of what was going on in the rear of the vehicle, then the expression on Devon's face certainly did. He had the look of someone who had just seen his team sore a winning goal in a cup final. To make things worse, within seconds of arriving on the drive of a luxurious Town House, Devon, exited the vehicle, one hand holding up his trousers while being led by the other to the front door. When they drove off, leaving Preston's friend at the mercy of the sex-hungry tigress, Bree could not understand why that inane grin was still plastered across his face. But Preston enlightened her. 'He did some ecstasy before we came out tonight and she has been feeding him with white powder in the bar. He will have the shock of his life when he wakes up in the morning.'

Bree smiled at his comment but nothing more, she knew that the thirty-minute journey back to Oxley would not be without small talk. She decided to continue discussing the desperate antics of Devon and the Wicked Cougar of the West End. It would fill the void and provide a welcome distraction to anything else on the driver's mind.

She knew that he would have to try his luck again though, people like Preston do not handle rejection well. When his vehicle pulled into the car park at Albermarle Court, he started a new line of patter. 'I really enjoyed tonight, but then I always enjoy being with you. But you know that already, don't you?'

Bree wanted to give him the whole, 'It's not you it's me,' spiel but decided to repeat the previous excuse she had given him. 'You are my brother's best friend, I told you before, it just wouldn't feel right.'

The six-packed athlete with the look of a bronzed God had anticipated the answer, his response was immediate. 'I think you are wrong, he often told me that you were the most precious thing in his life. I really think he would want me to look after his little sister.'

Bree frowned. 'You see, that's how much you know about me, I am his big sister, I am older than Jamie, twelve minutes to be precise.'

'He would want us to be together, Bree, I genuinely think he would give us his blessing.'

'Just because Jamie finds you good company and likes your sense of humour, it doesn't mean that he approves of you.'

The expression on Preston's face changed, just as it had done the night that he was the butt of the joke at the Charity Ball. 'And you are doing it again,' he said, shaking his head.

'Doing what?'

'Talking about him as though he is still here.'

'He is here, he is in my heart, Preston, he will never leave me, never.'

'I know it still hurts, Bree, I still feel it sometimes, but he has gone.'

'He hasn't left me. He talks to me all the time. If he could speak to you, he would tell you that you wrong, that you and I can never be together. He is disappointed with you, Preston, he thinks you should leave me alone.'

'But all I want...'

'October, last year! That's the last time you visited the crossing, nearly a year ago, Preston. You never even turned up on the anniversary in November.'

'I was on a skiing holiday, Bree, life has to go on, for both of us.'

'My life is with Jamie, it always will be. Don't call me again and don't send me anymore of those stupid flowers. I only throw them in the bin, so don't waste your money.'

As Preston's car moved off into the darkness, Bree searched her bag for her keys. She entered the flats through the communal gardens and looked up at the window of the room where her sister would be sleeping. She was thankful that she had returned early from her excursion into the real world.

Back in her protective mode, Bree realised that she had put things off for long enough, there was something that needed to be done. She took out the cheap throwaway phone she had confiscated from Cheyenne during the drug heist at the Marfield Estate and scoured the list of names. She set her sights on the one person that could make the world a safer place for her and her sister. She took a deep breath and finally plucked up the courage to call that number.

The phone rang several times before being answered.

CHAPTER FOURTEEN

'Liver and lights is opening the garden gate.'

The hushed voice was familiar, slurring, rasping, a hint of remote Scottish borders. A pungent smell, like that of drying whisky stains filled the night air. Poppy's head tuned on her soft pillow, her breathing was heavy, her slumber interrupted. She ignored the calling in her mind, but the eerie sounds returned and continued to torment her.

'Liver and lights is at the back door.'

A sudden gust of wind found its way through the slightly open window and breezed across her face, causing her to stir. No images, just a solid wall of darkness was all she could see in her head. But she sensed a presence, she felt eyes peering down on her, watching her every twitch and turn. She knew she was not alone. 'No,' she whispered gently, in fear of being heard. 'Go away.'

But the evil presence was going nowhere, it was in a playful mood, it continued to tease her troubled soul. The voice grew louder, huskier, it was more distinctive. She recognised that voice, she did not like that voice. She wanted to tell it stop but was afraid of the consequences.

'Liver and Lights is on the first stair.'

Poppy's head moved sideways into her pillow, her body began to itch and a small bead of sweat ran down her forehead and nestled in her neck, another followed a path along her cheek. Her heartbeat became more rapid and her arms more animated as she fought the demons inside her head. Hot and cold flushes ran over her body and all her limbs began to ache, as if she was being held inside a tightening grasp.

Suddenly, an image of a face from her past appeared in a blurry cavity inside her mind. A middle-aged man with ginger coloured hair and a greying beard. His soulless eyes were staring down on her, searing through the bedclothes, ogling her semi naked body. It made her feel nauseous, she wanted to vomit. She could feel his cold breath on her neck, it reeked of alcohol and stale tobacco. Her thoughts spun around, out of control, like a fast-moving roulette wheel inside her head, it landed in a distant time and place. A moment from her past that had come back to haunt her repeatedly. But this time it was real, this time he had found where she lived, where she slept. She heard the whimpering of a small girl sobbing in the background and then that familiar voice called out from the dark abyss of a broken memory and revealed the identity of her tormentor. Mister Donovan, the very mention of that name sent shudders running through her aching torso and caused her to beg for salvation. 'Don't hurt me,' she said in a small and shaky voice. 'Please, don't hurt me'. But the sinister ghost from her past ignored her plea.

'Liver and Lights is on the second stair.'

It had been more than twenty years since she had heard that voice. For Poppy the fear that lived within her mind had never gone away, it had remained dormant, but now it was real, Liver and lights was here, and he had come to seek his revenge. An image appeared to her from beyond the darkness of her subconscious.

She could see a face now, Sean Donovan, he was smiling. a sickly-sweet smile, he knew how scared she was.

He had told her, Donovan, that despicable care manager from the Bluebridge Children Home, he had told her that he would never forget. He promised her back then that Liver and lights would find her one day. He warned her that she could lock all the windows and bolt all the doors and he would still get into her house. The evil man said that Liver and Lights would show her no mercy and while she was sleeping, he would creep into her bedroom and would rip her heart out of her chest and then he would eat it.

Poppy's struggle with reality continued. She heard the cries and screams of a thousand frightened children. Faces pale and ghostly appeared and disappeared at speed through her head. Her limbs were gyrating, her whole body was soaking with sweat.

'Liver and Lights is on the top stair.'

It was her, that other girl, it was Lucy Jones, she was the cause of everything. Lucy was his favourite, Donovan used to spend all his spare time with her, playing games, teaching her magic tricks. He would give her bars of chocolate when he thought nobody was looking. It was their secret, they had lots of special secrets. It wasn't her fault that Lucy shared those sick secrets with the staff at the Children's Home.

But it was wrong, Poppy knew it was wrong, that's why she also had to say something, that's why she had to tell somebody. But she told Mrs Baxter, she was the manager, she was supposed to be there to protect her and the other children. She never knew why that woman did she not believe her. Mrs Baxter shouted at her and told her to stop telling tales. She said Donovan was a good man that he loved all the children that came to stay there. She said he loved them as if they were his own. But that wasn't love, not what he was doing to Lucy. She was only eight years old, just a small child. And then to make things worse Mrs Baxter told him, she told him everything, she told Sean Donovan word for word what Poppy had said she had seen. She was branded a liar, a troublemaker, but she knew her eyes had not deceived her. She knew what she saw in the utility room in the kitchen. She knew he shouldn't be doing what he was doing.

'Liver and Lights is on the landing.'

They were back inside her head, those terrible noises from that night, banging, shouting, screaming, wailing at the back gate. She wanted to look out of the window that night, but she was too scared. So, she hid, under the covers, just as she was hiding tonight. The darkness was her comfort. If she didn't see it then it would not be real, she told herself back then. But it wasn't her that he had come for that evening. That freezing cold night, just before Christmas. That terrible night that Lucy vanished and was never seen again. But now he was back, after all these years he had tracked her down, just as Donovan said he would. He was here tonight, his friend, Liver and Lights, was in the house. It was just as the sick and twisted caretaker said it would be. He told her she would never be forgiven that he would never forget. Every ounce of strength in her body had been taken and she would be helpless to fight him.

'Liver and Lights is opening your bedroom door.'

Everything suddenly turned cold, freezing cold, as if the whole room had been trapped in a large block of ice. It was just as it had been that night when Lucy vanished. She remembered that Donovan had come into her bedroom after dinner and told her that Lucy was going to have a visitor that night. She remembered his crooked smile, his yellowing teeth. She recalled his smelly breath and how he laughed that creepy, evil laugh. She hardly slept that night, buried beneath her blankets. She hid from the world, but she could not hide from the noises, those terrible sounds that followed the banging on the back gate. And then, in the morning, Lucy was gone, taken from her bed in the still of the night. It was as if she had never even existed. Poppy never spoke all that day and never asked Mrs Baxter any questions, terrified of what the answers might be. The worst thing was that with Lucy gone there was nothing to stop him. He had told her himself, that night, he had sat on her bed. He told her that she would be next. Poppy did not know what would be worse at the time, being Donovan's new plaything or facing up to his evil friend who had stolen Lucy away.

'Liver and Lights is leaning over your bed.'

Her heart began to thump so fast Poppy thought it would jump out of her chest. She could feel a chill in her spine as the icy room seemed to be spinning around her. 'Don't open your eyes,' she reminded herself. 'Don't open your eyes. If you don't see it then it isn't real.'

But she could sense his presence now, she could feel a cold breath on her neck. Her soaking wet body ached in every single bone, every muscle twitched as she heard that whisper grow louder and louder and louder. And then she felt a slimy hand touch her bare flesh…

'Liver and Lights has GOT YOU!'

Suddenly Poppy's torso sprung upwards as if it had been fired from a catapult. She screamed out loudly at the eerie darkness that surrounded her. Perspiration dripped from every crack in her skin. She could hear her heart pounding inside of her as if was attached to a large speaker in her brain. She reached out her shaking hand to find her bearings, a sharpened reality told her she was safe in her bed.

Poppy could feel that the sheets beneath her trembling body were soaked through. When she turned on the bedside lamp, she felt eyes staring at her from all angles. She focused on the two strange illustrations on her wall. The woman in those pictures seemed to know what she had experienced, but there was no pity in her eyes, none at all. When she looked down at her soaking wet tee-shirt she could sense the smell of fresh urine in the air, it was so strong she could almost taste it. She discarded her wet knickers and tossed them to one side, constantly keeping one eye on her bedroom door, just in case.

Without thinking the trembling woman yanked open the door and raced along the hallway to her sister's bedroom. She suddenly felt the need not to be alone. Safety in numbers, she thought to herself, he won't come back if there are two of us. When she opened the door to Bree's bedroom, she noticed a mop of blonde hair swing across the pillow as her sibling turned away to face the wall. She remembered that her sister had not been happy with her the previous night because she had re-visited Lulu. She hoped that Bree would turn over and look at her, if she saw the state that she was in she might have a mind for forgiveness. But her sister was being stubborn, unprepared to call a truce.

At least a minute passed before some words finally escaped from Poppy's quivering lips. 'Liver and Lights,' she said gently and then repeated herself a little more clearly. 'Liver and lights, he's here.'

But it seems that their earlier frosty exchange was still fresh in her sister's mind. 'Go back to bed, Poppy, I have to be up for work in a few hours.'

The unwelcome intruder had to think for a few seconds, she was still trying to appeal to her sibling's better nature. 'But my room is cold, like freezing cold'.

'For God's sake, Poppy! I showed you how to turn up the heating. Now go back to bed and let me get some sleep'.

Poppy looked back down the hallway, she couldn't go back, she was sure, but still not sure, scared, but not scared. Was he still here? She didn't want to take that chance. She tried again. 'Can I sleep in here tonight? Ya know, cause my room is cold and all that'.

The blonde head of hair in the bed was still angry, but she could see her sister's reflection in her wardrobe mirror, she could see she was shaking uncontrollably, a wobbling wreck. Her clothing was dishevelled, and her hair was all mangled. She looked petrified.

Poppy realised that she had to up her game if she was to find any sanctuary in this room tonight. She found a word that was a stranger to her vocabulary but most welcome to her sibling's ears. 'Please,' she said, her voice still shaky. 'It's just for tonight, I can sort out the heating thing tomorrow.'

Bree let out an exaggerated sigh and pulled back the bedclothes to allow her sister to join her beneath the cosy duvet. Poppy did not need a second invitation and scurried to the safety of the queen size bed. The girls lay back-to-back, no further words exchanged. Bree smiled, inwardly of course, she had no intention of letting Poppy off the hook for re-visiting the Marfield estate against her wishes. But she had seen something that night which pleased her, a weakness, a chink in the armour of her cold-hearted killer sister.

Even though Poppy had found a haven for the night she could not get back to sleep. There were thumping sounds starting up inside her head and she could hear small voices whispering in the distance. She stared long and hard at the back of her sister's bedroom door, hoping that there would be no shadows moving in the narrow gap at the bottom.

*

It is strange how some memories from our past stay in our minds and come back to haunt us when we least expect them to. After all, it is those things that we cannot see that scare us the most. A howling wind, a growing cancer, eerie noises in the cemetery, total darkness, the unknown. Donovan's tale lived long in the minds of those poor children that he had abused at the Bluebridge Childrens Home. A lifelong warning that would forever disturb the minds and souls of even the strongest of them.

Liver and lights never did visit Lucy Jones on that frosty December night, but the myth was enough to buy the silence of at least a dozen victims of the evil and twisted caretaker. The loud commotion at the back gate that night was that of Lucy's father who had driven south from Cumbria through two heavy snowstorms to be re-united with his daughter. He had been released from prison that morning, having served eighteen months of a three-year sentence for attacking a schoolteacher that his daughter had told him had been inappropriate with her. The teacher in question lost his job and was subsequently deported for his abuse, but never faced a jury to explain himself. The injustice of the world we live in can be so cruel sometimes.

The court had granted Mister Jones a custody order at 4pm that day and despite blizzard conditions and closed motorways he drove for nine hours without stopping, just to be able to hug his child. He called the Bluebridge Home on his mobile on route and relayed his intentions to a man with a gruff Scottish accent who was watching over the children. When he found the home closed on arrival, he banged furiously and shouted at the back gate to gain entry. When he finally entered the home, he was appalled to discover the that the boiler had stopped working the previous day and there was no heating inside the property. He was furious that his daughter and the other children there were expected to endure the freezing temperatures. Despite the protests of the care staff, complaining at the ungodly hour he had chosen to arrive, they could not deny him access to his child and allow him immediate custody. Gary Jones and his daughter spent that night in a local bed and breakfast where a kindly lady listened to his story of rough justice while his daughter slept soundly in a safe environment.

The pair enjoyed a hearty breakfast before driving home to Kendal in the North of England the following day. Life returned to normal, or as normal as it ever would be, for young Lucy.

She never did tell her rescuer about the atrocities that went on behind closed doors in that Children's Home. She feared that her father would react as he had done with the touch-feely teacher at her school and beat the living daylight's out of Sean Donovan. She did not relish the idea of her father having to go back to prison. But neither of them was surprised to discover that the Bluebridge Home was closed several years later, following several abuse allegations against its staff. Justice finally caught up with the wicked caretaker more recently, when a Paedophile Hunter Group caught him red-handed grooming two thirteen-year-old girls. He has served almost two years of a seven-year sentence and has just been placed in the isolation unit of the prison for his own protection

Lucy Jones had carried the unwelcome burden of being an exceptionally pretty child. Her shiny blonde hair, silky soft skin and beautiful blue eyes made her stand out in a crowd. It also made her a target for every sick pervert that crossed her path when she was placed into the care system. However, she coped better than most did and is now a strong-minded survivor of the torturous nightmares she endured during those eighteen months.

She is twenty-seven years old now and is married to the manager of a clothes store. She lives two streets away from her doting father who still visits her at least three times every week. She is a mother herself, twice over, and has two young children, both girls, one of which she named Poppy, in memory of a brave young girl who had once put her own safety at risk to protect her. She never fails to read her daughters bedtime stories, telling them tales of handsome princes and fairy queens who live idyllic lives in beautiful surroundings. But sometimes, just sometimes, when she slips those magical books into the drawer and kisses her children goodnight, it all comes back to her. She remembers Donovan's tale of Liver and Lights. And on those nights, she will always watch over her children until they are soundly asleep and at peace with the world, before joining her husband downstairs. Occasionally she will look out of her children's bedroom window, up at the surrounding darkness and utter a few words she keeps locked away inside her head. 'Fuck you, Liver and Lights, fuck you!'

Poppy was struggling to close her eyes in her sister's bed. She felt safer in this room, despite the unrelenting throbbing inside her skull and the peering eyes of those weird portraits hanging on the wall. She remained focused on the handle of the bedroom door, maybe saying a rare prayer, before her eyelids finally closed, and she found some salvation in a safer place inside her troubled mind.

CHAPTER FIFTEEN

Sultana pudding and custard.

That's what Neddy missed the most. Heaps of stodgy sultana pudding and lashings of runny custard. Nana Edwards would scold the lad at times, 'Elbows off the table, Neville,' or 'Close the back door boy, was you born in a barn?' she would say.

Thursdays was always their special day, time spent well. Nana would be playing her favourite tunes from the sixties while the pair would complete jigsaws. She would always let him find the corners of the puzzle and fit the last piece. He liked that! They would also play card games with the loose change in Nana's purse. Somehow, he would always win and end up with all of that cash in his pocket to take home with him. He never knew how at the time, he just guessed it must have been good luck. The cash didn't last long of course, most of it fuelling the habit for his sweet tooth at the local Co-Op store.

He remembered that she bought him a pair of shiny black shoes to wear at his father's funeral. His nana reminded him not to get them dirty at the cemetery, he was starting junior school the following week and she had told him he would need to make a good impression. Nana never said a word about his absent mother, not that day or any of the following days. Though he always sensed a tinge of anger in her voice whenever her name was mentioned.

Neville was excited that bright summer morning when a friendly couple came and bundled his clothes into the boot of a large shiny car. He thought it strange at the time that he would need so many shirts for a short holiday. But he never mentioned it, the young lad was looking forward to a change of scenery and had been promised that he would be taught how to fish in a big lake. The confused six-year-old boy did not know it at the time, but it would be almost a year before he would see his beloved Nana again.

As the years past, life changed, Neville became Neddy, the nickname he had not chosen but one he carried with pride. Unfortunately, like so many who have trodden that path of abandonment, the once well-mannered boy which the charming nature would discard his loving childhood and moral upbringing for a life on the wrong side of the tracks. Before the world ever had a chance to see him shine, the troubled teenager had become a drug-fuelled violent thug. And now, at an age where he should be sharing a home with a loving wife and bringing up his own children, he was a hardened criminal, rotten to the core. Neddy had become a ruthless enforcer for bad men who got rich on the pain and suffering of the weak and vulnerable.

Nana Edwards had always been the voice of reason amongst a thousand barks of condemnation and outrage. Despite her ailing health she had travelled long distances to see him in Children's Homes and never forgot his birthday when he was in the care of foster parents. She visited him regularly in a distant Youth Offenders Institution, where the growing lad assured her that he had changed his ways and regretted his crimes. But, as usual, he lied. She was there at his first very first court hearing when he was barely fourteen years old and, despite being very frail and barely able to walk, she was there at his final trial at the Crown Court.

Nana was the only living soul who believed that there was any good in him.

Images of his wayward life would often wash over Neddy as his head rested on that hard pillow in the cell at the maximum-security prison. He had time in there, lots of time to reflect on the bad decisions that had led him on to that crooked path he chose to follow. But, like many, his only regret was being caught. He felt no compassion, not for the victims of his crimes nor for his dirty deeds.

He cried the day he heard the news, inwardly of course, hard men like Neddy don't shed tears in public. So, he stifled his pain and anguish the morning he found out his beloved grandmother had passed away. His pent-up sorrow, however, soon turned to anger when he was informed that he would not be allowed to attend her funeral. His uncontrollable rage cost him seven days in the Segregation Unit for smashing up his cell and thumping two prison guards who tried to restrain him. And there, during that dark week in isolation, all he could think about was how beautiful that custard had looked covering his pudding and running over the side of the bowl. He could sense the unmistakable voice of Dusty Springfield in the back of his mind and hear his Nana repeating the story again of when she nearly won a fortune at the local bingo hall.

What Neddy wouldn't do to be six years old again, perched at the dining room table with his favourite desert.

Neville Edwards missed sultana pudding and custard. He missed his Nana.

But the oversized thug had no time to look back on his past today, his big problems were getting bigger, they were mounting by the minute. He was two weeks behind with payments to his main suppliers and the Bagman in charge of that operation was losing his patience. Neddy might run things on the Marfield Estate, but bigger fish in much murkier ponds controlled the flow of class A supplements into his back yard. He knew that without them his power and status would be gone.

Since arriving on the Marfield three years ago the cartel of Lithuanian drug couriers had become a real thorn in his side. They were cutting the costs to an army of dealers to flood the territory with cheap drugs and put his operation out of business. And to rub salt into the wound there were growing concerns about the increase in the local police presence. For several years Neddy had managed to 'buy off' prying eyes and gather inside information on surveillance operations from a couple of mid-ranking officers who enjoyed the financial fruits of their labour. But higher-ranking officials had put two and two together. They soon worked out that brand new cars and extended exotic holidays could not be achieved on an ordinary police officer's salary. This gave them enough ammunition to re-allocate his 'friendly' cops and they had now been transferred to Kent. And, to top it all, he still had to deal with Poppy. Her activities may not have cost him much in hard cash, but the fact that she had humiliated his gang had not gone unnoticed on the estate. More and more of their regular clients were either jumping ship for better deals from their Eastern European counterparts or were delaying payments. He needed to gain respect and stamp his authority on the new threat, and he needed to do it quickly.

But there had been a call out of the blue the previous night, a lifeline that might provide some breathing space and give him more time to regroup. Desperate times call for desperate measures and Neddy needed a change of fortune.

Most of the usual faces were on show at the firepit at the back of the industrial estate, a motley crew if ever there was one. Shark had collected all the cash due for his endeavours and found some sick pleasure in berating a couple of the minnows for their poor efforts on the streets of Woolwich. Cheyenne hated the heavy-fisted bully with a passion. She was fully aware of his abuse and degradation of young girls around the estate. She refused to answer to his tune and stood her ground. But, Fitz, the lad that had dished out a hefty beating to Poppy on her release was in Shark's camp. He said very little in front of Neddy, but in dark corners the pair were plotting the big man's downfall. The remainder of the dysfunctional drug family crew were undecided where their loyalties should lie. They feared Neddy as a man, but most realised that his respect in the community was waning. There would be uncertain times ahead!

As midnight drew close there was some commotion in the corner of the abandoned factory and a heated exchange between an odd couple could be heard from a dark alleyway.

'Get your hands off me,' a strange female called out, obvious to all onlookers present that she was a tourist to these squalid surroundings. Her speech and manner were certainly not from this part of town. 'Stop pulling me,' she said loudly as the pair came into view.

The scruffy man still carrying the bruises of a dog chain around his neck suddenly appeared, accompanied by the unlikeliest of female partners by his side. The angry woman was still wrestling with the tight hold he had on her as he led her to the centre of derelict building, as if she was about to be tried in some medieval court.

Bree shrugged off the grubby hands of her escort and gave him a stare that he would not forget in a hurry. 'This is Louis Vuitton, you know. You have got your dirty paw prints all over my jacket, you retard!'

Neddy sat on a makeshift Judges chair comprised of old milk crates and cracked a rare smile. 'Let her go,' he said. 'She aint going nowhere.'

The stranger to the venue brushed herself down and checked for scuff marks on her prized top, clinging tightly to her handbag as she looked around her. She was shaking with fear inside but had no intention of showing that to the staring crowd. Realising who oversaw this rabble of misfits she turned to face a stern looking Neddy.

The big man said nothing for a few seconds before sucking on his teeth and dumping a mouthful of thick phlegm on to the floor below. He did not seem surprised that the girl was there at all. Shark suddenly came to life and approached the out-of-place beauty, looking her up and down before unleashing the grin of a sick pervert. 'Girl, you is peng,' he said, clearly enjoying the view as he drew closer. 'Fit, very fit.'

Bree ignored his remark and turned her attention towards the large figure with the disgusting habit. She was still edgy and nervous, not that anybody noticed. 'You must be Mister Neddy,' she said.

A loud laugh erupted in the Kangaroo Court and spread to the other officials present.

'Well,' Bree asked. 'Are you the one in charge?'

Neddy didn't move a muscle, he sucked hard on his teeth again before raising his head to make contact. 'You bought the cash?'

'Not all of it,' she replied, producing a large brown envelope from her bag and tossing it towards the lanky leader of the bunch. 'I could only get three thousand out of my main account. I have to give them notice on my savings bond.'

Her comment drew more laughter from all in attendance, all those except for Shark, he had suddenly taken a real shine to the stunning interloper. He began circling around her, living up to his nickname as a creature of prey. Cheyenne suddenly rose to her feet, it seemed that she had an interest of her own in these proceedings and moved to confront the unknown visitor. 'That's her! That's the sket that was with that mad cow that fucked me over, She's the bitch who took my phone.'

Bree suddenly felt a breath on the back of her neck and sensed that Shark was behind her, his presence was unnerving. She looked over at Neddy who was counting the cash in the envelope. 'You need to get these morons away from me,' she demanded. 'I have done what you said, this isn't part of the deal.'

'Deal!' Shark asked, pawing at the back of her neatly groomed hair. 'What deal?

'Oh, Mister Neddy and I have struck a deal, isn't that right?'

The big man suddenly rose to his feet and called loudly at his second-in-command. 'That's enough' he explained. 'This is business, nothing else, just business.'

Bree smiled and removed Shark's hand from her lapel. 'See, I told you, can you move away from me now please, I don't feel comfortable with you here.'

Neddy tucked the envelope inside the deep pocket of his coat. He knew that money would buy him so more time with the Bagman. But he had demanded another three thousand and felt as if the woman who had called him that previous evening was playing him. He suddenly noticed an expensive looking watch on the visitor's wrist. 'Give me the time piece,' he said, 'to make up the difference.'

'No!' Bree yelled in a defiant manner. 'My brother bought me that for my twenty-first birthday. You're not having that.'

Shark suddenly reached out and grabbed her wrist, pulling hard on the bracelet of the watch. 'He said give us the watch you snotty-nosed skank!'

'Please,' Bree begged, struggling to keep her aggressors' dirty hands off her prized possession, 'don't take the watch. I will get you the rest of the money, I just need a few days, a week at most. Besides I have something more valuable if you let me show you.'.

'What?' Neddy asked. 'Tell me what you have?'

Bree stared harshly at Shark until he withdrew to a safe distance. She pulled out her mobile phone and fiddled with the digits for a few seconds before successfully sending a series of photographs to Neddy's mobile. The gang leader studied the pictures closely as she gave him a running commentary. 'The first three or four shots are just the kids you have dealing the drugs. There is a nice one of you there, Cheyenne, taking some money from a couple of schoolboys in their uniforms.'

Neddy's face was full of rage, but he let her continue as he scrolled further down the rolling collage of damning evidence.

'There's you, Mister Neddy, counting large bundles of cash. Careful, you almost smiled in those ones. And the one at the end is you again. I am not sure who the man with the expensive suit and the Audi TT is, but he definitely has a very big smile on his face when he is counting the money. I think he might have a personalised registration number on that car. He must be quite wealthy.'

Bree could see the anger in the big man's face, but she realised she had him where she wanted him. 'I've been told I am good at photography, especially close-ups. What do you think, Mister Neddy?'

Shark was back on his feet again, heading for the troublemaker who had infiltrated the gang. But as he got closer Bree lifted the phone high above her head. 'I wouldn't try taking my mobile. If I press send these photos will be on every local and national newspapers computer before you can say the words 'Clever bitch'. It won't be long before the police are all over this place and, well, there is enough on my phone for them to ask some serious questions. But, trust me, I have plenty more of these pictures, enough to put you all in prison.'

Even though the big man was seething with rage he could not help but praise the woman in front of him. 'You've got balls,' he said. 'Coming here, with this, you've got balls, gal, I'll give you that. But we said six grand, I still want the other three.'

Bree nodded. 'And that's it' she asked. 'That buys her safety?'

'I told you it would, didn't I?'

By now Shark had worked out who the cocky visitor was and what the money was for, there was no way that he was going along with this deal. 'Not for me it don't! Done is done, bruv, she's dead meat that nutty skank. I will carve her up bad when I find her.'

'You!' Neddy yelled, with an angry voice that woke the sleeping neighbourhood. 'You will do as you're fuckin' told, Shark. Now sit down and keep your fucking gob shut! Is that clear?'

The hefty man with the tattooed fingers was not pleased. 'But that bitch cut up…'.

'I said is that clear?' Neddy screamed at his insubordinate lieutenant, this time even louder, even firmer. His attention then turned to the woman who had set the cat amongst the pigeons that night. 'Seven days, that's all yer got, gal, seven days. Call me and I will sort out a drop off point.'

Bree nodded, aiming a smug smile in Sharks direction before exiting the gathering. She made her way along the shadowy pathways of the estate, constantly looking over her shoulder to make sure that she was not being followed. She began to wish she had parked Kendra's car further away from this den of iniquity. She desperately hoped it would still be there and in one piece when she returned. She checked the time and realised that she still had a few hours before she had to pick up her boss from Heathrow Airport. Her sister was safely tucked up in bed again that evening, so she had time to take in the night air and refresh her thoughts. She hoped that the money would convince Neddy to call off the attack dogs and end the bitter war between the Marfield crew and her sister. In her head she knew how addictive her sister found this place and all she wanted now was to make sure that Poppy had no reason to return to this miserable estate.

Shark was clearly angry with his leaders' soft approach to a sworn enemy. 'This is madness, bruv, people are laughing at us. What about the prosi skank, that Lulu bird, she still got off lightly. We need to take care of that skag-head. People on this estate need to know we aint no fucking pushovers.'

But the big man ignored his rant, he was busy counting the first cash pay-off, slightly amused that his visitor had written the words '*Mister Neddy*' in bold letters on the brown envelope. She was hardly a criminal mastermind in the making he thought to himself.

It was now obvious to Shark that his standing on the estate had been undermined. He felt humiliated by his leader and swore to get even. He grabbed Fitz and the two of them retreated to a badly disguised drugs den at the rear of the tower blocks. The pair shared a joint and a few pills and decided on which names they would enlist to assist them with their coup for power. Within the hour they had formulated a plan. Heads needed to roll. People need to be held to account. Neddy had to go.

*

The poorly lit housing estates of South Woolwich can be a daunting place for a street worker. Even though you need the roads to be bustling with potential punters, you find yourself looking around every corner, fearing that the bogeyman would be following your every move. It was worse for Lulu of course, either tripping up or coming down she lived her whole existence in a permanent state of fear. Her drug habits had given her a constant sense of paranoia, she saw ghostly faces lurking in the shadows the whole time.

Lulu's eyes were grey and misty when she set out in the late hours of that evening, rather like the dampening streets surrounding the run-down local docks area where she piled her trade. It had been a quiet night for business. It was a few days before the end of the month and many of her regulars would be relying on the salary to arrive in their bank accounts before they could take advantage of her cut-priced sexual favours. While most of the Lithuanian competitors, holed up in seedy bedsits along the waterfront, could charge between sixty and a hundred pounds for their services, Lulu had to settle for a fraction of that amount. She set herself a minimum target of one hundred pounds each night, enough to keep her body filled with lethal intoxicants and her head filled with warm thoughts.

In truth the streetwalker had not made much of an effort to impress that night. She had only prized herself out of her bed at eleven o' clock. A hurried makeover and a badly tied knot in her hairband hardly gave the woman the look of a glamour model. Despite what Mama Gillacuddy had told her when she was younger, Lulu no longer had the looks of someone that might grace the cover of a fashion magazine.

A warm summer evening had turned chilly and damp, Lulu wished she had had put on a thick jumper rather than the low-cut top and pencil skirt she wore to attract passing trade. A large vehicle had passed her by a couple of times, often a good sign. Third time around the nervous driver would usually pluck up the courage to ask those immortal words, 'How much love?' The deal could then be sealed. She had made up her mind that she would chance her arm and ask for thirty pounds if it was a new face. It was looking increasingly unlikely that she would be rushed off her feet that night, so she had to make the most of the situation. After all, she could always negotiate downwards if the punter looked like disappearing back into the night.

A man walking his dog gave her a harsh stare and uttered a few words of contempt as he walked past her for the second time that evening. She wanted to give him a mouthful of Glasgow's finest trash talk but could not muster the energy or the will-power to do so. And so, it looked as if the three times around the block theory was paying off for her. The long dark vehicle suddenly appeared from the deepening shadows, before stopping beneath a streetlamp along the road. She rubbed her hands together to warm them up, having learned that most clients complained if her bony fingers were icy cold when she prized their manhood from their underpants.

The car moved forward at a slow pace, veering towards the kerb as it approached. Lulu released her well-practiced smile to show that she was both friendly and willing for some business to take place. The vehicle came to a sudden halt around fifty feet ahead of her, its engine purring with a mellow satisfaction, like a large tabby cat having his tummy tickled. But as she began to stroll towards the car, she was dazed by its headlight beams that had switched on brightly and blinded her vision. In a spilt second the engine roared and the car ripped through its gears to build up rapid speed. Before the startled streetwalker had time to catch her breath, she found herself in a total state of panic. Almost instantly the vehicle mounted the kerb, just seconds before a terrified Lulu had the chance to think. The women's fragile body was swept up by the bonnet of the car and tossed ten feet into the air, spinning over like an injured trapeze artist, before crashing back to earth with a crushing force. The driver of the car pulled up sharply, the reality of the moment suddenly hit home.

The impact of the fall would have instantly killed people twice her size. But the plucky girl, who had been born and bred in the roughest housing estate in Glasgow was made of stronger stuff. Her arm lifted awkwardly at her side and a hand began to signal. Slowly she raised her head and looked beyond her twisted leg to see the lights at the rear of the car turn red. Even though she could barely see anything ahead of her she tried to make out the number plate of the car before it left the scene. But it would be in vain. Another noisy thrust of that powerful engine beneath its bonnet sent the car into a speedy reverse. It struck her for a second time, two of its the four spinning wheels making contact and crushing her battered body beneath two tons of angry metal. Within a few seconds the screeching of tyres ripped through the dank evening air as the weapon of destruction retreated to the safety of the shadows.

Lulu stopped moving. Her motionless body laying prostrate, like a discarded mannequin. Her eyes were wide open, but she would never be able to recount those final seconds of the troubled life. Her painful and pitiful existence had finally been bought to an abrupt end.

She was cremated ten days later after an autopsy had declared an open verdict on her death. Her fingerprints and crime file identity had revealed that Louisa McFadden was just twenty-eight years old when her life had been taken in such a cruel and undignified manner.

The detective handling the case was the only person in attendance at her funeral. The officer was due to retire the following month, a small villa on the Algarve was his reward for his loyal service. He had been working cases on the estate for more than twenty years and he knew every low-life scumbag and drug courier better than he knew members of his own family. He was sure that this had to be the nasty deeds of either the ruthless Lithuanian gang that had plagued these streets or a dissatisfied client of the deceased girl. The officer promised himself that he would not rest until he tracked down the driver of the vehicle involved in the hit and run. He knew. however, that little time and manpower would be allocated by his colleagues to a girl who chose to feed her heroin addiction with such a wayward lifestyle.

In the days that followed he did his best to solve the savage crime by scouring the area where she met her fate in the hope that he could track down some CCTV footage. He knew that time was against him and if he was not successful that Lulu's case file would be buried deeper than the ancient pyramids of Egypt. But for some reason this homicide affected his emotions more than others and he made the deceased woman a promise when her coffin was dragged into the flames. He swore that he would spend every waking hour of his final month of duty bringing her killer to justice.

But maybe for him the saddest reality of this tragedy was that he knew that nobody would ever miss her.

CHAPTER SIXTEEN

It would have been a surprise to anybody that knew Poppy Jarvis to see that she was both early and enthusiastic to fulfil her weekly obligation at Plumstead Police Station. But today was an important day, she was on a personal mission now, one that needed her to be at the right place at the right time. She certainly had no time for idle chat that morning. She answered all the regular mundane questions that the Custody Officer threw at her with a defiant, 'No.' Then waited for the nod to be given free reign for another seven days.

She boarded the same bus that had delivered her to her weekly ordeal and secured a seat for its return journey. She was not certain how the day would pan out, but one thing was for sure, it would brighten up an otherwise dull week. She mused over the predicament that Matt was in, feeling no sympathy at all for the cheating chef who couldn't keep his prick in his pants. She was certainly looking forward to seeing the look on the face of the skinny teenager from Chez Blanc. The scatty ex-waitress was going to be in for the surprise of her life. Poppy would be the last person in the world the little minx would expect to see. The last time they had laid eyes on each other was the night that Poppy completely lost the plot and trashed the restaurant, threatening diners with the jagged edge of a broken wine bottle.

Arriving at the familiar park on the outskirts of Eltham with a good twenty minutes to spare, she peeled off one of the notes she had held back from the Willow savings fund and treated herself to a bacon sandwich and a large mug of tea. She sat patiently and waited for the matinee to begin. She had a perfect seat, just far enough away not to be recognised but close enough to view the performance. The actors took the stage at exactly the same time they had the previous week. Matt parked his car in the same parking slot. Chantelle appeared from a small hut in the park with the toddler who was wearing the same football kit he had worn for the opening performance. Small talk was brief, and money changed hands once again, before Matt scurried off with the over-excited young boy to the world of adventure around the swings and slides. Chantelle made herself scarce for the best part of an hour and a half before returning with a small shopping bag from a supermarket.

As the performance reached its crescendo, Poppy watched closely as Matt hugged the child tightly and kissed his cheek before his chaperone scooped him up and placed him in a pushchair. She made her way back towards the park gates, constantly playing with her mobile on route. Matt waved furiously without a response from the toddler. The usually happy-go-lucky northerner looking slightly dejected as he walked back to his car. One final wave from the car window at a distance as Matt's car started on its return journey. But once again the small lad seemed completely oblivious to his parting gesture. Chantelle tidied the little boy's hair and wiped his mouth with some tissue before heading off in the direction of the small hut in the middle of the park. She showed little interest in her son, her attention more focused on the twitter feed on her phone. Poppy did not want to frighten the child so decided to bide her time. After all, what else had she got to do that day, she certainly wouldn't be following the instruction of her case worker and visiting the Job Plan Scheme representative.

Poppy moved a little closer to the park but still kept her distance, she wanted to fully appreciate the shock on the girl's face when she confronted her. Another hour or so had passed and Poppy was almost ready to pounce when Chantelle's phone suddenly rang. The conversation was brief before she dragged the little boy up on to his feet and began a stroll back in the direction of the play area. And then, what could only be described as a moment of confusion. A man in a cheap looking suit with wavy blonde hair approached her and grabbed hold of the child, hoisting him high into the air and swinging him around a couple of times. A brief conversation between the two adults, a slightly angry exchange, resulting in the man reaching in his pocket and producing some money, which he reluctantly pressed into Chantelle's grasping hand. She counted the cash and tucked it away in her pocket along with her other gains. And so off went the child with his second escort for the day, to enjoy another hour or so on the swings and slides. Poppy was no seasoned detective, but she sensed that something was wrong here. Her mind began to piece things together and without knowing the truth behind the façade, all she could come up with was three words to describe the teenage hustler, 'sneaky fucking skank.'

True to form, Chantelle kept her distance from the excitable duo in the playground and smoked a couple of cigarettes while making several phone calls. Poppy watched on for the hour and a half session, her mind working overtime. The man in the suit turned out to be a decent understudy for the actor who had appeared in the first performance that day, mirroring almost every action that the hapless chef had carried out. He was surely pressing for a leading role in this twisted tale. The child star, however, looked exhausted at the end of the show and almost fell into the waiting pushchair when his mother came back to retrieve him. More furious waving from another visitor was ignored. The poor infant was probably confused as well as knackered. He clambered back into the waiting push chair, no doubt thankful for some respite.

When the second visitor's vehicle was out of sight, the show was on the move. Poppy staying a full hundred yards or so behind Chantelle and the exhausted child. The plot was now in full swing, and Poppy began to wonder where this mystery tour would lead her. She didn't have to wait long, a fifteen-minute walk had led them to some maisonettes in a secluded part of Eltham.

Chantelle made a short phone call and watched on as an upstairs curtain open and closed. A large-framed woman in a tacky flowery dressing gown and fluffy slippers suddenly appeared. There was an instant reaction from the child who sprinted the full ten yards to be greeted by a pair of open arms. The small lads unbridled enthusiasm revealed the missing link to the story in just a few short seconds. This was without a shadow of a doubt his real mother.

The two women had a brief conversation and shared a few laughs, no doubt at the expense of the two men who had appeared in the earlier scenes. Time for another exchange of money, this time it was Chantelle's turn to hand over some cash.

And so, in true private investigator fashion, Poppy had cracked the case. Her initial feelings were of rage, a burning anger that this skinny slut could take her friends money under false pretences. But she couldn't help but feel a sense of admiration for the teenage grifter who had fooled two grown men. She wanted to confront her there and then and expose both women, maybe hand out a few well-deserved slaps and punches to teach them a lesson for the cruel scam they had devised. She began to feel a little sorry for Matt. It was an unusual emotion for her to handle. But she knew how much little Willow meant to him and she felt sure that he would not welcome this revelation with anything but deep sorrow.

Once the tardy mother and her son had disappeared into their home it was time for the final scene to be played out. Oblivious to her watching audience Chantelle sloped off towards the local shops, no doubt ready to spend some of her ill-gotten gains. But as she turned the corner, she felt a tight yank on the back of her hair and an arm thrust across her throat. Her attacker spun her around and threw her with great force to the hard concrete ground. Her instinctive reaction was to curl up in a ball and cover her face with her hands, anticipating a flurry of blows to follow. But there were none. She could hear heavy breathing above her and sense the presence of a raging bull.

'Get on yer feet yer filthy slag,' Poppy yelled.

The young girl began to shake, she still had no idea who her attacker was. Her hand reached down to her jeans, and she produced her takings for the day. 'I've got money, don't hit me, I've got money, just take it.'

Poppy swung a leg and delivered a hefty kick to the small of the stunned teen's back. 'I said get on yer feet, now!'

The clearly shaken girl followed the instruction of her aggressor, rubbing her back as she got to her feet. 'What's this about?' she asked, in a familiar shrilled voice which Poppy had once found so irritating. 'I aint done nothing wrong. I was just, oh no! Oh fuck! Oh shit! It's you aint it, it's you!'

The smirk on Poppy's face and the slow nod would stay long in the memory of Chantelle. If she was frightened at the start of the encounter, she was truly terrified now. She began to stutter, and her words became disjointed. 'I aint done anything to you, I just...'

'Shut up,' Poppy barked. 'Just fuckin' shut up!'

'What have I done?'

'Happy families, girl. I knew that weren't Matts fuckin' kid. You had better start talking or you are gonna get slumped.'

Chantelle's trembling hand reached inside her jeans pocket, and she produced another small handful of notes. 'You can have it, all of it, I didn't mean no harm.'

'Are you fuckin' kidding me, girl, no harm! Not one, but two fuckin' blokes, a right pair of mugs.'

'Yeah, that's what they are a proper pair of mugs, I was just trying to earn a bit of cash.'

'Who's that shitbag upstairs, the kids' mother, who is she?'

'My cousin, but I swear down, I was pregnant, Matt did get me pregnant, but I lost it, I had a miscarriage.'

'Bullshit!'

'It's true I swear down.'

'And the other mug?'

'He was just some bloke I met at a party.'

'Fuck, girl, you just drop yer knickers for anyone, don't you?'

'No, it aint like that, I liked him, I liked him a lot, but he was married, he just used me.'

'Like you are using them?'

'They are so fucking stupid, the pair of them, thick as shit. It was her idea, my cousin, I never saw either of them for a while and, well she had her kid about the time I would have had Matt's baby. So, I thought, fuck it, I aint got no job, just tell them it's their kid and see if one of them believes me.'

'Never thought how fucked up that is you dirty slag?'

'I know, but they both fell for it, I couldn't believe it, then I got used to having the dosh, three hundred nicker a month, me and my cousin split it.'

'Fuck, I still can't believe they bought it!'

'Yeah, but well, I could cut you in, look take all that money, they both give me forty quid a week, more if I say the kid needs new clothes and stuff.'

Poppy shook her head, she clenched her fist tightly, she really wanted to make this girl suffer. But then, as she stared down at the teenage face of innocence cowering beneath her, she suddenly had an idea. 'I could go sick on you girl, really paste you all over the place, but I'm gonna give you a break.'

'What?'

'I'll forget what I saw but you are gonna need to do something for me.'

'What, like hook you up with Matt or something. I knew you two were at it, you know, back then in the restaurant. I think everyone knew he was shagging you.'

'Nothing that simple, you need to meet me at the park, where you met those twats today. Meet me there tonight at eight o clock.'

'What for?'

'Just be there.'

'I will, I will.'

'Ya got a fake ID?'

'I don't need one.'

'Don't give me shit, girl, you aint fuckin' eighteen, I knew you was still at school when you spread yer legs for Matt.'

'I'll borrow my mates driving license, we look like each other. But why do I need ID, what are we doing?'

'Just wear something short, look tarty, and put plenty of make-up on. That shouldn't be hard for you, should it?'

'For fucks sake, you aint pimping me out to nobody, I aint doing that.'

Poppy grabbed the young girl's wrist tightly and gave her a stern stare and a solid warning. 'Just be at the park at eight o clock. Don't you make me come and fish you out, girl!'

'Alright, alright, I'll be there, let go of my arm.'

Poppy released her grip on Chantelle and picked up the money the frightened teen had dropped. 'Good, well fuck off now, before I change my mind.'

'Eight o clock, at the park, but just tell me, what we are doing.'

'Shark fishing.'

'What?'

In that moment the sinister smile that Poppy saved for special occasions had found its way back to her face. 'Bait, girl. We're going shark fishing and you are gonna be the bait.'

*

When Bree arrived home from work that evening, she could sense an atmosphere. She wondered if her sister was still angry at the fuss she had made about her untidiness that morning. But a messy room and unemptied ash tray was the last thing on her mind. She had news, big news, massive news, information that she was desperate to share with her sibling. But the nature of this revelation could work one of two ways, so she decided to break that bombshell gently.

Poppy scoffed down a plate of beans on toast, washed down with a few swigs of cheap vodka she had bought from the local supermarket. She would never tell him of course, but she had used ten pounds of the child allowance that Matt had coughed up that morning for the boy that wasn't related to him. She bagged a few essentials for her evenings meet-up with the teenage grifter from her past, before reminding herself she needed to borrow something from her sister. In her mind there was no need to ask, after all, she had lost count of the number of times Bree had told her, 'what's mine is yours.'

When her sister came out of the shower, she caught a glimpse of Poppy's jacket heading for the front door. 'I'm borrowing your motor, don't worry, I won't smash it up,' she said, as she scurried past her.

'But you don't have insurance, Poppy, and I need to pick up Kendra's car, I am collecting her from the airport in the morning.'

'I'll say I'm you if I get pulled over, stop stressing, I can drive ya know.'

'Then let me come with you, I can drive you, it will only take me a few minutes to get ready.'

'Nah, gotta be somewhere, missy, gotta get going.'

'Wait? There is something I need to tell you, it's really important, don't go out, Poppy, you really to need to hear this.'

'Tell me later, I gotta go, someone is waiting for me.'

This was certainly not the way she had intended to reveal the life-changing information she had uncovered but her sister had left her no option. 'Houghton, I have found him, Poppy, I have found Houghton for you, I know where he lives.'

Those few words did the trick and stopped Poppy firmly in her tracks. Just the sound of that name sent a thousand mixed signals scrambling through her brain. Anger, bitterness, hatred, pain, shame and humiliation were at the forefront of her emotions now. She found herself needing to get into the fresh air to clear her head. But despite that revelation she was single minded as she stormed down the stairwell in Albermarle Court, undeterred, her tormentor from her past would have to wait. Someone else had to suffer that night, the voices had made that very clear.

CHAPTER
SEVENTEEN

Whether Poppy would have ever asked her sisters permission to borrow her precious SAAB SUV if she had not come out of the shower that night was highly debatable. The fact that the keys were just sitting in the bowl on the table seemed to be an open invitation. Bree's monotonous gesture of 'what's mine is yours, sisters always share,' may well come back to haunt her. Besides, in Poppy's mind, that arrangement was only ever likely to be a one-sided affair.

It felt strange to be behind the wheel of a car again, especially one that had an engine that started first time and air conditioning that worked. It made Poppy wonder what had happened to her trusty old Vauxhall, the cheap but reliable vehicle that she driven for that year she had spent living with Cameron. She had bought the car during that rare twelve months outside the confines of a prison. It should have given her a real sense of real freedom for that time, a chance to visit new places and look up old haunts. But that time was wasted, a daily roundtrip to and from work and the weekly trip to the supermarket was almost as far as she got. She did once venture further afield and managed to trace an old boating lake where her father used to take her as a child. Maybe the mixed messages in her brain that day had told her that the ghosts from her past where best just left there, buried deep, in the past. But now that her sister had revealed that she had found him, found Houghton, the man who stole her innocence and robbed her of a soul, that would have to change now, she knew that she could not let that go. But tonight, it was to be payback time. Tonight, someone else would be paying for their sins against those she had loved.

She was in deep thought now, trying to ignore the squeaking voice of Chantelle in the passenger seat. Almost from the second she had picked her up from outside the park in Eltham the whingy girl had been complaining. But the feisty teenager had followed her instructions and worn a tight leather skirt and a low-cut top. In truth, she would not have looked out of place standing in Lulus old stomping ground in the red-light area close to Woolwich Docks.

Poppy's head was in a dozen different places that night, the voices were back, some offering advice, some chanting evil commands. She was having constant flashbacks of the night her best friend had ended her life after the humiliating video had appeared out of nowhere on the internet. All she could see in her thoughts was a terrified girl being passed around like a rag doll. All she could hear was the laughter of Billy Keyes as he egged his friends on. But one other image had stayed in her brain since the day she was released from prison. It would not leave her thoughts, it had woken her up at night. That hand with those letters inked on the fingers and that creepy voice that had belittled her defenceless friend as he pushed her head harder and harder until she gagged on his stale meat. And so, the time had arrived, retribution was on the doorstep. All she needed was for this bastard to arrive.

At exactly ten fifteen she realised that Lulu had been right, she obviously knew his ways better than most. Right on cue the star of the evening show appeared with several of his cronies. Two sets of eyes followed the paths of the small group of noisy football louts as they crossed the main road and headed for the entrance of the newly named Coconut Teaser Bar.

That day had not gone well for Steven 'Shark' Phillips, his long-suffering live-in partner had left the bedsit they shared that morning and returned to her mother's house in Staines. She had finally had enough of his abuse and infidelity. She had reluctantly given him false alibis on at least two occasions, when she knew in her heart that he had probably committed those sexual offences against defenceless young girls. He had shown no regrets for his actions and his suffering partner felt the full weight of a well-aimed backhander when she told him of her doubts. It was not the first time the bully had raised his fists to her. She knew damned well it would not be the last.

His day took a further downward turn when he discovered that two of his regular 'buyers' had skipped the estate and headed north on the M1 Motorway, rather than face him to pay their overdue drug debts. On top of this his masterplan to overthrow Neddy had come unstuck when his closest ally, Fitz, had jumped ship and sworn his allegiance to the man mountain who ruled the roost. Shark had got himself off the hook by saying that his loyalty was never in doubt, and it had been the booze and drugs talking that night he conspired to seize power. Neddy, ever conscious of the fact that the traitor in his ranks had family connections to the Keyes brothers, let the matter go. At least that's what he told his crew.

And to round off a terrible day for Shark, he had just watched his beloved football side, Millwall, be humbled four nil in a cup match, by Leyton Orient. The opposition should have been a walkover, on paper, a team that struggled in a lower league and had not previously managed to find the back of the net in the first three games of the new season. But Millwall had been well and truly played off the park that night and had not managed one single shot on target for the whole of the game. Shark was raging inside, angry at the whole world. He badly needed an alcohol intake or a gratuitous violent encounter to comfort his bruised ego. Surely his day could not get any worse!

Poppy made her instructions crystal clear to the skinny temptress in the short skirt, before reminding her to apply an extra layer of lipstick. 'All ya have to do is smile at him a couple of times in there, trust me he will do the rest.'

Chantelle was still complaining. 'But what if he doesn't fancy me?'

'Listen, ya only have to flirt with the cunt, don't make it too obvious. Then when he has had a few drinks, tell him ya need some fresh air and bring him down that alleyway to the car park at the back.'

'Then I can go?'

'Yeah, but don't fuck up.'

'You swear, I can go, if I do this?'

'Yeah, I said so, didn't I? Now get moving.'

'And you aint gonna say nothing to Matt about the kid and everything?'

'Just bring that big lump down to the back of the pub and were all square.'

'You said you was gonna surprise him.'

'Yeah, he will be well pleased to see me. But it has to be a surprise.'

'I look like a right slag, dressed like this.'

Poppy shrugged her shoulders, 'And...?'

'But I aint, really, I aint like that, I just...'

'Fuck off, girl! You've been slammed more times than a taxi door.'

'I knew I should never had come out tonight, I am gonna get hurt, aint I, he is gonna hurt me.'

Poppy ignored her comment and dished out her final instructions. 'Right, go in there now, I am gonna park the motor down the back road behind the car park. Remember, let him have a few beers before you bring him down there. I don't want the cunt turning up sober.'

'Fuck, I am bricking it...'

'Don't bottle out on me now girl, I aint come all this way to let you fuck things up.'

Chantelle left the vehicle with a face like a wet haddock and crossed the road to the pub, pulling down on the bottom of her skirt, which seemed to be getting shorter by the minute. She hesitated before looking back at the car she had arrived in, maybe hoping that Poppy would change her mind and not make her go through with this ordeal. But she could see her steely stare, even from across the street, she shook her head and entered the pub.

The newly born Coconut Teaser Bar and Music Lounge rose from the ashes of the previous public house, The Railway Tavern, during the peak of the Covid pandemic in 2020. Like many pubs and restaurants at the time it had struggled to survive through lack of revenue. A fresh approach was needed in a bid to attract a younger, more affluent clientele. A local businessman stepped in and refurbished the whole place The bar was now split in to two sections, one loud with a regular DJ blasting out music from the nineties, the other a more chilled-out vibe in a spacious lounge. Both bars attracted a mixture of youngsters and thirty and forty somethings, prepared to pay a bit over the going rate for a decent night out.

Chantelle took a deep breath when she entered the pub, checking her reflection in the cluster of mirrored tiles as she looked for her target. She heard him before she saw him, he was holding court at the centre of the main bar, moaning loudly about offside rules and what he would have done if he could have got his hands on the referee that night. Every other word out of his mouth was an expletive as ha showed his distaste for the officials. A loud sound system blared out in the background, as Chantelle, shaking inside, began to search for her fake ID.

Shark's tattooed fingers clicked furiously as he looked to attract the attention of a busty barmaid. He dismissed the angry expression of distaste she gave him and raised a twenty pound note high in the air to make sure he was next to be served. As he looked along the bar, he noticed the over-sized heels of a pair of bright white shoes supporting the legs of a pretty young blond with a petite figure. His beady eyes worked upwards, sighting skinny legs, a short skirt, a colourful low-cut top, squeezing two small breasts out of the front. He beamed with approval before he had even seen her face. Chantelle smiled first, she didn't want to, but the thought of failing this mission was not worth thinking about. She wanted to get it over and done with. Shark tilted his hand forwards in a gesture that seemed to be offering to buy her a drink. By the time she had nodded he had appeared by her side and introduced himself. The fact that he used his nickname told Chantelle she had found her target. She now realised why Poppy had used the expression, 'Shark bait.'

The small talk was just that, small talk, no world politics or thoughts on the current recession. It centred mainly around the music being played in the back room and the lack of other lively venues in the neighbourhood. At one point, when the heavy-set thug went to relieve himself in the toilets, the plan seemed to be falling apart. One of Shark's football friends began making conversation with the teenage Lolita. She was clearly enjoying the male attention and laughed out loudly, clearly taken in by his witty one-liners. But a pair of dark disapproving eyes appeared at a side window, reminding Chantelle that she was not there to have fun. Luckily, Shark muscled his way back in and re-claimed his prize, pulling her in to a quieter corner of the pub to pursue his lustful intentions.

An hour or more had passed and the bar had begun to fill with several mixed groups of smartly dressed men and an array of half-drunk women. Even though Shark had eyed up a few other candidates to provide some consolation for his bad day, his attention was still focussed on the girl at his side. Chantelle noticed that the conversation had become more course and that her new admirer's hands were beginning to wander. She fought off his advances and tried her best to remain calm. She was wishing at the point that she had followed her first instincts, to run in the opposite direction when she saw Poppy's face in the Saab that night. But she knew she would have not gone far before the crazed girl from her past caught up with her, not in those heels. She looked up at the side window again and saw that the same pair of eyes was still following the events of the evening through the smeared glass window of the pub. But this time they seemed to be smiling with a sick satisfaction. The plan was working, for Poppy, it was time to prepare.

At around midnight, Chantelle's loud and irritating squeaky voice could be heard above the blaring music as she stepped into the fresh air. Shark stood in the doorway of the pub exchanging crude comments with a few of his neanderthal pals, before the two of them headed for the dark passageway at the rear. It would seem appropriate that the letters on the big brutes' hands would spell LIONS, as that's exactly how he was when he escorted his newfound friend away from the bar. His vice-like grip on her arm likened to that of the king of the jungle latching on to his prey. But the teenager was still determined to see this through and strode towards the alleyway. It would be the first and only time she would be pleased to see the girl that had turned up out of the blue that day and wrecked her idyllic world, not to mention her money-spinning scam. Shark seemed to know the way, it was obvious that he was no stranger to the rear of this public house. Maybe Chantelle would not be the first victim of his to tread this path.

She was still fighting off the lumpy thugs' sexual advances when she lured him into the dimly lit car park at the rear of the pub. As the heavy-set man turned the corner, a sudden flash of grey and silver came out of nowhere at a searing pace and smashed across the side of his skull. Chantelle hardly had time to catch her breath to scream when a second blow from the heavy steel rod caught the big man across the forehead. He wobbled slightly and then fell to his knees. Chantelle froze, struck dumb by the level of violence at her feet. She shut her eyes tightly, knowing that this nightmare was not over. She was right. As the battered and confused thug tried to push himself off the concrete paving a much harder blow reigned down, this time across the back of his skull. The hard man crumbled in a heap. Poppy, weapon in hand, appeared from the shadows and immediately launched a series of brutal kicks to his head causing a large gash to open on the side of his face. Shark was barely conscious when he felt a tug on the back of his hoodie and found himself being dragged along the stony ground to the place where the empty bottles were stored. He was a weighty bastard, but with barely any resistance Poppy managed to twist both of his arms behind his head and locked the handcuffs around a stone pillar alongside the back wall. She delivered three sharp kicks between his open legs and watched on as the dazed bully groaned in agony.

Chantelle was afraid to move, her eyes were open now, she was witnessing this brutal assault just inches away from the beaten man. She was shaking, she wanted to run as fast as those heels would carry her. But she looked at the venom in Poppy's face and decided, wisely, not to move. Poppy took a small break from her attack, allowing her victim long enough to regain his senses. When she was sure he was conscious, she reached down and pulled his mobile phone from the pocket of his jeans and threw it across the floor at Chantelle's feet.

'See if it's locked?'

'Locked, err, no, no, it aint locked.'

'Get in on his Facebook thing.'

Chantelle was struggling to speak, 'Faa, face, what?'

'The live thing, ya, know, where everyone can see this shitbag.'

'Facebook Live?'

'Let's show the world want a cunt he really is.'

Poppy yanked off Shark's shoes and tossed them over the crates of empty beers bottle stacked in a large rack. As she unzipped his jeans he started to come around and for a few seconds, strangely, he found himself in a confused state of delirium. 'I like that,' he mumbled, oblivious to his predicament. 'Keep going.'

Seconds later he found his feet facing the evening sky as Poppy turned him upwards to yank off his jeans. He seemed to smile for a second or two, still trying to come to terms with his surroundings. He was at Poppy's mercy now, bound tightly by the solid steel cuffs, laying helpless, exposed, in his pale grey coloured briefs

Poppy gave him a crack across the ribs with the thick metal bar, his loud cry was one of confusion and pain. She retrieved a bright orange carrier bag and took out her next weapon, the ten-inch sex toy she had prized from Kayleigh's collection.

'Turn it on now,' Poppy said to a shaking Chantelle, who was clearly struggling to deal with the situation. 'Turn his phone on and put the camera on this fuckers face.'

Shark was slowly coming back to reality. He suddenly became aware of the danger he was in. He started to struggle, yanking hard at the handcuffs in a bid to free himself. Poppy delivered another hefty kick, this time to the side of his neck, then pinned down his arms by straddled his chest. She was surprisingly calm considering the level of punishment she had just dished out. Looking down at her prey she squeezed the side of his bleeding scalp and banged the back of his head hard against the cold surface.

'I want you to look at me, shithead,' she said, pure venom in her eyes. 'I want you to remember me.'

As Shark's senses began to return, he could feel the solid metal handcuffs cutting into his wrists and felt the inside of his head throbbing like the inside of a huge bass drum. His agony began to spread down his body, and he felt the sharpest of pains shoot through his ribs.

'Are you filming this?' Poppy asked a shaking Chantelle.

Her reluctant accomplice nodded. Her hand was unsteady as she hovered over the wounded victim to get a better view of his face. Poppy showed Shark the sex toy and goaded him. 'It's much bigger than yours mate. I just had a look down there. I'd say you got about half an inch and a dozen wrinkles.'

Shark was completely helpless now, securely restrained by the cuffs attached to the concrete pillar. He tasted blood in his mouth and found that his aching body was unable to move. But in true fighting spirit the heavyweight bruiser rolled some spit around inside his mouth and launched it upwards into Poppy's face. 'You are dead meat, girl,' he groaned. 'Trust me, I will fucking kill you.'

But the only reaction the bulky thug received was a sinister smile. 'I am gonna fuckin' enjoy this now,' she said.

Chantelle's hand was still trembling, she was a nervous wreck, but more afraid of fleeing than staying. She was praying inside that this chaotic nightmare would be over soon.

Poppy towered over her victim and her nostrils flared. 'How good is your memory shithead?' she asked, through gritted teeth.

'I remember you chivved up my cousin, I know it's you who banged Billy.'

Poppy smiled. 'Good, so you remember that night, do you? So, you will remember my friend, you will remember what you did to Nikita.'

'Fuck your filthy skaghead friend,' came the reply. Shark really was braver than he should have been at that moment. But this stocky heavyweight had been on the receiving end of several savage beatings from rival football gangs over the years, he was no pushover. He was also fully aware that the phone on his camera was recording this moment. He was not going to sacrifice his hard man reputation for anyone, especially the crazed psychopath hovering over him.

'I'm gonna refresh your memory, mate, see if you can think back to why I might be sitting here on your lardy arse body now.'

Shark tried to free his hands again but found himself wedged tighter than ever against the concrete post. Those handcuffs had certainly been worth the rummage through Kayleigh's lingerie drawers. And now the other stolen sex toy was about to play its part.

'Do ya need reminding, do ya need me to refresh yer memory, mate?'

Shark tightened his lips in defiance, he could see what his attacker was planning. Poppy leaned down and pinched hard on his nose while punching him hard in his aching ribs. It had the desired effect. Shark opened his mouth to gasp for air and in a split-second Poppy stuffed the large end of the dildo into his throat. She watched on as his eyes began to roll. His body shook violently, his face began to turn bright red as he struggled for breath.

'Gag on that, you ugly freak!' Poppy screamed. 'Do you remember her now, shithead? Gag on that you ugly freak!'

Poppy pushed the long piece of plastic further down his gullet and watched him choke. The pupils in his bulging eyes were growing in size and his face began to turn a shade of mauve. She had no intention of stopping until Chantelle screamed out loudly, 'Your gonna kill him, let him go now, he has had enough, stop now, Poppy, stop!'

Her panic-stricken screeches may just have saved his life. Poppy released her grip on the sex toy and Shark spluttered and coughed, gyrating his head in a bid to remove the offending object from his mouth.

'I want to go home,' Chantelle shouted, 'He has had enough, let me go home, its finished now.'

'Finished?' Poppy yelled. 'No, girl, it aint fuckin' finished yet'. With that she bowled over to the rack of empty bottles and pulled one out, smashing it hard against the slab of concrete above Shark's head, littering the big man's semi-naked body with tiny shards of glass. She made her way back into his view, grinning, she wanted to see the fear in his eyes that had been missing. A familiar voice in

182

her head told her that Nikita was not happy yet, she needed him to suffer more, he had to feel the pain that she had endured. That voice did not mince its words, it told her that he needed to be, 'done good and proper.'

Shark had switched his attention to Chantelle, maybe hoping she would provide a voice of reason. She was still filming the assault, but her hand was moving so much she was only recording small glimpses of the harrowing event. Despite the clear desperation showing in the big man's eyes, she knew she was helpless to rescue him. The frightened teen could do no more, she had said her piece, tried to save him any further punishment. But she realised now that Poppy would stop at nothing to gain revenge.

Suddenly, a laugh, a loud laugh, echoed through the alleyway, Poppy was amused. She had noticed a clear sign that Shark was more distressed than his foul mouth was revealing. 'He's just pissed himself!' Poppy yelled, pointing down at the growing wet patch on his grey briefs. 'That big fat shithead has pissed himself'. Poppy stood totally still for a few seconds, she was waiting for that voice to tell her that she had done well, humiliated the big lump, achieved some retribution for Nikita. Maybe this was enough. But the absence of any appreciation for her actions told her they needed more. This grisly show was not over.

Shark's eyes told her what his mouth wouldn't let him, he was sorry. He was begging her, pleading with her, he was truly sorry, even if he wouldn't tell her in words. She could see it all in the lines of pain and anguish that were etched on his distorted face. He remembered hearing about how she had sliced his cousin repeatedly, stabbing him more than two dozen times with a hunting knife. He didn't want to suffer that fate. For the first time in his life, the tattooed thug who feared nobody, was truly scared. In an act of desperation, he turned to the only person who might take pity on him at this time. He said a small prayer in his head and promised a god that he had never worshiped that he would mend his ways if he were to ever wake from this brutal nightmare.

Poppy towered over the defenceless man, she was still calm and composed, knowing that she could not leave things the way they were. Chantelle started to sob as she asked Poppy one more time to walk away, telling her again that he had suffered enough. But it wasn't just about Nikita now, she had remembered what Lulu had told her. He hadn't learned his lesson, people like him never do. She looked at the jagged neck of the broken bottle in her hand and knew what she had to do. As she leaned down, Shark tightened his legs together, maybe out of modesty, maybe out of fear. Whichever it was, it didn't work. Poppy yanked the urine-stained underwear from beneath him and threw his underpants into the bottle crates. She kneeled in front of his open legs, the way a midwife would crouch as she prepared to deliver a baby. At that second every moral fibre in Chantelle's body was telling the girl to run, to get out of there, break world speed records for a girl wearing heels. She did not want to witness this atrocity that she knew was about to unfold. But that dark alleyway looked a lot longer than it had done when she arrived here. An unequivocal fear kept her rooted to the spot. She shut her eyes tightly and remained as silent as she could.

And then, like a well-practiced surgeon, Poppy slipped the serrated edge of the lethal object beneath the big man's floppy genitals with one hand and took hold of his shrivelled penis in the other. And then, with one rapid upwards thrust she separated the plus-sized bully from his manhood. Shark could swallow his pain no longer and let out an ear-piercing scream that echoed all the way to the main road and back.

'And that's for that fuckin' school kid.' Poppy said, without showing the slightest hint of emotion. 'You sick fuckin' bastard!'

Chantelle's sobbing had turned to full blown tears. 'I just want to go home, please, just let me go home,' she begged.

Poppy stared hard at the quivering teen, a dark and evil stare that the terrified girl would remember for the rest of her life. 'Go, but you'd better keep your gob shut, remember, you are in this as well.'

'What, what do you mean?'

'You helped me with this, girl, if you are thinking about grassing me, remember, I will tell 'em it was the two of us.'

'No, no, please, Poppy, I aint gonna say nothing, I swear down.'

'You would get three or four years for this, ya know. But just think, you might end up in a cell next door to me. Ya wouldn't want that would ya?'

'No, no, sorry, I mean, no, no I aint telling no one, I swear down, I promise.'

'Well, what yer waiting for, fuck off then!'

Chantelle did not need telling twice, her skinny legs waddling at a speedy pace through the alleyway towards the safety of the streetlights in the main road.

Seeing his legs astride Poppy couldn't resist one last kick at the wounded animal beneath her. She strutted her way back down the side alley, tossing the neck of the broken bottle that was sporting fragments of shark's manhood over a garden fence. In the distance she could hear the clippity-clop of her accomplice's sharp heels as she retreated towards the other end of the pub carpark. She felt good about herself at that moment, she could hear the voices of those who doubted her telling her she had done well. She could make out the laughter and applause of Nikita. It gave her a warm feeling inside. But when she arrived at the end of the narrow side pathway which led to the street, Poppy was stopped in her tracks by something strange. It was a familiar odour, a fragrance that she instantly recognised. It wafted through the cooling air as if it might linger there all night. She looked both left and right but saw nothing. Maybe her mind was playing tricks on her, maybe not.

Before she entered her the car she treated herself to a celebratory cigarette, enjoying every last drag, with a smug look of satisfaction on her face. Those angry voices inside her head were silenced for another night.

CHAPTER EIGHTEEN

There is something quite breath-taking about the way the late summer sun sets over the Näsijärvi lake on the outskirts of Tampere. When the fading beams fall from the sky and dance across the water's edge, like nimble ballerinas waving fiery silks as they tread a path for the spectacle that follows. Then, without warning, the sun seems to plunge from the darkening sky, slowly at first, taunting onlookers with its magnificent aura, before being swallowed in one by the hungry gulp of the glistening waters below.

Krista had spent almost half of her life in this beautiful Finnish town, she had witnessed this sunset thousands of times, but somehow each evening seemed different. These surreal moments often filling her head with a thousand memories and mixed emotions. In her youth it had given her moments to dream, fantasies of a life full of success, love and happiness, preferably in that order for the bubbly and vivacious girl. The success became a speedy reality when she moved to England in her twenties, her clever mind and dogged determination helping her to soar to great heights in her career. Expensive clothes and exotic foreign holidays became her obsession as she flourished in the city with streets paved of gold. But love had somehow eluded her, her dreams of a happy life had been shattered by a man who was never free to keep his false promises. A man she loved, yet hated so much, that it turned their sordid tryst into a painful bittersweet relationship. Her future happiness would always be tainted by that experience, even though her childhood sweetheart, Per, had stood by her side and comforted her broken heart for more than twenty years. But even this mild-mannered gentleman had called time on their relationship of convenience when she found a reason to blame him for the death of her son at the railway crossing. Per had been tasked with keeping the wayward lad away from his volatile sister before Jamie set off for a travelling adventure in the Antipodes. His death certificate would show that Bree's twin had died just three days before he would have boarded the aeroplane to start his new life down under. Krista, absorbed by emotional turmoil after the tragedy, turned on the man she had known since eighth grade and somehow found a way to hold him responsible. It was the final straw for the gentile man who had played second fiddle for more than half of his shared life. He packed his bags and moved to Helsinki in the hope he could find some belated happiness in the country of his birth. In a strange twist of fate, he met up with an old schoolfriend of his ex-partner and was now, finally, in a mutually loving relationship. He had recently settled in Pirkkala, a small town less than twenty miles from where his former partner lived.

Krista checked her mobile, her daughter, as usual, had not been answering her calls or replying to her texts following their bitter argument. She knew Bree's mood swings well enough to know that any reparations would have to be instigated at her end. As a small child her daughter's stubborn resilience could be bought with an ice cream or a colourful comic. In her teens Bree would forget her grudges at the mention of a skiing trip or some new designer boots. But nowadays the anxious mother had nothing left in her armoury, her daughter was more distant than she had ever been. Krista did not regret the fact that she had spent four hundred thousand pounds buying and furnishing her daughter's beautifully designed apartment in Albermarle Court. She had used more than half of the money she made on the sale of the family home in Oxley Village, hoping it would kick-start a new and more fulfilling relationship. But the gratitude of her daughter lasted about as long as it would take for a coat of paint to dry on the walls of the bedrooms. Bree made it clear to her mother that she saw the generous gesture as an entitlement, not a gift.

And so, she tried to give Bree space and time, maybe hoping that her daughter would meet a handsome prince, preferably somebody like the ever-dependable Preston, who might provide the happy ever after. Maybe she would be asked to babysit their children in the future. Maybe, she thought, having her own offspring would be a wakeup call for her daughter and she would realise that a mother's love is truly unconditional.

Krista felt at peace with herself in her beautifully designed wooden house overlooking the lakes. She had bought this chic property with Per as a second home a few years after the twins were born. As a child, Bree had spent her summer holidays here surrounded by idyllic scenery and clean air. She had learned to speak the native tongue of her mother's birthplace at a weekend school. Something she complained about but excelled in. But even then, at that early age, it was obvious that all was not right with the headstrong child. Krista could never put her finger on it but the older her daughter became the more distant she became.

As she waited for the planned Zoom Call that might put her worried mind at rest, Krista looked across the lake and began to ponder on the 'what ifs' in her life. 'What if, she had never taken the job at the communications company in London, she would never have met Poppy's father. What if she had seen through him on that very first encounter, when he consumed more alcohol in one night than she usually did in one month. The warning signs were there. What if she had stayed on the pill, not played around with nature, not found herself in a situation where she loved a man with no hope and no future.

As she looked long and hard at the time on her laptop, she began to shake slightly, hoping that her fears were just fears. Reality seemed so scary at that moment. But one last 'what if' had screamed out to her almost every day she watched that breath-taking sunset. It was one that gave her a sickly feeling inside. What if she had followed her original plan and taken those tablets at the clinic on that frosty day in 1995. What if she had ended the lives of her precious twins before they had even begun. That thought had been locked away in a vault full of dark thoughts for more than two decades, but it seems that somewhere in her subconscious a calling spirit had found the key. She knew inside that she would never get over the tragic death of her son at the railway crossing. She felt as if her heart had stopped beating with his that day. That her body was merely a vessel that lived an empty existence. She desperately wanted to admit it, to her best friend Millie, and the numerous therapists she had seen, the blackest thought that had ever crossed her mind. But she never did, not even to her regular counsellor, who had surely saved her sanity on more than one occasion. But she began to wish more each day that it had been her daughter in the car that tragic night. She wished that Jamie was alive and well and still calling her at the strangest of times in the middle of the night, to ask her to pick him up from a party or because he needed to borrow some money. Or, as he often used to do, to remind her that he loved her more than anything in the world.

Krista always knew that her daughter protected the darkest of secrets in her own little Pandoras box of turbulent emotions. No professional counsellors, however renowned or expensive they were, could ever find the key to unlock that box. And so, here she was, a desperate mother, hoping that a renowned Professor of Psychology, based at Wisconsin University, might help her find the answers to her daughters disturbing behaviour. This might well be her last hope.

Suddenly, the sound of an incoming call on her computer screen made her jump. It was time to ask those questions.

'Hyvää Iltaa,' she said, as an elderly bespectacled lady's face appeared on her screen. 'Hello, from Finland.'

The woman at the other end of the call seemed to be adjusting her settings as if she had not heard her. She suddenly became clearer as she started to speak, her soft southern American accent soothing Krista's frayed nerves, 'Mrs Nylund?'

'It's Ms, actually, but please call me Krista. Thank-you for coming back to me Doctor Fiztgerald.'

'You seemed quite anxious. I know you have tried to reach me several times.'

'Yes, yes, I am sorry, I am a bit nervous I don't know where to start.'

'You mentioned in your email it was regarding one of my case studies.'

Krista's mouth was dry, she took a long sip from a bottle of spa water. 'My friend found you, well she is a friend of my daughter actually, she found your details.'

'OK, do you want to be more specific?'

Krista had her notes in front of the laptop, but she had read them so many times she could recite them word for word. She got straight to the point 'It is about Girl H.'

'Girl H?'

'You wrote about her in a case study, one you carried out in England, three or four years ago.'

The refined American lady hesitated before answering. 'But those reports are classified, I can't give you the specific details. I can discuss the content, but not the individual. You do understand that don't you?'

Krista was clearly nervous as she took another sip of water. 'Can you tell me more about your findings, you know, what you said about the genetic problems that might have caused her to be so violent?'

'I don't understand, what would be your interest in his girl?'

'It is important for me to know.'

'OK, I can see from all your calls and emails that you are desperate to know more, but I will need to know why. Are you thinking of writing some sort of paper on genetic imbalances in criminals?'

Krista lied, 'It is something like that.'

The woman in the large-framed glasses paused for a moment but then decided to feed her opposite number some of the details relating to the case. 'I interviewed Girl H several times in a prison facility just outside London. She was, she probably still is, one of the most fascinating case studies I have ever come across.'

'Was she crazy? Sorry, I shouldn't have said that. But, I mean, she did have mental health issues, didn't she?'

'I had two colleagues, between us we carried out a number of interviews and tests with Girl H. My gut feeling was that she was playing us, she knew what to say and when to say it. She was calculated, she was very calculated.'

'I don't understand, are you saying that she was pretending to be mad?"

'Heavens no! If you read my whole report, you will see that I diagnosed girl H, as a classic case of a sociopath with psychotic tendencies. Not everyone was convinced by my findings though.'

'Was her behaviour because of her upbringing, she was abused and rejected as a child, wasn't she?'

There was a stony silence from the other end of the line. Camilla Fitzgerald cleaned the lenses of her oversized spectacles and thought for a few seconds. She was conscious that she may be overstepping the line, providing the anxious woman with more information that she should be. But something told her that this was much more personal than her caller was letting on.

'You mentioned in your report some of the bad things that had happened to her,' Krista stated, keen to keep the flow of the conversation going.

The seasoned specialist looked slightly puzzled by the line of questioning. 'You do understand my interest in the case. A first grader could have identified, Girl H, as a sociopath.'

'Sorry, I didn't mean to...'

'Girl H did have a troubled upbringing, but her problems started from the moment she was born. She carries a gene, I won't bore you with the genetic breakdown, but it is a rare gene, a strand of MAOA-L. You are aware, Ms Nylund, that's what my research involves, the study of hereditary genetics. My case studies all centre around malfunctional chromosomes.'

'Sort of, I have been looking at some of your cases on the internet. So, Girl H, she got these bad genes from, from where?'

'Her parents, well in the case of Girl H, the bad gene as you call it would have come from her grandparents, grandmother to be more specific.'

'I am trying to keep up with you, sorry if I sound a little naïve.'

'I traced the girl's ancestry back to her great grandparents, it was all there, in the report.'

'The stuff about her grandmother, she, she was sectioned, wasn't she?'

'Sectioned?'

Krista suddenly remembered the very words that Poppy's father, Dean, had used to describe his mother's incarceration. 'She was deemed to be clinically insane.'

'That was more than sixty years ago, they don't use phraseology like that anymore. But yes, Girl H's grandmother was held indefinitely for the things she did.'

'She burned her husband alive in a locked room, set fire to the house, she almost killed her son and.' Krista had to stop herself her thoughts were running away with her.

There was another pause before Dr Fiztgerald opened the conversation again. 'The grandmothers' mother, Girl H's great grandmother, also had psychological problems. Records are hard to trace from that period, but I managed to find out that she had serious mental health issues.'

'Can you tell me?'

'It is all in the report.'

'I didn't get that far back.'

'She killed herself, she was only nineteen, she killed herself after drowning one of her children. She tried to kill them both, but one survived.'

'And that woman turned out to be her grandmother, girl H's grandmother?'

'Yes.'

'What happened to the grandmother?'

There was more hesitation, but the Professor of Psychology knew she had already said too much, so this would not change things. 'She suffered the same fate. They were moving her from one institution to another one evening and one of the guards left a tin of baked beans in a carrier bag in the vehicle. She stole the can when he was putting gas in the car, she hid it underneath her coat. When she got to her residence, she peeled the top off the tin and sliced her own throat with the jagged edge. I am not telling you anything that is not published in the report. I do have to ask though, this is more than a fascination in the case, I am right, aren't I? There is a personal interest here?'

Krista was not sure how to respond, there were many strange thoughts circling around inside her head. She was beginning to remember things she had forgotten about Poppy's father and how he had told her what a difficult child his daughter had been at times. Some things were making sense, but she still needed further answers. She was in too far now, she needed to know, she was desperate to know.

'So,' Krista said, trying to find a way back into the conversation. 'Girl H's grandmother committed suicide and so did her great grandmother. They both killed themselves after harming their own children.'

'Correct, it is such a tragic case and unfortunately it is not rare. I have made this breakthrough with at least three other families over the years of my research.'

'Did you find any other links to other people in the family of Girl H?'

'No, the parents only ever had one child, I did discover that the father died a few years back but that was of normal health issues. You see some people don't understand my case studies, these genes are not always present in all blood relatives. In this case the man can pass down the gene, but most males seem to have an immunity to the deficiency. Sorry, am I going too fast?'

'No, I understand, so men can be carriers but not be affected?'

'Exactly, the genetics, from my research seems to prove that point. My work is often criticised for its foundations because it is difficult to produce hard proof. But the facts in my case studies don't lie. None of the men in this cycle were ever affected. None of them ever had mental health challenges despite carrying the default gene.'

'OK, but what if.'

'If...?'

'If Girl H had a sister?'

'No, that's not possible, my research showed that she has no siblings, male or female'

Krista felt cornered, her head was spinning, she needed answers but realised she needed to come clean if she was to discover the truth and get her daughter the help she so badly needed. She had nothing to lose now so she knew she had to declare her interest. 'Girl H,' she mumbled, through her drying mouth. 'Girl H is Poppy Jarvis, isn't it?'

She didn't need the wisely professor to answer her question, the absence of a denial and the expression on her face confirmed what the concerned mother already knew. Fitzgerald decided to throw the conversation wide open. 'I can neither confirm that it is, or it isn't, what I can confirm, however, is that Girl H does not have any siblings.'

'She has a sister,' Krista replied, shaking slightly and struggling to speak. 'Well, she has a half-sister. Her father and I were,' she couldn't think of the best term to describe their tragic affair, so she used the words, 'we were lovers.'

An awkward pause ensued as Dr Fizgerald began to digest her revelation. Part of her wanted to retreat to her study room and cite the confidentiality act but she could sense the desperation of a mother who needed to know the truth. 'I find that hard to believe, my research showed that the girl's father and mother separated when she was around seven or eight, there was no record of him ever having more children.'

'It happened!' was Krista's blunt response, angered by the fact that she had been doubted. 'Why do you think I have been so desperate to get in touch with you?'

'How old is she, your daughter, how old?'

'Twenty-five.'

The professor gave her glasses another wipe which gave her some time to ponder on her next question. But the desperation in Krista's face told her that she already knew the question she was going to ask. She was the first to speak. 'She has had problems, in the past, my daughter, Brianna, she has had lots of problems.'

They were back on a level playing field now and Fitzgerald knew she had no escape route from the situation, if anything she had a moral obligation to follow this through. 'Mental health problems?'

Krista felt her answer sticking in her throat, she was doing her best not to show the pain she was feeling inside, it hurt her so much having to admit the truth. 'Yes,' she said, 'ever since she was a child.'

'Has she ever hurt anybody, physically?'

'No, not really, not people. But she was always very spiteful when it came to animals. We could never keep pets in our house when she was a child. She was expelled from the local riding school she went to because she once stuck a pony's eyes together with superglue. She said she did it because he was a bad horse. She told me that he looked at her in a funny way. I had to compensate them for the vet's expenses and to stop them calling the authorities.'

'But she never harmed people, friends at school, other children, that sort of thing?'

'No, not physically, but she has always been, I don't know how to explain it, she never mixed well with others, she could be really nasty without actually touching them. I always thought she was fighting for attention, but the things she did, they were not normal for a child.'

'Do you want to give me an example, you say she was never violent towards you or anyone else.'

'No, not physically, but she would do things to hurt me.'

'Hurt you emotionally?'

Krista remembered the first time her daughter had made her feel that she might be abnormal. It was something she had only ever told one counsellor, however, that therapist had dismissed what she had told him. But that event never left her, it was something that had always stuck in her mind, it had always bothered her. 'I shouted at her once, when she was around six years old. She walked out of a ballet lesson because the teacher said she was not performing well. So, I shouted at her, very loudly. I made her cry. I told her to wait for me in the car while I apologised to her tutor. But when I came out, she had gone, she had left the car, vanished, she just ran away. We had to call the police and everything, we were frantic.'

'Lots of children do stuff like that though when they don't get their own way. Did she come home herself?'

'No, we were sick with worry. The police finally found her four hours later, she was sitting on the side of a railway track.' Krista found her heart racing fast as the memory of that day came back to haunt her. 'My daughter was so calm when I asked her why she had run away. She told me she wanted the train to run her over, to punish me, she said she wanted to make me sad. She told me she would rather be dead than to live with me anymore.'

'And she was only six?'

'Brianna said, she said that someone had told her that it was the best way to hurt her mother, to make her mother cry like I had made her cry. She said that if she killed herself, it was the perfect answer.'

'But she never told you who told her?'

'She never said, she just said she heard someone tell her to do it.'

'Did you ever talk to her about it again, when she was older?'

'Yes, but that's not it.' Krista's head was full of mixed emotions, she reached for the bottle of water to quench her thirst, wishing there was something much stronger in that bottle to calm her nerves.

She had the professor's full attention now, Dr Fitzgerald would have liked to have been making notes but thought it would not seem appropriate 'You said, that was not all'.

'The railway crossing, where she went to, it was near where we lived. Three years ago, my son, her brother, her twin brother, he died there in a terrible accident. He was trying to help some people stranded on the tracks and, well, he just died. And Brianna was there, she witnessed the whole thing.'

'The poor girl, she must have been deeply traumatised.'

'Since then, she has, well, she has hated me, as though it was my fault.'

'But you can't blame yourself, that's what post-traumatic stress does to people, the poor girls head is reeling from what happened. She probably needs someone to lash out at.'

'She went to counselling, top people in that field, we spent a lot of money to get the best people to help her. But...'

'Let me guess, they assessed her behaviour as normal?'

'Yes, how did you know?'

'It is not uncommon, it follows a pattern, her sister is the same.'

'Poppy? God, no, she is nothing like her sister!'

197

'Girl H, she ran rings around the team who interviewed her at Bronzefield. That's how she managed to get released early from prison after she murdered that young lad. They deemed her just to have anger issues caused by her parents' negligence and abuse. They never ever thought to look deeper, they never asked her the right questions.'

'Deeper, oh, the fact that she may have a genetic, umm, genetic…'

'Defect, it is a defect, it is part of her makeup, where the girl has absolutely no conscience. Girl H has no feelings, no remorse for what she does, no compassion for those she hurts. It is as though she removes herself from the situation and sees it as somebody else committing those crimes. She is not alone. I have interviewed many psychopaths who showed similar characteristics. The ones that come clean often say that they hear voices. But Girl H, well, she was a smart cookie. You see she told me that if they knew what was really going on inside her head, she would have been locked away in a mental institution and never released. She knew she would never get out. So, she played the victim, gained the sympathy vote.'

'Do you think, Oh, my God, no! Do you think that my daughter has the same problems as girl H, as her sister?'

'It is impossible to tell without speaking to her at length. It may be that she is just mildly affected, that she can separate the default mode from her own personality, be two different people.'

'Like a schizophrenic?'

'Precisely, you see a schizophrenic can disassociate themselves from the reality of a situation, they can commit a crime, never believing that they were the person who did any harm.'

'But wouldn't the counsellors have spotted that?'

'No, not if they are not looking for it, not if they were trying to unlock the anxieties caused by her post-traumatic stress.'

'But, if she has, if she has this gene, she can be treated, there is a way of helping her, curing her?'

'In my opinion you can't rehabilitate somebody who cannot accept that their actions are wrong. It is perhaps fortunate that your daughter has no violent tendencies, that she only aims to hurt and supress people with words and insults. The mistreatment of animals may just have been a phase.'

'But what if Poppy leads her astray, makes her do things?'

'My God! You never said they know each other?'

Krista paused, the water in the bottle had vanished along with her hopes of finding the answer to her prayers. She wanted to get off the phone as quickly as possible and book the first available flight from Helsinki to be by her daughter's side. Through a drying mouth she found some words. 'They are living together, the girls, they are living together.'

Dr Fitzgerald was visibly stunned by her revelation. She chose her response very carefully. 'I can only advise you, of course, but I am sure you know for yourself, it is not good for these women to be together. They are likely to feed off each other's conditions. There is a saying I believe about the hazard of mixing burning oil with cold water. You need to separate them as soon as possible. I must go now to prepare for a lecture, but rest assured, Ms Nylund, I will be here, anytime day or night, if you need any further advice. I wish you luck. And, please, be very cautious.'

As the picture of the expert psychoanalyst disappeared the monitor on Krista's laptop displayed the screenshot of her and her daughter on a skiing trip to Aspen. Somehow, after that call, her daughter looked different now, she didn't know why, but the expression on her face looked as cold as the frozen slopes in the background.

When darkness fell on the waters of Lake Näsijärvi that night, the memory of the enchanting sunset had evaporated from Krista's thoughts. A thousand unanswered questions about her daughter's erratic behaviour over the past twenty years had suddenly become clearer. The worried mother had found some answers, but she had no readymade solution. She so desperately wanted to be close to her daughter at that moment. To hug Bree so tightly, that all the pain and badness inside her would simply disappear.

Seconds later she was back on the computer, spuriously looking for the next available flights to Heathrow. There was no time to lose now, her daughter's safety and well-being was her only priority.

CHAPTER NINETEEN

There had been an atmosphere at the flat during that week, neither of the girls, it seemed, were happy with the other. Bree was disappointed with her sisters seemingly blasé approach to the revelation that Houghton was alive and kicking and living in a detached house near Gatwick Airport. She had assumed that the moment she revealed she had found the sick piano teacher that had sexually abused her sister she would want to seek immediate retribution. She had even re-arranged her work schedule that week in case Poppy was hell-bent on gate-crashing her tormentor's property.

But Poppy was going through a bad time. She hadn't slept well for the past few nights, plagued by constant night terrors. The thumping migraines were not helping either, she seemed to be taking more and more paracetamol each day to clear them. Her limbs ached, she constantly felt tired and weak. She was irritable and snappy. Bree had been on the end of her sharp tongue on more than one occasion that week. The slightest thing seemed to tilt her mood swings.

Her sister laughed at her when Poppy said she might have a brain tumour, causing a heated argument between the siblings. But something inside her head was not right, she knew it. she had even resisted the urge to buy alcohol for five days, despite her cravings. Strangely she seemed to have no problem sleeping. The comfort of her warm duvet seemed to be the safest place in the world to be most of the time.

On top of her ailments, she was still feeling trapped in the flat. Boredom was setting in, the mind-bending routine was becoming almost as bad as being in prison, it was draining the life out of her. She knew what time the postman delivered to the flats each day and she felt you could set Big Ben to the monotonous daily routine of the neighbours. She would never tell a living soul, but she was looking forward to her weekly trip to the police station. Her sanity was being tested at every level.

And now, to make matters worse, the banging in her head had been replaced by a continuous banging at the front door. Whoever it was, they had bypassed the downstairs security door and by the loudness of the knocking were clearly in no mood to be turned away.

As brave as Poppy was, she still peeped through the spyhole to make sure the intruder was not Neddy and his crew. She was suffering inside and felt far too weak for conflict. She would rather face another monotonous afternoon of dull television programmes than face her dreaded demons head on that day.

She had only opened the door a few inches when Kayleigh barged her way in, arms flapping around her, shouting at the house guest. 'I know it was you, Poppy, so don't lie I know it was you!'

Poppy grabbed a large apple from the fruit bowl and stood at the doorway to her bedroom. Let this crazy bitch have her say then send on her way, she thought.

The frumpy mother from the ordinary house began showing a side of herself that others had rarely seen. Red faced and breathing hard, she held out the palm of her hand and offered Poppy a get-out option. 'Just give me the money you stole, and I won't tell

Bree.' she demanded. 'You can keep the other stuff you took out of the drawer. If that's what turns you on, keep it. I just want Willow's money back.'

Poppy said nothing, she stared long and hard at the mousy girl with the mousy coloured hair and took another large bite of her juicy green apple.

'The money!' Kayleigh said again, this time raising the tone of her voice in a bid to sound more threatening. She pushed out the palm of her hand towards Poppy's face. But the only reaction her plea received was a sneer from the girl she hated more than anybody in the world. Then suddenly her new-found bravado began to shrink, in those few seconds she recognised the lifeless look in Poppy's eyes and remembered that dark stare that she had encountered that evening in the Chez Blanc Bistro. The night her opposite number had dished out a vicious headbutt that had disfigured her for life. She remembered being surrounded by bright lights in the ambulance and the searing pain that lasted in her cheekbone for several weeks. Her uncommon show of bravery began to evaporate, and she took a step backwards. She knew that this girl could never be intimidated by someone of her stature. That she would be on the losing end of any scuffle that followed. All she had left was words. 'He told me, that boy in the alley, he said he saw you go into the house.'

Still nothing from Poppy, still enjoying her fruit supplement, maybe slightly disappointed that the lairy lad she had taught a life lesson to had turned out to be a grass.

Kayleigh had lost the high ground and was now struggling with her battle of words. Her insecurities came to the fore, maybe this was the real reason she had come here on the warpath. 'I know about you and Matt, you know, he tells me everything.'

Poppy greeted her comment with a shrug of the shoulders, still more interested in her appetite.

'Matt told me you were fuck buddies, when you worked at that restaurant together. Just fuck buddies, Poppy, nothing else. He said you was cheating on your boyfriend at the time. That don't surprise me. He said It didn't mean anything to him, he said you was just an after-work shag.'

Finally, there was a reaction from her counterpart, but not the one she expected. 'Yeah, that's right, just fuck buddies. Tells you everything, does he, Matt, tells you everything?'

'We have no secrets, he loves me, Poppy, real love. Me and Willow are his life.'

Poppy was desperate to bring this intruder down a peg or two, shatter her idyllic world in one swift sentence. But she decided to keep Matt's Wednesday afternoon escapades a secret. Throwing her apple core into the bin, she readied herself for conflict.

'Is that it then, ya said want yer wanna say?'

'I just want the money back, Poppy, sixty pounds. I know how much it was because I count it every week. Do you think it fair to steal from a baby?'

'It's gone.' Poppy said bluntly. 'I spent it.'

Kayleigh's face began to turn a deep shade of red, she was struggling to come to terms with how calm her opponent was 'Well, I want it Poppy, otherwise I will have to tell Bree. She will give me the money and you can owe it her.'

Her comment did not go down well. 'Listen, girl, don't come round 'ere shouting the fuckin' odds at me. You mouthed off at me once before and look where that got ya. This is as much your fault as it is mine. I have been out over a month now, you and silly bollocks said you would find me a job, but you aint. I am skint, so I nicked a bit of money, so fuckin' what!'

'I got you that interview, at the diner in Bexley Heath, you never turned up'.

'It was 'alf way across the fuckin' country. Three fuckin' buses to get there, I wouldn't have got home 'til two in the morning'.

'Bree said she would pick you up when you finished your shift each night'.

'I don't wanna rely on her, fuck me it's bad enough living 'ere with that dozy bitch'.

'Beggars can't be choosers, Poppy. It was a decent job. The money was good for that line of work'.

'Listen, girl, I don't beg to nobody, never have done, never will do.'

'I didn't mean it like that. I just meant, it's not easy to find you a job with your, well you know, your history.'

'Cause I've done time?'

'Not just that, Poppy, everyone knows you, as soon as I typed your name on an application form, people knew who you were.'

'What about Matts place, the vegan gaff, I bet you never even tried.'

'He asked the owner, Poppy, honestly, they are fully staffed.'

'I aint lazy, I just want a job, get me the fuck out of 'ere each day. It's doing my head in, she's doing my fuckin' head in. That's probably where all these fuckin' headaches are coming from.'

'That's ungrateful, Poppy, Bree is trying so hard to make you feel welcome here.'

'And why do you do that, why do you stick up for her? I aint stupid, I can see she walks all over you, talks shit about yer behind yer back, takes you for a right mug.'

'She is my friend, Poppy, I have known her most of my life.'

'Trust me, girl, she aint nobody's friend.'

Her comment silenced Kayleigh, she wanted to defend her bestie but deep down inside her heart she knew she was right. Bree had used and abused her for most of the eighteen years they had known each other. Her harsh putdowns and snidey bullying had got worse over the years and she hardly recognised her now as the one half of inseparable duo that used to hold hands proudly when they walked to school together.

Poppy stood silent in the doorway to her bedroom, she wondered why her visitor's dramatic entrance and full-blown confrontation had fizzled out so tamely. Part of her wanted Kayleigh to strike her or at least start hurling worthwhile abuse in her direction. Anything to break the mundane monotony of being left alone in the flat. But there was nothing, the girl with the Plain Jane identity kit looked forlorn and tired. Bree had been right about one thing – her best friend certainly did resemble a mouse right down to her non-descript hairstyle and her timid nature.

'So,' Kayleigh asked much more politely than she had before. 'Will you be giving me the money back from Willow's nest egg?'

Poppy was slightly amused. 'Wouldn't have thought so. Best you run along and grass me up to your so-called mate.'

'She will only defend you,' Kayleigh sighed. 'But you know that don't you? God knows why, but you can do nothing wrong in her eyes. You could have been a mass murderer and she will still support you.'

'Yeah, shame innit!'

'Even Matt is in your corner.'

'So, he knows me, you don't. You are just a little miss fuckin' 'judgey', thinking she knows what I'm all about.'

The two girls stared long and hard at one another from opposite ends of the hallway, a moment passed without a word being said. Suddenly, without warning, Kayleigh found her feet carrying her forward at great pace until she came to an abrupt halt just inches away from her nemesis. She stood motionless for a few seconds, staring deep into the merciless eyes of her host. Then, in one crazy unexplainable moment she lunged her head forward and pressed her lips fully onto Poppy's, closing her eyes tightly as if she wanted to savour a sensuous kiss.

Poppy never moved an inch, nor did she push her away, their lips remained locked for a dozen seconds or more. Kayleigh's surprise move had certainly caught her off-guard, weakened her defences, yet heightened her senses. A small tingle ran down her spine. It was a surreal moment where neither woman knew what to do next.

Reality returned in a split second and a blushing Kayleigh found herself retreating to the safety of the front door. 'Sorry,' she said in a shame-filled manner. 'I just needed to know, I just, I just needed to know.'

'Know what?' Poppy asked, slightly breathless from the moment of madness.

'To know what it is about you that everybody loves so much. To find out why you have got so many people under your spell. I still don't know what they see in you, what makes you so special.'

'Wait!' Poppy yelled at her fleeing visitor, causing the mousy girl with the ordinary life to turn and face her embarrassment head on. Seeing the uneasy look on Kayleigh's face Poppy lowered the tone of her voice as the two girls stared long and hard beyond the space between them. 'Ya don't have to go, not if yer don't want to.'

A tiny crack appeared in Kayleigh's lips and turned into the smallest of smiles. Slowly she made her way forward and found herself in the arms of her sworn enemy. It was the strangest of feelings, as if she had found sublime safety in the mouth of a raging volcano.

The women retreated inside Poppy's bedroom and fell in a heap on the unmade bed. It was an awkward encounter, neither seeming to want to take the lead as they sheepishly removed one another's clothes. Kayleigh ran her fingers gently over her enemy's erect nipples before licking them with her tongue. Poppy felt a tingle run through her body and instantly forgot about the throbbing pains still rolling around inside her head. When both girls were fully naked they shared a long lingering kiss before their lips explored every inch of their partner's flesh. The ordinary girl was shocked at first at the sight of Poppy's bruised and scarred torso. She found herself touching those parts with the finest caress before nestling her head between her rival's legs, sending her into a frenzy of heightened sexual satisfaction. Poppy moaned, gently at first, but let out a small scream when the mousy girl's soft tongue found a magical spot just outside her soaking wet crevasse.

It seemed like much longer, but the girls spent less than an hour in bed together, sharing one another's bodies and fulfilling the craziest of sexual fantasies. Their bodies lay entwined in an erotic embrace for several minutes before Poppy left the scene to find some clothing, her legs buckling slightly as her feet found the floor.

Kayleigh was even more red-faced now that when she had entered the flat in a steaming rage. But the redness was more out of physical exertion than embarrassment. She may appear timid and weak, but she had certainly not been shy between the sheets, that's for sure!

'That aint your first time,' Poppy said, taking a long drag on her cigarette, completely unperturbed by her sisters previous telling off for smoking in the flat. 'You've definitely done that before.'

'A long time ago,' Kayleigh replied, with her tainted innocence laid bare. 'When I was at college. I sort of, well, I sort of had a crush on this girl and well one night we both got drunk and, to be honest, I can't remember too much about it.'

Poppy seemed to find their erotic encounter amusing. 'Not sure what Matt would make of it,' she said. 'It would probably give him a stiffy for a month if he knew.'

Kayleigh felt strangely at ease and laughed. 'It will be the first time he has had a boner in a long time. God, did I really say that out loud? Did you, sorry, I mean, was it in prison where you? I suppose what I'm saying is, has this been a regular thing for you. You know, like, how many times?'

'Dunno really, only a couple of times, when I was locked up in Bronzefield. I think I thought that I was never get out of that prison, so I thought well if this it for the rest of my life, I might as well give it a try.'

'Was it, I mean was I, was it, erm, you know, was it OK for you, today?'

Poppy laughed. 'Fuck me girl, ya not looking for marks out of ten are ya. I'd say a solid six, maybe seven at a push.'

Her comment bought another smile to Kayleigh's face. 'It's just that, I don't know, but me and Matt, it's just not the same anymore. He, he, Oh, nothing, I just ramble on, don't I?'

'Blokes are like that, girl, you know, hot and cold.'

'It's just since Willow came along, well, before that really, he hasn't really been near me.'

'He's alright, Matt, trust me girl he is one of the gooduns. Probably just going through a funny phase.'

'I saw him, you know, when you came over to our place that time, he couldn't take his eyes off you.'

Poppy dismissed her fears. 'Give yer head a wobble, girl, he loves the bones of you and that kid, anyone can see that.'

When she had finished her cigarette Poppy ran her fingers slowly up along her new lover's cheekbone. Kayleigh closed her eyes, not wanting to tell her sworn enemy how good it felt to be touched by a caring human hand. She was, however, slightly bemused by Poppy's observation. 'Yer know something, I think I did ya a favour, girl, ya know, when I nutted ya. It's given ya face a bit of character, makes ya look, dunno, bit sexier I suppose.'

For just a few short seconds the ordinary girl from the ordinary house felt like a Royal Princess, showered with gifts, showered with compliments, still tingling inside from their sexual tryst. She wanted to stay, to repeat their sexual workout but she had left Willow with her mother that morning and she had the baby's medication in her bag. As she lifted herself from the sweat-soaked sheets and began to get dressed she felt a warm glow inside her body. She hoped it would stay there all day or at least until she had to face the ordeal of changing a dirty nappy when she had picked up her daughter.

Poppy had made herself comfortable for the day, stretching her legs out on the sofa in the living room and switching on the big screen television. She had seen their unexpected sexual jaunt as a welcome excursion to her mundane existence but took it for exactly what it was. Two sex-starved women enjoying the thrill of a forbidden escapade. There was no romance and it was unlikely that there would ever be a repeat performance. She felt slightly subdued and at peace with the world at that moment. But as Kayleigh began a farewell speech Poppy's mood was about to turn darker than the blackest storm clouds.

'I have put my mobile number in your phone, Poppy.' Kayleigh remarked, feeling a sense of guilty misjudgement inside when she saw that her rival only had one contact number. She also added her thoughts on her hosts current predicament. 'Don't steal any more money, if you need a bit of help just call me. And please give Bree a chance. I know she can be a bit highly strung, but your sister is alright. She is truly trying her best to help you.'

'Half-sister,' was the response, as Poppy scoured the channels for something to watch. 'She's, only my half-sister.'

'But there is one thing, Poppy, something you should really talk to her about.'

'Spit it out, there's a film coming on after the news.'

'It's really not my place to say. I want to, Poppy, really, I do. But it is up to Bree to tell you. You just need to ask her the right question. Ask her about Chichester, I can't say more than that.'

But the woman on the couch was not listening to her visitor, she was absorbed in a news report on the split screen in her line of vision. One side showed a police mug shot of a pale looking girl with blotchy skin, the other a cordoned off area in a side street next to Woolwich Docks. Poppy recognised both immediately. A police officer was giving an interview about the event and a contact number for anybody who held information about the incident was listed below the pictures.

Poppy did not need that number, she flew out of her cosy position and ran to the kitchen, turning the drawers inside out until she found what she was looking for, a carving knife with a ten-inch blade. She was burning up inside with rage.

Kayleigh was half-way down the second flight of stairs when she heard a howling scream bellow out from above. It was far louder and much more ferocious than the sensual screams she had heard in the bedroom.

CHAPTER TWENTY

The sisters had not exchanged a single word since they had turned off the M23 motorway and passed Gatwick airport. The sight of low-flying aeroplanes seemed to have had a profound impact on Poppy and she puffed nervously on her cigarette once they arrived at their destination. She was still seething about the death of Lulu but needed a clear headspace and more time to plan her revenge on Neddy and his gang. Today was the turn of a wicked ghost from her past to face her wrath, the rage had been building up inside of her for most of the hour-long journey.

Bree had deliberately parked her car next to the fourteenth century church in Chapel Street, a hundred yards or so from a large cottage surrounded by a small white wooden fence. Poppy had the impression that her sister had visited this place more than once before, she seemed to know her way around the one-way system and the route from the town centre to the outskirts of Horley. Bree was applying some lip balm and checking her hair in the car mirror for the third time that day, while Poppy stared aimlessly at the surroundings streets. The sound of the nearby church bells rang out loudly close by, the three hourly chimes told them both that their 'plan' was about to start.

'This has to be the place, Poppy, you must recognise it,' Bree said, picking up her handbag from the rear seat.

Poppy lied to her sister, she was having second thoughts about how the day might unfold. 'I only lived there for a few months, it was such a long time ago.'

'Look, Poppy, it wasn't easy to find him, Kayleigh never stopped going on about how much trouble she could get in for getting us the information. The Houghtons' that live here fostered children about the time you said, and he is a retired music teacher. I know you think that the name is spelled differently but let's face it, Poppy, spelling is not exactly your strong point.'

'Yeah, but I don't get why you have done what you have done. Ya know, like booked a piano lesson with him and all that.'

'The siege of Troy, Poppy!'

'What the fuck?'

'I go in there, all dressed up, flutter my eyelashes at the old perv and suss it out. Then, he thinks everything is on the level, I make an excuse, open the front door and you come in, all guns blazing. Then we confront the sicko and...'

'Call the feds, you said we would call the police.'

'He needs to be punished for what he did. Remember, Poppy, you were probably not the only one, they fostered quite a lot of young children at that time.'

'I told you, the police aint gonna take my word against his. It was nearly twenty years ago.'

'You said his wife would speak out against him, if she knew what he was really doing.'

'Yeah, she seemed OK from what I remember, I think she would believe me.'

'You don't have anything to lose. Maybe, just maybe, if you see him locked up for what he did it will help you in some way.'

Poppy did not answer, something had suddenly caught her

attention. There in the garden, behind a series of neatly trimmed hedges she could make out the shape of that small windmill, its sails barely turning due to the lack of any breeze. She suddenly remembered when she used to look down from her bedroom window and think how out of place it looked. Just then a low-flying plane coming into land at nearby Gatwick airport made everything seem real. She knew for sure now that this was the place, this is where the final shreds of her childhood innocence were ripped apart. In an instant her demeanour had changed, and she had a stealthy determination in her voice. 'Do it,' she said. 'Do it now. Just give me a sign, when to come in.'

Bree smiled and checked her hair one last time, applying a final coat of cherry lip balm. 'Showtime!' she said, producing a sickly smile that would not have looked out of place on an evil clown.

When Poppy watched her sister stroll up to the large white house, she suddenly realised that she was dressed in the shortest skirt she had ever seen her wear. She couldn't help wondering if her sibling was getting some sort of sick pleasure out of this painful experience.

The SAAB was parked far enough away to hide her identity but close enough for Poppy to see the exchange at the front door. She felt her teeth clench and her fists tighten as the occupant appeared. It was him, it was Houghton, just the sight of him made her feel sick to the pit of her stomach. Now here he was sharing pleasantries with her sister less than a few hundred feet away. She had to work hard to fight the venomous instincts she was feeling inside

The first thing Bree noticed when she was ushered into his lair was the smell of white spirit. Her host was quick to point out that he had been re-painting the banisters on the stairs that morning and had accidentally spilled some of the cleaning fluid. He didn't look like a sexual pervert to Bree, but looks can be very deceptive. Thinning grey hair perched on a wrinkled forehead told her that her that her host was somewhere in his mid-seventies. The bowing rims on his spectacles had seen better days and he dressed like a man who had no self-respect. Bree wanted to give her professional opinion on the badly matched trousers and cardigan he had chosen to wear that day, but there were other, more pressing matters at hand.

Several pictures adorned the walls of the spacious detached cottage, it had a real rural feel about the place. A log fire blazed away in the middle of the living room. Houghton stoked it a couple of times with a thick metal poker and threw another couple of log pieces on to keep the flames alive. With the introductions and pleasantries over and done with Bree made an astute observation. 'It's a bit warm for a fire isn't it, must be seventy degrees out there today.'

Houghton raised a friendly smile. 'Oh, I feel the chill more these days, must be my old bones.'

'How old are you?' Bree asked, not sure why she should be so forward.

'Seventy-six, old in places but still young at heart.'

'You look much younger,' Bree said, in a flirty manner meant to lower his defences.

'Thank-you. that is a nice to hear, especially from such a beautiful young lady, but it won't get you a discount on your lessons.'

'Oh, sorry,' Bree said reaching inside her bag and pulling out some notes. 'We did say thirty pounds for the first hour, didn't we?'

Taking the money Houghton offered a sickly smile. 'My pension doesn't pay much so every little helps. I don't do many of these lessons nowadays, not since, well...'

'Since what?'

Houghton hesitated for a few seconds, he seemed to be getting slightly emotional. 'My good lady wife, Alice, she died last year, it has been a bit tough really, but I soldier on the best I can.'

'I am so sorry to hear that.'

'That's her, up there,' Houghton remarked, pointing to two photographs sitting either side of a marble urn. 'We would have been married forty-five years next Friday. This place feels so empty without her. I suppose having her ashes so close to me reminds me that we all must go someday. I know we will see each other again. I know she will be waiting for me up there.'

Bree completely ignored his sombre tone, if this really was her sister's abuser, she had nothing but hatred for this vile pervert. Besides, if everything her sister told her was true, his wife would be waiting 'up there' a long time for this man. His kind only end up in place and it surely isn't heaven.

'There is no piano,' Bree observed looking around the living room.

'No, not out here, I have a special room, my music room, its over there in the corner.'

Bree followed his lead, taking a long hard stare at the pictures of his departed spouse, wondering deep down if she knew what sort of man she was really married to.

'You said on the phone that you can play a bit, some simple stuff, you said that on the phone, didn't you?' Houghton asked.

Bree laughed. 'Real basic stuff, you know, like Frere Jacques and Chopsticks. I am good at that one, I liked playing Chopsticks, but I haven't played anything since I was a small, like seven or eight years old. Is that, OK?'

There was an awkward silence, Houghton seemed to be looking her up and down, his wayward mind most likely picturing her in a primary school uniform. Bree noticed his wandering eye, she felt queasy. It made her skin crawl as the pair entered the music room and Houghton declared, 'Oh, I bet you was such a beautiful child.'.

'I am a bit warm in here, can I take my jacket off?' Bree asked.

'Of course, there is a coat rack next to the front door.'

Bree left Houghton arranging the seats by the piano in his special room and headed back into the warm living area. She slipped her coat over a hook on the rack before unlocking the front door, leaving it slightly ajar. Taking a deep breath and tugging her short skirt down slightly she returned to the arena.

The frail old man ushered her to the two chairs parked closely together and closed the door. 'Now, before we start, let's see what you can do. Do you know how to run up the scales on the piano?'

'No, but I can do this,' she replied, and began pounding away at the keys on the finely tuned piano. The distorted racket caused the tutor to wince as she produced a horrendous rendition of Chopsticks. To make matters worse she insisted on making a loud sound on every note. 'Dah dah dah dah dah dah, de de de de de de, dah dah dah dah dah dah, dah'.

Houghton laughed and tried to give her some encouragement 'Yes, that is Chopsticks but you are out of key. You need to take your time, take things slowly.'

'Watch me,' he said. 'Like this, gentle strokes, let your fingers glide across the keys.'

A growing hatred was building inside her as she checked his smarmy smile and studied his evil withering old fingers. She needed to release that mounting rage within. She vented her anger on the keys of the piano, this time thumping each key much harder and singing much louder than before. 'Dah dah dah dah dah dah, de de de de de de, dah dah dah dah dah dah, da'.

'God, I am really terrible at this.' she said pretending to be upset. 'I just wanted to learn something special to play for my mother on her birthday, but I am really hopeless, aren't I?'

Suddenly, Bree felt a clammy set of fingers touching her skin and looked down to see Houghton's hand on her bare knee. He quickly removed the offending body part and apologised. 'Tut, tut, clumsy hands,' he said apologetically.

Bree gave the old man a harsh stare but played along with the game. 'You really should know better at your age, Mister Houghton.'

Meanwhile, Poppy had entered the property through the open front door and was standing in familiar surroundings. The furniture may have been replaced but those harrowing memories hadn't. She studied the photograph of the late Mrs Houghton, remembering how the large-framed woman taught her to cook eggs and bake cakes. Despite displaying a warm smile in that picture, her eyes told a different story, they seemed full of sadness. Poppy remembered how her husband would shout at her when she spoke out of turn or when she spent too much time on the phone to her sick mother. She never saw him raise her hand to her, but she could tell that his wife was frightened of him, often retreating to the safety of her bedroom when he was in one of his foul moods.

Poppy had a head full of painful memories and bad thoughts as she crept stealthily around the living area. The only thing she found strange was the smell of the cleaning fluid in a bottle on the mantelpiece. Mrs Houghton had always had three or four vases full of bright fresh smelling flowers on the tables when she had lived here, but they had been replaced with insignificant ornaments and tacky table mats. She screwed up her face as she heard the terrible din coming from the music room. Her sisters' horrendous piano playing really was creating a noticeable distraction, which allowed her to survey her old abode uninterrupted. When she turned towards the fireplace, she saw the metal poker in the hearth. It was the same one that he had once threatened her with when he was scolding her for misbehaving.

In Houghton's lair, the old man was becoming increasing frustrated with the antics of his new pupil. She seemed to be ignoring his tutoring and continually pounding the keys on the piano like a one-year-old child with a brand-new toy. He was beginning to wish he could put an end to this torturous lesson. But every time he showed Bree some sample hand movements she would revert to a thumping version of Chopsticks, accompanied of course by her out of key voice. He decided it better to let the hour play out its course and then make his excuses if any further lessons were booked.

But just then, a moment of silence, peace and quiet, all that could be heard was the bottom of the music room door as it brushed across the badly worn carpet. Both master and pupil turned as one to face the truth. Houghton recognised the long poker in the hand of the intruder but for those first few seconds he did not recognise the angry face staring down at him.

'Oh, I think you know my sister,' Bree said, in a smarmy, self-satisfied tone. 'Say hello, Poppy, say hello to Mister Houghton.'

The smiling eyes on the withering old face soon lost their sheen as the music teacher put the name and the face together. He began to tremble slightly as Poppy walked towards him, the angry expression on her face warning him that Karma had finally found him out. A sense of impending danger suddenly washed over his body. But before he could open his mouth to speak, he felt the full force of the poker catch the side of his neck, it knocked him sideways off the piano stool and on to the hard floor. He wobbled slightly as he tried to get to his feet, but then a second blow reigned down om him, catching the base of his skull. The impact caused him to him to yank hard on the bookcase and a hundred or more music books fell on top of his fragile old body. A head full of cheering voices goaded Poppy on, reminding her of those terrible crimes he had committed. As the assault gathered pace, Poppy dropped the poker and aimed a few well-placed punches and kicks into his ribs and chest. Bree busied herself by striking the keys of the piano, she was completely out of tune, not that anybody was now listening to the awful racket she was making. 'Dah dah dah dah dah dah, de de de de de de, dah, dah dah dah dah dah, dah. It was another clumsy and ham-fisted version of her new favourite song. She didn't care what others might think, she felt she played it so well. She smiled blissfully, thumping the badly collated chords repeatedly, drowning out the groaning and moaning noises to the side of her chair.

Suddenly, Poppy halted her assault, she was slightly out of breath and her knuckles had begun to bleed. She took one step back and saw the frightened old man cowering beneath her. His face was covered in blood. Houghton's wiry old fingers began dragging his beaten carcass across the floor. He groaned loudly as the break gave him a chance to absorb the excruciating pain in his chest. Realising her sister had ceased the attack, Bree stopped playing. She turned her head slowly to survey the damage that had been done. She looked at the helpless old pensioner sprawled out on the floor. A pitiful expression on the pervert's face seemed lost on the sisters now, they could clearly see that the old man was fighting for his life. When Bree raised her eyes to catch her sister's stare, a sinister and heartless smile appeared. It was one Poppy recognised, it was the same one she had seen before in the mirror. 'You have to finish this now, Poppy, you know that don't you, you have to finish this, now.'

Those scratchy voices reeling around inside her head agreed, they applauded her sibling, demanding that Poppy do what her Bree had told her to do. They had waited for this day for almost twenty years. 'He needs to die,' they screamed. 'You need to do this.'

There was a moment of silence and confusion. Houghton was breathing was heavily, he was clearly struggling to keep his eyes open. He stretched his fingers out in Bree's direction as a final plea for salvation. He could sense his time on this earth slipping away. Poppy, however, resisted the urge to continue her revenge attack, she was done with him. 'He is weak now,' she said. 'Just a weak old man, he can't me hurt me no more. We need to go. We need to leave now.'

She looked down and took one last look at the pathetic pervert. In her twisted and confused mind, she questioned why she had ever let the evil things this man did to her dictate her whole life. He was feeble, he was weak. She suddenly felt ashamed that she had not done this sooner. Her sister was right about one thing, she felt better now. She felt as though a large dark cloud above her head had finally moved away and let in vast rays of warm sunshine.

As Poppy made her way back to the car she had one last task, she headed for the windmill. Gripping hard on one of the sails she ripped it from its stanchion before repeating the exercise with the others. She was hell bent on destroying the whole feature, but suddenly something stopped her in her tracks. A sound, long lingering chimes of enchanting beauty, haunting, mystical, magical. She felt her feet turn back towards the door of the house. Something was calling her, beckoning her back to the music room. She found all her other senses has stopped working, as if she was in a trance. Those hypnotic notes were luring her back into the house. As she reached Houghton's room of evil doings, she saw her sister, perched in an aura of magnificence on the chair. She saw her perfectly groomed blond locks swaying gently on her shoulders as her head moved gently from side to side. Her eyes were closed tightly, not that there was any music to see, nor required. Bree seemed to know each heartfelt chord as if she had played this song ten million times. She brushed her nimble fingers, gliding them majestically across the piano. She stroked each key with such grace, caressing every single note that bought perfect tranquillity amidst the craziness and brutality unfolding inside this den of evil today.

Poppy stood in the doorway of the music room, she was dumbstruck, completely in awe of the amazing spectacle. It had captured her heart, released her soul from torment. Her head slowly cleared of dark thoughts and was filled with vivid daydreams of open fields and sunny days. She could see a busy boating lake, hear the laughter of small children, the smile of her father as he arrived with two oversized ice creams. Happy days, such happy days.

Houghton shuffled his body sideways beneath her feet as he turned his head to view this golden goddess sat on his creaky music chair. His eyes misted over. He too felt every single beautiful note as if it was being played by the very angels that he hoped were waiting for him. He allowed himself a small smile for being so foolish to believe that a creature of such flawless elegance could ever have tricked him. This was indeed the most beautiful rendition of Beethoven's Moonlight Sonata he had ever heard. If this was to be his final calling, his last day on earth, then he was thankful that the tones of this melodic masterpiece would still be in his memory. It was like a beautiful sorbet refreshing the pallet after a poor meat feast.

As the song reached a triumphant crescendo, Poppy looked long and hard at her sibling, still pulling at heartstrings with the adorable magic in her fingertips. She realised that her sister was indeed talented, a shining star in a universe of darkness. She knew that Bree could have had the world at her feet and that she could master anything and be loved and adored by all those that fell humbly at her feet. She should have been proud to share the same blood as this music maestro.

Almost as sporadically as it started the music came to an end, those final few notes playing out in harmonious symmetry. Bree clasped her hands together, her head held high as if she was embracing the applause of a concert hall full of music lovers. It was nothing less than she deserved, it had been a perfect, she knew that, Houghton knew that, even Poppy, who had never heard a classical ensemble played in her life, knew that. But the strangest of thoughts ran through Poppy's head during those few seconds. She was in no doubt that her sister was indeed talented beyond anything she could have ever imagined. The simple beauty of that performance had moved her like she had never been moved before, stirring hidden emotions from the depths of her battered body and her tormented soul. But she also realised at that moment that her sister had lied to her. That Bree's mother had been telling the truth all along. That deceit did not sit well with Poppy, it did not sit well at all!

Bree gently closed the lid of the piano as if she was closing the chapter of a book. She looked across the floor at the crumbled old man, his face covered in blood, his feeble arms and ancient hands outstretched, begging for assistance. His eyes pleading for some mercy to be shown. Bree scowled at him and turned her head to see that her sister was no longer standing in the doorway. She turned her attention back to the frail old carcass lying on the floor. Houghton's old bony fingers were scraping at the carpet, he was trying to pull himself to a place of safety. He suddenly found the strength to say a few words, words of hope, words of desperation 'Please,' he mumbled. 'Please help me.'

But his plea went unheard. Bree was angry that her sibling had let this man off the hook. She thought for a few seconds before rising from her seat, kicking over the music chair as she made her way into the living room. Houghton pulled harder on the strands of carpet as he dragged himself a few inches nearer the door. He hoped that his ordeal was finally over. But those thoughts vanished when he looked up and saw Bree standing over him, her two hands clasped tightly around the urn carrying his wife's ashes. The beauty had vanished from her face and replaced with a cold callousness. Once again, he asked for salvation. 'Please, please help me,' he begged.

A small shake of her head confirmed what the stricken man already knew. 'You said you wanted to be reunited with your wife, didn't you?' she asked, raising the vessel above her head. In an instant Bree used all the strength in her arms to bring the urn crashing down on to his wrinkled head. A plume of grey dust filled the air as the ashes of his wife covered the room.

Bree brushed herself down and cleared her throat, retreating to the living room as the old man inhaled the dust particles of his dearly departed. But she had not finished. She returned with both the bottle of white spirit and a smouldering log which had been sitting in the hearth of the fireplace. Almost unconscious, Houghton watched on as she sprinkled generous drops of the liquid in the bottle on to his large collection of music books. In the calmest of manners, she then sprinkled a small stream of the inflammable solution across the carpet. At that moment her plan was put on pause by the sound of the horn in her car, her sister was clearly getting impatient and wanted to get away from the scene of the crime. But there was a stealthy determination in Bree's face, she had not come all this way to let this evil man get away with his sick crimes against her own flesh and blood. She lowered the slow burning log downwards towards the path of noxious fluid and watched panic set in. All hope of salvation had now disappeared from Houghton's eyes.

'Oops,' she said dropping the fiery end of the stick onto the floor. 'Clumsy hands, silly me.'

It took less than ten seconds for the liquid to ignite and run a rapid path across the music room floor. The old man had by now accepted his fate and closed his eyes. Maybe he was hoping that his ever-forgiving wife would be waiting for him at the pearly gates. But his star pupil told him in no uncertain terms where she thought he would be heading. 'Burn in hell, you filthy bastard,' she said, as she calmly left the room.

Poppy was very animated as she watched her sister give herself a final wipe down before getting into the driver's seat. She had been fighting off those demons inside her head again. They were angry with her for not delivering the final retribution they had demanded for Houghton. Poppy was desperate to get away from the property, for her this was over now, she had done what she came to do.

But her sister was not in a rush, brushing her hair and checking her reflection in the mirror before applying a top-up from a new stick of cherry lip balm. She checked the wing mirror on the Saab and could see plumes of grey smoke rising out of the side window of the cottage, as the flames ripped through the music room. And as cool and as calculated as she always was, Bree started the engine on her car. 'I'm famished,' she said with a cheeky smile. 'Let's find a nice place down on the coast for a late lunch.'

CHAPTER
TWENTY-ONE

An uneasy silence ensued as the fading lights of a lone streetlamp guided two figures through the dark and damp alleyway. As the pair came to a sudden halt, their shallow silhouettes retreated to a place of safety, finding refuge amongst the deepening shadows. There was an ill wind that had bought the sisters to this place. Since leaving the idyllic cottage in Horley they had spent most of the time avoiding any discussion surrounding the events of the day. Bree had given her car a decent run-out that afternoon, driving all the way to Brighton and along the coastline in search of a suitable place to eat. Apart from ordering food and beverages and a limited amount of small talk, nothing was said. Even on the return journey, when a speeding motorcyclist swerved in front of the SUV, both remained tight-lipped. But now, as night fell, here in the relative security of a walkway behind some small local shops in Oxley, they both knew that things needed to be said. As restless minds worked overtime the women found themselves face to face. Words were not spoken but the sisters shared a glance that told its own story.

Suddenly the hollow barking of a stray dog and the frantic screams of a nearby police siren bought a feeling of harsh reality to this dark place. Bree busied herself on her mobile phone, frantically checking the Surrey newsfeed for any updates. The fact that there was no news was good news.

Poppy perched herself on a small red brick wall and watched her sister bury her thoughts inside the tiny handset. Her head was a tumultuous sea of rage and confusion, there were things that bothered her now. She twisted back her honey brown hair and sucked hard on her bruised knuckles, wincing slightly at the taste of her own blood. She was first to break the stony silence. 'She never smiles,' she said in a hushed voice, almost as if she was speaking to herself. 'The girl in the pictures, she never smiles.'

Bree glanced down at her sister, ignoring her remark, she re-focused her attention to the screen on her phone.

Things needed to be said. 'She never smiles,' Poppy repeated. 'That girl in the pictures, she should be happy, but she never smiles.'

'What are you wittering on about?' Bree asked, shaking her head at her sibling's seemingly trivial remark.

'Why don't she never smile? Not in any of those pictures, that don't make sense.'

'What?'

'The girl, the one in all of them pictures on your walls.'

'My Luna Sard collection?'

'Yeah, that's it, all of them pictures are the same girl, but she don't ever smile, not in any of them.'

Bree flicked back her hair and rolled her eyes, she was slightly agitated by her ramblings but decided to humour her sister 'And, and, what...?'

'You, you said, you told me that geezer painted them, the weird bloke, the one who thought he was supposed to be a woman. You said he was trapped in a body he didn't wanna be in. He wanted to be someone else.'

'Really, Poppy, have we got time for this nonsense?'

'Just saying, she should be happy, but she don't smile, that don't make sense.'

Bree laughed at her sister's strange observation. 'Oh, I see, sorry Poppy, I didn't realise you was such an expert on post modern art. You must have forgot to tell me about that. Did you do a university degree while you were sitting in your prison cell?'

Poppy felt awkward now, it showed on her face, but it didn't stop her sister poking fun at her expense. 'Maybe we will see you on the television soon, on one of those art programmes, giving your opinion on Henri Monet or Claude Matisse. It seems you have a hidden talent after all.'

Poppy was fed up with her sisters put down, she knew she could never win an argument against Bree's superior intelligence. She knew she could not win that battle, but she decided to fight back, determined to wipe that smug expression from her face. 'Maybe that's you in the pictures, maybe you like them weird pictures so much cause it's you that's trapped in a body you don't want to be in. Maybe it's you that wants to be someone else.'

'What, like you!?' Bree scoffed. 'You really think I want to be like you, Poppy?'

'Not me, nah, nah, not me. Like Jamie, I think you want to be like your brother. I think you were jealous of him. I think you still are.'

Bree moved closer, towering over her sister, she began to raise her voice, clearly not appreciating her siblings' comments. 'Don't talk about Jamie, you didn't know him, you have no right to talk about him.'

'From what you told me, he was alright, your brother, he was an OK bloke, he weren't cracked in the head like you are.'

'Oh, I see, cracked in the head am I Poppy?'

'Yeah, you're fuckin' cuckoo girl, just full of lies and shit and definitely cracked in the head.'

'You are the crazy one, Poppy, you, it's you that is cracked in

226

the head. Normal people don't go around bashing up drug dealers and beating up helpless old men.'

Poppy smiled, the strangest of smiles. 'What do normal people then, missy? Send themselves slushy valentines cards from their dead brother, is that what normal people do?'

Brees face turned to thunder, and her voice went up at least two levels. 'How dare you, Poppy Jarvis! How dare you go down my personal things. All I do for you'.

'Ya see, I couldn't work it out first, you know, where I had seen that writing. Then I remembered, all of them letters you sent me when I was in prison. It was that one word, *always*, and that letter *Y*, nobody does a curly tail on that letter like you do.'

'Oh, I see Poppy, an expert in handwriting as well as an art critic. Whatever next my sweetest sister? Seriously, I think the adrenalin rush has gone to your head today. You do have the strangest of notions.'

'Deny it then.'

'I don't need to justify myself to you.'

'Nah, cause its true, ya know it's true, ya sent them cards to yourself, yer mad bitch.'

'All I ever try to do, Poppy, is help you and protect you. I just want to give you the best life I can.'

'Yeah, right, like that shit today?'

'Oh, sorry, are you going to thank me for finding him, your tormentor?'

'You fuckin' knew, didn't ya?'

'Knew what?'

'Ya knew there was no way I would call the filth. Not when I saw him, not when it all came back to me.'

'He deserved everything he got.'

'Maybe, but that's what you wanted, weren't it? All that banging on about police and justice, it was just bullshit.'

'I can't help it if you can't control your temper, Poppy.'

'I don't try to be something I aint. Ya see I am working you out, girl, all this shit with you and your brother, it aint right, it's fucked up.'

'Shut up about Jamie, you didn't know him, so shut up about him. He still talks to me, he guides me. You know he told me he doesn't like you, Poppy, he said I deserve better.'

'He's dead, for fucks sake girl, get it into your thick head, he's dead, he aint coming back, he's dead.'

'You don't know what me and Jamie have, you could never know, Poppy, because nobody has ever loved you like he loves me.'

'And now he is dead.'

'No, he is still with me.'

'He is dead, missy, dead, get it into your thick skull. Jamie is dead, just dust and bones in the fuckin' ground. He is dead, dead, dead, dead, dead...'

As that final word left her mouth Poppy found herself on the receiving end of a forceful smack as the palm of her sister's hand connected with the side of her face. In an instant Poppy rose to her feet just in time to prevent another swipe at her. She grabbed her sister's wrist and held it tightly. They were inches apart now, lips were twitching, eyes locked in a duel of their darkest hidden thoughts. 'That's the first and last time ya ever get away with that, girl, I swear down,' Poppy said, through gritted teeth, before releasing her grip on her sister's arm and turning her back to walk away. She left her sibling with a parting warning. 'He is coming for you, missy, trust me, that big bad wolf is coming for you.'

'What are you talking about?'

'I don't need your shit anymore, I am gonna get myself totally pissed and a good hard shagging. Don't wait up for me.'

'Come back here, Poppy, don't walk away from me!'

Her sister ignored her request and stepped into the shadows. 'If your dead brother really does talk to you, he will tell you that you're cray, you're a fuckin' fruit loop. Keep taking the pills, girl, keep taking those fuckin' pills.'

'You are the crazy one, not me, it's you Poppy, you are the crazy one!'

'Watch out for that big bad wolf girl, he don't take no prisoners.'

'Don't you dare walk away from me, Poppy Jarvis! Come back here, come back here right now!'

*

Their argument had left a bitter taste in both the siblings' mouths. Neither one of them could understand the actions or words of the other. Bree had expected her sister to be eternally grateful for giving her free reign to carry out her own brand of justice on the sick music teacher that had caused her so much pain. Poppy felt trapped, knowing that her sister had set her up to do exactly what she had wanted her to. She felt no obligation to be thankful to her sibling, she did not feel in her debt. If anything, she wished she had never made the journey to Horley that day to visit those ghosts of her past. She needed a drink, a very large drink to help her forget what had happened.

Bree needed to find some comfort too, she re-visited the only place where she could relay her thoughts to someone who truly understood her. She arrived at the Maple Crossing just in time to see the 11.06 rattle between the barrier gates. Her excursion gave her a few moments to digest the events of the day. She was furious that her sister could not understand the connection she still had with Jamie. Angry that she refused to accept that he never left her thoughts for one single second, that she felt his pain as he waited in eternity for his soul mate to join him. She was sad that Poppy would never understand the undying love that the twins had for one another.

Poppy only managed to achieve one of her two aims that night. Several unsuspecting patrons of the Rising Sun public house, a few miles outside Oxley, had been happy to buy the lone stranger in town a few drinks. But when the alcohol had taken hold, her outrageous flirting and filthy gesturing came into play. She made several unruly advances towards a few regulars of the pub which got her evicted from the bar. She ended the night alone, clutching a large bottle of vodka she had stolen from a late-night mini mart. The amount of alcohol she had consumed that evening would have floored most people. But she was looking to put another dark day behind her and gave no second thoughts to the consequences. She had certainly drunk enough to dismiss the threat of another of those banging hangovers she had been suffering all week.

By the time she found her way back to Albermarle Court she was in no fit state for a reconciliatory conversation. She had no intention of making the peace with her sister that night. The flat was in total darkness when she let herself in. Poppy was in a playful mood. A bell sounded inside her head telling her it was time for round two.

'Oh, Breeaannna,' she shouted, as she wobbled her way into her home. 'Breeaannna, it's time to play.'

As she switched the lights on in the hallway the first thing that she noticed was broken glass and a badly disfigured picture on the hall floor. She made her way to the living room where she found that two more pictures had been ripped from the wall and were in a similar condition. The door to her bedroom was half open, just enough for her to see that her sister had decided to take her rage out on the complete collection of weird illustrations that had no logical reverence. Poppy laughed and took a swig of the stolen vodka. Treading over the fragments of shattered glass she made her way to her sister's bedroom. She was not going to let the tantrums of a spoilt child ruin her fun for the evening. She did, however, lower the tone of her voice as she entered the room.

'Oh, Breeeaaannna, are ya coming out to play?'

But Bree was not in the mood for her sibling's cruel banter. Her face pushed tightly into the dampened pillowcase beneath her head. Her beautiful blonde locks seemed to have lost their sheen and been replaced with a dangling tangled mass. The space beneath her eyes was red raw as though she had cried herself to sleep.

Poppy could see that the final two pictures from the collection had been smashed in unison with their counterparts and were hanging loosely from opposite walls in the bedroom. She noticed the pretty flowered bin in the corner of the room was tipped over and saw the covers of the greeting's cards had been bent and torn and had been discarded. She crept past her sister's bed and leaned down to survey the damage. Another gulp of alcohol was devoured, not that it was needed. Poppy placed the half-empty bottle of vodka on the floor and began to collect the self-written tokens of love. She carefully unfolded each card and did her best to straighten them, trying hard to repair the damage that had been done. She had to focus hard to make out the writing. 'I will love you til the, I think that says sands, yeah, I will love you til the sands of time run dry. I like that one, it's my favourite'. she said, in a mocking voice. 'Oh, yeah, and that word again, *Always*, with the curly tail on the *Y*. And kisses, don't forget the kisses.'

Poppy did her best to unfold the cards, she placed them in a neatly presented exhibition on her sibling's dressing table, as if today was a day of celebration. 'Ahhhh, see that's nice, missy,' she said, proud of her display. 'See, he really did love you.' Poppy laughed to herself. 'You really are a fuckin' looney tune, girl.'

As Poppy leaned over Bree's bed, she saw a close-up of the damage that the argument had caused. Her sisters' snores were broken by the tiny snuffles of an uncleared throat, she had never seen her sister so broken. Strange thoughts ran through her mind, perhaps it was the first time that she realised a sisterly connection really existed between the two of them. It was a rare emotion that she felt, for a few seconds she began to regret the things she had said, despite the fact they needed saying. Maybe she never realised just how fragile her sister was.

Poppy's voice was slurry, there was an unusual hint of empathy in her tone, almost caring. 'Ya see, girl, I wouldn't let nobody hurt ya, I think ya know that. But that big bad wolf, he aint gonna be on your doorstep, he aint gonna come knocking at the door. Ya see, missy, he is inside your head, like he is inside my head. Like he has always been inside my fuckin' head. I can't stop him.'

Poppy reached out her hand and stoked the reddened skin on her sibling's face. 'But there's two of us now, girl, we are gonna be OK, me and you, we will be alright.'

As Poppy stumbled her way across the floor and retreated to her bedroom, a tear, a large tear of sobering pain and sadness escaped from the corner of Bree's eye and ran along her cheek.

CHAPTER TWENTY-TWO

The past is a long and winding corridor littered with small rooms, some with doors you chose to open, others, maybe those carrying warning signs, that you chose to ignore. But you cannot change the fact that you are here now. That you have reached this place in your life and that the decisions you make today will determine your fate tomorrow. Should you open the door on your left or your right or simply let others make those decisions which will shape your future.

There had been an unnatural silence since a worried parent arrived at her daughter's flat that morning. Neither of the women knew what the other was thinking. Maybe that was a good thing. Bree had decided to offer her mother an olive branch and had agreed to spending time with her to resolve their issues. She asked for three things from her parent, these were unconditional requirements for her to activate a truce. Honesty, however brutal it might be. If she wanted more information about her real father, it must not be muddied in the murky waters of her mother's own perception of the three yearlong sexual relationship.

Secondly, there must be no mentions whatsoever of further counselling. Her mother could no longer bribe her as she had done since she had been a small child with the enticement of expensive holidays and high fashion clothing. There were to be no bargaining tools placed on the table. She made it clear to her mother that she knew she still suffered with mental health issues, left hanging and unbalanced, since Jamie's sad death. But her destiny was to be left in her own hands.

The third demand was that her mother had to accept that Poppy was her sister, her true flesh and blood, and that she would be a permanent fixture in her life. Krista would find this the hardest demand to adhere to. She would have liked to have asked her offspring one question. Which of them her daughter would choose if a decision had to be made? But, in truth, that answer was probably the only thing that was crystal clear in her head when she boarded the plane in the early hours of that morning at Helsinki Airport.

Their hour-long phone conversation the previous evening was by far the longest the two of them had spoken to each other in many months. It started in a formal manner but began to move forward when Krista suggested that she would do her best to address her daughter by her shortened name. She knew that would be a struggle for her, but she would make any sacrifices she needed to get her foot back in the door at Albermarle Court. There was no mention in the call of either Dr Fitzgerald or the shocking revelations of the report.

During the flight to England, Krista began to wonder where everything had turned sour in their relationship. She remembered how quickly her daughter had gone from being a sulky child to a rebellious teen, often starving herself for days if she did not get her own way. However, every time Krista saw a happy memory from her daughter's childhood flash through her head, she countered it with dark thoughts. There were too many bad things that had happened over the past decade to put them all down to co-incidence. There were questions she never dared ask her daughter in fear that the truth would be too heart-breaking for her to handle. Krista never knew why those flickering flames of anger her daughter had displayed as a child turned into a raging wildfire of hatred. To make matters worse it seems as if Bree would pour the salts of bitter resentment into her own wounds. She truly believed that her daughter thought that by hurting herself she would make her mother suffer more.

It had been refreshing to see her offspring greet her with a warm smile and a tight hug when she entered the flat, a good start, she thought. Bree explained, without holding back on any of the details, that it was Poppy's signing day at the police station so she would be gone for a few hours and the two of them would not be interrupted. Her mother was surprised to see that the series of Luna Sard paintings had all been taken down and been replaced with enlarged family photographs from their old house. She never asked her daughter why but assumed that it was part of the 'fresh start,' she had mentioned during their call.

Bree opened the conversation with a small apology. 'I am sorry about the crystal piano. It was a really nice thought, I just lost my temper, so I am very sorry.'

Her mother was quick to take the blame for her daughters' previous outburst. 'It was my fault. I should never have said what I did. Of course, I will never love anybody as much as you and Jamie. You two were always my whole world, you always will be.'

Bree looked disappointed at her mother's remark. 'We said honesty today, mother, total honesty.'

Krista nodded, wondering how strong that newfound understanding would last when she revealed the truth about the genetic disorder that her daughter might have. But for the time being she was happy to play along with the rules of the game.

'Coffee, mother? 'Bree asked, the warm smile returning to her face. 'I bought some of that special Columbian one, you used to like that one.'

'Perfect' her mother replied. 'To be honest I feel a bit tired after that journey today. That flight seems to be getting longer or maybe I am just getting older'.

'Are you staying with Aunt Millie, tonight? I would say you could stay here, but with Poppy staying and everything.'

'It's fine, darling, Millie is expecting me, I said I would be over at hers sometime this evening. She is making dinner, meatballs in her special sauce.'

Krista studied some of her daughter's photography folders that had been left out on the table, thumbing her was through a montage of gritty pictures of life in the gutter. She smiled broadly when she thought how talented her daughter was but did not comment on her fine work in fear of upsetting then mood of the day. She accepted a small tray with a large coffee mug and a plate with a few plain biscuits on the side.

'No coffee for you, Brianna? I mean, sorry, Bree.'

'Bad for my anxiety apparently. I have been cutting down a lot, just two cups a day now. I think it is helping.'

Krista saw an opening and took it. 'I was going to ask about your anxiety, but before you say anything I am not going to preach to you about counselling.'

'I have good days and bad, like before really. I have realised that it's something I have to learn to live with.'

'But you are sleeping better, no more of those terrible nightmares.'

'I sleep like a baby mother.'

'Speaking of babies, I must call in to see Kayleigh and her lovely little Willow. How old is she now? She must be three months or more.'

It became obvious to her mother that Bree had not appreciated her comment. She was finding the strains of their re-ignited relationship harder than she thought she would. She suddenly became tearful, the coffee cup in her hand was visibly shaking. 'I am so sorry, Brianna, I mean Bree, I am going to try, really I am.

I have done a lot of thinking these past few weeks. I know I have made mistakes, a million of them. But I just want my daughter back. I realise now that it is my fault, I lost you, a long time ago. I just want you back in my life now.'

The two women did not hug, and that moment passed. They sat down together and Bree showed her mother a collection of photographs that she had printed out that morning, some of which she revealed would be in the next issue of Kendra's magazine. Krista had never been a fan of her daughter's boss. They had clashed the one and only time they had met. She thought it best to keep her thoughts to herself and simply admire the artistry of her a high-class fashion photographer that just happened to be her daughter.

They shared the biscuits on the tray and discussed upcoming fashion events for half an hour. But Krista was struggling to finish her second cup of coffee. She told her daughter she was feeling tired and woozy, the jet lag seemed to be kicking in. 'I know the flight is only three hours but getting to Helsinki was a nightmare this morning and well, the traffic from Heathrow, that was horrendous. That journey really has taken its toll.'

'Crash out for an hour if you like, I've just changed the sheets on Poppy's bed.'

Krista felt a little dizzy when she got to her feet and her daughter was quick to assist. 'Are you sure you weren't at the vodka on the plane, mother? You are all over the place.'

Krista laughed, a faint laugh 'I really must be getting old, I am so sorry darling, maybe a little nap will bring me back to normal. I just feel tired, that's all.'

Bree drew the curtains, leaving a small gap in the middle to let in some fresh air from the open window. 'Take your time, mother, Poppy won't be back for ages yet. I have some work to do anyway.'

'Bless you, darling, I am so pleased we had that chat on the phone, I feel so much better about things now.'

Bree smiled as her visitor stretched out on the freshly made bed. She watched on as her mother's eyelids slowly lost their battle with the daylight beaming through the small gap in the curtains. Even though the temperature was soaring outside there was a bitter coldness in the room when Bree's painted on smile disappeared without a trace. It was replaced with a look of hatred and contempt. Then, as her mother lost her battle to stay awake, Bree began to whisper small words, hardly legible, almost incoherent. It was if she was talking to somebody else sitting in the corner of the room.

Her plan had worked, so far. Despite the fact she knew that there was absolutely no logic in the action she was about to take, she knew that there was nothing stopping her now. Her mother now peaceful in a heavy slumber, laying helpless, totally unaware of the evil thoughts racing through her daughter's head.

*

Bree sat in silence in her living room for the next couple of hours, her mind was in the hands of others now. Part of her wanted to fight the demons inside her head but she knew she was not strong enough. A slam of the front door revealed that Poppy had returned from her weekly trip to the police station. She was not in a good mood and was more than happy to share the reasons for her anger. 'Cunts!' she screamed. 'All of them, just cunts!'

Her sister was amused by her tantrum, 'What have they done now?'

'I gotta go on some fuckin' course, aint I, all the way to fuckin' Streatham.'

'No, what's that for?'

'Some job search shit they do, if I don't go, I don't get no money. This is all down to you, you and that fuckin' Kayleigh, you said she would sort me out a job.'

'I thought you said they were OK with you at the Work Programme Centre.'

'I hate the geezer at the place. I swear down, if he laughs at me again next week, I will deck him.'

'Did you eat when you were out, did you get something?'

'What with, shirt buttons? I'm fuckin' skint aint I? Have to pay me own fuckin fares now as well.'

'You're hungry then, do you want me to…'

'Starving. Don't worry I'll make myself some beans on toast.'

'Beans again, Poppy, that's the fourth time this week.'

'What are you the fuckin' food police? I like beans.'

'Sit down, I will make it for you.'

'Cheers, ears.'

'We have a visitor today, remember, I told you.'

'Oh yeah, that's why you aint at work, your old girl was coming over from, em ehh…'

'Finland, Poppy, I must have told you twenty times she lives in Finland.'

'Yeah, that's it, Finland. What happened did she blow you out?'

'No, she's here, that's her bag on the side. I don't think she's very well. She is asleep. I put her on your bed, I hope you don't mind.'

'Nah, that's alright, I am going out later anyway.'

'I thought you didn't have any money.'

'Well, you can sub me a few quid, cant ya? I'll pay yer back when I sort out the job shit money.'

'Your personal banker as well as your personal skivvy, what next, do you want me to chauffeur you to the shops and back?'

'For fucks sake, don't get all shitty about it, I won't ask ya for any dosh then.'

'I didn't say it was a problem, Poppy, I just don't like being taken for granted. Of course, I will sort some money out for you.'

'Cheers. I will pay yer back, once I've sorted things.'

Poppy opened the door to her bedroom to see that her sister was not spinning her another yarn, while her sister served up a generous helping of baked beans surrounded by triangles of toasted bread. She also bought her a large scoop of her favourite desert to help wash down the taste of the basic meal.

'I will have to get some more of this ice cream, Poppy, that's the second tub you have got through this week.'

Her sister said nothing, she was too busy woofing down the food her sibling had prepared. The whole plate was cleaned off in less than a minute.

'Do you know, I wasn't going to tell you this, but my mother really upset me today. She was saying really nasty things about you, Poppy.'

'Like what?'

'Very nasty, I don't really think you want to hear them.'

'Tell me, tell me what the bitch said!'

'She, my mother, she told me that you probably deserved to be abused as a child. She thinks you probably encouraged the men who did it. She kept saying, 'People like her'. Really nasty, she said you deserved everything you got.'

'Fuckin' bitch don't wanna say that to may face, I'd lamp her, old woman or no old woman.'

Poppy was side-tracked with the mint chip ice-cream. She noticed that her sister looked a little perplexed. 'What aint ya saying?'

'It's horrible, I shouldn't tell you.'

'Just spit it out for fucks sake.'

'My mother said, Oh, God, this is really bad Poppy. She said your dad, probably, you know, used to do things to you when you were young. She said she thought he was a paedophile.'

'You better get her out of here, girl, I will fuckin' rip her apart!'

'I think you should, Poppy.'

'What!'

'It would solve all our problems. I think you should finish her off.'

'Aye, what yer saying?'

'I saw a documentary the other day. It's easy, Poppy, you just put a pillow over her head and hold her throat, so she can't breathe properly. She is fast asleep now, completely out of it. You would be too strong for her. It would all be over in a couple of minutes. She deserves it, for all the bad things she says about you. She deserves to die.'

'Nah, don't be a twat, I'd give her a slap for badmouthing me. I aint gonna do her in, am I?'

'You've killed before.'

'Nah, that was different, ya know it was.'

'You have to do it, Poppy, you have to do it right now. If not for you then for me. You owe me, remember, you owe me. I found him for you, I found Houghton. Now you owe me, just this one thing and we are all square.'

'Give yer fuckin' head a wobble, girl. It aint gonna happen.'

'Now, Poppy! Now! You have to do it right now!'

'You are fuckin' cuckoo, girl, aint ya? I aint banging yer mum, not now or never.' Poppy said, giving her sister a stare of disbelief. She sprung her legs up on to the sofa and found herself an alternative source of amusement for the afternoon. Switching on the television, she turned up the volume to maximum, completely insensitive to the sleeping guest. Bree did nothing. She sat in stony silence and folded her arms, just like a petulant child that had lost all her privileges. The angry woman never moved an inch for the best part of an hour. Her beady eyes never left her sister, that burning hatred never left her gaze.

Krista was struggling to find peace in her slumber as she laid on top of Poppy's duvet. Weird echoes and strange thoughts raced through her brain, and she could hear muffled laughter. Her head began to sway gently from side to side as she sought some respite from a chorus of sinister noises. Her mind was awash with blurry images and tiny whispers. As she slept, a large shadow seemed to block out the light as though a sudden darkness had fallen within the room. She felt a sudden hefty weight on her legs, it moved slowly upwards and rested on her chest. It was not a comfortable feeling, it felt very heavy on her small frame. She was desperate to see what was causing her body such pain, but she found her eyes would or could not open. She thought she heard a familiar voice above her head. it confused her, it seemed to be a friendly voice, but it was using poisonous words of pure hatred.

A sudden clasp on one side of her neck was joined by a much tighter grip on the other side. It was uncomfortable, painful, she tried to raise her hands to free herself, but her arms could not leave her sides. She suddenly found herself in a vice-like grip, she needed air, her chest was aching, her heart pounding heavily, faster and faster. She wanted to scream but could not prize open her mouth. The pressure grew as that grip around her neck tightened harder and harder. She tried to struggle, she wanted to kick out, she could feel the life draining from her body. And then, that voice became more familiar, telling her she was hated, that she had always been hated. Krista stopped struggling, she stopped moving, and then a small tear slithered down her cheek, as she realised in those final seconds who had been saying those angry words.

CHAPTER TWENTY-THREE

'**W**ake up!'

Poppy heard a familiar voice above her shoulder and felt a sharp nudge in the side of her ribs, her head was beginning to spin. The voice spoke again and told her to open her eyes, but her brain needed rest and told her to keep them closed. The voice grew louder and became more persistent. 'Wake up! They will be here soon. Wake up, you need to know why.'

A sickly taste in her mouth made Poppy want to gag, she spat out a dark shade of saliva and her eyes peeled open. She found herself sitting on the floor, her head resting on the corner of the sofa. The lights from the lamp above her head were blinding, heavy weights seemed to be dragging down on her eyelids. A humming sound started up inside her skull and reverberated all around her brain. She forced her eyes closed for some respite.

Her sister was persistent. 'You need to know why, Poppy, why it had to be this way.'

'Just let me sleep,' came a croaky voice from the floor. 'Tell me later, I'm knackered, just let me sleep.'

'No! You need to know, before they come, you need to understand why I had to do this.'

Poppy was rapidly changing her mood from agitated to extremely angry. She looked up at her sibling, perched above her on the sofa, a strange expression of self-satisfaction on her face. She pushed down on the floor to get to her feet but found herself stumbling and ended up flat on her back. Bree gave her one of 'those looks,' the ones she saved for Poppy when she was displeased with her.

True to form Brianna Nylund had chosen to keep her darkest secrets close to her chest and wait for that rainy day to unleash the downpour of misgivings she had been hiding. Well, those heavens had now opened. A monstrous monsoon was about to be unleashed.

'All I wanted,' Bree said calmly, 'was for me and you to be like proper sisters. Was that too much to ask, Poppy, really was that too much to ask?'

It took all her strength, but Poppy managed to sit herself upright. She felt weak, she was confused, strange thoughts were racing through her head. She could feel her heart beating fast, but she had no energy, she could hardly summon the strength to talk. She felt disabled, she felt like an invalid.

Her sister seemed to have a well-rehearsed speech prepared 'That's all, Poppy, just me and you, like real sisters, nobody else. Look at all the things I have done for you, I got you out of that hell-hole of a prison, I gave you a nice place to live, bought you a new phone, new clothes, everything you wanted...'

'I never asked you to,' came a small, muffled sound from beneath her. Poppy had cleared her throat and finally found a voice, albeit, not much more than a whisper.

'But you never said no, did you, my ungrateful sister. You never said no.'

'Get me some aspirin, I feel like shit.'

Bree laughed loudly. 'Oh, you are going to need more than aspirin to deal with this headache, trust me.'

'I feel fucked, like really fucked, get me some pills.'

'I don't think so, Poppy. You see you will be going soon, you are going to have a new home, not as nice as this one, one with lots of bars and scabby women.'

'What the fuck you chattin' about?'

'You see, my beautiful, but so selfish sister, all I asked you to do was one thing and you couldn't even do that for me.'

'You asked me to top your mum, you crazy fuck!'

'One thing, just one thing, for all the things I have done for you. You would never been able to find Houghton without me. You would never have buried the ghost of what that man did to you without me.'

'You are seriously sick in the fuckin' head, girl.'

'Maybe, maybe I am, so I had to do it myself.'

'What?'

'She won't be plaguing my life anymore. She has finally got what she deserved. I suffocated the bitch, she is lying on your bed, finally at peace with herself. Disappointing really, she didn't even put up much of a struggle.'

Poppy tried again to push herself to her feet, but she was still drowsy, her brain was sending signals, but her body wasn't answering. Her head had started throbbing and she was fighting a losing battle to keep her eyelids open. She needed to move but still couldn't. 'You aint got the bottle, missy, people like you are all talk.'

'Wrong, my simple sister, so wrong. It was easy for me. I just pressed down hard on her neck until she stopped breathing. You see, she couldn't fight back, she had some...' Bree laughed to herself. 'Well, she had some of your 'special' chocolate sprinkles, you know the ones you like in your ice-cream.'

'What yer fuckin' talking about?'

'Peclosaperidone. It's a long word, much too long for you to spell, Poppy. Mind you, 'disloyal' and 'betrayal' are probably difficult for you to spell.'

'Aye, what yer saying, I don't get it.'

'Never wondered why you slept so well, without alcohol? Have you never wondered why you had all those headaches?' Bree mimicked her sibling's morning tantrums. 'Oh, get me the pills, missy, my head hurts. Maybe I have got a brain tumour. No, Poppy, no brain tumour, you need to have brain to have a brain tumour.'

Poppy looked around the room, everything seemed to be out of focus, her eyes spotted the empty ice cream bowl beneath the sofa. She suddenly realised why her body had stopped listening to her brain. She could barely move a muscle. In that split second, she felt a burst of rage rip through her torso, she tried to lash out at her sister, but her arm had no strength, she just felt weak, very weak. 'Why?' she asked her gloating sibling. 'Why the fuck?'

'You see I found those pills when I was at my lowest point, when I couldn't sleep, no matter what I did. I didn't mind the headaches. They were worth it just to be with him again.'

'Who?'

'Jamie, of course, Jamie. Every night he would be in my dreams, every night. I could be back with him whenever I wanted.'

Poppy sighed and shook her head slightly. 'Mad as a fuckin' hatter, girl, you're just fuckin' bonkers.'

'But those dreams started getting nasty. Jamie, he started getting nasty. The trouble was, darling sister, I never knew when the nightmares started and when they ended. That's why I had to stop. But I knew the power of those pills, I knew how to keep you under control.'

Reality began to dawn on Poppy, she suddenly realised what had been causing her to have so many hallucinations and why those nightmares had all seemed so real. Her head was starting to spin, and she found she had no feeling in her toes, but it didn't stop her trying to get herself up off of the floor. 'I swear down, I am gonna fuckin' kill you! I aint messin' this time, you are dead girl!'

Bree shrugged off her sisters' threats. 'God, you were tough to manage, Poppy, you were becoming immune to small doses. I had to cut up two, sometimes three tablets at a time to keep you in line. You see, at first, I just wanted to stop you going back to that awful place to see all your junkie friends. But then, well, then I just decided that you could be my little puppet. I could have some fun with you. And then I realised you were the answer to all my prayers. But you and your nasty temper, you nearly messed things up. You know, with that Shark fella. I got some good photos of that little mishap. But I couldn't have you going back to prison, I had to keep you safe, until you had done my little deed.'

'Killing your mum, fuck, all this can't just be about that.'

'No, of course it wasn't, but let's face it my beautiful but deranged sister, this was never going to work, was it? You and I, it was never going to be.'

'Bitch!'

'No, Poppy, you are the bitch. You could have made this easy, I just wanted her gone, you knew that you knew how much she hated you. You've killed before, it wouldn't have bothered you. With all that violent shit in your head you were bound to be going back to prison again at some point. Why, why couldn't you just do what I asked.'

Poppy suddenly found enough energy to force a grin and she taunted her sister. 'She aint dead. You aint got the bottle. It's just more of your bullshit, more of your fuckin' lies, Your mother aint dead.'

But Bree was determined to have the last laugh, that monstrous rainstorm had finally reached its crescendo, a veritable tsunami had now arrived. 'No, my beautiful, but so fucked up sister, my mother is dead. But yours isn't, she is alive, Poppy, your mother is still alive.'

Poppy tried her best to swing a punch at her sibling, but her arm barely left her side. Her face was filled with rage 'Don't talk about my mother, you aint got no right…'

'She is alive and well, Poppy. I say well, she had a hip operation last summer, but she gets around OK.'

'Liar, more shit outta that lying gob of yours, fuckin' liar!'

'She is a dinner lady at a primary school, she lives in a lovely little place called Chichester, its right by the coast.'

'Bullshit, just more fuckin bullshit!'

Bree moved swiftly and collected her mobile phone from the dining table, scrolling down her photo gallery she found what she was looking for. 'Hannah Samuels, that's what she calls herself nowadays, Hannah Samuels. She lives with the caretaker of the school'. Bree turned the phone around to show her sister a picture of a middle-aged couple posing close together in a school playground. 'That's her with Gary, he is her, well, her new man, I suppose. Very cosy, don't you think?'

'Nah, that's just crap, you do things with photos, you muck about with 'em to make things look different, I've seen ya do it. That aint her, she's dead, I know my mother's fuckin' dead, don't say no more about her.'

Bree studied her montage of pictures more closely. 'They knew, of course, they both knew, Kayleigh and Matt, they have known for ages. It was Kayleigh that found her for me, I told you she had some good contacts in social services.'

'You are just fuckin' nasty, girl, when I get up, I swear down I am gonna go sick on you, I am gonna plaster you all over the floor.'

Poppy tried to push herself up, but her body was still too weak, unwilling to respond to her urges. Her sister pushed her back down. 'Sit there until I am finished with you. The police will be here soon, this might be the last chance for me to tell you some home truths. Bree's face lit up when she found what she was looking for amongst the photographs on her mobile. 'Oh look, here it is. a close-up of your mother. Look just there, Poppy, see that little kink on her nose. Remember you told me our wonderful father broke it that time? Recognise her now?'

Poppy was trying to look away from her sister's phone, but something drew her to that photo. She suddenly felt sick inside, she felt a pain, like a sharp dagger slicing through her heart. Strange emotions began to wash over her body, she found herself wanting to cry, to laugh and to scream all at the same time. She had to shut her eyes tightly to stop a runaway tear showing the weakness and despair she was feeling inside. And then her sorrow turned to anger, as a tidal wave of hatred raced through her, she swung her arm out wildly, narrowly missing her sister's head.

'Don't you find it weird Poppy that she is surrounded by kids at that school? I have seen her with them, she really loves them children. Don't you find it strange that she is happy amongst all those kids, but she never wanted her own child in her life?'

Poppy turned her attention to the Mulberry bag on the dining room table and then switched her gaze to the door to her bedroom.

'Oh, she can't help you, Poppy. I know you don't believe me, but I told you, she is gone. There will be no more droning on about those bloody sunsets in Tampere and trying to find me new therapists. She is out of my life now, forever, like you will be soon. Unfortunately for you, Poppy, you will be held responsible. I can see the headlines now. 'A drug addict with a history of violence finally meets the woman who had an affair with her father and split her family up.' The jury won't need to be as clever as Einstein to work out the rest.'

The broken girl on the floor was struggling to come to terms with all of the revelations. 'Why?' she asked. 'I thought me and you was alright now. Why?'

But before her sister could answer her question the sound of a screaming police siren shattered the peaceful tranquillity of the road outside. Both girls suddenly turned their attention to the large window to see the reflections of the blues and twos arriving in the courtyard

'It's time to go, Poppy, it's time to go.'

Bree composed herself, took one long deep breath and then suddenly ripped the sleeve of her Versace top, pulling off a couple of buttons from the front for good measure. One yank and a shake of her golden locks messed up her perfect hair. To complete the task, she ran a wet finger across her eye liner to make it look as if she had been crying. Her smile of self-satisfaction beaming down on her helpless sibling, still desperately trying to find some power in her legs.

'I guess I'll have to face that big bad wolf on my own after all.' Bree said, ignoring the steely daggers in her sister's eyes.

Bree answered the intercom as if she was responding to a curtain call. Taking a bow before giving her best impersonation of a distraught and vulnerable girl, whose mother had been cruelly stolen away from her by the monster on the floor. Her performance was, as with everything she ever did, executed with perfection, right down to the sobbing and shaking body that greeted the police officers as they arrived on mass.

When they entered her flat, Bree's acting skills reached their peak as she begun to spin her pre-planned tale of woe. But suddenly, a loud crashing noise was heard on the outside of the building. Rushing through her home, she looked down to see that Poppy was no longer sprawled out on the living room floor. A cold panic set in. Her sharp instincts took her immediately to the open door of her own bedroom where she could see her window was wide open. With two officers looking over her shoulder she looked down to see the wheelie bins below had all been overturned. The garden area was in almost total darkness, but the shadow of a limping figure could clearly be seen slipping over some bushes and heading towards the open fields. She wanted to scream at her rescuers to get after the offender, but a sense of reality told her to hold her tongue. Within seconds, her acting skills kicked-in again and the weeping victim was playing her part. A nearby WPC offered a shoulder to shelter her crocodile tears.

A couple of eager police officers raced down the stairway to take up the chase, radioing the driver of one of the nearby vehicles to meet them at the entrance. Pandemonium ensued as another set of flashing lights arrived at the entrance to the flats and the rear doors of an ambulance were flung open.

In Poppy's bedroom the scene was chaotic. A uniformed officer was straddled across a limp and lifeless body, lying motionless on the bed, his hands pumping furiously on Krista's chest. Another policeman was barking instructions down his radio, desperate to gain some assistance in their attempts to resuscitate Bree's mother. All seemed lost as a grieving daughter fought desperately to enter the room to be closer to the situation. But just as she managed to slide past the WPC who had been comforting her, Bree heard the hopeful officer on the bed utter the words that would bring an alarming reality check to the poisoned mind of the would-be murderess.

'I've got a pulse, it's not strong, but I have a pulse and shallow breathing,' he yelled. 'For God's sake get those bloody paramedics up here as quick as you can!'

CHAPTER
TWENTY-FOUR

S he didn't know where she found the strength to launch herself from the bedroom window, nor why she wasn't feeling much pain from her crashing fall. Maybe it was the adrenalin rush kicking in, or maybe just the aftereffects of those drugs that her sister had been cutting up and mixing with her ice-cream. But even though she felt no real pain in the parts of her body that shielded her fall, Poppy could feel a familiar throbbing inside her head, thumping away, growing louder by the second.

If anyone had deserved a bit of luck that night, it was Poppy. It came in the shape of an unsuspecting Uber driver that had left his car engine running while he escorted an elderly woman into the newly built retirement home on the outskirts of Oxley village. Her original intention had been to dump the vehicle when she was far enough away from the scene of the crime. But her eyelids were growing heavy weights and her body was beginning to shut down. Poppy had been on enough drug benders in her teen years to realise that she was not in control of her actions. She just about made it to a patch of waste ground hidden by some trees and bought the car to a sudden halt. Within a few short seconds her body slumped forward over the driver's wheel, and she lost her battle with the Peclosaperidone intoxicants that were still coursing through her veins.

As she slept, ten thousand images entered her troubled mind, most of them distorted and twisted faces from her misspent youth and time spent in prison. But now new heads appeared to be mocking her. Kayleigh and Matt had joined in the motley crew of misfits, pointing at her, laughing at her. The voices became louder and louder, she wanted to scream, to push them all away. But she found a strange comfort in their humiliation, she didn't know why. And for the first time in two decades, she had a vision of her mother, not aged, as she looked in her sister's photograph, but just as she remembered her the day she walked out of her life. Poppy became lost in that illusion, desperate to feel her mother's warm embrace one more time. But the image faded before she had the chance to reach out her arms and the emptiness returned to her bruised and battered body.

Strangely, when she awoke, she could not separate fantasy from reality. She had suffered so many nightmares in the past few weeks that she fully expected to see her self-righteous sister standing over her with a glass of water and a packet of Nurofen. But her aching head was not going to be cured that quickly. Her survival instincts told her she needed to stay awake, she needed to be alert.

As the effects of the drug began to wear off, she felt fresh bruising to the side of her neck and the base of her spine. She realised that her leap from her sister's window on to the plastic bins below had not been achieved without injury. The pain in her body though was a nothing compared to the agony inside her heart. Poppy had always assumed her mother had died. She had never forgiven her father for the torturous life she had endured while they were a family. But as much as she was in denial, she knew that that photograph on her sister's phone was genuine.

The slight dent at the end of her mother's nose and her tiny earlobes were unmistakable. And to make it worse, a thousand times worse, her mother was smiling in that picture. She rarely remembered her mother smiling. But now she had made a new life for herself, a happy life, with other people around her, with children at her feet. In that very moment she shared her sibling's hatred for her maternal parent, cursing the woman that bought her into the world. Maybe all mothers were the same, she thought. She suddenly felt the slightest tinge of sympathy for Bree. Maybe, she thought, Bree's mother really was the bitch her daughter had painted her out to be. Maybe all mothers are like that. Her faith in humanity was at the lowest point it had ever been at that moment.

But other thoughts, not good ones, made their way through her scrambled brain. Matt and Kayleigh, they were far from blameless in this whole mess. They were in on it, they had known the whole time. Those blurred images inside her head were becoming clearer. And now an unknown voice told her that they were laughing at her behind her back. They should be punished for their deceit, but how? The revelation about Matts' weekly excursions to another family life would not cause enough pain to mirror the heartache she was feeling inside. There must be a harsher retribution for their betrayal.

Suddenly, she felt a vibration in her front pocket and realised that she had not left the flat empty handed after all. She checked the mobile, knowing full well that it would be her sister calling her. She looked at the smarmy smile on the face on her handset and cursed at the caller, but she didn't answer. Poppy needed more time to think

As she felt new stabbing pains in her side and shooting pains in her legs, her sisters words came back to haunt her. They knew, they knew all along, Matt and Kayleigh, two people, maybe the only two people in her life she felt she could trust, had betrayed her. A smouldering volcano began to build inside her head and by the time it reached her fractured heart it was ready to erupt. She should never have let her guard down, she realised that now. The voices, she thought, they were always right, they had guided her well, they had told her never to trust people

And then she felt the sharpest pains, the pains of reality. It was as it has always been in her troubled life, people using her for their own gains. Bree's conniving plan to use her as a scapegoat for her mother's murder. And now Kayleigh had used her to explore her sexuality. She felt sick to the stomach to think that she had let that mousy girl into her bed. But why didn't Matt tell her about her mother? What gain was there for him? The two of them had been close once, confiding in each other all of the time. Why would he keep her sisters' cruel and twisted secret safe? She suddenly thought back to the cluttered living room of the ordinary house in Anerley and remembered the face she had seen staring at her on the screen of Kayleigh's laptop. She remembered who it was now, the busybody psychiatrist who visited Bronzefield Prison. She could hear her twangy American accent bounding around inside her head. Why, why the hell would Kayleigh be looking at that woman's files? Her brain was being overloaded, she could find no rhyme nor reason for anything, she felt as if her head was about to explode. Poppy suddenly let go of her pent-up emotions, she unleashed a very long and extremely loud scream and suddenly felt slightly better. She repeated the exercise, this time banging her fists furiously against the steering wheel of the car. It worked, the minefield of chaotic thoughts inside her head were calmed.

She hated them all now, Bree, Matt and Kayleigh. But they would have to wait. Her sister would no doubt be giving an Oscar winning performance at the local police station in her bid to put her back behind bars. Condemning her to at least another dozen years or so of purgatory. She could already see the sickly smirk on Callard's face as he handed her a new prison uniform. It made her furious inside to think that he would ever be allowed to wallow in her misery.

But Poppy Jarvis was never one to feel sorry for herself for very long. In an instant that well practised self-preservation mechanism kicked in. She was single minded now, totally focused. Even though her body ached from head to toe, and her brain was giving her countless mixed signals, Poppy knew that to get out of this mess she would need to find strength and resolve that had always served her so well in the past.

Desperate times call for desperate measures. She needed a plan. Poppy needed a bargaining tool.

She knew exactly where to find one.

*

Anybody that knew anything about Matthew Jameson would say that he had a heart of gold. A gregarious fellow with a permanent smile on his face and a laugh that could be infectious even in the direst of circumstances. He was generous to a fault and always the first to offer his support to those in need. He found it hard to see bad in anybody and would always defend the underdog in a conflict. Few people, apart from Kayleigh, knew that he also cried real tears after watching the ending of sad films or when he was touched by the emotional lyrics of a song. The big man might have appeared a menacing figure when he was stood upright, but in truth he was really nothing more than a big softy.

So, despite his sobering discovery he didn't curse and shout loudly that afternoon when Chantelle broke his heart into a thousand pieces. To be fair to her, the cunning teenager looked full of remorse when she revealed that the young boy that he had spent those precious hours with each week for the past year was not his child. He wanted to scream out loud at her, to tell her that she was a money-grabbing bitch for taking his weekly contributions, when all that time she knew that there was a possibility that the child might be the biological son of somebody else. He wanted to, but he didn't. It wasn't in the gentle man's make-up. What Chantelle failed to tell him of course was that it was never the fathers DNA check that was in doubt, because the poor boy in the ill-fitting football kit already had two parents. And so, Matt did what he had done with other cruel twists in his life, he took it on the chin. He wished the scheming ex-waitress well and sent her on her way, choking on his words as he told her that he hoped that her and her apparent son enjoyed a happy life together. And, despite the fact his heavy heart was breaking inside his chest, he even handed her the toy car that he had bought his fake son that morning. He told her that he was given one the same colour and model when he was a child. After all, it was not the poor lads' fault that his 'part-time' mother was a two-faced liar. So, Matt Jameson did not scream and shout that day. But when Chantelle was out of sight, the big Geordie lads heart melted like butter in a frying pan. He sat on the steps of a run-down church and wept large salty tears for at least a half an hour.

But however broken Matt felt at that moment he knew he had to find the resolve to deal with the matter. He did have the consolation of knowing that the other child, that one that he knew without doubt was his, was waiting at home for him. At that moment he was desperate to get back to Anerley and squeeze his tiny bundle of love with the tightest hug ever.

His world had been shattered that day and, maybe selfishly, he was hoping for some consolation from the partner he had pushed to one side recently. Matt, being Matt, felt it was the right thing to do to tell her everything. After all, the truth has a nasty habit of catching up with you when you least expect it. At least now Kayleigh would know the reason for his mood swings and why he never had any spare money. He felt some strange relief in knowing that he would never have to lie about his Wednesday excursions again. So, he was prepared now, to come clean, to beg her for forgiveness and hope that she would understand. Maybe, if he was completely honest about the situation, Kayleigh would find it into her heart to give him the chance to make amends. He hoped that she might even help him overcome the trauma of the cruel revelation. His journey home was much slower than the one to the park that day. He took the scenic route rather than a direct one. He was buying time, he needed to find the right words to open that awkward conversation.

Unusually, for early September, the temperatures had taken a sudden rise and the ordinary cul-de-sac in that tidy suburb in South London was littered with small children. They played happily along the pavements, sporting colourful Tee-shirts and shorts. Some of them were making the most of their last few holiday days before they had to return to school. Kayleigh had never been a fan of the humid weather and welcomed the occasional breeze rushing through the open back door of the house. She sat, as she often did, glued to the screen on her laptop in the living room. But there were no internet searches being carried out for friends and relatives today. No job searches, no delving into the world of psychology reports for criminal misfits. No, she was going to relax and enjoy the sunny afternoon. This was a rare bit of 'Kayleigh time.'

It was strangely quiet in the adjacent alleyway, the noisy youths seemed to have found a new location to torment homeowners. So, with the much-welcomed silence returning to the area, Willow was deep in slumber in the middle of a napping hour. The baby was enjoying the fresh air in a shaded alcove in the garden. She looked peaceful as she slept soundly in her bright coloured carry cot. Her mother saw the sudden return of peace and tranquillity outside her house to be a blessing. She had found it strange, however, that the teenage delinquents had decided to take their loud music and weed smoking gatherings to another location.

With Willow dreamily following the sleep patterns introduced by her parents and with the work chores done for the day, Kayleigh, headphones in place, was catching up on some YouTube clips and singing along to some her old favourite rock songs. She had ignored her boyfriend's first couple of calls, she was still angry with him for failing to notice that she had been to the hairdressers and had her roots coloured the previous day. She was feeling increasingly insecure at this moment in time. Her and Matt seemed so distant in their relationship now and neither of them seemed to be trying to hide their angst for the other. She knew that he had become fed up with her constant nagging. When they did have any kind of conversation, he seemed to be looking straight through her, as if he only saw her as the mother of his child and not the red-hot lover of his fantasies. Neither of them wanted to admit it but the introduction of the sex toys and role play had made things worse. After all, Matt was like most men, he would retreat into a perfectly designed neanderthal cave whenever his manhood came into question. She was convinced that there must be someone else. The lack of money told her that he was spending the security of his child's future on another woman. He had mentioned the name of a girl that had started working at his restaurant several times over the past month and her mind had gone into overdrive. After all, that's exactly how things had started off with Poppy and her partner when they had worked together. And there was, of course, the other elephant in the darkened room of her overthinking brain. Kayleigh was still finding it difficult to come to terms with the fact that she had ended up in Poppy's bed. Their steamy sexual encounter was still fresh in her mind, and she had begun to question her own sexuality. Maybe her out-of-control hormones were playing tricks on her mind. She knew that she did not want a repeat of the steamy sex session with her arch-rival, but at the same time wondered if she would ever be able to be fully satisfied by a man again.

Her mobile rang twice more before the distraction became an irritation and she removed her headphones to speak to her boyfriend. Perhaps, she thought, she should try harder, suggest they hire a babysitter and have an evening out, it seemed like ages since they had had some fun together. Don't just be civil, she told herself, make some real conversation, ask him how the catering course went today. But those thoughts vanished the second she heard the tones of his voice. She found the first words out of her mouth to be a continuation of the barraging she had dished out that morning. 'That gate is going to fall off soon, Matt. There are children playing outside and you will be responsible if one of them falls over it.'

Matt ignored her comment, he sounded more distant than usual, the pauses in the opening conversation told her that there was something wrong. 'I am going to take the night off work, Kayls,' he explained, in a serious tone that his girlfriend found concerning. 'I thought we could have some you and me time, you know, so we can talk.'

'That sounds great, hun, but we really need the money from those extra shifts.'

'I know, Kayls, but, well, I just don't feel good today.'

'Me and you both hun, but we are relying on that money.'

'It's just, I am not sure…'

'Are you ill, is that it, is there something wrong with you?'

'No, I am OK, well, not really OK.'

Matt did not want to drop the bombshell on the phone, he knew he needed to do that face to face, his partner was not making that easy for him. He changed the subject, maybe biding his time in the hope that the right words to explain his predicament might jump into his head. 'I thought you was seeing Godzilla today, going to a spinning class or something.'

'I don't know what's happening, I haven't heard from Bree all week. The last time I spoke to her was at the weekend, she told me that Poppy was really bad-mouthing her mother and she was thinking twice about letting her stay.'

'Poppy doesn't mean any harm, you know, her mouth works before her brain does. She says things, she doesn't mean all of them.'

Kayleigh was not happy with that comment. 'Why do you always have to do that, Matt, defend Poppy, before you even know the facts.'

'The girl has had a shit life. She just needs people to get off her back. I am not defending her, Kayls, she just needs a break. Anyway, how is our little babycakes today?'

'It's almost half-way through her hour now, she is being such a good girl. I really think those pre-planned naps are doing her a lot of good. She seems a lot less grouchy.'

'We need to keep a check on her stools again, she has been doing funny coloured poos lately.'

Kayleigh smiled at his comment and made her way to the garden, she was conscious that the sun was burning down, she felt the heat might make her sleeping princess uncomfortable. Her and Matt continued their chit-chat, but she sensed from the small pauses and the tone of his voice that he was holding back. In her head she told herself she needed to cut him some slack and listen to what he had to say for himself when he returned home. But as she made her way into the garden, she was greeted with a sight that would stay in her memory until the day she died. As she looked down to check on her daughter, a wild scream ripped through her brain and rushed down her head before becoming trapped inside her mouth. Her body began to shake uncontrollably, before she suddenly released a howling cry of pain.

'Kayls, what is it, Kayleigh?'

But his girlfriend couldn't speak, she was rushing around the garden like a headless chicken. She opened and closed the back gate at least three times before falling on to her knees. Finally, Kayleigh found enough saliva in the dry roof of her mouth to allow her to scream out the words that would rip out the already shredded heart of her boyfriend.

'She's gone, our baby's gone!'

*

The fuel tank in the stolen taxi was now on reserve, rapidly running out of petrol. Poppy seemed to have been driving around in circles for the best part of three hours trying to work out her next move. Her head was still aching, and her body felt weak. She was trying to remember how much cash she had left in her pocket but could not concentrate fully due to the screaming baby on the passenger seat. She had tried singing, making funny noises, shouting, even screaming, to calm the child. But tiny Willow was having none of it. Red faced and clearly distressed, her bawling reached new levels. Poppy suddenly realised that this was not a good idea, in fact it was the worst idea she had ever had in her life.

Her haphazard road trip now took her into South London and familiar territory. She wasn't sure why she wanted to be back there, it seemed to be her only option. When she passed her old block of flats, she suddenly felt safer, she didn't know why. But as she turned the corner into the estate, she spotted a police car and hurriedly retreated the way she came. Her attention had now switched from her noisy passenger and was firmly on the car mirrors. She was worried that the police car had spotted her and was now on her tail. Putting her foot down and reaching perilous speeds for a built-up area, she headed further south, not sure where she was going or why she was heading there. Several times she checked her mirror and expected the police to swoop at any moment. Then, she heard them again, soft voices, heckling, laughing inside her head. They seemed to be amused by her predicament. She cursed them loudly, but they ignored her. The chorus grew louder as the faces from her past began queuing up to poke fun.

She had lost count of the number of times her phone had rung, but she had nothing to say to her treacherous sibling. She wished she had enough petrol to return to Oxley Village, to find that girl and crunch her bones under the full weight of the vehicle she was driving. But a check of the faltering petrol gauge and the sound of a spluttering engine told her that this journey was all but over.

The car spewed out its final breath and came to an abrupt halt as it approached the entrance to the Sewardstone Reservoir. Poppy found herself shouting out loudly, with baby Willow her only audience. She began to lose control of her emotions, banging the dashboard with clenched fists and cursing everyone. She hated her sister, Kayleigh, Matt, even the Uber driver for not leaving the car with a full tank of petrol. She realised she had next to no money, her body ached from head to toe, and she couldn't bend her left leg. But worst of all she had no real plan.

Poppy slammed the door of the vehicle as she got out, aiming a vicious kick at the paintwork. She fell to the ground as the scathing pain in her back reached her legs and made her crumble. Dragging herself sideways she began to realise that the aches and pains she was suffering were not going to be fixed with some aspirin and a decent night sleep. Every bone in her body seemed to be calling out to her to quit this charade and give herself up. But the thought of going back to a ten by eight cell was not an option for her. She needed to clear her head of the laughing hyenas and think out her next move.

Her phone log showed fifteen missed calls, all from the same number. Suddenly, the shock of reality set off alarm bells in her head. Something told her that her sister always seemed to know where she had been all of the time. And then she remembered that familiar odour at the end of the alleyway where Shark received his comeuppance. She cursed her sister, not for the first time that day, when she realised there had been a tracker inside her mobile. It had to go, the phone, it had to go. As she looked down the banks of the reservoir to the giant bathtub of swirling waters below, she heard the screams of the baby start up again. Her mind went into a state of panic and confusion, she knew had to get rid of the phone as soon as possible. She would, but she needed to make one call before she switched it off and tossed it into the rushing waters beneath her. There were only two numbers she could choose from. The choice was simple.

CHAPTER
TWENTY-FIVE

Nobody in the room wanted the phone to ring, yet everyone present in that tomb of despair in Anerley was desperate to hear its ringtone sound out. Complete silence reigned.

Five pairs of eyes remained glued to the tiny handset laying on the dining room table, it was the one and only link they had to the abductor of baby Willow. Matt reached around his partners shoulder and tried to pull her closer to him to comfort her, but she resisted, brushing him aside. Her face was ashen, red raw beneath her eyes, the result of a million tears of despair. She rocked backwards and forwards in her chair, clutching her daughters comfort teddy bear so tightly it left imprints on her tearstained top. The neatly presented Detective Sergeant Kerr had said nothing since they had heard that first call. The angry voice on a small hands-free speaker which sent panic through their hearts and minds. The call that assured them that all of this mayhem and madness was really happening. This was not a nightmare.

The silence was broken by the sound of teaspoons ratting on the tray as a tall and slender WPC appeared from the kitchen armed with refreshments. 'I didn't know who took sugar, so I bought the bowl,' she said, in a soft voice that nobody heard. Her eyes peered upwards at the senior officer, but the chiselled expression on his face was giving nothing away.

Despite falling in line with the sombre mood set here, Bree was restless, constantly checking her own mobile to see if her sister had attempted to make any contact. She hadn't, why would she? The fact that her mother was fighting for her life in an ICU bed at the nearby hospital seemed to be of little consequence to Bree. It should have been playing heavy on her mind, but it didn't.

'She said tell the truth,' Kayleigh suddenly remarked, in a cracked, half broken voice that pulled at the heartstrings of all those present. 'She said, tell the truth, babe, what did she mean by that?'

Bree felt awkward, she did her best to give an impression of a concerned friend. 'I wish I had never bought her here, I am so sorry, I didn't…'

'What did she mean, Bree?' Kayleigh asked again, this time more firmly. 'When she called, she told you to tell the truth and shame the devil, those were her words.'

'She is messed up, we know that. I never thought she would do something like this. But I am sure she wouldn't hurt Willow. She is just bluffing.'

'Bluffing!' Matt yelled. 'Bluffing! She just threatened to drop our fuckin' daughter in the river!'

The police officer felt it was time to intervene 'We all need to calm down' he said. 'We have alerted the Special Task Unit, they will be at the reservoir by now. Everything is going to be OK,' he added, in a kind of vague monotone voice which convinced nobody.

Kayleigh was not done, she wanted answers. 'Bree, you said nothing, nothing at all. She said she would give you ten seconds to tell the truth and you said nothing.'

'It was just a threat, Kayleigh, she wouldn't have really thrown your baby into the water, I know her, she is crazy but not that crazy.'

Matt banged the table with a clenched fist and raised his voice. 'I told you we should have told her, I kept saying she had the right to know about her mother being alive. You are to blame for this, Bree, you, and you too Kayls, we should never have kept it secret from her.'

Kayleigh had a burning anger in her watery eyes as she faced her partner. 'How dare you defend her, Matt, after this, how dare you!'

The detective Sargent put his hand down on Matt's shoulder to reassure him. 'I know everyone is upset but this isn't doing anybody any good.'

Kayleigh now switched her attention back to her best friend, there was no warmth in her expression. 'What is the truth, Bree? What did she want you to say?'

Bree shrugged the comment off and looked back down at her phone, she was clearly not enjoying the hostile eye contact from her bestie. She noticed that she had two missed calls, both from Kendra. 'I don't know, I really don't know.'

The solemn silence returned for a few moments as the five pairs of eyes fixed firmly on that object in the middle of the table, as the steam evaporated around those mugs of fresh tea that were lukewarm by now. Kayleigh suddenly began to shake uncontrollably and found Matts grasping hand a comfort. 'She will die without her medication, she will die. Is that what you wanted, Bree? She is probably dead now, I know she is dead, Willow is gone, my beautiful baby, she is never coming back, she is dead.'

Matt realised that the Brees' presence was upsetting his girlfriend. 'Shouldn't you be at the hospital?' he asked her. 'Your mother, you should be there with her, nobody wants you here.'

'I want to be here for my friend, thank-you, Matthew Jameson, if that is OK with you? They said my mother is stable, she is in good hands. I need to be here for Kayleigh.'

The atmosphere was becoming more tense by the moment, a powder keg of raw emotions ready to explode at any second. Then suddenly the loud ring tone of a mobile suddenly shattered the new calm. But it was not the phone they were all hoping to hear. DS Kerr reached inside his jacket pocket and answered the call.

Everyone looked up at the concerned officers' features, hoping for a good sign, praying for a small smile to appear on his weary face. But his expression of concern told them a story they did not want to hear. The heart inside the hardened detective's chest felt a squeezing hand wrap around it as he relayed the news to the waiting parents. 'They are at the reservoir. They have retrieved the carry cot from the water. I am so sorry, but there is no sign of the baby.'

A howling scream of excruciating pain could be heard the length and breadth of Marlow Close as Kayleigh fell forward and collapsed on to the floor.

CHAPTER
TWENTY-SIX

The price of freedom can bring the cruellest twists. Poppy was no longer an inmate, incarcerated in a dingy institution, locked away for up to twenty-three hours each day. But in her head, she was still a captive. She was, she always would be a prisoner of the horrific memories of her past. Encased in a fortress of vile abuse and neglect from which she could never escape. She had trodden those damp paths in the fields of damnation all her life, hoping for blue skies to appear. But she never knew when, or indeed if, they ever would.

She found herself in more familiar surroundings, sitting on a dampened stretch of grass at the rear of what remained of the Eagle Public House, close to Cranford Fields. She had hoped that dropping her mobile phone at the side of the gushing reservoir would delay the hunt for her. The police would need to retrieve the carry cot from the water and consider whether she had jumped in herself. It would buy her some time, but to do what? She was done now, her body was busted and broken, her will power weak. She could no longer consider her options because there were none.

Her head began to reel as she recalled the words of her threat to the concerned party at Kayleigh's house less than two hours ago. She had given her scheming spiteful bitch of a sister ten seconds, ten whole seconds to tell the gathered crowd the truth. It was a generous gesture, it was more than enough time, she even counted slowly. But it was not an idle threat, despite the urgings of those tormentors inside her head she did throw the carry cot into the raging waters below. But not Willow, the stolen baby was wrapped in the Uber drivers smart leather jacket he had left in his taxi and was cradled in her arms.

The baby had stopped crying, it was a blessing. The baby had stopped crying, it was not a blessing. She was silent now, Willow, she had not made a murmur since they left the reservoir. Maybe she was asleep, Poppy couldn't tell. Or maybe, just maybe she had just made things a whole lot worse for herself. Perhaps she should have not shaken her so hard, maybe the babe in arms would never wake up. A thought crossed her mind, just for a few seconds. Perhaps she should have jumped herself, headfirst, into the dark waters of that reservoir, ended this life of constant pain and torment once and for all. It was not the first time that thought had crossed her mind. In the past her natural survival instincts would not allow her to feel pity for herself, suicide had never been an option. But she began to feel the walls closing in on her, she had crashed and burned one too many times. The cold comfort of a mortuary slab would finally bring an end to her misery.

A distant police siren suddenly reminded her that she was not at these familiar surroundings to feel pity for herself. She needed to be strong, she had to find some money to help her get away, to anywhere, just as far away as she could. Something suddenly caught her attention in the distance, she realised that her fate might not be in her own hands. Headlights, dull but brightening by the second, a vehicle approached from the far end of the old field, it seemed to be locked in on her destination. Poppy felt the searing pains of her earlier tumble from the window and realised she was not up to outrunning the police this time. She looked down at the pallid face of the peaceful child in her arms and relayed her thoughts to the silent infant. 'I think this is it, Willow, mate, I'm fucked, I can't run no more. I think it's time for me to go back where I belong.'

Two doors slammed firmly on the dark coloured van and four small shadows appeared, slowly they grew in size and stature. One of the arrivals stood out, he was clearly much larger in size than his associates. Poppy raised her eyes, knowing that she didn't have the strength to face her opposition. But she wouldn't let the police handcuff her without a struggle. She would let them know what she thought of them before they locked her up.

The largest of the figures from the vehicle suddenly bellowed out an order to his followers. 'Get back!' he yelled. 'All of you, get back in the van.' Poppy realised that she recognised that voice, it sent a lightning bolt of panic through her aching bones.

Some of those in attendance were not happy with the orders that had been given. Keelan was the first insubordinate, he was adamant their prey needed to suffer. 'Nah, dat bitch gotta pay, Neddy, she gotta get merked, that sket gotta fuckin' pay good.'

'This is my beef, I am gonna take care of this myself,' the familiar voice responded.

Another unhappy soldier in the ranks also made his thoughts clear, this time it was the angry voice of Fitz. 'Done is done, bruv, she nearly put Shark in the ground. Man's gonna spend his life with half his dick in a jar. She done wrong, blud, gotta bang dis loopy bitch, gotta finish her.'

Neddy stood his ground and asserted his authority. 'I said get back in the fuckin' van! All of you, now!'.

The dejected squad of delinquents followed his orders and dragged their feet back to their vehicle. Three scowling faces, clearly unhappy, as they cursed their leader under their breaths.

There was a moment of time for reflection, just a few seconds before this one-sided battle would commence. Poppy knew her options were limited. She wanted to let go of the motionless child in her arms, to at least put up a fight. But she had no weapon, she was sleep deprived and had little energy. She was barely able to stand, yet alone defend herself. She realised she was beaten, she would never ever admit it, not to anybody. But she knew she had finally reached the end. It was time to accept her fate.

Neddy moved forward, slowly, quietly, as if somehow, he was trying not to disturb the small bundle wrapped in the jacket resting in her lap. And then, nothing, he just stood there, towering over his prey, like a hungry vulture waiting to pounce. Poppy looked at Willow and touched her cheek, maybe to comfort her, maybe not. A distant moment from what seemed a lifetime ago suddenly seeped into her head, causing ten thousand mixed emotions to race through her weary mind. Neddy was sharing that moment, she could tell he was by the strange look on his face. 'Do you ever wonder?' he asked, staring hard at his bitter rival. 'You know, do you ever think about…'

'Don't start, Neddy, don't go there.'

'She would be nearly twelve now, going to big school and all that.'

'Shut up, just shut up, Neddy!'

The big man looked long and hard at his foe with the baby in her arms. He wanted to say more but remembered he had an audience sitting in the vehicle behind him. He changed the subject, he was, after all, not here to make friendly gestures. 'Fuck me! You don't do things by halves, do you, gal? They are looking for you everywhere, it's all over the radio and TV. That poor bird in Anerley, she is going spare, she is out of her fuckin' mind with worry.'

'You aint here about the baby, we both know that, just fuckin' get it over with.'

'Fuck, gal, you have always had bad attitude, real fuckin' attitude. You have always been a headfuck, Poppy, a real loose cannon, but this aint you, stealing a fuckin' nipper.'

'Don't expect me to beg, Neddy, I don't beg to no one, especially a cunt like you.'

'Jesus, you have caused me so much agg, so many fuckin' problems. Why couldn't you just take the beating when you come out of prison. That's all they were there for, just to give you a good whacking for what you did to Cameron. I told 'em, no blades, I told 'em not to merk ya. You should have just taken your punishment.'

Poppy found a reason to smile. 'How is that piece of shit, Cameron, still eating through a straw?'

'You heartless bitch! He was in a wheelchair for six months, gal, still needs sticks to walk. You fucked him up bad, really bad.'

Poppy shrugged her shoulders. 'That bully got what he fuckin' deserved.'

Neddy couldn't take his eyes off the babe in Poppy's arms, he was still seeing images from the past. There were things he had never said and may never get the chance to again, so he just said them. 'I would have looked after you, and the baby, you know, if you had decided to keep it, to keep her.'

'You're a soppy cunt, Neddy.'

'I would have stood by you, I told you that.'

Poppy laughed. 'Oh, what and told Cameron when he got out of prison that you had been shagging his bird. Don't think that would have gone down too well, mate, do you?'

'We could have…'

'Nothing, Neddy, nothing! We would have nothing! I was fifteen years old. I was fucked up to the eyeballs on gear. I didn't want a fuckin' kid, don't you get it? Social services did the right thing taking her away. At least she was adopted, not another fuckin' unwanted brat in care.'

'It could have been different, I could have got a proper job, got a flat and stuff, looked after you.'

Poppy laughed, 'A job! Get real Neddy, get fuckin' real. You have been pushing pills and bashing people since you were a kid, what fuckin' job could you have got?'

'I could have changed, gal, I know I could have been a better person, I just needed…'

'Oh, and what about Cameron, I suppose he would have been OK with it all. The three of us could have gone for long walks and picnics in the park with the baby couldn't we, all played happy families. Don't kid yourself, Neddy, me and you only shagged because we were both off our heads. It weren't no fuckin' love story or nothing was it? It would never have happened if Cam hadn't been locked up'.

The big man closed his eyes for a few seconds and took a deep breath, he was pleased he finally got a chance to release those thoughts that he had been holding back for more than a decade. A sudden whirring sound in the darkening sky made them both look towards the heavens where they watched a roving police drone hover past. Neddy suddenly found something amusing. 'Do ya know, I always wanted to be a pilot when I was a kid. You know, like a fighter pilot or taking those big Jumbo Jets to Australia and America. Fuck, I am thirty-two next week and I aint even been in an aeroplane.'

Poppy wasn't really listening to his strange anecdote, she was more concerned about the footage the disappearing drone might be relaying to the hunting pack of police cars. 'Do what ya gotta do, Neddy, it's gotta be over today, 'cause you know I can't let things go, especially after what ya did to Lulu. Fuck that girl weren't no saint, mate, but she never did no harm to no one in her fuckin' life.'

Neddy looked puzzled. 'That weren't none of my crew.'

'Bullshit! No point lying about it, if it weren't you yerself, it was one of yer fuckin' gorillas.'

'Why would I do that, gal, why would I top her when she spent a monkey a week with me? Why would I fuck that business up? That girl had problems. She had a lot of enemies. The Lithis tried to bang her out before, it was probably those bastards that did for her.'

Poppy stared long and hard at the menacing figure above her, she really didn't believe him but was trying to work out what he had to lose by lying. Her thoughts now turned to the dilemma she found herself in and there was something troubling her more than the presence of the large-fisted lump that towered over her. She looked down at the tiny bundle in her lap and touched Willow's face, swiftly moving her hand away as her fingers began to tremble.

Neddy noticed she had stopped rocking the child. 'She needs to go home, gal, it's over now, she needs to go home.'

Poppy looked shaky and her voice was a little croaky. 'She's cold, Neddy, she is so cold, like ice.'

Neddy crouched down as low as he could, his eyes met Poppy's and for the slightest of moments his gaze took away the daunting reality of the situation.

'Why do I do this stuff?' she mumbled. 'Why am I such a bad person?'

The big man did not have an answer, all he could offer was a sympathetic look and two large open hands. 'Give her to me.'

Poppy shook her head. 'Maybe its cause if what I did, maybe cause, you know, I gave away the baby and things, this is him punishing me. This is God, paying me back.'

'That's rubbish, gal, you know that. Give her to me, she needs to move around a bit, warm her up.'

'She aint gonna warm up, Neddy, is she? She aint ever gonna warm up.'

The giant of a man leaned forward and carefully prized baby Willow from her arms. She offered no resistance, none at all, she was still shaking. Neddy stared down at the clearly beaten girl on the ground. He was awash with anger but could not help but feel an overwhelming sense of pity. He knew more about the harrowing experiences she had endured in her life than most. Seeing her so vulnerable was a strange experience for him.

Poppy refused to be humbled, 'Just do it Neddy, don't say nuffin, just do it.'

The big man wrapped the stolen coat a little tighter around the baby, rubbing her freezing cold cheeks, before placing her gently on the grass. He looked over his shoulder at the revenge-hungry pack of baying hyenas waiting for him in the distance. He knew that Poppy was right, things had to end today, she was becoming a massive liability to his illegal operations as well as his reputation. He thought long and hard before he leaned across the grass and reached deep into the pocket inside his long coat. Poppy closed her eyes tightly, her heart was racing fast. But she knew that her body was a spent force, she couldn't have fought for her life even if she wanted to. A few seconds seemed like minutes as they passed by, maybe Neddy was taunting her. Suddenly she heard a small noise and felt something brush against her legs. When her eyes peeled open, she could see a large brown envelope nestled in her lap. Neddy cleared his throat and released a large ball of messy phlegm onto the grass, he needed her to listen to every word he was about to say.

'There's nearly three grand in there,' he said in a hushed voice. 'It will help you get away from this place. But you need to get your arse moving, gal, the feds will be all over these fields soon and you don't look like you're in no fit state to outrun them.'

If Poppy looked bewildered, it's because she was. But before she could make any sense of what was happening, she watched Neddy take another look over his shoulder to make sure his subordinates were too far away to hear his plan. 'Listen to me carefully, Poppy, you need to remember what I am saying, you need take this in. You need to get your arse to Swansea, it's in Wales, its hundreds of miles away, you can get the train from Paddington. There is a bar, it's down by the beach, it's called the Castle Keep. You will be safe there, I promise.'

Poppy was momentarily distracted looking at all the crisp fifty-pound notes in the envelope. 'What, Swansea, what the fuck is that?'

'You need to go tonight, Poppy, before all the shit hits the fan. The last train from Paddington leaves around half past eleven. I know that cause I've done the trip before.'

'Why Swansea, what's there? Is this some sort of fuckin' trick?'

'Do you remember, Smudger, Big Bazzas' mate from the pub?'

'Yeah, the small geezer that used to do all the karaoke.'

'That's him. He's a good bloke, he owes me. I sorted out some aggro he was having last year, so he owes me a big favour. He owns that bar in Swansea Harbour. Remember, Poppy, it's called The Castle Keep. I will call him later, let him know you will be there in the morning.'

'Castle Keep, it's a pub, yeah, Swansea, near the sea?'

'Get a taxi when you get to Swansea station. Remember, it's next to the harbour, don't forget Poppy.'

'Paddington station, you said, eleven o clock.'

'The last train goes about half eleven, get there earlier if you can, but don't stand out. Hide in the toilets or something. The old bill will have everyone looking for you.'

Poppy looked beyond the big man to his impatient troops waiting in the van. 'What about those shitheads?'

'When I push you, Poppy, just lay backwards in the grass until the van is out of sight, they don't need to know nothing.'

Poppy's eyes were glued to the tiny ball of clothing wrapped around the baby, there was no movement, nothing at all. She felt some strange emotions stir inside her for those few seconds. She felt a deep sorrow for Matt and Kayleigh, but not enough remorse to make her shed a tear. 'And the baby?' she asked.

The big man did his best to spare her any further guilt. 'I will sort the baby out.'

'What the fuck, Neddy, why, why are ya doing this for me?'

The big man did not want to admit what he was truly feeling, but something inside him stirred when he saw her clasping the tiny infant in her arms. A different time, a different place, a crazy world from a dozen years before, that had suddenly felt like a dozen centuries. But he had already let his guard down once that day and wearing you heart on your sleeve is not a good look for a man with such a nasty reputation.

'For old times' sake, gal,' he said, displaying a lifetime of rotting tooth decay, in a broad smile that had not been seen for many years. 'Just for old time's sake.'

Neddy leaned down and looked his old friend in the eye. This pair of social misfits once shared a sadness that had been hidden deep beneath a drug-fuelled hazy existence. It was something that only the other could fully understand. 'When I push you just lay backwards and don't move a muscle,' he said. Poppy nodded and offered him the best grin of gratitude she could muster. Despite the fact her body ached all over and she was still confused, she realised that he was offering her a lifeline. This was one time when she had to listen to a real voice of reason rather than those strange echoes rolling around inside her head.

With one firm shove in her chest the large man with compassion in his heart sent Poppy reeling backwards. He screamed some abuse down at her as her head hit the turf. She laid in silence, her head nestled in the grass, her body remained motionless. Poppy's sister, it seems, was not the only one who could carry off a dramatic acting performance when she really needed to. Neddy had one final warning for the woman that had caused him so many problems, a warning he uttered in little more than a whisper. 'And' he said, as he turned to leave, 'don't ever come back to my estate again, cause then I really will have to fucking kill you, ya mad bitch!'

CHAPTER TWENTY-SEVEN

t was, just as she knew it would be. She hoped that it wasn't, but it was. The scene that her daughter had described so matter of factually in her text message the previous evening was coming to life and there was nothing in the world she could do to stop it. It was too late for prayers now.

Her beautiful child had said in the lines of her final contact that nothing would look different from the outside, there would be no sign of the discovery that needed to be unveiled. Bree had insisted that her mother be accompanied when she entered the property, she would need to contact the police or at least a neighbour to escort her through the door. But even though this demand was marked out in capital letters, in her broken heart, Krista knew she had to face this ordeal alone. Glancing up from the corner of the building at the bedroom window, a clearly shaken mother could see that the curtains in her daughter's bedroom were fully drawn. There was no movement, none at all, but none was expected.

Tiny footsteps carried her shaking legs, almost in slow motion, to the rear entrance of the flats. She would not need to check that text message to find the number that would open the security door, those four digits were engraved inside her troubled mind. The smell of freshly cut grass filled the warm morning air as she entered the communal gardens. The gardener had been right about his decision to delay his planting of seeds and the sidewalks spawned a mass of colourful Alpines. Happy looking flowers for the saddest of occasions. Krista looked at the neatly cut lawn and remembered how she had shared a chilled bottle of Prosecco with her daughter the day she received the keys to the flat. They didn't argue that day, it was a rarity. But she remembered that occasion clearly, not one single word was wasted in anger. That warm sunny Friday evening the previous August was a time to celebrate, a time for hope, a time to dream, a time to put the traumas of the past behind them and look to a bright future. The renewal of the broken relationship between a mother and daughter. Yet, here she was, in that very same garden, with every skeleton from a closet full of tarnished memories coming back to haunt her.

As she headed down the pathway a strange thought crossed her mind. She suddenly remembered that the young man delivering the Thai takeaway meal that night had remarked how similar the two women looked. How they both had the most sparkling eyes he had ever seen and that it would be a very long time before he would forget making that delivery. They enjoyed their food and their wine on the lawn that evening, as if it was a picnic. They found a rare happy moment in their volatile relationship, sharing real heartfelt laughter and planning a shopping spree to buy curtains and bedding for the new home. It was a memorable evening. If only she had known that it would turn out to be the last time that they would ever share a meal together.

Today was not a day for drama, something else that was made very clear in the text message. There must be no screaming or wailing, no uncontrollable tantrums. But most of all there must no crazy notions of joining her on the journey she had decided to take. The calling was hers, let her take this journey unaccompanied. Let today be about letting go and being happy that she might find the peace and tranquillity somewhere in a quiet corner at her final destination. Prayers would be accepted, but not for anything other than the hope that she could finally be reunited with her one true soul mate. After all, eternity can be a very lonely place for one person to exist alone.

It may have been the sound of a small child's voice in the distance that sent a cold chill running through Krista's bloodless veins at that moment. It re-ignited distant memories of a small family that once played crazy games on their own lawn less than a mile from this place. Images of two happy-go-lucky twins that lived their childhood surrounded by love and joyous moments. Krista smiled as she remembered Brianna sprinting around the garden in the pretty white dress that she had worn in a school play. Her long flowing golden locks bouncing off her perfectly rounded shoulders, her eyes beaming brightly in the hazy sunshine. Jamie was chasing her, water pistol in hand, tormenting her, as was his way. Shouts and screams of hysterical joy. Her daughter fell over that day, on a loose slab of newly laid paving stone, cutting her knee and drawing blood. She never blamed her brother, who was chasing her, in fact she never blamed Jamie for anything. Krista could not help but think that if it had been her son had been the one to fall that day there would have been laughter after tears. Jamie was an uncomplicated child, he accepted life for its ups and downs and never held grudges. But his sister was the total opposite, she could remain stone-faced and downright petulant for weeks on end. And so, the incident was deemed to be her mother's fault for employing bad workmen to carry out those jobs in the garden. Krista could still remember the heartless scowl on her daughters face as she applied some antiseptic cream and a plaster to the small wound. Bree did not speak to her mother for five days as punishment for her bad judgement.

In another vivid memory, Krista could see the small wooden children's playhouse that had been erected at the rear of their garden. She remembered how the tiny siblings would sit in their until it was way past their bedtime, sharing their stories, hopes and fears with one another. Jamie never was very good at keeping secrets, everybody knew exactly what bothered him and why it bothered him. But even back then she knew that Brianna would never reveal what was truly going on inside her head. She was such a flawless and beautiful child, skin deep. But the beauty inside her body seemed to be shallow, she seemed totally uncaring about those around her. Krista suddenly felt a tight grip of guilt around her heart. As a mother, she should have known back then, known that her daughter had problems. She should have known, she should had acted sooner, not left it until her child reached puberty. Good counsellors may have been able to prevent her daughter from becoming the vindictive and self-obsessed creature she became. But now it was too late.

Her hope that the number for the security door was wrong and that this had just been some crazy disturbing prank was dismissed when she entered with ease. Krista found herself at the stairway that would lead her to the face the stark reality that lay waiting for her. Her footsteps had not gathered pace, if anything they were even slower than before as she climbed the two flights of stairs that would take her to a daughters final calling. This place had meant to be a haven of untainted virtue, a new start, a breath of fresh air in the lives of two women that had already been torn to shreds by one tragedy. But now it would only ever be remembered as a cold tomb of despair.

The spare key, the one she had been given by the estate agents, but told never to use, opened the door she did not want to open. But Krista would do her best to stay true to her daughters wishes. Today would not be a day for drama. It would be as if she was visiting her child for fresh coffee and a chat about an upcoming fashion show. Yet in her aching limbs she knew that once she entered that flat her life would be forever changed, her heart would be broken beyond repair. A haunting memory from her son's funeral suddenly appeared in her head, she looked down to see that her hands were shaking. A sick feeling raced through her body and landed in her throat as she pushed open the front door to number three. She hesitated for a few seconds, but knew that today, of all days, she had to be strong.

Krista crept through the hallway, not wanting to make a sound, despite the fact she knew that there would be nobody to disturb. A lasting memory suddenly flashed through her mind of the day she first came to view this property. The sheer excitement and anticipation of a new chapter of her life. It was the first time in many years she had seen that missing sparkle shine brightly in her daughter's eyes. She shuddered slightly when she realised that sparkle would never be seen again.

There was one last hope and she hoped beyond all hope that it would not be there, the hand-written sign. But it was, just as the lengthy text message said it would be, it was posted on the outside of her daughter's bedroom door. Her mind began to play tricks on her as a lasting memory of a distant children's birthday party came to taunt her mind as she took tiny steps to where the sign beckoned her. The familiar sounds of a small girl's laughter and shrieks of delight echoed through the hallway. The sign on the door did not alarm her, she knew that it should have done, but it didn't. It said, in simple verse, in handwriting she wished she did not recognise, '*Call the police. Do not come in alone.*'

And with those carefully scripted words she accepted that her daughters torment was finally over. In the cruellest of twists her first-born had detailed her own mortality, addressed line for line in that text message, like a twisted tragedy transformed into a sick screenplay.

The door seemed to open before it was pushed. When Krista entered Bree's bedroom she wanted to look anywhere, everywhere, but not at the bed. A hint of almonds told her that her daughter had still had time in her planning to spray a generous squirt of her favourite perfume. She didn't know if she would hate the smell of that scent now or hold on to its lingering fragrance as a beautiful memory of her daughter's presence.

It was not the first time she had seen loose pills scattered across the floor of her child's bedroom. Not in this abode of course, until now, this had been a happy place. But there had been three occasions after Jamie's death when she had been bought to a state of panic. She began to hang on to the faintest of hopes that this was a false alarm as it had been back then. A badly broken girl simply craving attention. But as much as she wished and as hard as she prayed, inside her head she knew that her faith in a miracle would not be answered this time.

Krista was trembling, her eyes slowly lifted from the shiny laminate floor and followed a path, from two perfectly joined Christian Louboutin heeled shoes, across the silky bedclothes. A sudden chill found its way into her bones when the vision of her daughter's bare legs came into view. Beautifully toned, with just the right amount of fake tan, they were outstretched, at a peculiar angle. She wanted to straighten them so that her child looked more graceful, but she was fearful of her reaction to touching her daughter's cold flesh.

The memory of seeing her son in an open casket before his funeral returned to her cloudy thoughts at that moment. She remembered how handsome he looked that day, almost as if he was attending his own wedding rather than his own funeral. She was pleased that she had taken time to compliment the funeral parlour that had pieced her sons broken body back together and let him be buried with some dignity.

She looked down, hesitant at first, before her eyes ran the full length of her first-born's static torso. Her gaze moved along the curvy bold daquiri Gucci dress she had chosen for her final act. They say that the strangest of thoughts run through your head when all hope is lost. Krista looked down at her daughter, lying prostrate, in the deepest of slumbers and thought for the tiniest of moment of her as Sleeping Beauty. But as she looked closer at her child's pallid skin and saw that all life had been drained from her once beautiful features, she suddenly realised that no kiss from a handsome prince would ever bring the colour back to those cheeks.

Brianna was a perfectionist in every way, but in her final thoughts she could not have foreseen a minor wardrobe malfunction. Krista took out a clean tissue from her handbag and wiped some sloppy drool from the bottom corner of her daughter's mouth. It was obviously not something Brianna would have anticipated, otherwise there might have been an instruction in the words of the text message. But she needed every ounce of inner strength inside her body to push down her daughter's eyelids and bring the final curtain down once and for all.

By now her head was spinning and strange voices began to call out to her, she had lost all sense of reality. She could hear a tiny voice in her head, calling her name, it seemed to know she was in pain. She slipped off her shoes and placed them next to her daughters in front of the mirrored wardrobe. Climbing on to the bed without disturbing the resting body, she laid down next to her child. Their heads met in the small gap between the fluffy pillows. Krista stretched out her arm and reached out for her daughter's hand, clasping her fingers tightly. She closed her eyes and wished in those few seconds that she could join her in this final journey. She wished that the text had not been so demanding and that she could make her own choice on where her own destiny should lie. But this was her daughter's finale, she knew she would not want to share this curtain call with anybody else. Besides. she needed to be practical for her daughter's sake. Otherwise, there would nobody there to make the funeral arrangements.

But then, suddenly, in that moment of unequivocal sorrow, Krista became confused. Bright lights flashed across the inside of her eyelids, a whisper, a tiny murmur, reciting her name. And then, just when she had thought that all was lost, she felt a small throbbing feeling, like a heartbeat. There was a hint of warmth in those fingers that were wrapped around her hand. She breathed in deeply as she felt them squeeze her tightly. Inside her head she could hear another whisper, and then she felt a bright beacon of light, it was stinging her eyes, searing through her brain, her head was full of fuzzy echoes.

That soft mellow whisper suddenly became a tiny voice, it seemed to be reaching out to her. It grew, slowly, increasing in volume until she could make out the words more clearly. She became confused, the voice was calling out her name. But it was not a sound she recognised, the one she was so desperate to hear cry out to her, it was not the voice of her daughter.

'Krista, Krista.'

Her eyelids began to peel open as the distorted sounds inside her head became more balanced. She peeked through a tiny slit in her eyes but closed them sharply when she was blinded by bright lights. Her mind was in a state of confusion, she could sense her throat was dry and her lips were trembling. She forced her eyes back open and looked upwards to see the beaming smile of a stranger in a nurse's uniform. 'Krista,' she said. That's all, just her name, but she repeated it twice more. 'Krista, Krista.'

As those noises slowly became shapes, she suddenly became aware of her surroundings. A busy team of white clad staff scurried frantically around inside the small brightly lit room. Some were citing numbers, while others were checking the heartbeat of their patient. Krista was puzzled, there was laughter, they all seemed to be so happy. They were in a state of delirium, as if they were celebrating a major triumph. Then suddenly a brass band seemed to be playing overtures inside her head as thumping drums and cymbals clashed angrily together. Krista tried in vain to raise her hand to move the oxygen mask strapped to her face, breathing deeply as she began to come to terms with what was happening. But as she looked beyond the medical team that had bought her back from the brink of death, she saw the face that made her head sink back into the security of the warm pillow beneath her head. Bree's dark eyes were staring at her from the other side of a glass window. The cold and heartless expression on her face reminding her that her own daughter had tried to squeeze the life out of her that day. She was still drowsy, unaware at that moment that it was the very drugs that she had warned her child of that had subdued her. But she would never be told that her haunting nightmare had been the result of the Peclosaperidone. Krista was in a state of subdued confusion. She didn't know if it was better for her to be here in this bed, protected by the staff of the hospital, or back on that bed of sorrow in her daughter's flat.

Bree looked on anxiously through the viewing window of the Intensive Care Unit, a worried young woman who had suddenly had the weight of the world placed on her shoulders. Poppy was still on the loose and her mother was still breathing. This was not how she had planned this day. She did her best to smile when she received a reassuring squeeze of the arm from a passing doctor. 'She is back with us, Miss Nylund, you don't need to worry now, your mother is going to be OK,' he said. Her fake smile fooled the elated physician, but it vanished the moment he disappeared down the hospital corridor. Inside she was burning up with fury, her hatred had reached insurmountable levels. She suddenly realised that her safe and cosy world was about to implode.

The silenced ringtone on her phone had not stopped calling out to her for at least three hours. The text message box in her mobile was filling up fast. Kendra was persistent, determined to speak to her protégé. In a dazed state, Bree was trying to plan an exit route from the Emergency Room. It didn't seem to matter now if she answered that call. Her concerned boss seemed relieved to hear her voice. 'Bree, Bree, are you OK, cutie? I have been so worried about you.'

'Hi Kendra, I'm sorry I didn't take your calls. I am at the hospital. they, eh, they have just bought my mother out of a coma.'

'Oh, darling, that's fantastic news, I am so happy for you. Listen, sweetest, I know you have a lot going on now, but this is really urgent. Two detectives came to my house this morning and seized my Mercedes. I have been at the police station for six hours now. They say the car was involved in a hit and run and some poor girl died. Bree, Bree, Bree, are you there…?'

CHAPTER
TWENTY-EIGHT

L ies, dark lies and black lies, that's all they had been. Poppy knew now that her sister's manipulation and cruel and twisted lies had got the better of her. The meanness of the self-obsessed woman, hell bent of ridding her life of her mother, certainly knew no bounds. She hated her sister with a passion now, she wished she could summon the strength and the energy to exact her revenge. Part of her still wanted to return to the scene of the crime and commit a real murder. Her sibling needed to be punished for her betrayal. But as bitter as she was at that moment, strangely, she got it. She understood fully why her sister had done the things she had had done. She would probably have done the same herself. It wasn't particularly clever, and Bree had obviously not thought her plan through, otherwise Poppy would be sitting in the corner of a police cell now with her whole world about to collapse around her. However, a couple of women had been gossiping at that same bus stop she was seated in and had and set her mind into overdrive. 'Critical but stable condition,' those were the words they repeated from a radio broadcast. 'Critical but stable condition'. So, Krista was still alive, Bree's masterplan had failed or at least been put on ice. If her mother is still alive, she will tell the police the truth, tell them who had really tried to finish her off. Or would she? Maybe she hated Poppy enough to back her daughter, to forgive her treachery. Or maybe Bree would blame it on her medication, give her mother the tight hug she was so desperately craving and the two of them would be reunited. It would be mother and daughter against the world.

The pain was excruciating, Poppy could hardly move, since sitting upright in the dank and chilly bus shelter in Woolwich Docks. The consequences of her fall were beginning to become apparent now. Her leg had cramped and practically seized up. Her neck had stiffened and one whole side of her body felt battered and bruised. That sharp pain in her ribs was back too, confirming that the previous damage she had encountered there had never really healed up. Maybe the broken girl should find it amusing that, where dozens had tried and failed in the past to disarm her defences, she had ended up with self-inflicted wounds. She certainly didn't feel like laughing. She winced as she recalled her dare-devil leap from the bedroom window. Maybe those drugs her sister had given her had several unlisted side effects, damn right stupidity, being one of them.

She had watched two buses come and go since she arrived at Woolwich Dockyard Bus Terminal. Buses that would have taken her away from this madness. They would have taken her to board a train that would deliver her to some weird place she had never heard of, to meet a man she barely remembered from a decade before. But something had stopped her boarding those buses, she was perplexed, in a state of total confusion. She looked down at that large brown envelope full of cash. Neddy was not lying, she had counted the money twice and that two thousand eight hundred pounds would buy her some time and some new friends. But it wasn't the fifty-pound notes that she was studying closely, it was those letters on the front of the envelope. She ran the broken nail on her grubby finger around that curly letter *Y*, the one she recognised from those self-addressed greetings cards. Why would Bree do that? Why would her sister give all that money to a low-life drug dealer? She wanted to believe that it was to buy him off, to keep her safe to carry out the crime she had planned for her to commit. But nothing made sense, she knew it wasn't just about that, she knew her little sister would do anything to protect her from harm. She remembered that Bree had once said to her that she might have been better off staying in prison. She felt that she knew how to handle everything around her in those familiar surroundings. That she could not stray off the path that was laid out for her. It seemed strange to think that such a crazy notion could be true. But Poppy was starting to remember how uncomplicated things were when other people made decisions for her, when she didn't need the voices to guide her. She was safe within those four walls and the world was safe from her.

And that's when she started to realise. Not just that her thumping headache had packed up and deserted her, nor that there were no cloudy images in her vision. But they had gone, the voices had abandoned her, even Nikita was no longer goading her, even she had moved on. For the first time in a very long time the thoughts inside her mind were still. They were as calm as the boating lake she had visited as a child. It gave her a chance to evaluate her situation, to think of what was really happening in her life.

Maybe the pain she was feeling on the outside of her body was masking the twisted agony inside her heart. She wished that she had never learned that her mother was still alive. It hurt her so much to think that the woman who had given birth to her had never made contact, never attempted to find her. It wasn't as if she would have been difficult to track down, she had made the front page headlines in at least three national newspapers. Even her abusive father made an effort to make contact with her before he died. And now her mother was happy. living in her own ideal world somewhere by the coast. It was as if she had never even given birth to her. And that reality made her thoughts then turned to her own daughter. She wished that Neddy had not reminded her of her own child that was taken from her arms before she had even had the chance to see her smile. She remembered the terrible pains she went through giving birth to her baby and how she swore at the midwife, telling her that she would never, ever, have sex again, if there was even the remotest chance she might fall pregnant. She worried for the tiniest of moments if her child had been treated well by her adoptive parents, if she had managed to live a normal life. And, although she had no right to be giving her rejected daughter a place in her memories, she felt a morsel of comfort in knowing that she had given desperate people the chance to have a family. Poppy wished she could forget the past, all of it, to start her life over again and make better choices. But her wishes had always fallen down a bottomless well. She knew that good things only ever come to good people.

A third bus passed by without stopping. Poppy reached inside her jeans for her phone to check the time, then remembered it had been discarded at the side of reservoir. She looked over at the large clock on the side of the nearby church, it was nearly half past ten. She would need to get a taxi to the mainline station now if she was to have any chance of fleeing London tonight.

But other thoughts were bothering her now, even though those dark clouds had disappeared. She began to recall the damage she had caused over the past two days. She started to see an image of Neddy digging a small shallow grave for the lifeless body of tiny Willow. She tried hard not to think of the distraught look on Matt and Kayleigh's faces when the police broke the news to them. She would have liked the time to explain why she took such drastic measures to get her sister to confess. But she knew they would never believe her. They would never forgive her.

She didn't know whether it was the effect of the drugs racing through her broken body, but irrational thoughts began to spin through her head. Life hadn't been so bad in the flat in Albermarle

Court. She enjoyed watching films on the massive television screen, the food was free, the bed was comfortable, and she could lose herself in the power shower. She was even getting used to her siblings' constant ramblings about her flourishing career and expensive shopping sprees. God, she thought to herself, she was even starting to like the taste of Tofu.

Why couldn't things have panned out differently for her? Was it really too much to have a normal life, to find a steady boyfriend? Someone who didn't expect her to push drugs or take pleasure out of using her as a human punchbag. Maybe a regular guy, someone like Matt or Preston. Men who knew how to make their partners feel special. She had never need to buy a vase because nobody had ever greeted her with flowers. No handsome hunk had ever served her breakfast in bed. Nobody had ever rubbed her feet with scented oils and asked how her day had been. There had been no Prince Charming's in her life, even Cameron had turned out to be a low-life loser.

Despite what her sister had thought she didn't relish the idea of returning to Wallsgrave. Bully boy, Callard, would be chomping at the bit at the news, gloating from ear to ear. This time would be worse, she would be labelled a child murderer, even though she had never intended for it to happen. She could see a weeping Kayleigh and Matt, re-united by grief, standing opposite her in a court room. But child killers get no respect, she would face one long, very long, sentence. She would constantly be looking for broken glass in her meals and checking each dark corner and corridor on her way to the shower rooms. She was tired of prison life now. She knew that she couldn't go back there. Especially after she remembered what had happened to her young cell mate. And that's when the sharpest dagger of reality plunged into her heart and sent her thoughts reeling back to the night at Wallsgrave Prison, the night it happened.

She remembered that her fragile cellmate had endured a particularly hard few days, having clumps of her silky black hair ripped from her scalp as she narrowly escaped the clutches of two vengeful inmates. The petrified girl knew that Poppy was due to be released the following week. She realised that any sanctuary she had enjoyed sharing a cell with the hard-faced prisoner would be gone. There would be nobody there to watch over her, to protect her. She would be left at the mercy of a bunch of feral savages, baying for her blood. Even though she had known Poppy less than a month, the terrified prisoner was aware of her fearsome reputation inside Wallsgrave. Just one word from her cellmate and she might be spared the punishments that were threatened. When the timid inmate approached her, all Poppy could remember seeing was a broken young girl, a small child in a young woman's body. The faith had gone from her eyes. She had been hoping her cellmate would offer her assistance in one of the only two options she had left. Unashamedly, the frightened young girl knelt on the cold floor of their cell and pressed her hands together. She looked up with tears in her eyes and she begged. She begged to Poppy and when Poppy ignored her, she begged to God, to the God she had previously denounced. And then in desperation, she begged to any God that might listen to her. But Poppy was resolute, it was not her fight, it was not her problem. She felt the helpless girl had no right to ask her for anything. After all this was Poppy Jarvis. She owed nothing to anybody in this world and was owed nothing in return. It was the way it always had been. It was the way it would always be.

Poppy remembered the sound of the alarms screaming through the walkways to the cells. Four prison officers ushering the residents into the courtyard while her cell mates mangled torso was covered up before being loaded into a black body bag. And for some reason, Poppy could not get that image out of her head. She should have done something back then, she knew, just a token offering, she should have done something. Then Poppy suddenly realised that she had seen that look of hopeless despair again, more recently, only this time it was disguised. A clever masquerade to hide the thoughts of a broken soul. She ran her fingers across the handwriting of the envelope and felt a cold chill run through her bones. She suddenly felt empty, she felt very sad, it was an emotion she was finding it very hard to come to terms with. Maybe that cold breeze that rushed over her body was the first time she had ever truly felt the burden of guilt.

As the bells on the church chimed twice, telling Poppy that it was half past the hour, she knew it was time for her to make her move. She dragged her wounded carcass off of the damp seat in the bus shelter and limped to the side of the road, raising an arm, in agony, to hail the first black taxi that she saw.

Poppy never knew whether this would be the end of the beginning or the beginning of the end, only God could decide that now. All she knew was that she could not be stranded in no-man's land, she had to make it to her destination before that train arrived.

CHAPTER
TWENTY-NINE

This was no longer an ordinary house in an ordinary suburban street in South London, far from it. A media circus had descended on Marlow Close and were camped outside number twenty-one. Camera flashes lit up the darkening sky each and every time there was a hint of movement behind the drawn curtains. News crews and comment hungry reporters flooded the front garden desperately hoping for that one picture or quote that would make a headline for the unfolding story. The reeky gate had since long lost the battle to hold on to its hinges and lay prostrate in the grass.

Bad news travels faster than good, everybody knows that, and tonight was no exception. The cul-de-sac was lined from one end to the other with spectators from the neighbouring streets. Spiteful chit-chat amongst themselves. Some were saying that they knew the couple well. But in truth Matt and Kayleigh had barely even been on 'good morning' terms with anybody in their local vicinity. The street had become so busy with onlookers and do-gooders that several additional police officers had been called to the area to keep the crowd under control. The local residents seemed desperate for the culprit to be named. They were after blood, but they did not know for sure who should be spilling it. Rumours were rife, but in truth most of those lining the pavements only knew half of the story. Not everybody in the growing crowd was expecting or even hoping for a happy ending, of course. There will always be those heartless souls amongst us who will take pleasure from the misery of others.

The sight of an infant smothered by gushing water would not have been an image that would leave you easily. So, the police team draining the reservoir were relieved when there was no sign of the baby. They had retrieved Poppy's mobile phone which had now been secured in an evidence bag. But for those members of the highly experienced Special Task Unit in attendance in Anerley, they knew that time was running out. A three-month-old baby had been missing for more than eight hours by now and was in the hands of a known criminal psychopath. The lack of any real hope could be seen clearly on their faces. None of them expected this day to end well.

DS Kerr found himself surrounded by a small group of well-meaning bodies inside the house. Social Care Workers, Family Liaison Officers and a couple of well-disguised members of the press. They chatted aimlessly, all spouting their own theories on the tragic situation. Fortunately, Kayleigh could not hear their morbid conclusions. She was in a complete state of shock and could barely stay on her feet without the aid of her mother, who had been there most of the evening. During those desperate hours of waiting for news Kayleigh had argued bitterly with Matt and told him to leave the property. She had endured enough torture and torment to last her a lifetime. So, when he dared to defend the actions of his crazy so-called 'friend' again, she finally snapped. She completely lost control of her senses and threw a large ornament across the room which caught him on the side of his head. To make matters worse,

Preston had arrived to offer his support, having spent the best part of three hours searching the areas surrounding the reservoir. Matt and his gym buddy had also clashed, as the testosterone levels in the front room had reached heightened levels.

The local news channels had already carried out a couple of live TV interviews from the outside of the property that day, but the distraught parents could barely bring themselves to speak. One of the news channels had returned and asked the couple to make a direct appeal to the abductor of their child. Reluctantly they paired up in the space where the missing gate should have been and did their best to show that they were unified in their grief. Kayleigh did not tell her partner that she had found some real comfort in his arms as he pulled her closer to him before they looked down the lens of the broadcast camera. Her mouth was as dry as a sandpit and she was clearly struggling to speak, so Matt took the lead. He cleared a large lump in his throat and looked awkwardly around at the gathered masses, wondering why he had never noticed any of these 'so-called' neighbours pass his house before.

'We,' he said, trying desperately to keep his composure. 'We, we want to say…'. Realising he was mumbling Matt checked himself and started the interview again. 'We want to say to everybody that has been out today searching for our…'

He was clearly struggling to speak when the Detective Sargent appeared from the background to finish the interview 'We want to express our gratitude to all those people that have given their time to…'.

But now it was the policeman's turn to be stopped mid-sentence as a loud shout went up from a dark corner at the end of the cul-de-sac. An eerie hush started and spread like wildfire through the gathered bystanders, ending in a few seconds of sombre silence. The stunned crowd seemed to turn their heads as one as a woman's voice halfway down the close broke that silence. 'The baby,' she yelled. 'He's got the baby.'

The whole audience froze, rooted to the spot, as a large figure in a full-length trench coat and dirty laced-up boots trod the white lines in the middle of the road. Nobody, apart from the approaching stranger moved an inch. He was single minded, taking small, measured steps, an unbroken stride, never losing eye contact with the large crowd ahead of him. As the shadowy figure grew larger in stature and came into full view, Kayleigh's body began to shake uncontrollably. She slipped free from her partners grip but almost immediately felt into the arms of a WPC who yanked her backwards and held her in a tight bear hug. Several worried glances were exchanged as the man from the shadows came into clear view. The Detective Sargent waved his arms at a couple of officers and before anybody could say a single word a pair of tasers were removed from their holsters and were pointing in the direction of the oversized stranger. Two bright red beams began dancing merrily over the big man's torso, then rested just beneath his neckline. It stopped him in his tracks. Neddy had felt the scorching stings of those beams before, he was not in the mood for a repeat of that punishment today.

A uniformed man broke ranks and moved to the middle of the road, he was followed by his colleague. 'Armed police officers, put the baby down, put your hands behind your head and kneel on the floor,' he yelled.

The second man with his weapon drawn repeated the order, more direct and much louder than his colleague. But the big man stood his ground. The silence was deafening, not a word, not a sound. The tension was mounting by the second.

Kayleigh could be held back no longer, she broke free of the arms around her and rushed forward at the pace of an Olympic sprinter, swerving past two uniformed officers and ducking under some flimsy police tape at the edge of the police cordon. She moved swiftly forwards but came to a sudden standstill when the sight of this huge man holding her precious daughter in his arms became clearer. She paused for a few seconds as she saw Willow's pastel pink bonnet poking out beneath the brown leather jacket. She took one huge intake of breath before reciting a small prayer inside her head. Kayleigh walked forward, slowly, trembling every step of the way, every fear she had ever had come to life in these few short seconds. She was desperate to speak but could not find her voice. She was closer now, less than four feet, she stopped and reached out her arms.

As their eyes met, neither one of them expected anything of the other, an ominous cloud of darkness hung over the close. The atmosphere was palpable. And then that silence was broken, just a tiny sound, but it was a chord that was more beautiful than the chorus of a thousand heavenly angels. It was the sound of a baby's cry. A whimper at first, then a small snuffle, before the familiar scream that had kept her parents awake at night, as Willow bellowed out a screeching tune that nobody in that close would ever forget. The onlooking crowd felt a warmth run through their hearts as if they were one, united in their relief and happiness. Neighbours hugged strangers and small children were pulled close by their parents and held tighter than ever. Even the toughest of men in the street found a lump in their throat and a large tear in their eye.

Neddy could not help but grin. 'She is cold,' he said to the distraught woman in front of him. 'Cold and probably hungry, but she is OK though. She just needs her mum.' He stretched out his arms and offered the squealing child to her emotional wreck of a mother. He added some immortal words of cold comfort. 'She would sleep through anything that bloody kid, tough as old boots.'

Kayleigh grabbed Willow so close to her bosom she was in danger of squeezing the life out of her infant. A paramedic tried to wrestle the baby from her arms but her grip on her child was so tight it would have taken a dozen bodybuilders to prize her from her daughter.

Neddy arched his back and fell to his knees, clasping his hands together behind his back. He didn't need to say anything more, but he felt a compulsion to reveal what he truly believed. 'She wouldn't have hurt her, ya know,' he said with a crooked but meaningful smile. 'Poppy, she wouldn't hurt a little baby.' As those words left his mouth the giant of a man felt a thumping clenched fist catch the side of his face. Another followed as Matt waded in with punch after punch before being hauled away by a couple of burly police officers.

As the handcuffs snapped around his wrists, Neddy found himself looking up at the star lit sky. He may have been mistaken or simply dazed by those blows to the head. But he would swear that at that very moment he could smell fresh sultana pudding and hear the dulcet tones of Dusty Springfield belting out a classic tune.

CHAPTER THIRTY

A growing mist had engulfed the lifeless trees that surrounded the railway sidings at the Maple Crossing on this warm murky evening. There always seemed to be a morbid silence at this place these days, broken only by the rattling of the passenger trains that passed through at the turning of each hour.

One forlorn figure, a lost soul, stood motionless on one side of the railway tracks. She was not a stranger here, an ever present on all occasions and in all weathers. This was like a spiritual home for Bree. She never bought flowers to this sacred venue. Her brother had once ridiculed her for buying him a rose when his valentines date let him down at short notice, she never forgot that. Instead, she would read out the messages that others had left him on sympathy cards and tributes at his funeral. Those heartfelt words would bring back cherished memories of their lives in younger years. Reminding her of times when it had just been her and Jamie against the world. Her mother had always found the scene of her sons' final moments too heart-breaking to visit, or so she said. She preferred to make large charity donations in Jamie's name, in a half-hearted effort to keep his memory alive. Preston had, until the previous Autumn, been the only other regular visitor to attend this place of sadness. But even he was now found that this location tugged too hard at his emotions. He preferred to remember his best friend in happier surroundings, holding a bottle of lager in his hand while singing loudly, out of tune, and dancing, badly, to the music in the background. Despite what Bree thought, he truly missed his best friend.

The sound of a car door opening and closing suddenly caught Bree's attention. It was on the other side of the bridge near the entrance to the crossing. Headlights shone brightly in her direction, but then swung around as the vehicle turned and made a hurried exit. She was anxious, nervously expecting small blue flashing lights to surround her at any moment. Time was of the essence, but she knew in her heart that the train would not be late.

All tokens of love and remembrance may have been a thing of the past to some people, but Bree still found comfort here, albeit cold comfort. She felt close to him, just being here. She checked the time on her mobile and saw that there were still a few precious moments for her to relive her most beautiful memories of her brother. Retrieving a small mirror from her bag she tidied her hair and applied the smallest layer of lip seal. Her reflection was still being kind to her, but it was beginning to show that the traumas of the past twenty-four hours were taking their toll. Her energy and zest for life had been drained from her body, as had the confident smile from her face.

She heard another sound from the distance, it sounded like the howl of a wounded animal. It was unsettling at first, but she was not scared, she knew that nothing could hurt her here. A sudden rustling of bushes, somewhere in the darkness, made her look again. More swift movements in the ruffage and a hushed voice, as if someone had disturbed a poacher looking for game. But Bree remained composed. She was resolute, nothing could stop her now, she knew that. And then, in the corner of her eye she caught a glimpse of a shadowy figure beneath the flickering lamplight on the opposite side of the tracks. It was moving slowly, heading towards her. It was too large to be an animal, it grew in stature until the dimmed lights at the edge of the railway siding finally revealed the identity of her unwelcome visitor.

'How did you know?' she asked her sister, who was clearly struggling to stand upright on her injured leg.

'Where else would ya go this time of night?' Poppy replied.

Bree stared hard at her opposite number before turning her head, hoping she would find some comfort in the headlights of an approaching train. 'It's never late, this train, it's always on time.'

'So ya said before.'

Flicking her golden locks back behind her ears, Bree was finding it hard to look her sister in the eye. She started to wonder what the next few moments would bring. 'I know you hate me now,' she said, her voice slightly broken and distorted.

'Can ya blame me?'

A shake of the head was all that was required. 'I wish it could have all been different, you and I, I really wish that we could have just been like, well. You know…'

'Never gonna happen, missy, was it?'

'I suppose not.'

'But this aint the way, ya know that. This don't solve nuffin.'

Bree looked down at her phone again, wishing those waiting minutes would turn in to seconds. She did not fear her sister's retribution, nor did she doubt the decision she had chosen. She had a determination inside her that night that could not be blunted. For her this was the way, it was the only way she could be free. She suddenly felt an obligation to justify her actions to her sibling. 'When I was young, I just wanted to be that little girl that made everyone smile. To make my mother proud, to do good things. That's all I wanted, that's all I ever wanted. I didn't want to be the little girl that heard the voices all the time.'

'I know, trust me, I know what ya mean. But this aint the way.'

'I can't go to prison, Poppy, you know that. Those women, they would eat me alive in there.'

'You need help girl, fuck, they will love you inside there, they will be falling over themselves to get you help. Ya know, like proper help.'

'Don't patronise me, Poppy, please don't do that.'

'You would get all the right people looking after you. Ya like that don't ya, being the centre of attention?'

'What, you mean I could be like a circus freak or something?'

'It aint your fault, the way you are. It's like me, ya know. I have had them quacks trying to work me out for loads of years. How the fuck can they work me out when I can't even work myself out?'

'The rest of my life in prison, Poppy, it's not for me.'

'Nah, nah, ya got money, girl, ya can get a good brief. Ya might get a seven stretch, you could be out in three, four tops. But you still need to sort your nut out.'

Bree smiled, that sanctimonious smile that irritated her sister so much. 'Oh, my naive and beautiful sister, you have no idea, do you? I have done so many bad things.'

'Yeah, but if you fess everything up to them it goes better for you. Like, if you tell them that you're sorry, ya know, for all the things ya done.'

'But that's it, my sweetest sister, I am not, I am not sorry.'

'Look, nobody's perfect, we all do bad shit, only some of us get away with it longer than others.'

Shaking her head, Bree allowed herself a small grin at her sister's naivety. 'Oh, Poppy, Poppy, Poppy, you just dont realise, do you? Even the day you were released from prison I still had bad thoughts. I could have just picked you up at those prison gates, we could have gone to a nice restaurant to celebrate your release. But something in my head told me I had to let you suffer first.'

'For what?'

'For all those times I came to visit you and you pretended to be ill, or got in to trouble, just so you wouldn't have to see me. So,

I watched them, Poppy, I watched those brutes give you what you deserved before I came to your rescue. I sat in the car and waited, I enjoyed it, I loved every minute of it. I laughed while they were beating you up.'

Her siblings face told her she was angry, but Poppy shrugged her shoulders and accepted the revelation for what it was. 'Probably deserved it then, didn't I.'

Bree checked the time again. Those minutes were moving faster now, the sands of time were coursing rapidly through the middle of the tiny hourglass of her life. The women stared long and hard at one another for a few seconds, both knowing that the train would be arriving at any moment. Poppy looked down at the same stretch of railway track as her sister, there was a slight hint of panic in her voice. 'Ya could forget all this shit and come with me. Look, I got a stack of cash here, we can run away together.'

Bree instantly recognised the large brown envelope in her sister's hand and wondered how she had it in her possession. Could she really have got the better of Neddy? She asked one question. 'He told you then, Neddy, he told you?'

'That don't matter now. So, what about it then, me and you, we jump on a train, go away, like far away. We could buy a couple of bottles of booze for the journey, play another drinking game if ya like?'

'Didya, wouldya, couldya?'

'Yeah, but no shit answers, right? You know what 'appens if yer give shit answers.'

A sudden breeze rushed through the railway sidings and Bree had to tidy her hair. She looked over at her sister and despite the poor lighting she could clearly see how badly battered her sister's body was. It was at that moment she realised how cruel she had been to her own flesh and blood. The feeling of guilt had rarely washed across the souls of either of these women, but Bree found a sudden compulsion to be honest. 'I lied, Poppy, about your mother, I lied to you. She isn't happy. I lied about that. When I went to see her there was a sadness in her eyes. I think she would love to see you again, maybe to explain why she had to stay away. It's not too late you know, Kayleigh has her address, you should find her.'

Poppy shrugged her shoulders. She had already resigned herself to one truth that could not be disputed. 'She obviously never gave a fuck about me, did she?'

'I think you should at least give her a chance. She is lonely inside. I truly believe she would want to see you.'

Poppy ignored her sisters' ramblings, there had been far too much time pass by and too many bad things happen to her for her ever to forgive her mother for abandoning her. That past was better left behind her. She had other priorities, she realised that she needed to get her sister away from here and she needed to do it now.

'You know your mum will forgive yer, don't ya?' Poppy said, determined to stop her sibling from acting out her crazy fantasy. 'Like when she gets out of hospital, yer know, and she has a chance to talk to ya. She will forgive ya, I know she will.'

'I don't want her forgiveness, Poppy, I want her to suffer. That's why I have to be here tonight.'

'All she wants is a hug. She needs yer now, missy, more than ever, don't she?'

'She doesn't deserve anything, Poppy, nothing at all.'

And then, beyond the darkness, the small but distinct lights of the train could be seen. They came to life like a runaway star in the middle of the blackest night. They were distant at that second but were growing steadily. Their appearance bought the warmest of smiles to Bree's face. 'You see, Poppy, I told you it's never late.'

But the worried looking woman opposite felt the need to respond. She needed an answer to a question that had bothered her since the moment the siblings had first met. 'But not that night, the train, it weren't on time that night, was it?'

Her sister's demeanour suddenly changed, her smile turned inwards and her bottom lip started to tremble. 'No' she said, her voice breaking more with every word that left her mouth. 'Not that night.'

'He never drove the car, did he, Jamie? It was you that pushed them other people off the tracks.'

Bree could not answer, her face seemed to have lost its colour, as if an unfriendly ghost from her past had just crossed her path. Her eyes glazed over, and she seemed to shiver as if an ice-cold breeze had rushed through her body. Slowly, she nodded her head and found a few more words stumbling out of her mouth, 'You could never understand.'

'Make me understand. I aint gonna judge ya, am I? Remember, tell the truth and shame the devil.'

Bree hesitated at first but then realised it was finally time for the truth to be heard, however painful that truth might be. 'He had been so nasty to me, Poppy, like really nasty. And then he wanted to leave me, to go away, because of the things I had done. You see he knew everything, everything.'

'But you told everybody that he...'

'It rained that day, all day and all night, just non-stop. Rain, rain, so much rain! The roads were flooded, that's why we came this way. But that's why the train was running late, it should have gone through here before we arrived. But all that wet weather, it was more than twenty minutes late. I had picked him up from the pub, you see, he was steaming, blind drunk. I was taking him home, looking after him. I always looked after Jamie. But he was going away, that weekend, going to Australia, going away forever. He told me I needed to sort myself out, to get help, while he was away. But I knew he was never coming back. You see, he was laughing at me, Poppy, my brother, my one true soul mate, was laughing at me. I couldn't let him go away from me. They told me, inside my head, they told me, I couldn't let that happen.'

'So, ya killed him, ya killed yer own fuckin' brother?'

'The car, that jeep, it was stuck on the tracks. There was a little girl crying in the back seat, I couldn't get her out. I tried to wake him up to help me, but he kept falling asleep. Too much drink, he liked his drink, Jamie, he really liked his drink. I knew then what I was going to do. You see, I came here a long time ago, but the voices didn't win that day. I knew that they would bring me back here. I always knew that. This place, they kept telling me, it has always been my destiny.'

'But why didn't you fight them, you loved Jamie, I know you loved him, you loved him more than you should have done.'

'Not that night, I hated him! God, I hated him so much that night, Poppy. I used to love him so much but at that moment I despised him, I wanted him to suffer.'

'Jesus wept!'

'I wanted to go with him, you must believe that. You see, Poppy, he was the one, the only one, I could never ever love anybody the way I loved Jamie. I know you will never understand, but I couldn't let him leave me, I couldn't share him with the world. You see, he was weak, he wasn't strong enough to keep our secrets safe. So, that night, it was perfect. You see, this is my place, it has to end here for me, I have known that since I was a little girl. He looked so peaceful in his sleep, so handsome. I sat in the car with him and held his hand, so tightly. But when the train lights got closer, I, I...'

'What, you just got out, you just left him on the tracks?'

'It all happened so quickly. Every day, every single day, Poppy, I miss him, every single day. I knew you wouldn't understand.'

The lights on the train had grown by now, the sight of those glowing headlamps making both girls have different reactions. Bree stood tall and proud, pushing back her hair again before taking one step forward and finding her feet in the small granite stones in the middle of the railway track. She reached inside her jacket pocket and found her lip balm, softening her perfectly shaped lips for one final time.

Poppy was visibly distressed, shaking her head furiously and reaching out her arms. 'Get off there ya nutter, this aint what Jamie would have wanted!'

Her sister's eyes lit up and a smile of satisfaction returned to her face. 'He is waiting for me, I know he is waiting for me. He has been lonely on his own.'

'Nah,nah, nah, he aint waiting, girl, he aint waiting. This aint no fuckin' fairy tale, there aint no happy ending here!'

Bree nodded her head slightly. 'We both know that it has to end this way for me.'

'What about me? You can't do this, you can't just leave me.'

'You're a survivor, Poppy, you always will be, you will be OK.'

'Nah, this aint right. Get off the tracks, get off now, please, get off now!'

'You can't save me, my beautiful sister, nobody can.'

'We can do this, ya know, me and you. We can do our time, get out and get another place together. I can be better, I promise, I get it now, I can do cleaning and help and things, try harder. Don't leave me, please, don't leave me!'

Suddenly, the rails beneath them began to rattle as the full face of the approaching locomotive appeared down the line. The flickering lights getting closer and closer as the train seemed to gather momentum. Poppy's heart began to race, and her head was filled with a thousand images of all the people she had hurt and all the bad things she had done in her life. She wanted to scream, louder than she had ever screamed before. But somewhere amid all the surrounding madness and mayhem she suddenly found a strange calm. 'Take me with ya,' Poppy said, in a mellow voice her sister barely recognised. She reached out her arms towards her sibling, there was a look of sublime sadness in her eyes. 'I aint got nothing here if ya go, nothing. I wanna come with ya. Please, take me with ya.'

'Why?' her sister asked, looking bemused.

Poppy was panic-stricken, she seemed as if she was desperate not to be left alone, it told in her breaking voice. 'Cause yer my sister, Bree, my little sister. I am supposed to look after you, aint I?'

Bree felt a warm glow in her heart and forgot about the world of complete chaos and impending danger for that split second. She did, however, feel a strange compulsion to correct her sibling. 'Half-sister.'

In the darkest of all their darkest moments her comment made the women share a small laugh. Poppy's chin wobbled slightly, and her bottom lip began to tremble. She spoke softly again, this time almost childlike in her manner. 'I'm coming with ya,' she said, dragging her injured leg and taking two small steps forward to join her sibling on the broken stones in the pathway of the oncoming express. That was the second time the girls' eyes had met across the tracks, and for those few seconds they felt a strange and endearing infinity to one another. It was as if they had lived a hundred lifetimes together and knew exactly how the other felt. They could see the heartache in the other's world, they could feel their siblings pain. It was if they had cried one another's tears and knew that they were the only person in the world that could offer solace and comfort. Despite the approaching danger a warm glow encircled their bodies and they suddenly found themselves wrapped together in a tight embrace in the middle of the railway track. Their steamy breaths warmed each other's necks, a tiny morsel of comfort as their destiny drew closer.

As the speeding train thundered towards the Maple Crossing the driver suddenly had a clear view of the obstacles ahead of him. He pressed the warning alarm horn repeatedly, pushing so hard that he almost broke it. A screeching groan echoed through the darkness as the panic-stricken man did his best to bring the three hundred tonnes of speeding steel to a halt. But he was losing his battle with the clock. He began shouting into the darkening abyss as he realised that time was not on his side.

Bree tightened the grip on one of her sisters' hands and used the other to tidy her hair. She was determined that the onrushing gusts would not spoil her immaculate features for her final act. When the women's eyes met again, they squeezed each other's fingers tightly to provide some reassurance. But at that very second the tiniest hint of doubt showed on one face, causing immediate concern on the other. The train was almost upon them, there was no time for hesitation, not now, no chance to ask the question that needed to be asked. In the blink of an eye, one woman released her hold on her sister's fingers and shoved her forcefully with the palms of her hands. The impact sent her sibling reeling backwards down towards the railway sidings. With just seconds to spare and with the grating of the train's brakes getting ever louder, the woman stranded on the railway tracks had to shout to be heard by the other. 'Your mother needs you more than I do. Don't forget me, I will be waiting for you.'

'Always?' the other asked her sister, screaming back from the grass verge where she had landed. 'Always?'

'Always,' her sibling confirmed, with a mesmerising smile that assured her sister that she was not afraid to face her end.

The humongous weight of the locomotive suddenly met an unwanted target on the railway tracks. The upright figure didn't move a muscle, she was carried for more than a hundred yards before being dragged beneath those large crushing wheels of steel. Her body became entangled in the underbelly of the first carriage as the momentum of the train slowed rapidly, but not in time for the woman to be spared. Her torso was mangled savagely by the weight and ferocity of those jaws of solid metal. Her limbs were ripped apart and strewn across a lengthy stretch of the railway tracks. As the train was finally bought to a juddering halt, the echoes of an ear-piercing scream of unbridled pain went unheard.

It was over, for one of them at least, their sad life of torment and heartache had finally come to an end.

A dark shadow shrouded the Maple Crossing that night and grew in stature until it had encased the whole of the surrounding area. Residents living close to the scene gathered to pay their heartfelt respects to another poor victim of the intersection's poor safety measures. Many believed the place to be cursed and petitioned the local council to close the level crossing for good. None of them would ever know the truth behind the two tragic souls that had died there over the past few years, nor would they ever meet the survivor.

*

Maybe the line between sanity and insanity is so fine that we dare not believe it truly exists. Yet, one tiny step, one small footprint, can take us to the darkest corner of our minds. Hushed whispers that will haunt you, blurry images that will break your spirit and leave an indelible engraving on your heart and soul. For most of us, we can all witness the simple beauty of life and be thankful. We can see the blue skies above us, feel the warmth of the sun against our skin, tread a safe path on the solid ground beneath our feet. But in your mind, you should know that it could be waiting for you. Somewhere, beyond the darkness, an unknown voice, calling your name, taunting you. Waiting for the time when your weakness carries you across that threshold. And once you cross that sacred line you can never step back. You can never return to the normal. Whatever the normal truly is in this crazy existence we call life.